Chieftain

G·K
Hall
&Co.

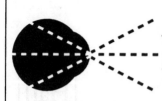

Chieftain

Arnette Lamb

G.K. Hall & Co.
Thorndike, Maine

Published in 1995 by arrangement with Pocket Books, a division of Simon & Schuster, Inc.

G.K. Hall Large Print Paperback Collection.

The text of this Large Print edition is unabridged.
Other aspects of the book may vary from the original edition.

Set in 16 pt. News Plantin.

Printed in the United States on permanent paper.

11491

PS
3562
.A4218
C45
1995

Library of Congress Cataloging in Publication Data

Lamb, Arnette.
    Chieftain / Arnette Lamb.
        p.   cm.
    ISBN 0-7838-1279-5 (lg. print : lsc)
    1. Great Britain — History — Edward I, 1272–1307 — Fiction. 2. Large type books. I. Title.
    [PS3562.A4218C45   1995]
    813′.54—dc20
                                                                    95-2474

To
Lou Ann Williams,
my good neighbor and constant helpmate

Acknowledgments

Special thanks to Alice Shields for her expertise, her encouragement, and her friendship.

Thanks also to Pat Stech for her generosity, her honesty, and her eagle eye.

And to the best of all editors, Caroline Tolley.

Prologue

Scarborough Abbey
Summer 1301

Death stalked Clare Macqueen.

It dulled her honey brown eyes and turned her skin waxy white. Even her flowing golden hair had lost the luster of life. Usually tall and stately, she now seemed frail and childlike, swallowed up by the narrow bed.

Shrouding the ache in her heart, Sister Margaret pressed a cool cloth to the scratches on Clare's cheek. "Are you in pain?"

"I cannot feel my legs. Are they broken?"

"Nay, child." The half truth came easily, even to an abbess, for in two years, fate had dealt this injured girl enough misery to last a lifetime. "You haven't skinned a knee."

A bittersweet smile curled Clare's lips. "You patched up enough of those. Every time Johanna and I climbed the harvest oak. Where is she?"

Sister Margaret's chest grew tight. Strong, capable Johanna. What would she do when she saw her sister, Clare? She'd fall prey to temper, for

Johanna had always been Clare's champion. "She's stabling the horses and getting your servants settled in the guest cottage."

Clare's eyes drifted out of focus. "A wolf spooked my mount. I fell."

The horse had trampled her spine. Once the inevitable infection set in, sweet Clare would die. Praise God it would be a painless passing.

Sister Margaret blinked back tears. "You couldn't know a beast lurked in the shadows."

"I should have stayed in the cart, but I wanted to ride."

At ten and five, Clare was still more child than woman. Neither marriage nor motherhood had settled her restless spirit.

"Where is my son?" Clare asked.

"In the next room with Meridene. He's taken a liking to goat's milk."

"Meridene loves children. Her husband should fetch her. 'Tisn't fair that she was wed as a child, then brought here and forgotten."

"True, but Meridene's safe, just as you and Johanna are." Questions plagued Sister Margaret. "What of your husband?"

Tears pooled in Clare's eyes. "Taken by the king."

Edward I. The mere thought of him brought fresh pain to a wound fifteen years in the healing. Sister Margaret clenched her teeth to stave off the ache. The walls of the infirmary faded, and she was once again a carefree Highland lass who'd caught the eye and inspired the passion of Alexander III, the king of Scotland.

Oh, Alexander, she lamented, *your merciful soul abides in these girls.* His complexity of character had been passed on to his fair daughters: Clare, with her penchant for game and glee, and Johanna, inspired by her dedication to love and law.

Through a haze of seasoned misery, Sister Margaret stared down at one of her two children, who both favored a Scottish king long dead.

"Did you hear me, Sister Margaret? The king ordered Drummond taken to the Tower of London."

Again and always Edward. Now that he'd vanquished Wales, the king had turned his armies and his wrath northward. The Hammer of the Scots, they called him. Clare's husband, Drummond Macqueen, was only the latest victim.

Sister Margaret cringed when she recalled the cruelty of which Edward the Plantagenet was capable. Upon the death of their father, Alexander, the twin girls had been found by one of Edward's many royal spies. Only by taking the veil and swearing secrecy had Margaret been allowed to accompany her daughters to this remote abbey in North Yorkshire.

Johanna and Clare knew nothing of their birthright, not even their family name. A pity, for their blood was as blue and their lineage as royal as any crowned at Westminster Abbey.

Thinking of that cruel deed, she feared for Clare's three-month-old son. "Will the king come for your boy?"

"Nay." Clare swallowed, fighting back tears. "Like everyone else, he thinks Prince Ned rather than Drummond Macqueen sired my child."

"Is it true?"

Transfixed by the tapestry on the far wall, Clare spoke softly and with great regret. " 'Tis true I was unfaithful, but Drummond had planted his seed the month before. In exchange for my favors, the prince promised me he would go to his father. He said the king would spare Drummond." Her mouth pursed in disdain. "The pervert lied to me. My sin went for naught."

"So you were allowed to keep your son."

"Yes. The king gave me a writ granting us a demesne in Dumfries." Lifting a weak hand, she pointed to her traveling bag. " 'Tis in my pouch. Will you get it please?"

Sister Margaret retrieved the rolled parchment and read of the king's meager bequest and his condemnation of Clare's husband. "Why didn't you go to this place?"

"I know no one in the Borders, and the king forbade me to take any of Drummond's people. Not that they would've followed a known adulteress. Drummond denounced me publicly. I was ashamed, lonely, and afraid. I thought only of coming to you."

"Bless the Virgin you did. All will be well. Rest now."

Clare's eyes drifted shut. Sister Margaret expelled a breath and began to pray for the soul of her daughter.

Sometime later, she heard voices in the next room. Taking the royal scroll, she tiptoed from the infirmary and found Johanna and Meridene huddled around the baby's cradle.

Johanna looked up, her brown eyes clouded with concern. "How is she?"

"Dying."

Meridene gasped and scooped up the babe.

Making a fist, Johanna punched the air. "She had no business riding that trail at night. She knows better. What kind of a beast is her damned husband to have so little care of her?"

"Johanna!"

"Sorry, Sister Margaret." Johanna folded her arms at her waist, jostling the ring of keys that dangled from a leather thong. "Lord Drummond should have traveled with her."

Johanna possessed a maturity beyond her years and a logic to rival any Oxford scholar. Although younger than Meridene and only five minutes older than Clare, Johanna had always been the leader.

"Where is her husband?" she asked.

Sister Margaret waved the parchment. "Lord Drummond is taken by the king. He could not have seen to her welfare." She relayed Clare's tale of woe.

Her jaw taut with anger, Johanna held out her hand. "May I see what our generous sovereign has left her?"

Sister Margaret handed over the document and reached for the babe. Meridene kissed the boy's brow and placed him in Sister Margaret's arms. Her grandson was a handsome child with a grin as big as the Highlands. What would the future hold for him?

Johanna squared her shoulders and moved to the door. "I'll sit with her."

Sister Margaret visited Clare's servants, Mr. and Mrs. Stapledon. Two years ago, when the king himself had taken Clare to the Highlands to wed the dashing Scottish chieftain, she had convinced the Stapledons to come with her to her new home. But Macqueen Castle was now ruled by Drummond's younger brother.

Bertie Stapledon scratched his beard. "The king'll execute Lord Drummond, do ye see. What'll become of the babe then?"

A chill passed through Sister Margaret. "I do not know."

According to the writ, Lord Drummond's family was prohibited any congress with Clare or the child. Meridene would help Sister Margaret raise the wee Alasdair. Johanna was too busy overseeing the farmers and shepherds who occupied the abbey's land.

By the next evening the deathbed vigil had begun. Practical, dependable Johanna paced the room, swearing under her breath. Meridene held the child, plying him with a wooden rattle and humming a lullaby. Sister Margaret prayed.

Clare's complexion now glowed with the flush of fever, and her skin felt hot to the touch. In a voice drained of feeling, she called for her twin.

Johanna hurried to the bed and leaned close. Sister Margaret fought back tears at the sight of her daughters, both fair haired and as lovely as a summer day. Johanna had stayed at Clare's side through the night. Their whispers and occasional laughter brought back memories of their youth.

"Tell them, Johanna," Clare whispered.

"Later," she said, stroking her sister's brow.

"Tell us what?" Sister Margaret insisted.

When Johanna didn't speak, Clare said, "When I —" She swallowed, then took several shallow breaths. "When I'm gone, you're to say Johanna died. Mark my grave with her name."

Meridene began to cry.

Sister Margaret crossed herself. "Nay."

Clare's fever-bright eyes pleaded. "You must agree, Sister Margaret. Let her take my son. Go to that land in the Borders. She could raise Alasdair. Help him seek his destiny."

Quietly, Johanna said, "Who's to know 'tis me rather than Clare?"

"Anyone who has ever spent five minutes with the two of you," hissed Meridene. "You may favor each other in physical appearance, but in temperament you're as different as moonrise and sunset."

"Oh, please, Sister Margaret," Johanna pleaded. "Clare abided by the king's wishes. She never told anyone in Scotland that she had a sister. She never revealed that we chose the name

13

'Benison' for ourselves because it means 'blessed.' We have no blood kin, save little Alasdair. Do not deny me the chance to have a life outside the abbey."

A refusal perched on Sister Margaret's lips, but she paused, swayed by the plea in her daughter's voice. Johanna was as capable as any man at running an estate. She was fair in her judgments and honest in her ways. No one knew her in Dumfries; the land lay in the Borders between England and Scotland, far from Scarborough Abbey and farther still from Castle Macqueen.

And she deserved a life of her own. One thing held Sister Margaret back. Years before Edward had branded both Clare and Johanna with a hot iron and declared them wards of the crown. The symbol, a blunted sword no bigger than a thumb, signified the conquests of Edward I. The only trouble was, Clare's brand appeared right side up, Johanna's upside down.

"What of the brand?" Sister Margaret asked.

Johanna's hand flew to her shoulder. "Clare's husband will be hanged," she said. "Who's to see the mark?"

"True," said Sister Margaret. "But it could be dangerous. Should any who know Clare come to visit that place, you'll be found out."

A familiar confidence twinkled in Johanna's eyes. "The Stapledons will go with me. They know all of the Macqueens. Should any of those Highlanders defy the king and come to Dumfries, Bertie can alert me." She blotted her sister's brow.

In her typical authoritative voice, she added, "I'll see that your son makes a fine man, Clare."

Clare closed her eyes and smiled. "You will not. You'll teach him to swear and skip Mass."

Tears streamed down Johanna's cheeks. Her composure faltered. "I'll tell him an angel left him on my doorstep."

"At least you won't have to deal with his father," Clare whispered.

A candle sputtered, the tiny flame struggling for survival, much the same as Clare clung desperately to life. The stone walls seemed to close in on Sister Margaret; how could she, in the space of a day, send one of her daughters to God and the other to an uncertain future? Desperate to keep one, she said, "Johanna, there is much you do not know about Clare and Lord Drummond."

"Not so. She has told me all I need to know about the chieftain," said Johanna. "I'll raise Alasdair to believe his sire was a legend among men, although I know it for a lie."

"Oh, Johanna, you have it crosswise," said Clare, so near death she gasped for breath. "Drummond isn't bad. He hates only me." She closed her eyes and sighed. "And with good cause."

Chapter
1

Seven Years Later
Fairhope Tower

The door to the buttery slammed open. "A stranger's just come, my lady," said Amauri, the porter, as breathless as if he had run all the way from Carlisle. "He claims he's your husband."

Johanna turned around so quickly the wide cuff of her surcoat tipped over a crock of honey. Fighting back panic, she righted the jar before the sticky contents spilled onto the workbench. Were it not for the fear in the servant's eyes, she would have accused him of teasing her. "He said nothing else?"

Amauri's mouth pinched with disapproval. "Only that he was Drummond Macqueen was all."

Drummond Macqueen was dead, hanged years ago by King Edward I. Although she'd received no formal notice of Drummond's execution, she

16

hadn't expected condolences from the Crown; the ruthlessness of Edward I toward his enemies was legendary. The arrival of this imposter did seem oddly timed, since the old king had been laid to rest himself last year. The new king, his son, Edward II, had recently been crowned.

Surely the man played some jest or hoped to profit by posing as her husband. He'd soon learn that the widow Macqueen was no easy mark for tricksters.

"You mustn't worry, Amauri. Show him to the hall. Have Evelyn serve him the everyday ale, but she's not to chat with him. And you're not to carry his luggage."

"Aye, Lady Clare." He bowed and turned.

Johanna had answered to that name for so long it sounded natural. She did not regret losing her own identity; in taking Clare's name she kept her sister's memory alive. But more, seven years after the fact, Johanna knew she was fulfilling her own destiny.

The porter stopped. "What shall I do with his elephant?"

"His what?"

"His elephant." The servant put his hands on either side of his head and wagged his fingers. "Massive beast with huge ears, a snout as big as last year's Yule log, and beady eyes."

Johanna glowered at him. "I know what an elephant looks like. I've seen the drawings in Alasdair's books."

Embarrassment turned the servant's complexion pink. He fumbled with the laces on his jerkin. "Sorry, my lady. I meant no offense. Everyone knows you're as bright as the king's own chamberlain."

At any other time she would have scoffed at his praise, but considering the meeting ahead, she needed every scrap of confidence she could muster. "And you're a prince among porters, Amauri. Where is the creature now?"

"Chained to a post in the outer bailey and drawing a crowd. The workmen from Saddler's Dale dropped their plows in the field and swarmed the creature. The cobbler's wife swooned."

Johanna imagined the excitement the beast would cause. She also wondered where the visitor had acquired the odd animal. She had heard of only one elephant in the land, and it was housed in the Royal Menagerie.

Alarm pricked her senses. The Royal Menagerie occupied a part of the Tower of London. Drummond had been taken there for execution. But what, her common sense demanded, would a man posing as a Highland chieftain be doing with an elephant?

Trying to still her racing heart, she dismissed the porter. "Fret not about the beast unless it causes trouble. Its owner won't be here long." Then she carefully rolled down the sleeves of her bliaud and stepped into the afternoon sunshine.

In the castle yard the wheelwright haggled with the blacksmith over the price of nails; the randy potboy bartered with a comely goosegirl over a more personal and earthy commodity. From the laundry shed came the fresh scent of lavender soap. An infant wailed. A horse whinnied. A small herd of sheep fled before a yapping dog.

The familiar sights and sounds soothed Johanna's jangled nerves and inspired rational thought. Once she had lived in fear of discovery, but after seven years she'd grown comfortable with the identity of her twin sister. Everyone, from the lordly sheriff of Dumfries to the poorest cabbage farmer, was loyal to her and protective of Alasdair.

At the thought of her son, she grew fearful again and paused near the rabbit warren. This had been his favorite place to play, until he saw the butcher slaughter an old buck. Alasdair had sworn never to eat rabbit again. Although she hadn't given birth to him, Johanna considered herself his mother. She had paced the floor and comforted him when a budding tooth made him fretful. She had watched with joy in her heart and tears in her eyes when he'd taken his first wobbly steps. She had made mistakes. She had showered him with too much affection. She had, in sum, spoiled him.

What if this stranger tried to take Alasdair? That possibility brought her to the point of panic. Comfort came with the knowledge that Alasdair was absent from the castle. After the midday meal, her son had gone fishing with Bertie Stapledon, but they always returned before dark. Instinct told her to get rid of this stranger before her son came home.

Eager to do just that, she pulled off her soiled coif and picked up the hem of her work dress. Then she hurried across the yard and raced up the steep steps to the hill fort. As she made her way to the upstairs hall, she laid out a plan for dealing with the man who awaited her. She would greet him kindly. She would listen to his preposterous story. She would name him a liar and order him off her land. If he refused she would have her guards subdue him. Then she would send word for the sheriff and insist he earn his retaining fee by sending back the pretender and his elephant from whence they'd come.

But the moment she saw the stranger, even from across the hall, she was forced to rethink her strategy.

In profile, he bore so striking a resemblance to Alasdair that Johanna grew panicky all over again. His straight nose with its high bridge and gently flaring nostrils marked him as a relation. His pitch-black hair reminded her of her son's unruly mane. A sensitive mouth and strong, square jaw confirmed the likeness. But more than his features, his intensity of concentration as he examined the needlework on the fire screen swayed her the most. Bending from the waist, he looked just as Alasdair had when he'd first seen a turtle draw into its shell. This man appeared interested and inquisitive. And breathtakingly handsome.

Without doubt, he was a Macqueen.

Terrified, she could not yet step into the room and announce her presence, but continued to watch him unnoticed. Rather than trunk hose and jerkin, he wore trews of soft leather and a full-sleeved shirt of loosely woven wool. His long legs were lean, his flanks trim; yet his shoulders were as broad as a blacksmith's. In his hand he held a Highland bonnet, ornamented with three tattered feathers and a shiny silver badge bearing an emblem she couldn't make out, but suspected was a wolf rampant, the symbol of Clan Macqueen. The device was repeated on the palm-size brooch that secured his distinctive tartan cape at his shoulder.

Over the years she had created fictional stories about Drummond, tales designed to inspire pride in a fatherless boy. To Alasdair, his sire was a heroic figure, pure of heart and strong of will. Would this man, surely a Macqueen cousin or uncle, refute or enlarge upon the legends?

"I see improvement in your needlework, Clare," he said, still studying the framed tapestry.

Startled, Johanna stepped back. Then she caught herself. She would not fear this man, neither would she allow his breach of etiquette to go unchecked. "I pray the same is true of your manners, sir, for you haven't the right to address me with so much familiarity."

He stood upright and strolled toward her. With an outwardly casual air, he studied her from head to toe; yet his blue eyes were intense in their inspection. "I haven't the *right,* Clare? You seem to have forgotten just how many rights I hold where you are concerned."

She felt invaded and clenched her fists to keep from slapping him. "Who are you?"

He tisked and shook his head. "Shame, shame, my dear. Not that I expected you to welcome me with open arms. You preferred to save your embraces for other men."

A pigeon landed on the sill of the open window. Seeking a diversion from the compelling man and his just accusations, Johanna shooed the bird away. Casually, she said, "I asked your name, sir."

One side of his mouth curled up in a smile. "I haven't changed *that* much. You know precisely who I am. Why pretend otherwise?"

Resisting the urge to call him a knave, Johanna summoned patience. "Because Drummond Macqueen is dead. The old king hanged him."

"Not so. Edward the First, rest his soul, chose to be merciful. His son proved benevolent and upon taking the crown, set me free." Anger glittered in his eyes and tightened his jaw. "But then, as I recall, you have intimate knowledge of our new king, do you not? Have you presented him with more bastards?"

He was referring to Clare's affair with the Plantagenet prince who was now the king. With dread Johanna remembered that all the Macqueens knew. Thank God their lands were far away in the Highlands, for her heart wrenched thinking Alasdair might be scorned for another's sin. Yet how dare this brute be so rude as to bring up Clare's mistake? Johanna had no intention of addressing her sister's indiscretion. She sighed and lifted her chin. "Who are you, and what do you want?"

With no more vigor than a carpenter choosing wood, he said, "You have a brand here — a wee blunted sword." He pulled his shirt aside and touched the thick muscles above his right collarbone. " 'Tis why you wear modest gowns."

Seeing his strong hand and remembering the passion Clare had attributed to her marriage bed, Johanna fought back a surge of longing. She would not risk losing her independence or revealing her true identity, not for the sake of passion. "Your knowledge of the mark proves nothing."

"You cannot possibly have forgotten me." A trace of vulnerability laced his words and his massive shoulders jumped.

Sensing a weakness in him, she took advantage; Clare had risked her immortal soul for her husband, and Johanna had too much to lose. "Forgotten *you*, an imposter?" she scoffed. "You may be memorable in some circles, but here . . ." She let the insult trail off.

The troll laughed, a hearty sound that seemed natural. "Very well. I offer you more intimate proof." He plopped down on a bench. Resting his arms on his knees, he stared into the mug. "You suffer dreadful cramps during your menses, which are as regular as Sunday Mass. You used to cuddle beside me in bed or lie awake until I joined you. Who else but a husband could know that?"

Appalled, Johanna felt herself blush. Unlike Clare, she didn't suffer for being a woman. That he knew the particulars of Clare's cycle created the first doubt in Johanna's surety. But she hadn't built a successful life by withering before every man who challenged her. "You are not my husband."

Surprise lent elegance to his rugged good looks. He took a long pull on the ale. "Have you annulled our marriage?"

She wanted to rail at him; instead she began to pace the rush-strewn floor. "How long, sir, will you continue this farce? I am not your wife."

He chuckled, but the sound held no humor. "You're not a very *good* wife."

"Enough of your rough talk!" She whirled and marched over to him. "I can see you are a Macqueen. I give you that much."

"Then I've made progress. Hurrah for me."

"Which Macqueen are you?"

He stared at her breasts. "The only one you know in the carnal sense — at least I believe that is so."

The insult deserved a like reply. "Have you come here for money?"

He almost choked, and his gaze leaped to her face. "Money?"

She'd made him uncomfortable. Hurrah for her. "If so, you've made a useless journey, for I haven't

24

a mark to squander on a man who cannot earn an honest wage."

He craned his neck in an exaggerated examination of the tapestries on the walls, the brass brazier, and the diamond shaped panes in the windows. "You expect me to think you are poor, amid all of this prosperity? The largesse of the Plantagenets, I assume."

To build the keep, she had sold all of her jewelry and Clare's. When that had not been enough, she had indebted herself to the neighboring laird of Clan Douglas. During the construction she and Alasdair had lived in a crofter's hut. She had repaid the debt, and to this day, worked as hard as anyone in her demesne. "You know nothing about me or the origins of Fairhope Tower."

"You needn't explain, Clare. 'Twould seem we have the same benefactor." His expression grew hard, and he slammed down the tankard. "But I will not share you again."

His possessiveness gave her pause, for Clare had spoken at length about her husband's jealous nature. Perhaps it was one of many family flaws. Clare had loved Drummond more than life. She might still be alive were it not for his warring ways. The old heartbreak returned. "You have the poisoned brain of a madman."

"An interesting observation," he growled. "Especially from a faithless wife."

Suddenly afraid and desperate to get rid of him, she said, "I'll summon my guards."

He waved her off. "Summon your new king, should it suit you. He bids you well, by the way. But I'm certain you often receive his *greetings*."

She had seen Edward II only once. He'd been a prince back then. The truth came easily. "I haven't had the honor of seeing His Majesty since I came to this land."

It was the wrong thing to say. His eyes narrowed, accentuating the length of his lashes. "Come now. Our gracious new sovereign cannot say enough about the way in which you *honor* him. He was particularly verbal about his sojourn last year in Carlisle."

In January of 1307, the old king had convened Parliament in the nearby city of Carlisle, but neither he nor his son had communicated with her. What game did this man play? At a loss for a convincing denial and weary of defending herself to a stranger, she again spoke the truth. "You have been misinformed. Ask anyone here."

"I'll not reap the truth from them. These people will be loyal to you." He gave her a sugar-sweet smile. "But that will change. This land, the keep, and all in it belong to me."

"Mother!" Alasdair's voice boomed through the keep.

Johanna gasped. The stranger lifted his brows.

She heard the slap of boots on the stairs. Her heart hammered in tune with the footfalls. A moment later, Alasdair burst into the room, a huffing Bertie Stapledon on his heels.

Hair in disarray, blue eyes bright with wonder,

her son skidded to a halt, scattering the rushes. "There's an elephant in the bailey, Mother." He lifted his arms. "An *elephant!*"

The stranger looked awestruck. "As the Lord lives," he murmured, "that lad is my son."

Johanna glanced at Bertie, the servant who had accompanied Clare to the Highlands years before. To Johanna's great dismay, he doffed his cap and bowed. "Lord Drummond," he stammered, and shot Johanna a worried frown. "We thought you dead."

"So I'm told. You're Bertie, if I recall."

Johanna went weak with fear. The man *was* Drummond Macqueen. He had spent seven years resenting his wife's infidelity while languishing in prison. Johanna's demesne had prospered under her care, and Alasdair had grown to a good-natured, precocious boy of whom any father would be proud; Drummond had a right to claim both. Could she convince him that she was the wife he hated and whose body and spirit he knew intimately?

She must entice him into leaving. Either way, she'd do her acting without an audience. "Alasdair, go with Bertie." She tipped her head toward the door.

As if he hadn't heard, the boy approached Drummond Macqueen. His chin up, boyish pride shimmering like a bright mantle, Alasdair said, "Who are you?"

Drummond seemed fascinated by the lad. "I'm your father."

Alasdair peeked behind the man. "Where are your wings, then?"

"My wings? Why would I have wings?"

Flapping his arms, Alasdair sighed dramatically. "Because if you're my father, you must be an angel. Mother said 'twas so."

Surprise and amusement twinkled in Drummond's eyes. "She did?" He shot her a measuring glance. "'What else did she tell you about me?"

Alasdair shrugged. "Stories. Hundreds of them. No — thousands." Turning pleading eyes to Johanna, he said, "Is he my father?"

Her throat as dry as last summer's bracken, Johanna tried to swallow. Gathering courage, she kept her voice even. "We'll discuss it later, Alasdair. You are excused."

"He *is* my father." He hooted with joy and turned his back on her. "Is that elephant yours?"

Still wonderstruck, Alasdair's father gave the lad a genuine smile. "Aye. He's called Longfellow."

"I want to ride it." Alasdair tucked his small thumbs into his belt. "I ride very well, you know."

Drummond coughed discreetly, but Johanna saw the humor behind it. She needed to talk to him privately, seriously. "Alasdair, leave the room with Bertie."

When the lad didn't budge, Drummond's expression grew fierce. "Do as your mother says."

Alasdair rocked on his heels and grinned slyly. "Will you let me ride the elephant if I do?"

"Let's put it this way," Drummond said with false civility. "Should you harbor any desire of getting within a bishop's mile of that elephant, you'll obey your mother. Now."

Controlling the situation became vital to Johanna. She took Alasdair's arm. "Out with you. You've lessons with Brother Julian."

"But —"

"Go!" She pointed to the door.

As Bertie led him from the room, her son looked back over his shoulder at Drummond Macqueen. Johanna shivered, just thinking his name.

Clare's husband was here. Wait. Not Clare's husband. Johanna's. No. Oh, goodness.

She knew nothing about being a wife and less about guarding her every word. Perhaps he'd merely come here to taunt her.

"He's not a Plantagenet bastard."

She walked to the dining table and, from a footed bowl, picked up two hazelnuts. Rolling them in her palm, she said, "Nay. He's *my* son."

Rising, he came toward her, his boots softly crunching the fresh rushes. "My apologies. Rest assured I'll not deny him my name, nor my protection."

His nearness made her uncomfortable, for she felt small beside his towering form. He smelled of leather and warm summer air, and her mind whirled with pictures of the intimacies he would expect, intimacies she had dreamed of but never thought to share. Confused by her own romantic musings, she fought for command of

29

her emotions. "Alasdair has no need of *your* protection. I've managed quite well."

He took a handful of the hazelnuts. "You've indulged him."

Her temper flared. "How dare you judge me. He's all I have."

Much too reasonably, he said, "Not anymore. You have me . . . again." He cracked the nuts.

The sound made Johanna jump. "I do not want you. If our new king has indeed set you free, then go back to your Highland kin."

He picked the nut from the shell and put it on the windowsill. "Now why would I do that when I have a prosperous estate, a son, and a comely wife . . . here?"

Comely wife? The compliment spelled doom, for how could she make him believe that she was his wife and at the same time speed his departure? So daunting a task made her bold. "Do not waste your pretty speeches on me."

"You doubt me?" He feigned innocence, his expression so reminiscent of Alasdair that Johanna despaired.

"I don't even know you," she said.

He slapped his hand over his clan badge. "Never have truer words passed my lips."

How could he be so glib when her future was at stake? "The past doesn't concern me," she said through gritted teeth. "I'll have Evelyn prepare you a room."

"You've clanged."

Her heart catapulted into her throat. Did he

suspect her for an imposter? No, he couldn't; under order of the old king, Clare had not told Drummond she had a twin sister. Edward I had been explicit in his wish that no one know of Johanna's existence, and Sister Margaret had agreed. The irony of the ruse was a balm to Johanna, for she had called *him* a pretender. "That's hardly surprising, given your seven-year absence, for I was only fifteen at the start of it."

"You've matured handsomely. And you are different."

Uncurling her fingers, she let the nuts drop into the bowl. Dampness from her palm had turned the shells noticeably darker than the others. "I've changed more than you know."

An understatement, Drummond thought, as his gaze again strayed to her slender waist and generous breasts. A true bounty of wifely assets, especially to a husband who'd been denied those charms for seven years. "Then I await the opportunity to explore the *new* Clare."

Her brown eyes flashed fire. "You'd fare better exploring a hedgehog, my lord."

By all the sacred relics, she had changed. "What has happened to my malleable bride?"

"Of necessity, she has thrived in your absence."

She'd been naive and convent bred. Now she trembled with indignation. Drummond relished the challenge of peeling off her armor of self-control and gaining revenge for her sins against him. Most men accepted the role of cuckold, especially if a Plantagenet was the one swiving their wife. Not Drummond Macqueen.

With four brothers and twice that many uncles, he'd had little in his youth to call his own, save a drafty room in a Highland stronghold, his weapons of war, and a finely bred horse. Then, in an effort to forestall England's conquest of Scotland, he'd taken the virgin Clare to wife.

The voice of reason intruded and reminded him that she'd borne him a healthy son, for no one would doubt the boy's parentage. She would, by God's grace, give him others.

A noise interrupted his thoughts. The fat gray pigeon again lighted on the sill, cooed, and snatched up the nut. In a flutter of wings, the bird flew off. Drummond was reminded of the noisy crows that inhabited the Tower.

Dark memories intruded: the constant baitings by English guards; an animal, they'd called him, and a wild creature. Early in his incarceration, he'd begun to believe them. They had flaunted their women before him and once brought him a diseased whore.

"She should be to an animal's liking," they had said.

The young and virile Drummond had turned his back on the unfortunate woman. The guards had never brought him another female. At least not a human, and they had never stopped calling him an animal.

He glanced down at his wife and found her studying him. He grew uneasy at her steady, self-assured gaze, felt as if his tongue were tied in knots. Others parts of him, however, reacted in typical, if unwanted, fashion. He pictured his fingers sliding through her silky golden hair. He remembered making love to her and nipping her shoulder at the spot where she bore the mysterious brand. Her compliance in their marriage bed had been any man's dream. A return to those days seemed appealing in the extreme.

His sudden desire for her made him cross. "Then you will surely thrive under my husbandly guidance."

"I do not need a husband."

"Oh, but you do," he spat. "And a lord and master as well."

As confident as a queen at court, she did not waver. "I believe you are Drummond Macqueen, but I cannot imagine what you want with me. The housemaid, Evelyn, will show you to your chamber."

Drummond felt like a troublesome guest, easily dismissed. "What will you do?"

"The same as I always do. I'll manage my estate." She turned to go.

He grabbed her arm and spun her around. "Fairhope Tower is *our* estate. I'll accompany you."

Chapter 2

Only through sheer strength of will did Johanna keep her composure as he led her down the curved stairway. With a stone wall on her left and a new husband on her right, she felt trapped. She needed time alone, time to think, time to plan. But how could she manage a spare moment if Drummond insisted on following her like a cat after a milkmaid? He couldn't possibly come into her life to stay. Could he?

The answer made her stomach grow tight; as her husband he could do as he pleased — with her, with Fairhope Tower, and with Alasdair.

"This keep looks new," he said, staring at the red stone walls.

Pride in her home eased her worried heart. " 'Twas finished about five years ago."

"The stone is an odd color."

" 'Tis from the quarry near Dumfries. Sweetheart Abbey gets its name from the color of the stone."

He paused at the second level and peered through the open door into the kitchen. Evelyn sat at a table cleaning a still-wiggling trout and humming a popular lay. At the walk-through hearth, which separated the kitchen from the main hall, the spit boy cranked the handle that turned a haunch of venison over the fire. Bundles of drying herbs hung from the ceiling. Leather and wooden barrels lined the curved walls — all in readiness for the successful return of the huntsmen.

Evelyn looked up and glanced curiously from Johanna to Drummond. "Alasdair and Bertie made a fine catch, my lady," she said.

"I can see they did. Have the cook prepare it with leeks and butter sauce. I'll see if the market has fresh berries for a tart."

The maid seemed absorbed in Drummond's tartan. "Shall I set another place at table tonight?" she asked coyly.

Before Johanna could reply, Drummond said, "Aye, at the head."

Evelyn sucked in her breath and her hands flew to her cheeks. "My lord! You're supposed to be dead and buried." The fish plopped onto the earthen floor. The spit boy dashed to retrieve it. The lovestruck lad cast a crestfallen gaze toward Johanna.

"I'm very much alive," Drummond said to everyone in the room. "And I'm fair content to be home."

As calmly as she could, Johanna said, "Contain

yourself, Evelyn, and tell Amauri I said to fetch his lordship's luggage."

Taking her arm, Drummond led her back to the circular stairs. "How long have you lived here?"

Although she expected to cause discord, she couldn't avoid the subject of his incarceration. She couldn't help lying, either. "When I had recovered from Alasdair's birth, I came here straightaway and hired a builder."

"You? You accomplished all of this without counsel?"

Taking control of the situation came as natural to Johanna as bathing. But just now she must pretend to be the Clare he remembered, and Johanna's twin would have offered an explanation for bold behavior. "After your arrest, my circumstances changed."

"Who designed the keep?"

Should she hesitate, as Clare would have? Yes. Drummond must believe that time and events had brought about the differences in his wife, but she would have to go slowly to convince him. "Simon de Canterbury."

Drummond nodded his approval. "He has a good reputation in London. Why did you name it Fairhope?"

At that moment, Johanna felt capable in the role of his wife, for Clare had spoken at length of her brief time as his bride. "Because we discussed it on our wedding night."

He lifted one brow and gave her a cocky grin.

" 'Twas the extent of intelligent conversation between us, if memory of the occasion serves."

As the object of his heated gaze, she grew flustered. "Not so, my lord. We discussed the white heather the maid put in our bed for good luck. We also discussed the children you would give me."

He chuckled. " 'Twas the *making* of the children that dominated our speech and our actions. Once you grew comfortable with the act, we never left the bed."

The act? Embarrassment and confusion plagued her, for Clare's version of the night had differed greatly. She had spoken in romantic terms, told of them worshiping each other and exploring every facet of love. In a dreamy remembrance, she had used words like *cherish* and *adore*. Drummond's offhanded account tarnished the second happiest event of Clare's short life. Only Alasdair's birth had ranked higher.

Why couldn't Drummond, Johanna thought with sadness, allow himself one loving memory of the past? It was a poor tribute to a woman who had gone to her grave with his name on her lips.

Incensed at his callousness, she hurried down the stairs and through the common room to the main entryway of the keep, where she snatched up her basket and her mantle. "I thought you wanted to accompany me to the village."

"Oh, I did and still do." He took the wrap and dropped it over her shoulders. "But your talk of making children distracted me."

So frustrated at him she thought she might scream, Johanna counted to five, then took a deep breath. "I shan't distract you again, my lord."

His gaze moved to her breasts. "I'm sure," he said, meaning the opposite.

Her first impulse was to challenge him, but Johanna thought better of it; she intended to keep a distance between them.

Hooking her basket in the crook of her elbow, she preceded him out the door. "What would you like to see first?"

You, naked and writhing beneath me, Drummond wanted to say. Instead, he stifled his base urges. Before he took Clare fully to wife again, she would reveal the details of her adulterous affair with the man who was now the king. Then she would beg her husband's forgiveness. But by all the saints, she was more enticing today, and she belonged to him.

On that gratifying thought, Drummond pulled the door closed behind him and surveyed his surroundings.

Built in the modern concentric design, Fairhope Tower stood on a high mound. At the base of the hill, instead of a moat, a hay-strewn lane ringed the keep. Beyond the now empty thoroughfare and butting up against the thick retaining wall was an assortment of timber post-and-beam houses, still so new they did not sag. Tradesmens' huts and merchants' stalls interspersed the residences. The soldiers' barracks comprised the largest building. It was flanked by a prosperous smithy on one side and the stables on the other.

Outside the ten-foot-thick circular wall, rye and millet prospered in the bailey, even though herds of fat sheep and cattle grazed there. Close by, the elephant, Longfellow, with Drummond's crusty companion on his back, stood amid a crowd of curious town dwellers and farmers. Farther out still, another wall, thicker than the first and crenelated for defense, circled the whole of the estate.

Impressed, Drummond looked down at his wife and again wondered how she had accomplished so much, for the keep was as fine as any in the Borders and far richer than he had expected. The Clare he remembered couldn't cipher or plan well enough to manage even the smallest of households. This defensible and flourishing community stood as futher testimony that she had changed or had received the guidance of an expert.

Clare, his faithless wife and the mother of his son.

A weight seemed to press in on Drummond at the thought of the lad, his only surviving son. He found himself softening toward the woman beside him.

She had always been lovely, her skin smooth and unblemished, and given to maidenly blushes, her hair thick and shimmering like precious gold. Yet now, her lovely brown eyes surveyed him with caution, and even had she tried, she could not conceal the intelligence there. When and from whom had she acquired it?

His gaze dropped to her lips, and he thought them fuller than he remembered and more prone to an appealing smile than a missish pout. She seemed dignified, self-assured, and passionate. That aspect of her brought a halt to his admiration. She had lain with the man who was now the ruler of the land. What if Edward II intended to keep her for his mistress?

She shifted the basket from one arm to the other. "Must you stare? You make me feel like a sow at market."

Drummond couldn't help but laugh. "Any man who likens you to a pig deserves to languish in a sty, and I'd be lying if I said other than you are a pleasure to look upon. 'Twas always so."

She started down the steep steps. "Thank you for that, my lord. Have you questions about the keep?"

He had dozens, and he had also years to obtain the answers. "What was here before?"

"A thriving crop of bracken, with heather and gorse for color and peat bogs for aroma."

He chuckled at her lighthearted reply and received a smile. The wordless exchange was oddly satisfying and completely unexpected. "How much land do we hold?"

She glided gracefully down the steps, a gentle breeze lifting her coif and revealing a coil of wheat-colored braids at the nape of her neck. And she smelled of heather, his favorite fragrance.

"I own the land and control the water within

one day's ride in all directions, according to the writ the old king granted to *me*."

Me. Her stressed use of the singular verified her new independent nature. He'd break her of that bad habit, too. "How much of it do we farm?"

"I lease it to the tenants. In exchange I reap first fruit of their labor."

If she wanted a contest of wills over pronouns, he'd gladly oblige. "What do we do with the profits?"

"With last year's tallage, I built four new houses, from which I now collect rents." She stopped halfway down the hill and pointed to several of the buildings that he had admired moments before. "I also set aside enough money for liming of the fallow fields. 'Tis proven to enrich the soil."

Her businesslike account of her stewardship of the land shocked him as much as his own desire for her. Exploring her charms would have to wait; for now he would delve into her mind. "I thought assuming responsibility made you sore at heart."

Her lips tightened, drawing his attention to her finely angled jaw. He'd like to put his mouth there and taste the flowers of Scotland on her skin.

She stared at the gatehouse. "It once did, but thanks to you, circumstances forced me to overcome my weaknesses."

She was condemning him for defending his culture and his land against Edward I and leaving her to fend for herself. "Had you not bedded

41

a prince, the Macqueens would have taken you in. You could have lived in safety in the bosom of my clan."

A shrug rippled her mantle. "I'm happy here." Picking up the hem of her dress, she hurried down the remainder of the steps.

In the interest of harmony, Drummond dropped the subject of what she should have done. Although he had spent years anguishing over the state of affairs of Clan Macqueen, he had eventually given up hope of returning to the Highlands. A lifetime of loyalty pulled at him, and like dried leaves tossed on hot coals, his yearning for Scotland burst into a fiery need. If she would but admit her infidelity, he would gift her with this demesne, take Alasdair and head north. His family would welcome him. They would also name Alasdair the son of a whore, for they all knew she had given herself to an Englishman.

For years Drummond had hated her for that. "Who helped you?" he snapped.

At his angry tone, she drew back and glared at him. "A league of Roman engineers rose from the dead and bade me let them build this keep," she snapped back. "I sat upon a tufted silk throne and nibbled pomegranates and figs while they struck up the castle of my dreams."

A moment after his mind began working again, Drummond choked with laughter. How queer, he thought, that she had become so entertaining and distracting.

She crossed the well-tended lane. "I learned many skills at the abbey."

Did she regret the preposterous outburst? Why? Suddenly he felt driven to know more about her. He thought of the stories she'd told of her childhood. "You learned from Sister Margaret?"

"Some knowledge came from her."

She obviously didn't want to discuss it, which was peculiar, because her childhood had been a favorite subject. "Then was it one of your friends there? Meridene or the other lass. What was her name? Juliana?"

Seemingly uncertain of their destination, she scanned the row of dwellings against the wall. In a quiet voice, she said, " 'Twas Johanna."

He sensed a change in her mood, a return to the wariness he'd seen before. "Aye, I remember her now. You always swore that Johanna could outfit and manage an army on crusade."

In answer, she whispered, "She could," and headed for the butcher's shop. "The archers will return soon. I'm certain you'd like to meet with the huntsman. He'll come here first — if they were successful."

Idle chatter had once been her favorite pastime. Now she seemed worried. Determined to learn the source of her distress, he caught up with her. "Now why would I enjoy the company of those fellows?" She glanced up, and he saw tears in her eyes. "Why are you crying?"

"I'm not crying." She made a lie of the statement by brushing tears from her cheeks. " 'Tis

43

only the harsh light from the sun."

"And I'm a Venetian moneylender. Tell me why the mention of your friend at the abbey upsets you?"

"Leave off, Drummond. I simply miss the people there."

"Then invite them to visit." Unable to resist taunting a reaction out of her, he added, "You have my permission."

Her eyes blazed indignation and her complexion flushed the same color as her faded red surcoat. "Perhaps I shall."

If he were clever and careful, he could find out from the townsfolk if any man visited her regularly. "Then we are in accord. And after we see the butcher, you can introduce me to everyone else in the village."

"Introduce you? You told none but Amauri that you are my . . . husband?"

He resisted the urge to touch her and vanquish her hesitance. "I saved the pleasure for you."

She opened her mouth to snap out a retort but changed her mind. Her momentary control disappointed Drummond, for he liked this new, fiery Clare.

"Of course," she said, as if complying with a mundane request. Then she ducked beneath the flycatcher and disappeared into the butcher's shop.

Drummond fumed. She should make a production of his homecoming. She should present him to the people with all of the respect due the lord of the keep. She should be grateful that her husband had taken her back.

"Are you coming, my lord?"

The cheeriness of her tone set his feet in motion. Once inside the structure he found her standing beside a bearded man whose upper arms were as big as the hams that hung from the ceiling beams. His thick brown hair was closely cropped with a striking patch of white at his left temple. He wore a soiled apron slung low over a rounded belly, and when he smiled, Drummond thought it genuine.

Motioning him forward, Clare said, "My lord, meet John Handle, a solid Christian and our right goodly butcher."

The man fairly beamed. "Welcome home, Lord Drummond, and praise God. What happened? We thought you dead."

Drummond hadn't expected mercy from Edward I. Edward II, however, probably sought some perverse glee in returning Drummond to the wife who'd made him a cuckold. Even if it were common knowledge, he'd not address it with a butcher.

"I escaped the old king's justice."

Handle nodded vigorously. "An' hid out in the Highlands waiting for him to die. Bless his son for favoring you. The new king does, doesn't he?"

"Aye. He'll not lay siege to Fairhope Tower." Unless he came for his mistress, thought Drummond.

"Her ladyship has told us all about you," the butcher went on. "My favorite tale is the one about you slaying a wild bear with only a dirk for weapon. 'Tis Alasdair's favorite, too. She made you a saint for the lad."

Shocked, Drummond stared at the woman beside him. Her head bowed, she toyed with the pink ribbons that adorned her basket. Why had she concocted such a story? It was pure fantasy, for no sane man would challenge a boar without a pike and a sword.

On the heels of confusion, Drummond felt a surge of pride, for she had spoken well of him to his son. Knowing he must comment, he said the first thought that popped into his baffled mind. "My lady flatters me overmuch."

John Handle smiled fondly. " 'Tis her way, my lord. A more kind and generous soul never drew a breath. She rations peat with the rest of us. When it comes to protecting her, I'd trade cleaver for sword."

Drummond had expected scorn from these people. After his release in April, he'd dawdled in complying with Edward II's command that he reside at Fairhope Tower. Longfellow had grown fat on the lush English countryside.

Drummond hadn't expected objectivity from the people of Fairhope, either. He must test their loyalty. Could this butcher confirm Drummond's suspicions that his wife still entertained the newly crowned Edward Plantagenet? To that end, Drummond pointed to the slabs of meat.

46

"Your wares look fit enough for our new sovereign."

John Handle cocked his head to the side. "The pork? Doesn't he have a taste for beef?"

So, the butcher had knowledge of the king's preferences. No doubt he took special care to please the monarch's palate every time he languished at Fairhope Tower. Glancing at his unfaithful wife, Drummond felt the old anger rise. To the butcher, he said, "Did His Majesty say as much to you?"

Looking like he'd been poked, the man grew stiff. "The king don't speak to the likes o' me."

Now that he was about to catch her in the first lie, Drummond relished his victory. Casually, he said, "Then how did you know he prefers beef to pork?"

"Brother Julian said 'twas so. He heard it from the prior at Sweetheart Abbey, who heard it from the archbishop himself when he was in Carlisle making a saint of that Welshman. Know you of it differently?"

Drummond floundered, suddenly adrift in a sea of misconceptions. His wife looked away, but not before he saw the disappointment in her eyes. He felt ashamed of himself and groped for something to say. The butcher seemed oblivious to both Drummond's ploy and his wife's reaction to it.

Hoping for the best, he plastered on a smile. " 'Tis true the new king takes beef over pork, but I imagine he'd change his tune, should he see these fresh hams."

Clare rolled her eyes and huffed in disgust.

The butcher sucked in his paunch. "Thank you, my lord."

Eager to extricate himself and his wife, Drummond held out his hand, "Shall we, my dear?"

Ignoring him, she said much too sweetly, "John, send over a haunch of that meat — for *my gracious lord.*" Then she left the way they'd come.

Once in the lane, she walked toward the weaver's shed. Over the clickety-clack of the looms, Drummond tried to verify Edward Plantagenet's stories about his dallyings with Drummond's wife. The weaver proved loyal to Clare, as did the cobbler, the market maid, and the chandler. To Drummond's dismay, each of the people he spoke with had a tale of his bravery that rivaled or surpassed the story told by the butcher. With a frayed and rotting rope, he had descended a treacherous glen and saved a wayward child. And all of the heroic episodes had come from Clare Macqueen. Why would she make him a cuckold and then create such tales?

When they exited the candle shop, she turned on Drummond. "These are good people, and they do not deserve to be used as pawns in your senseless game."

She spoke the truth, for he found the townsfolk likeable, open, and truly thankful to have him in their midst. But their gratitude didn't absolve her. "Do you deny your liaison with Edward?" he demanded.

"I do not deny that a thirteen-year-old bride can easily fall prey to a royal prince."

"A decent Scotswoman would never willingly spread her legs for an Englishman."

"What about all of the Douglas heiresses who have married English earls?"

How dare she sound so educated and so reasonable about cuckolding him, as if she'd had no choice in the matter. "I care nothing for those Lowlanders."

"And I had no choice."

"You should have sought my counsel," he ground out.

She moved so close to him that their clothing touched. "I swear on Alasdair's soul that *I* could not seek you out, Drummond."

Her piercing gaze touched his soul, and he thought again about how much she had changed in demeanor, and the more he looked at her, the more certain he was that her appearance had also changed. She'd lost her girlish freckles, and she no longer fluttered her eyelashes to gain his attention and his admiration. Obviously, she wanted neither.

But he'd have what he wanted from her. "That's a bold challenge, coming from you."

She gave him a fake smile. "You're a bold man."

He found that he liked the way the sun turned her skin the color of cream, and any man would admire her warm brown eyes and expressive mouth. His life would be easier if her disposition were as pleasing and her morals were suddenly flawless. "I can get bolder still," he grumbled.

"Then show your mettle to your son," she said curtly. "I'm certain he will appreciate your display of animal behavior more than I."

He cringed at her description of him. "You're angry with me?"

She dropped the now full basket. "Yes, I am. I've spent the better part of the day watching you connive to make a whore of me in front of my own people. They respect me and seek my guidance. Now, if you will excuse me, I have ledgers to balance and servants to oversee."

Only his father had given him so chilling a set down. "Have your steward do it."

"I *am* my steward."

His mind skidded to a halt. "You?"

A bell rang out. " 'Tis four o'clock," she said. "Alasdair will have completed his studies. You promised to show him your elephant. I hope you'll not disappoint him. We sit down to table at eight."

With that, she whirled and started up the steep steps to the keep. Drummond watched her go, her back stiff, her hips swaying, her arms empty. "You forgot something," he called out.

She stopped and turned to face him. Her righteous anger stirred his blood, for she looked like a woman defending her home.

With complete irreverence, he said, "According to the chandler's tale, when I rode into battle against Edward the First, you always rewarded my chivalry with a parting kiss. I assume a return

50

from the dead deserves an equal show of affection."

She marched toward him. Feeling like the gallant in every story he'd heard today, he prepared to receive her favors. Then he'd rebuke her, or perhaps he wouldn't.

But rather than offer him the kiss he anticipated, she snatched up her basket. "Go whistle!"

When she turned away again, her steps quicker and more determined, Drummond continued to admire her. He had been wrong to draw conclusions, but damn if she didn't make him feel like a useless ornament in his own home. She also brought out the playful lad in him, for he wanted to race up the steps and pinch her pretty bottom. From past experience, he knew what she would do in response.

On that enticing thought, he anticipated the evening to come.

Johanna had just pressed seal to wax on a letter to Sister Margaret informing her of Drummond's return, when Bertie Stapledon entered the solar.

Cap in hand, a worried frown creasing his brow, he leaned against the closed door. He wore a bulky tunic belted low on his hips and trunk hose that he'd patched himself. "I should have been here to alert you of his arrival."

Warmed by his loyalty, she attempted to make light of the situation. "Then who would have taken Alasdair fishing?"

51

A fun loving man with a penchant for fat trout and a fondness for the hunt, the widower had been a constant in Johanna's life. As always, he fell into the role of mentor. "You've thought about what to do?"

"I've thought of little else. 'Twould seem I must learn to be a wife to him."

"Evelyn said he insisted on taking your place at table tonight."

She shrugged. "I always thought it mere ceremony."

"And a carrot to dangle before Alasdair when he gets an itch to roam the tower battlement late at night."

A gentleness settled over Johanna. She could not love Alasdair more, even if she had nourished him in her own womb. When the trials of motherhood troubled her, Bertie was always there to help. "I doubt he'll soon bedevil us with that threat. An elephant is surely more exciting."

"How did Lord Drummond come by such a creature?"

She stared at the clothes chest that seemed to dominate the room, much the same as the owner governed her thoughts. "I know not, but 'twill give me something safe to discuss with him."

"How is it for you, Lady Friend?"

The endearing name for her had been coined on the night his wife died. Bertie had been downhearted and lonely. Johanna had encouraged him to talk. The sad event had sealed their friendship.

" 'Tis confusing, Bertie. I feel vulnerable, as if I'm a breath away from botching it all."

He moved a wooden stool near the table where she sat. "I imagine you were shocked when you saw him."

"Not half so much so as when you called him by name. I had condemned him for an imposter."

Bertie laughed, but when she did not join in he grew serious. "Pardon, but I suspect he was just as disturbed as you."

Johanna felt a burst of relief. "I hadn't thought of that."

" 'Tis natural you didn't."

Her past mistakes danced before her like demons around a Hallowmas fire. "I should have inquired after him — at least once in all these years."

"Why? They didn't call the old Edward the 'Hammer of the Scots' because he fancied himself a carpenter. He hated the Highlanders more than the Welsh. No one would have expected him to spare the chieftain's life, and the less Clare Macqueen said to that Plantagenet, the better. Had you written in her name you might have attracted the attention of his son."

Bertie knew of Clare's affair with Edward II, and he'd been correct about the danger in her calling attention to herself. According to Drummond, Clare's royal lover had not forgotten her.

Johanna had bigger trouble now. "Drummond is convinced that I am the new king's mistress."

"Why would he think that?"

"It seems Edward told him so."

"Heaven help us all then, for even the kindest of men say he'll make a dreadful king. I remember him as a useless prince."

Under normal circumstances she would have fretted over the dire predictions regarding the new king's rule. Just now she had her own troubles. "Tell me what you remember about Drummond."

"I wasn't that close to him, do you see? And he did have a passel of younger brothers and kinsmen in that Highland stronghold. And they were off raiding or warring more often than not. But even in a crowd he stood out — proud as a man freshly knighted the day I first saw him. Destined for greatness, his father said."

"Did Drummond believe it?"

"If I'm remembered of it correctly, he laughed and swore 'twas the burden of being birthed on Whitsunday."

"He was popular?"

"Aye, but he was the firstborn son, with his father's blessings. A fair demon he was with a sword in his right hand and a wicked dirk in his left."

Needing a crime to offset Clare's sin, Johanna said, "He had mistresses, I suppose."

"I wouldn't know about those doings," Bertie said much too quickly and defensively.

"We can be certain, of course, that he's gone decent now."

"To be sure, for he brought no woman with

him. Just a garble talking Welshman — name of Morgan Fawr."

"Will Mr. Fawr need quarters in the keep?"

Without rancor, Bertie said, "Nay, he's a stable dweller." He tipped his head toward the trunk. "I don't suppose Amauri's been too busy to carry Lord Drummond's luggage up."

To which chamber, she asked herself for the hundredth time. When no answer came, she again faced the grim truth that she had no idea of what to do with Drummond Macqueen. "I haven't set Amauri to it yet."

"You could move Alasdair in with me and have his room to yourself."

Fairhope Tower had no guest chamber. When Red Douglas or Sheriff Hay visited, Johanna followed custom and relinquished her chamber for important guests. Bertie had given her a temporary solution to the problem of sleeping arrangements. "Have Evelyn move Alasdair's belongings to your room and my things to his — before she sets the table, and tell her she's to keep my business to herself or I'll send her back to her family."

"I'll tell her, but she cooed like a dove just moments ago when she spoke of Lord Drummond. Sooner or later she'll tell him whatever he wants to know. If she doesn't, young Alasdair will."

It was true, and Johanna must have ready answers to all of Drummond's questions. But first she must know more about him. "Do you

55

think he loved Clare?"

Bertie stared at the ceiling. "He never told her so, although she asked often enough. They were young when they wed — he three and twenty, and Clare almost three and ten. He treated her well enough, but he never gave up his dallying women. One of them bore him two sons. Poor mites both died before they crawled, or so the gossip had of it."

Johanna knew how she would feel if her husband took a mistress and gave the woman children. She'd feel betrayed, and she would doubt her own worth. Poor Clare. Such misery might lurk around the corner. Of necessity, she grew more determined to speed Drummond to the Highlands and into the bosom of his clan.

"I doubt he'll stay," she said.

"I doubt he'll leave."

Fear engulfed her. "Do not say that, Bertie. He must go before he finds out I'm not Clare."

"You've won over bigger trolls than him, and canonize me if the sheriff offers his congratulations of it. I say he'll quaff a few when he hears the news."

Ramsay Hay, the sheriff of Dumfries, had been her devoted champion until she had packed away the trappings of mourning. Then he had turned erstwhile suitor. Although she had been blunt and insistent when refusing his attentions, he had been equally persistent. She seldom worried about other men approaching her, for Ramsay kept most of them at bay. But could he chase off a husband?

She tapped the stack of letters on her desk. "I've written him a message. I wrote to Sister Margaret and Meridene, too."

Tenderness wreathed Bertie's weathered face. "The abbess'll wear out a rosary praying for you. Mistress Meridene will picture it on one of her tapestries."

Never had children been so fortunate as Clare and Johanna, and later Meridene, for Sister Margaret had cared for them as any mother would. She had been so protective and nurturing that Johanna sometimes thought the abbess had chosen wrongly in her vocation. "I asked her to visit."

" 'Twould be grand if she did, and without haste, for Ramsay Hay will run his horse to ground getting here. Pity any who runs before his mission."

Moved by a fierce protectiveness toward her home and her son, she walked to the window and scanned the outer bailey. "Ramsay's first visit should prove interesting and diverting. When he arrives, I'll tell Alasdair he can patrol with the watch."

"He'll pass up a custard for that."

"If there's trouble between Drummond and Ramsay, it won't do for Alasdair to witness it."

Bertie's eyes twinkled with glee. "We should also bar swooning women and fretful babes from the table that night."

Johanna only half listened, for she had spied the elephant at last. Her heart clamored in her breast, for the animal appeared as a small gray dot on the horizon.

Drummond was taking Alasdair for a ride. What if he took him for good?

She whirled and raced for the stable, fear rising like bile in her throat.

Chapter
3

Perched on a padded saddle, his son before him, Drummond sat atop Longfellow's broad back. A specially woven carpet with tassels and tinkling bells protected the elephant's spine and further cushioned the passengers.

The slow pace and high vantage point afforded an unobstructed view of his holdings. Summer ripened fields turned the land into a sea of swaying grain. The loamy soil would support any number of crops, and he wondered why she did not vary the plantings. Peas and beans would thrive in the furrows. She could even graze cattle on this land.

On the western horizon lay Solway Firth. In the distance to the north, a sizeable loch looked like a giant platter of silver. Closer, and straight ahead, a rocky banked and tree lined burn wended through the countryside. Longfellow plodded toward the water.

A gentle old bull, he obeyed Drummond without hesitation, and only occasionally did his enormous feet stray from the hard packed wagon road.

"I want to stand up." Alasdair drew his knees beneath him and moved into a crouch, preparing to stand.

Patience, Drummond had decided, was a rare gift when dealing with a seven-year-old lad. "So you've said, Son, at least a dozen times."

His skinny ass in the air, Alasdair looked over his shoulder at Drummond. Freckles dotted his nose and cheeks, and a familiar defiance twinkled in his eyes. "Then say yes."

Alasdair had been blessed with his mother's mouth, which was now drawn tight in frustration. He'd also inherited her willfulness. Her *new* willfulness, Drummond amended, for she'd been quiet and tractable when he married her. "Sit down, Alasdair!"

"Listen, Father. I could be persuaded to serve as your squire, should you be persuaded to let me stand."

"Nay."

"But if I'm to steward this land someday, I should know all of the farms and the herds." He flapped his arms, as if exasperated. "How can I, unless you let me stand up and see them?"

The lad could negotiate himself out of a sealed barrel. But could he wield a sword? Eyeing him cautiously, Drummond said, "I could be persuaded to forgo shining your bottom with a leather strap, should you be persuaded to sit down."

Miraculously the lad did as he was told. Then

60

he spoiled it by grumbling, "You're afraid of what Mother will say."

The statement was so unexpected that Drummond almost laughed. Had he, as a lad, spoken so disrespectfully to his father, he'd have been cuffed soundly, then given the dreaded task of cleaning chain mail. "You have the manners of a cornered badger."

As precocious as a prince, Alasdair again moved into a crouch. "She will not yell at you, you have my word of honor on that. Mother seldom yells."

Mother. The sound of that word sparked another oddity. In the last hour Drummond had heard it said more than he would have in a week's time at Macqueen Castle. The patriarchal clan system had specific places and duties for women, and indulging their sons was certainly not one of them.

"Next year, when I'm older, I'm also going to scale a castle wall."

Drummond sent his son a threatening stare, then waited until he resumed his seat. "Also?"

"Like you did when the evil Viking lord kidnapped Mother."

Caught off guard, Drummond merely stared at the crown of his son's head and the mop of wavy black hair that played host to an assortment of twigs. Alasdair was obviously referring to another tale his mother had told.

"You burned his sails so he couldn't escape with her."

61

A reply worked its way through Drummond's confused mind. "Macqueen Castle lies three days' ride from the sea, and it has no dock."

"So?"

Drummond had wrongly responded with logic. He was quickly learning that nothing about the fables his wife had created had anything to do with logic.

"She gave you a piece of a kiss," Alasdair said reverently.

"You mean a kiss of peace."

"No." He shook his head. "Heckley, the fletcher, says the best thing a girl can give a lad is a piece."

At Alasdair's age Drummond had understood adult innuendo; he'd also witnessed his father and his older kinsmen taking their manly pleasure of the wenches that were always about. Infidelity had been an accepted practice, and Drummond had given it little thought. Until his wife had lain with another man.

When his wounded pride stirred, Drummond tamped it back. "You should listen to me, not this Heckley fellow."

Alasdair scrambled to face Drummond. "I could listen better standing up. Why won't you let me?"

Longfellow picked up the pace; he was eager to reach the water, which had been the reason for the long ride. "Hold on."

Disdaining the rope handles woven into the carpet, Alasdair kept his hands at his sides. "Mother

says an adult should always answer a child's —
a young man's — questions."

"Your father says a child should always obey.
Now take hold of that handle."

He did. "Now may I stand up?"

"Absolutely and irrevocably, nay. Never. And
if you ask me again I'll punish you."

The lad's mouth fell open. "Me?"

Now that he'd made an impression, Drummond
relaxed. "Aye, and severely."

"How?" Alasdair leaned close, excitement dancing in his eyes. "Will you put me in a cage and
let the women of the village poke me with their
broom handles?"

"Where did you hear of such a ridiculous punishment?"

"Do you not remember? That's the justice you
meted out to the evil black knight who stole all
of the children's sweets."

Oh, Lord, in fable Drummond had progressed
from rescuing damsels to sparing children the pain
of losing their tarts. Was there no end to his
wife's imagination? "Does your mother tell you
stories about anyone else?"

He nodded. "She said an angel left me on her
doorstep. There's also a funny story about the
sheriff. He drank too much ale and on his way
home to Drumfries, he fell asleep on his horse.
He awoke in Carlisle."

"Do you like the sheriff?"

Alasdair smiled. "He taught me how to piss
off of the curtain wall and not splatter my hose

and boots." Solemnly, he added, " 'Tis manly business."

Drummond felt a stab of jealousy toward a sheriff he'd never met and the time the man had spent with Alasdair. The future, however, belonged to Drummond. "Who else teaches you manly things?"

"Brother Julian and Sween, the huntsman. And Bertie takes me fishing."

Drummond would come to know all of those men, and henceforth he would dictate Alasdair's studies. "I saw Evelyn scaling the trout you caught today."

His lip curled in distaste. "If she leaves the heads on, I'm not eating any."

The lad was as strong willed as his mother. Drummond scratched his nose to hide a smile. "Why have you not learned to clean your own fish?"

He looked absolutely insulted, his mouth pursed, one eyebrow cocked. "A man provides the meal," he said sagely. "The women prepare it."

"Who told you that?"

"Sheriff Hay."

Again, Drummond felt the sting of envy. "What if the women are ill or too busy with other things?"

"Mother is never ill, and everyone always hurries to do her bidding."

Just as she would rush to do as Drummond commanded her.

"Look!" Alasdair pointed behind them. " 'Tis her."

Tightening his hold on the lad, Drummond twisted in the saddle. A single rider raced toward them, leaving a trail of dust in the road. Drummond commanded the elephant to halt, then waited.

She rode astride a lathered gelding, her fingers clutching the animal's mane. She'd lost her coif and her combs, and her braid had begun to unravel. Moving abreast of Longfellow, she managed to stop the horse. Although her chest heaved from the breakneck ride, she calmly said, "Alasdair, come down from there."

Alasdair turned around, his back again to Drummond. "Nay."

Worry made her anxious, and the horse sensed her mood, sidestepping and tossing its tail. She seemed oblivious to her mount's distress. "Put him down, Drummond."

The command snapped the last thread of Drummond's frayed patience. Being sassed by an ill-mannered child was one thing, taking orders from a woman was something else. "Nay. I promised him a ride to the burn."

Having his position defended made Alasdair bold; he folded his arms across his chest and stared at Longfellow's flapping ears. "We're on manly business, Mother."

Strands of golden hair whipped about her face, but she paid no attention. Her skirt rode high on her leg, exposing her knee, but she didn't seem to care. Her anxious gaze flitted from her son to her husband. Beyond her distress, Drummond sensed fear. But of what? Did she think he couldn't protect the lad?

"No harm will come to this insolent child," he said. "At least no accident will befall him."

"If you give him to me, you will not be troubled with his safety or his headstrong nature."

"Headstrong?" Drummond laughed. "You have a gift for understatement."

Through gritted teeth, she said, "And you have none at all. Give me my son."

My son, as in *my tenants, my keep,* and *my land.* The possessiveness of it fueled his anger. If she wanted a battle of wills he would gladly oblige her, for Drummond had no intention of losing. With a sturdy stick, he lightly tapped the elephant's withers. Longfellow started forward again. "We'll return before dark."

"Wait!" The stiffness went out of her, and she gave Drummond the most insincere smile he'd ever seen. "Since neither of you will come down, it must be because you're having fun." She slid off the horse. There was no saddle. "So, I'm coming up."

"Hurrah!" Alasdair patted a spot on the carpet in front of him. "Sit here, Mother. You can see all the way to Loch Linton."

As Drummond watched her horse canter back toward the keep, he wondered where she'd learned to ride so well and so daringly. He also toyed with the notion of reprimanding her for it. But Alasdair was tugging on his shirt and demanding that they stop and help her up.

Resigned, Drummond halted the elephant, then replaced the rope ladder and watched her climb aboard. Longfellow swung his massive head toward her and sent his trunk to take a whiff. As Drummond expected, the beast returned to his favorite pastime: eating grass.

When she reached the top, Drummond grasped her waist and put her across his lap. She squirmed in a way that melted his anger and hardened his loins. He held her tighter.

"What are you doing?" she protested, clutching his arm.

Her hair caught the wind, and the loose strands felt like silk against Drummond's face. The pleasing fragrance of heather wafted around him. He had to clear his throat to speak. "You'll block Alasdair's view, so I'm putting you between us."

She surveyed the carpet. The handles were out of her reach. "What will I hold on to?"

Drummond returned the fake smile she'd given him moments before. "Me."

"I'd rather sit there — between your legs."

His smile turned genuine and his mind made a lusty picture of her words. "Be my guest. You can even bounce up and down if you like."

She sent him a confused frown before moving off his lap and situating herself between his knees. He considered pulling her back and wedging her pretty bottom against his manliness, but decided against tormenting himself. Instead, he stared at her wind tossed hair and wondered what she would say if he offered to tidy it.

When Longfellow started down the road again, she said, "Where did you get the elephant?"

"He got it from the king," said Alasdair. "Longfellow took a liking to Father, and when he left Londontown Longfellow missed him so much he butted down the gates. The king made Father come back and fetch Longfellow. Now he's our elephant."

Drummond leaned forward and softly said, "Why have you never taught him to respect the conversation of adults?"

Alasdair chirped, "But I know the answer. You told me before we even got on him."

"I do not remember anyone addressing a question to you." Lowering his voice, Drummond said, " 'Tis rude and presumptuous to let him believe that he can interrupt at will."

Her backbone stiffened. "He's just a lad, and he loves you well."

She spoke casually, as if it were natural for a son to love a father.

Alasdair murmured, "It's very rude to whisper, even I know that."

For the remainder of the short ride, Alasdair chatted constantly, but only once did he try to stand. "Get you down, Alasdair Macqueen," his mother scolded. "Or you'll be old and toothless before another dish of custard passes your lips."

The threat worked until they reached the burn. Alasdair stood and scrambled down the ladder.

Longfellow plunged his trunk into the water and began to drink. Drummond descended and helped Clare to the ground. Then he moved the saddle and carpet and put them beneath a rowan tree.

A moment later Longfellow siphoned water into his snout, arched it over his head, and doused his back with water.

"What's he doing?" asked a wide-eyed Alasdair.

Longfellow was making so much noise, Drummond had to yell. "He's giving himself a bath."

"I want to go swimming," Alasdair declared.

His mother examined her fingernails. "I could be persuaded to let you go swimming if you could be persuaded to study Latin for an extra hour."

His eyes snapping with intelligence, Alasdair paced before her. "For how many days?"

So that was where Alasdair had learned his bargaining skills. An interesting aspect for a female, thought Drummond.

"For two days," she said.

"Done." Alasdair tore off his jerkin and shirt and pulled down his hose. Kicking off his boots, he left his clothes where they lay and walked into the stream. Above the waist his skin was brown; below, his thin legs and buttocks were as white as a goose's belly.

His mother gathered his garments. "Stay close to the bank, Alasdair, and come out before you turn blue."

Drummond couldn't resist saying, "Shall we join him?"

She glanced at him. The wind stirred her hair, and the dappled sunlight made of it a nimbus of gold. "You may if you like, Drummond, but I prefer to watch today."

He wondered what she'd do if he tossed her in. Probably bluster and curse him to hell. But now that Alasdair was out of earshot, Drummond had other matters to discuss. "You thought I was taking Alasdair for more than a short ride."

She tossed the lad's hose over her shoulder and began folding his shirt. "I didn't know what to think when I saw you so far down the road."

"And if I had exercised my right as his father and taken him anywhere I chose?"

Matter-of-factly, she said, "After an hour or so, you would have begged me to take him back." When Drummond sent her a look of disbelief, she added, "He's never been away from home before."

That probably explained his stubborn nature. "Never?"

"Not without me."

"You've coddled him."

Clutching the clothing to her breast, she sat on a boulder and watched the lad frolic in the waist deep water. He flapped his arms and turned in a circle. "Perhaps so, but I had no instructions in the rearing of children. I was taught —"

"To obey your husband."

She sent him a sideways glance. "Yes, and other gentler duties."

"Like riding a horse without benefit of saddle and bridle?"

"No. I wasn't taught that at the abbey."

"I forbid you to do it again."

To his surprise she rubbed her hip and gave him a crooked grin. "You needn't spare a worry over that, my lord. I expect I'll suffer the consequences for days."

Congeniality had always come natural to Clare, but when flavored with sincerity, it became an especially appealing quality. Drummond was drawn to it, and he wanted to reply in kind, but he couldn't quite let himself.

She hesitated another heartbeat, her expression open, and for the moment, trusting. Then she turned back to their son, and her eyes softened with motherly love.

The breeze turned cool on Drummond's cheek. Like a window thrown open briefly, the opportunity to befriend her had passed. Perhaps it was just as well, but he couldn't help feeling as if something precious had slipped from his grasp.

"What shall we feed Longfellow?" she said into the silence.

Drummond moved to stand behind her. "The grass in the outer bailey should satisfy him for a week or so."

Her laughter rang hollow and insincere. "That's far enough, Alasdair," she called out.

Only the lad's neck and head were visible. He bobbed up and down, the movement carrying him deeper into the stream. She called to him

71

again and began rubbing her hands together. "Alasdair!"

"Come in and get me." He waved his arms. "I'm drowned, Mother. I'm as drowned as a rat."

"I'm not coming in after you."

The lad giggled. "I'm never coming out," he singsonged. "I'm never coming out."

Her mouth twitched with laughter. "Then you'd better grow fins and call yourself Alasdair MacTrout."

He floated onto his back and beat the surface with his hands. "You'd better rescue me."

"No." She glanced at Drummond. "Not today."

"Do you swim?" he asked.

Keeping a close watch on her son, she pulled her hair free and started to replait it. "Well enough to keep afloat and indulge my son."

Drummond let the sarcastic remark pass; the lure of her golden mane proved too tempting. He pushed her hands away. "Let me do that." When she tensed, he added, "While you tell me why you made up stories about me."

A sigh lifted her shoulders. "In the beginning they were for Alasdair, to lull him to sleep . . . and to feel pride in himself and you. You weren't here, and he was always asking questions about you. 'Tis natural for a son to be curious about his father."

Her thoughtfulness gave Drummond pause, and he had another reason to regret that she had been unfaithful to him; her exile from the Highlands had deprived Alasdair of the company of his kin. "You could have simply told him the truth."

"He's too young to understand the strife between England and Scotland. I meant to tell him when he was older, but at the time he needed someone to look up to."

"A flesh and blood man cannot live up to those tales, Clare."

She chuckled. "I think you'll find that slaying dragons is easier than being a good parent."

"A good parent. The term seems peculiar. In my experience, women bear sons, fathers and uncles raise them. But guardians never accept responsibility for a disappointing charge."

"Yet you are quick to say that I have coddled, spoiled, and indulged Alasdair."

"You have."

"And you have two ways of looking at the issue, both of which conveniently support your position."

"Which is?"

"Whatever you do is correct, or 'tis not your fault. By omission or absence, you contributed to his growth or lack of it."

A valid argument, he was forced to admit. But not to her of course. He finished braiding her hair. "What reason did you give Alasdair for my absence?"

"I simply told him you had gone to heaven to be with God."

"Rather than telling him I was imprisoned for treason against the English."

"Yes. As I said before, he's too young to understand politics. It was better that he thought you had gone to heaven."

Only Clare Macqueen would liken prison to paradise. "If you thought I was dead, why did you not find another husband?"

A butterfly landed on her head. She spoke quietly. "I was a dreadful wife, even you said as much. Why would I wed again?"

"Perhaps 'tis because you knew I lived."

She turned so quickly she almost tumbled from the rock. The butterfly flitted away. "I knew nothing about you."

Again he glimpsed her sincerity, but out of the corner of his eye he saw Alasdair easing into the center of the stream.

"I'll get Alasdair out of the water." He turned to Longfellow and said, "The king's a pox ridden maggot."

As expected, Longfellow threw up his trunk and trumpeted loud enough to make ears ring. Alasdair squealed and made a hasty retreat from the water. His mother pulled off her mantle and held it out for him. Arms pinned to his sides, his knees knocking, his little penis shriveled to a nub, he let her wrap him in the faded red wool.

"That'll teach you to mind me," she said, rubbing him dry.

His eyes looked inordinately large and wary, and the sun had turned his nose and cheeks bright red. "Longfellow gave me a fright."

"He was obeying your father's strange command."

Alasdair's fear melted, and he gave Drummond a gamin grin. "Longfellow behaves better than me, does he not?"

So direct and honest a question smacked of his mother's influence. This time, Drummond jumped at the chance to reply. "Aye, but he's much older and reaps no pleasure in taunting his betters."

Alasdair glanced up at his mother. "If I had a little brother I'd be his betters, would I not?"

She spent a long moment studying the lad. She looked young enough to be his sister and innocent enough to be a bride. "You would have to look out for a sibling and share your treasures."

Alasdair cast an inquisitive gaze to Drummond. "Father, would I truly have to share my toys?"

"Not if you had a sister."

The lad beamed. "Then I'd like a sister. Will you get me one?"

"Aye," Drummond said.

"Nay," said his wife.

Her quick refusal made Drummond rethink his strategy. He needed no plan to bed his wife; she had no choice in the matter. Why then was she so determined to deny him? He suspected she was hiding something, and he knew just the way to learn her secrets.

She might naysay the sister, but she'd have no more control over the sex of the children

Drummond intended to get on her than she would have over his intentions. He'd bed her, and she'd welcome him with open arms. He knew Clare better than she knew herself.

Chapter
4

The perfectly cooked fish tasted like vellum in Johanna's mouth, but she'd eat every last morsel before she'd reveal her discomfort. The ale was fresh and the goblets kept ever-brimming by a diligent Evelyn, who circled the table like a hungry hawk at twilight. The maid seemed fascinated by Drummond Macqueen, as did most everyone at the table.

Determination pushed Johanna to act as if her world were a dream come true, rather than an unfolding nightmare. She must keep her composure and pretend that life was proceeding as it should.

Seated to the right of Drummond and across from Alasdair and Brother Julian, she listened intently to the conversation that centered around politics but occasionally strayed to local events.

Garbed in a plain robe woven from the wool of black sheep, the bearded cleric couldn't say often or effusively enough that in returning

Drummond to his family, God had answered his prayers. He'd spent so much time talking he didn't notice that Alasdair had eaten most of the fish from their trencher.

Bertie, who sat to her right, had been silent throughout the meal, but with encouraging smiles and an occasional wink, he lent her his support and his understanding.

She no longer worried that Drummond might take Alasdair away; now she agonized over what Drummond expected of her. The closer bedtime came, the more troubled she grew.

Drummond appeared comfortable at the head of the table, looked as if he'd been born to command more than the attention of the small group in attendance. He confirmed what Clare had said: Had the king of England not interfered with his destiny, Drummond would have ruled all of the Highlands.

The fanciful notion spurred Johanna's own fantasy, and she took a moment to ponder how differently this day might have unfolded. She could have been his faithful wife, who had pined in his absence; he could have been her devoted husband, who had been unjustly imprisoned. Their reunion would have been a cause for celebration, rife with loving glances, tightly held hands, and even a stolen kiss or two.

Drummond would be wearing a fine surcoat that she had stitched and embellished with fancy embroidery. She'd hold the office of his personal barber and trim his shoulder length hair. He would give her a winsome smile, and she would live to do as he bade her. Side by side they would rule their kingdom, spreading love and peace to all who abided here.

Was this uncomfortable evening the start of her penance for the sin of coveting her sister's life? Regrets turned to melancholy, and Johanna staved off a wave of self-pity. She would take each day as it came. The nights, however, struck fear in her heart. He would expect intimacy; why else had he promised Alasdair a sibling? The irony of the situation struck Johanna as oddly funny, for her education as a woman was progressing backwardly; she knew how to raise children, but was ignorant in the begetting of them.

She must stall as long as possible, and when that failed she would simply brazen her way out.

"What if the angels want you back, Father?"

Alasdair's latest question drew her attention.

"I'll simply tell them I'm needed here," Drummond answered.

Around a bite of carrot, Alasdair said, "Aye, you have to get me a sister."

Johanna grew stock still. She could feel Drummond watching her, waiting for her reaction. Bertie shifted on the bench, causing it to rock. Evelyn let out a lovestruck sigh. Brother Julian pasted on a benevolent smile.

"Aren't you?" Alasdair wheedled, looking from her to Drummond. "You promised me a sister."

Praying her hand didn't shake, Johanna reached for her goblet. "Alasdair, 'tis not suitable conversation for the table."

Drummond winked at his son, then sent her a knowing grin. "Your mother is correct. She and I will discuss the matter privately."

A contented Alasdair picked at his trencher. "Father, who's guarding the gates of heaven?"

Hoping to make Drummond as uncomfortable as she was at the moment, Johanna grinned. "Who indeed, Drummond?"

He ran a finger along the high neckline of his shirt, gave her a disgruntled glance, then cleared his throat. She wondered if he would go along with the excuse she'd given for his absence, or would he explain to his son that he'd been imprisoned for the last seven years? Had Johanna not been so troubled about her own situation, she might have pitied him.

Looking like a disarmed warrior who'd fallen to his enemy, he groped for an answer. At length, he said, "Are you worried that devils might get in?"

A vigorous nod pitched Alasdair's hair into his eyes. "Brother Julian says the devils are everywhere. They make mischief — even in young lads."

Relieved laughter rumbled in Drummond's chest. "Like yourself?"

"Well . . ." Alasdair raked his hair off his forehead and gave Johanna his sweetest smile. "I'm not evil, only headstrong and sometimes troublesome."

His father asked, "How does one punish a headstrong and troublesome lad?"

As crestfallen as the day his first puppy had died, Alasdair stared at his meal. "He doesn't get any custard."

Drummond's handsome features softened, and in the dim candlelight he appeared younger than his years. Seeing him thusly, Johanna couldn't resist asking, "Did your father make you forgo custards when you were wicked?"

He cocked an eyebrow. "In his own fashion. Who is your overlord?"

She wondered at the change in topic, but didn't dare question him. "James Douglas the Red. His lands lie to the north in Dumfries proper."

"He has a reputation for yielding to the English. How many soldiers do we furnish him?"

She expected him to find fault with her; he had ample reason to condemn his wife. But she had not anticipated his antagonism toward a fellow lord. Defense of her neighbor came easily. "I send him no men-at-arms. Thanks to his leadership, we are at peace."

Brother Julian put down his napkin. "It has not always been so, my lord."

"There was bloody war everyday," declared Alasdair. "Women cried and children went hungry. Foolish men got their heads stuck on pikes. Why did you not come and help them?"

Johanna's stomach roiled. "Alasdair, please. Not at the table."

"What think you of this Douglas?" Drummond asked Alasdair.

The boy waved a carrot to punctuate his words. "He's a goodly man. He has a passel of daughters and a very fine dirk, with rubies in the handle and a dragon on the blade."

Sliding a quick glance at Johanna, Drummond said, "You did not give the lad my dirk?"

He was referring to the weapons that Clare had carefully packed away and asked Johanna to keep. She had intended to give them to Alasdair one day. Now she would yield them to Drummond. "Of course not. He's too young yet."

Tapping his knife on the table, Drummond seemed to consider his next words. "Have you spoken to this Douglas about fostering Alasdair?"

"Nay. He will not be fostered out."

"Precisely. I'll teach him what he needs to know."

She abhorred violence, had every intention of sparing her son the trials of battle and the hatred the Highland Scots felt for the English. "We'll discuss it later, my lord."

Alasdair interrupted with, "Give me a sword, Mother, for I want to rule the people."

Johanna said, "And you will, but a great lord must do more than wield a sword."

Drummond's lips curled in an indulgent smile. He turned to Alasdair. "What must a great lord know?"

"He must know how to make alliances and settle disputes."

All rapt attention, Drummond put down his knife. "How will you make alliances?"

"That's easy." Alasdair put his wrist to his forehead. With too much drama, he said, "I'll flatter the ladies until they swoon at my feet. A well brought up man never tells a lady she stinks, even if she smells like the privy." More seriously, he added, "A gentleman must have his principles."

Humor brightened Drummond's eyes. "A most admirable practice. How will you settle disputes?"

Alasdair blinked, as if confused. "Just the way Mother does."

"Tell me."

He squirmed on the bench and collected his thoughts. "I'll be fair, and if the Anderson lads again scatter MacHale's herd of sheep, I'll command them to gather up the beasts. Then they must rethatch his roof."

Drummond turned to Johanna. His earlier scrutiny of her paled. The absence of malice or prejudice gave his new examination a probing quality. Clare had sworn that he was a fine judge of character and a leader of men. Johanna hoped he had maintained those qualities, that he'd kept his high moral standards even through years of capture. But how could she know for sure?

His blue eyes shone with sincerity, and she could not turn away. Admiring him came easy, for few men were blessed with so many appealing features. His brows flared gently and his strong jaw framed a mouth softened by sensuality. She thought his lips were made for the shaping of tender words and suspected a horde of women had vied for his attention. Was it possible, she wondered, that a man so physically alluring could also be good to his core? And how, her woman's heart queried, could she ever learn the answer when circumstances dictated that she avoid the very intimacy that would allow her the means to find out?

Drummond speared a leek with his knife and held it out to her. "Here. You've hardly eaten."

His cajoling tone lured her. Forcing a smile, she took the offered food. "Thank you, my lord. The onions are particularly sweet this year."

He stared at the blade as if he'd just noticed what food it held. "How nice that in my absence you've acquired a taste for leeks."

Clare had hated leeks. The moment of congeniality fled. Once again, conversing on even the most mundane topics proved a chore, for Johanna felt as if she were walking barefoot through a field of thistles. "You must be mistaken, my lord. I do love leeks."

She hoped to see his eyes cloud with confusion; they narrowed with challenge. "Seldom have I been mistaken where you are concerned."

Disappointment threatened. She fought it back and gathered her gumption. "This, then, 'twould seem to be one of those times."

He leaned closer. "You said you hated leeks, refused to eat them."

To keep him off guard, she gave him a honey-sweet smile. "You're correct, of course. I'd forgotten our brief time together." Using her knife, she raked all of the onions to his end of the trencher. "Satisfied?"

He stopped, his hand between his plate and his mouth. A different sort of intensity glimmered in his eyes, and his gaze fell to her breasts. "Hardly."

"Why are you talking about leeks?" said Alasdair.

Drummond continued to stare at her. "Why indeed."

Unaware of the tension between them, Alasdair plunged onward. "Mother, are these different from the leeks you had at Papa's home?"

Drummond said, "As I recall, your mother found little in the Highlands to like."

"Oh, nay. You have it wrong, Father. She always says Macqueen Castle was a glorious place. You won all of the jousting tournaments and led the hunt. You always laid the kill at her feet."

Still watching her, Drummond said, "Did you say that, Clare?"

This time the burr in his voice sounded more pronounced when he said the name Clare. By comparison, Johanna thought her own name bland. But she had never heard it said by a Scotsman. Nor would she ever. That fact confirmed her earlier suspicions about losing her own identity. With so many possibilities to consider, how could she maintain it?

"Did you?" Drummond prompted.

She welcomed the distraction. "I told him he would be proud of his father's heritage."

"I see. Even though you had no taste for Scotland or her people?"

Johanna grew weary of the charade. "I've changed, Drummond. How often must I remind you of that?" When he continued to stare, she searched for the name of a dish with origins in the Highlands. "As proof, I'll ask the cook to prepare a haggis."

He propped his elbow on the table and rested his chin in his palm. Leaning close, he said, "You know very well that I loathe the taste of haggis."

He'd bathed since their return from the burn, and he now smelled pleasantly of the minty soap she herself had made. That so absurd a thing as his smell would rule her thoughts brought a new fear. She rebelled against it. "Perhaps you will learn to like the dish, just as I have learned to like leeks."

"I hate haggis, too," said Alasdair. "If you make me eat it, I'll vomit on the floor."

Seeking a respite from her husband's probing gaze, Johanna looked at Alasdair. He wanted so much to be like his father. She couldn't fault him for that, but she could stop him from acting peevishly about it. "Then you'll clean it up."

His skinny neck stiffened. "Evelyn will clean it up."

Bertie leaned forward. "A true and gallant knight never vomits in the presence of a lady."

Like a thirsty sponge, her son absorbed the new bit of wisdom. "If I promise not to retch, will you promise to give me a sister?"

Aghast, Johanna slapped her palm on the table. "Alasdair! Mind your manners."

"What think you of Fairhope Tower, my lord?" asked Bertie.

Drummond seemed to accept the change in topic, for he shrugged. " 'Tis fair enough, but I wonder why we own so few cattle."

Johanna jumped to her own defense. "We haven't the fields to support livestock."

"What of that bottomland near the loch?"

So, he *had* been investigating her estate — the one subject that came easily. "I grow grain there and flax."

"And with no small success," Brother Julian put in. "Each spring a merchant comes all the way from Glasgow to buy my lady's white linen cloth. 'Tis highly prized."

Drummond emptied his goblet. "Cattle would prove more profitable."

Johanna waited for Evelyn to pour him more ale. "But it will not support the families who earn their winter livelihood by making flax into cloth."

"We could do both. Why not halve the land and import a small herd of Spanish beef? Grow your flax if you must, but raise cattle, too."

How dare he try to alter her well thought out plans? He cared nothing for the people here, their welfare and their self-respect. He should take his modern ideas and foist them off on his beloved Highland kin.

"I'll think about it. How fares your family, my lord?"

"Well enough." He shrugged, popped another onion into his mouth, and turned his attention to Brother Julian, who'd begun sawing at the trencher he shared with Alasdair. "Your ministry prospers?"

"Indeed," he said expansively. "My lady has provided a fine place of worship." Then Brother Julian resumed his favorite topic. "Some of us in the spirituality believe the new king will favor a peace with all his subjects."

" 'Tisn't faith, but an empty treasury that concerns our sovereign," said Drummond, casting a glance Johanna's way.

Did he expect her to comment? The troll could expect whatever the devil he wanted. She gave him a bland smile.

"Why does His Majesty demand more revenues?" Brother Julian asked.

Drummond picked a bone from the fish. Holding it before the light, he turned it this way and that. "To pay off the debt Edward the First left him. 'Tis said it's two hundred thousand pounds."

"I want to go to Londontown and meet the king," said Alasdair. "Can we go, Father?"

"Only if your mother craves to see our sovereign again."

"Again?" Brother Julian dropped his knife. "Know you the new king, my lady? You never said as much."

Evasion seemed her only escape, for the topic

was too dangerous for casual conversation. "Now where would I meet a king?"

Drummond didn't move so much as an eyelash, but his expression screamed accusation. "Pray let me refresh your memory. Edward the First brought his son with him to Scarborough Abbey when he fetched you to me. Both the king and his princely son escorted you to the Highlands and attended our wedding."

Her throat seemed to close. Gaining time to form a reply, she drank. "I had eyes only for my betrothed."

Drummond hadn't expected flattery, for his face went blank with surprise.

"Did the old king give you a present, Mother?"

Recovering, Drummond said, "Aye, his son stayed with us for the better part of one winter. Your mother knew him well."

Fear stole Johanna's breath. She couldn't hold his gaze.

Like a torch on a bleak night, Bertie's voice flashed into the darkness. "They say the new king favors rustic crafts."

She could feel Drummond staring at her, compelling her to look at him. She stared at her left hand, which bore no ring, because Drummond hadn't bothered to give one to Clare.

Absently, Drummond said, "Edward the Second has been known to chop a tree and dig a ditch. Surely my lady can confirm that he is an accomplished sportsman?"

Too distraught to reply, Johanna called for Evelyn to serve dessert.

During the commotion of clearing the table, Johanna dredged up an old memory. She had met Prince Edward, but only by accident. Upon arrival at Scarborough Abbey, his father, King Edward I, had summoned both Johanna and Clare for a private audience. After studying them for the longest time, he had commanded Johanna to keep out of sight for the duration of his visit, and he made Clare swear never to reveal to anyone in the Highlands that she had a twin sister. When Johanna questioned him, he warned her that kidnapping and blackmail were common practices in the Highlands. He feared that the Macqueens or their enemies would abduct her and use her in their political schemes. He teasingly swore to marry Johanna off to a Turk should she disobey him and show herself.

Both girls had been surprised that the king knew of their existence and that he wanted Johanna's identity kept a secret. They had asked Sister Margaret, a Scotswoman, to confirm the information, but the abbess had been too upset over Clare's leaving to address the questions. Johanna had comforted the older woman until she slept. Still wide-awake, Johanna had gone to the larder to be sure there were enough provisions to feed their royal guests.

Strange voices had interrupted her inventory of the stores. What had come next still chilled her to her soul.

"You look far away."

At the sound of Drummond's voice, she jumped. He leaned close and whispered, "And perplexed."

She was, but he'd never know why, for she did not herself understand the events of that long-ago night. Nor would she ponder them now.

Nibbling the berry tart, she considered all that Clare had told her about him and drew upon a solid fact. "I was merely wondering if you still have a sweet tooth."

He didn't believe her, his closed expression told her so. "And I," he said obliquely, "wonder many things about you."

Feeling badgered and on the brink of losing control, she rose. "That's very interesting, my lord. But if you'll excuse me, I'll check to see if the huntsmen have returned. Bertie will show you to your chamber."

She exited the room and raced down the stairs. When she reached the entryway she heard footsteps behind her.

"What did you mean by 'my chamber'?"

"We will occupy separate chambers."

"When badgers fly!"

"I have fulfilled my wifely duty. Alasdair stands as proof of that."

"As will his brothers and sisters to come."

Johanna froze. "You cannot possibly expect me to —"

"To what?" he said, suddenly standing so close behind her she could feel the warmth of his body. "Fulfill your wifely duty? You took to it well enough, Clare. Even in travail, you offered little complaint, or so I was told."

Speechless, Johanna stared at the main doors. The lighted lamps mounted in sconces on the wall cast shadows on the portal: a man towering over a woman. The images appeared ordinary, a direct contrast to the unusual problems that raged between them. The taller shadow moved, closer, and as she watched, her heart hammering, she felt his hand snake around her waist. Then his lips touched her neck.

She gasped and twisted free, only to be pinned, facing him, her back against the heavy wooden portal. The ironwork braces pressed into her shoulder blades. His hands framed her face. He leaned against her, a bold challenge in his eyes.

"Cry peace with me, Clare," he whispered, "and for the sake of our future, I will try to forgive you."

Caught in the trap of his masculine power, she longed to bolt, but her legs wouldn't obey. From somewhere inside her, the unfulfilled woman yearned for the contentment he offered, and while she knew next to nothing about Drummond Macqueen, she instinctively knew that on this matter he spoke the truth.

How could she beg forgiveness for a sin Clare had committed in the noblest of causes? Yet how could she not when her future and all she loved and had strived to achieve hung in the balance?

Oh, Lord, she had no answers, not when her life had been turned tapsal-teerie and his nearness made her insides churn with longing.

He leaned closer and tilted his head to the side. Then she felt his lips on her neck, his fingers moving the high neckline of her bliaud aside. She trembled beneath the velvet touch of his mouth and her mind whirled with exotic visions. She swayed, and he hauled her full against him, his heated breath escaping in a rush.

The embrace was a maiden's dream, being swept up by a man whose desire for her overrode his loathing. Being that woman seemed a treasure too precious to relinquish, no matter the risk.

"Ah, you do remember that I am the master of your passion."

His acceptance of her as his wife fired Johanna's courage. Of their own volition her fingers walked up his chest and plunged into his hair. Like a visitor seeking entry, her virginal dreams stood on the threshold of fulfillment. In an instant she could step completely into the role of Clare Macqueen, wife.

What, her soul cried out, would become of Johanna, then? As he continued to caress her, she knew that by yielding to him, her own identity would irretrievably slip away.

When his mouth moved to hers and he hummed a manly groan, she stopped thinking about who she was and who she was supposed to be. Images of the woman she would become and the man who would shape her future filled her thoughts.

The stories she had told Alasdair of his father might well come true. Drummond would become her gallant knight, slaying life's dragons and pledging his love to her.

He stopped and drew back. His eyes glowed midnight blue and his lips shone with dampness from the kiss. "You taste sweet, like honey."

She stared at the finely worked brooch securing the Macqueen plaid at his shoulder. " 'Tis the dessert tarts. I make them with honey."

"You once said such chores were the work of servants."

Yes, Clare would have said that, but unlike Johanna, the amenable Clare had always stepped forward to accept the responsibility of visiting the sick and entertaining guests at the abbey. In her youth, Johanna had easily grown bored with the idle conversation of clerics, and she had no time for social calls. However in the past seven years she had come to enjoy both, for the villagers repaid her kindness with respect and loyalty.

At a loss for anything but the truth, she said, "I am not the naive girl you married."

"Nay, you're not. You've become a desirable woman."

He kissed her again and held her tighter, his hands roaming her back and circling her waist. As if intrigued, he mapped the slope of her ribs and the flare of her hips, and when his tongue nudged her lips apart and raked a slippery path across her mouth, Johanna felt her judgment flee. Her fingers tightened in his hair and the strands felt thick against her palms. When his tongue thrust forward and invaded her mouth, she thought it the most heavenly intimacy imaginable. She tasted honey on his lips, and the sweet flavor made her want more.

Following his lead, she glided her tongue against his and awaited his next move. He jerked and drew back a little. She lifted heavy lids.

A confused frown marred his brow. "Who taught you to enjoy kissing in the French fashion?"

She'd received only two adult kisses in her life, both just now from Drummond Macqueen. A gamble seemed her only option. "You did."

Disappointment chased the glow from his eyes. He did not speak, but she could see his denial and knew that Clare had not enjoyed what he called the French way of kissing. In her eagerness Johanna had erred. Common sense told her she would do so again, and probably often. Pray her future mistakes were minor ones.

Desperate for a return to their momentary accord, she gave him a smile. "It was you, for I know no Frenchmen, save the almoner at Sweetheart Abbey."

He glared at her, the heat in his eyes both intimate and distanced by mistrust. She also saw weakness and distraction there. For the first time in her life, Johanna felt the power of a woman to stir a man and turn him from his anger. The desire that smoldered in his eyes was dampened by the questions unanswered. If she used her newfound power, seduced Drummond or allowed him to seduce her, could she retain her lands, her

95

son, and hold on to her true identity?

He shrugged. " 'Tis a small matter. I always did like kissing more than you — unless we were in our chambers with the door bolted and the lamps extinguished."

An odd comment, for surely any woman would enjoy his amorous attentions. Evidently Clare had been choosy in her displays of affection. Pondering the why of her sister's objection would only complicate Johanna's already formidable task.

His hands circled her wrists and he pulled her hands free. "Perhaps we should retire."

It was too soon. She needed time to explore her new powers and learn her alternatives. "Retire to where?"

He guided her hand to the waist of his leather trews, then lower. "You haven't lost the ability to rouse my passions, Clare. In truth, you're better at it now."

Aghast at where her boldness had led, Johanna jerked her hand away. "I assure you," she stammered. " 'Twas not my intention to . . . to do any such thing. We hardly know each other."

A knowing grin softened his features. "Coyness sits well upon you. 'Tis an appealing trait in a wife, so long as she leaves it outside my bedchamber."

The last two words made her shiver.

"Do you quake from cold or from desire, Clare?"

She'd suffer a stoning before she'd confess the feelings he aroused. Ducking under his arm, she headed for the stairs. A nasty lie sprang from her lips. "Neither, my lord, and I will never beg your forgiveness or share your bed."

As if he were taking a leisurely stroll, he moved toward her. "Aye, you will — at my command." He grabbed her then and pulled her roughly into his embrace.

The kiss was a crude parody of the gentler ones they'd shared moments before, and she wondered if he hadn't been suddenly possessed by a demon. His lips were everywhere at once: on her face, her neck, her breasts, and his hands followed in pursuit. She backed away, but he crushed her against the curved stone wall. The harsh sound of his breathing echoed in her ears.

Horrified by the change in him, she moved her head away and opened her mouth to scream. His lips crashed down on hers and his hands turned viselike on her arms. Against her belly, she felt his hardness.

Suddenly she knew what he intended to do with it. The word *rape* blared in her mind. "Stop!"

"I cannot, Clare." He pulled at her clothing and wedged his knee between her legs. "It's been too long, and you belong to me."

When he lifted her skirt, she grew desperate. Pulling on his hair to get his attention, she yelled, "I do not. Save your breath and your pawings, for I have no wish to be mauled by an animal."

He grew as still as a post. "What did you call me?"

Now that he seemed to have gained control

of himself, Johanna's fear turned to anger. "An animal."

Perspiration glistened on his brow. "I'm no animal."

The despair in his voice puzzled her, but she refused to dwell on it; she had to put a distance between them. Harsh words seemed her best weapon. "You tore at my clothing. You mauled me."

He moved away and ran his hands through his hair. Pressing his palms to his temples, he murmured, "I am not an animal."

Seizing the moment, she picked up her skirt and started up the stairs. At the landing, she looked back. Still clasping his head as if in pain, he dropped to his knees. Had she not been so afraid she might have felt concern for him.

As she continued her retreat, she heard him murmur something that sounded like a pledge, but she was too far away to discern the words.

Chapter
5

I am not an animal.

As if he'd drunk too much ale the night before, Drummond felt weak, his stomach sour, his head spinning with regrets. Exhaustion added to his misery, for he'd sat on the floor in the entryway and stared at the torches until the flames had burned themselves out. Then he'd made his way here, to the solar.

He hadn't tried to sleep, knew he couldn't, not indoors. Every night since his release, he'd slept in the open. In Dunstable he'd purchased a fast horse and kept the stallion at the ready. He half expected the king's men-at-arms to overtake him, bringing word that Edward II had rescinded the order of clemency.

Dwelling on the prospect that he might be returned to prison was merely a diversion, for Drummond knew what had caused his current distress: her accusation and the painful memories it spawned.

To deflect his thoughts, he again studied his surroundings. In the rosy light of dawn, the sparsely furnished solar appeared functional, and not what he had envisioned. No musical instruments graced the room, no trinkets and games. This was a working room.

The ledgers were neatly kept, the figures correctly totaled. Frugality had enabled Clare to earn a profit after her third year at Fairhope. Last fall she had commissioned a new chapel and still managed to post a handsome surplus, part of which she sent to her overlord. She hadn't, as Drummond expected, squandered money on padded furniture and costly gowns. The quills were plain, the ink of common making; she'd even abandoned the looping style of fashioning her letters. The only extravagance in this room and throughout the tower was the glass.

The east facing windows served as a portal for the morning sun and offered a clear view of the main gate. Moments before, the huntsmen had returned, an impressive roe buck slung over the withers of the leader's horse; braces of squirrels and partridges adorned the other mounts. A messenger had rushed into the castle, and even now, the servants were stirring, carrying water and clanging pots.

Would his wife arise soon? Would she come here?

Last night when he'd first kissed her, she had been yielding, as she had years before, but this time he'd noticed a curiosity and a willingness to participate and explore. That had surprised him more than his own loss of control. She had been the last woman he'd possessed prior to his capture, and in spite of what had occurred last night, or perhaps because of it, the thought of seeing her again awakened his morning lust.

He had been eager, but his actions had not been beastly, not in the way she meant. A man should desire his wife, and Drummond's action had nothing to do with animalistic behavior. He'd never before been blinded by his desire for her; Clare had accepted her wifely duty, but she had never before encouraged him.

She thought and acted differently now. Her shallowness was gone, replaced by intelligence. Selfishness had matured to strength of character, and wifely obligations had ripened into feminine need. Why, then, had she rejected him?

Because he'd mauled her.

Nay. Never. He closed the ledger and pounded his fist on the wooden binding. He had not hurt her. He'd frightened her, but how? She knew well his passions, had suffered them in their marriage bed — except during the daylight hours or upon waking. She had always declined his lovemaking first thing in the morning. But Clare had never liked rising early.

And what of her refusal to bear him more children? That affront wounded him to his soul. She had enjoyed her pregnancy; her skin had glowed with impending motherhood, and she often cajoled him into fetching her tarts and cheeses in the middle of the night.

He didn't seem to know her anymore. It was almost as if another woman had stepped into her body. That absurdity made him smile, but his humor was short-lived.

Had he changed as much to her? Probably, but she'd made him a cuckold and never expressed regret. She'd passed herself off as his widow and never bothered to confirm his death. She'd left him to rot in the Tower of London.

He picked up a yellowed parchment, the royal writ signed seven years ago by Edward I, granting her this property. The writ also prohibited her and Alasdair any congress with his kin. That order rankled, for it had served no great purpose. Drummond's younger brother had not yielded to the old king, but had been waiting to face him in battle when Edward had died while bringing yet another army northward.

The damage done by Edward I's writ involved a simple sadness, a family tragedy. He'd separated a man from his son and a lad from his culture.

Now Drummond must right the wrongs of a dead king without angering the living one. Teaching Alasdair about his heritage should prove easy, for the lad was still young enough to mold. Stepping back into the role of husband afforded a greater challenge, for Drummond's wife wanted nothing to do with him. He must change that.

But sometime later, when she entered the room and halted just inside the doorway, Drummond could only stare.

She wore an underdress of crisp, white linen; the high, rounded neckline and the edges of the long sleeves were embellished with tiny embroidered leaves. The rust-colored bliaud turned her eyes a tawny brown and accented the golden hues in her hair, which she'd wound into a simple coil at the nape of her neck. She looked slender and youthful, and as distant as the moon.

"Good morrow," he said, rising.

She crossed to the desk, her gaze scouring the papers he'd been examining. "What are you doing here?"

"I couldn't sleep, and —" Incensed that guilt would induce him to explain himself, he resumed his seat. "I like this room, Clare."

She picked up the ledgers and the royal writ. "I hope you haven't smudged the ink on my papers."

He noticed that her hands shook, and he relaxed a little, for she was obviously as uncomfortable as he. "*Our* papers."

"You're correct, of course." She slipped the official document into the top ledger and returned the stack to the wall shelf. Then she headed for the door.

"Wait. I want to talk with you."

Halting, she placed a hand on the door frame. "How delightful."

"Sarcasm doesn't suit you."

"Pray tell what does, husband mine?"

Husband mine? She made being married to him sound like a cross to bear. "Common courtesy

103

would be a helpful start."

"Common?" She turned to face him. "A quaint word, and precisely the way I feel, after . . ."

"After I tried to exercise my husbandly rights?"

She looked bewildered, her lips slightly parted, her brows arched in confusion. "If you expect me to be grateful, you are mistaken. You promised to honor me in word, deed, and prayer. By your signed oath, you obligated all of Clan Macqueen to do the same."

When had she begun reading Highland law? And had she always been so appealing in the light of morning? Disgruntled at his lovestruck observance, he stood his ground. "You also made promises in your trothplight. You agreed to obey me."

Her confident smile portended disaster. "I do not recall receiving an order from you last night."

Cleverness had never been among her attributes; as his bride she'd been better at pouting to get her way. "I do not recall your being so direct."

Her dainty nostrils flared. "Then your memory is faulty on that point, too."

"My memory is fine!"

Her chin went up, and the glare in her eyes promised retribution, but her voice was honey-sweet when she said, "You're correct, of course."

"Stop being so compliant."

"Compliant," she repeated, as if contemplating the meaning of the word. "Am I to take it that you no longer wish for an obedient wife?"

104

"Blast you for a quick-witted wench. But know this, dear wife, twisting my words will gain you nothing."

"Then hurrah for me, because *nothing* is exactly what I want from you." She snatched up her basket and started to walk away.

"Come back here."

As indifferent as an Englishman on Hogmanay, she sent him a blank stare. "Yes, my lord. Have you a command for me?"

Peevishness overwhelmed him. "Aye. Sit down."

She surveyed the room. "On what? You've taken the only seat."

The room was devoid of benches or stools, save the one he occupied, and he'd be damned for a heretic before he'd admit his error. "Then stand. I want to talk to you."

She waved her hand. "Talk away."

Feeling like a tongue-tied fool, Drummond didn't know where to begin, so he started with a truth. "You're different, Clare. What has happened to change you so?"

"I haven't the faintest notion of what you are referring to."

He found himself grumbling, "Last night."

"Last night." She toyed with the words. "Would that be before or after you tried to rape me?"

"That's absurd. A man cannot rape his wife."

"He most certainly can — if she is unwilling."

"You were willing, Clare. Why else would you

fondle me and kiss me with your tongue."

She knotted her fists. "I did not fondle you, Drummond Macqueen. And you enticed me to kiss you in that . . . that fashion."

"*Entice.* A most interesting word, and completely fitting."

She stared at the empty coal bucket. "Perhaps in your twisted vocabulary."

"Twisted?"

"Yes. You enticed me. I enticed you. The event proved a terrible disaster. And it confirmed what I have always known."

"Which is?" he growled.

"That you prefer Scottish women over me."

His manly pride screamed for retribution. "You once applauded my powers of seduction and praised my experience."

"Me and half the women in the Highlands. Do you deny having mistresses?"

"You begrudge me a mistress, after all these years?"

Deadly serious, she pointed a finger at him. "You begrudged me."

There it was, her admission of guilt. But somehow she'd managed to put the onus on him. He intended to give it back. "My taking a mistress is not the same thing as your taking a lover. A woman must be faithful."

"And what must a husband be?"

"He must be a good provider and protector of his family."

Cool disdain gave her a queenly air. "As in

106

providing a keep, such as Fairhope Tower? As in protecting *my* son from those who would do him harm? As in planning for his future and assuring the well-being of all of the people in *my* care?"

Drummond felt cornered and wondered how he'd lost control of the conversation. But more, how had she become so bloody capable and so demanding? "We were discussing the manner in which you kissed me last night."

She opened her mouth to voice an angry protest, but paused. Then she calmed herself, folded her hands and bowed her head. "You're correct, my lord."

Witnessing her exercise such self-control when he possessed so little made Drummond want to scream. "Will you cease saying that!"

"Of course, my lord."

"Look, wench." He rounded the desk and stood before her. "You enjoyed kissing me. Do not deny it."

Without the slightest flinch, she declared, "From the bottom of my wench's heart, I do deny it."

As the Lord lived, she wanted to anger him. But why, for it only drove a wedge between them. He almost slapped his forehead; she wanted them at odds. "Lying is the second poorest of wifely practices."

"Then I shall strive to practice harder, for I've had little practice at being a wife."

He caught a whiff of heather. Like water on

a fire, the pleasing fragrance doused his ire. He considered telling her why he'd lost control last night, but realized he didn't trust her enough to completely bare his soul. He did owe her an explanation; she'd spoken the truth about the short time they'd lived together as man and wife. Flattery had always succeeded with Clare.

He took her hand and found her skin cold to the touch. "Seven years is a very long time to be deprived of your considerable charms, Clare."

She blinked slowly. "Save your blandations, Drummond. You cannot condemn me for a faithless wife and in the same breath expect me to believe that you want me."

To make his point, he leaned back and examined her from head to foot. "Any man would want you."

She radiated confidence. "But you aren't just any man, are you?"

"Nay. I am the husband who must forgive you."

"Or else what?"

He hadn't considered more than one alternative, hadn't thought their quarrel would degenerate this far. Yet he couldn't voice the option that would force her to do his bidding; threatening to take Alasdair from her was his last option and his inherent right. Besides, he wanted her willing and penitent.

She yanked back the sleeve of her bliaud. "Or else you'll bruise me?"

A mark the size of his thumb colored her wrist. So that was the reason behind her anger. Although he felt guilty, he also felt driven to say, "That doesn't hurt, and you know I did not do it on purpose."

"Not all wounds are of the flesh, Drummond. Words can be as painful as blows. They linger, too."

She'd also become a deep thinker, in his absence. In response, he lifted her wrist to his lips and kissed the mark. "I never meant to harm you. I'm sorry, Clare."

In a quiet voice, thick with hesitance, she said, "Will you swear never to do it again?"

He had begun the conversation hoping to exact an apology from her, but that was before he realized how deeply she'd been affected by his loss of control and how much she resented wanting him. "Aye," he said. "You have my word."

She sighed with such profound relief, he grew puzzled anew. More so when she said, "Now that that's settled, I'm sure you'll want to bathe and change your clothes."

"Do I smell?"

As if their quarrel had not occurred, she gave him a playful grin, then sniffed and pretended to cough. "Not if you intend to revel with the huntsmen. They've been in the woods for days. You should make good companions."

He had other plans for the morning, but he doubted she would approve of him taking Alasdair to the blacksmith and commissioning the lad's battle gear. He did need a bath, though.

"Will you perform the office of chatelaine and bathe me, Clare?"

Color blossomed on her cheeks. "I regret I cannot."

He took pleasure in her maidenlike response and knew he could grow accustomed to her shy reaction. "Another time, perhaps?"

"Duty calls me elsewhere."

He noted her evasion but let it pass; she had not refused him outright. "Where are you off to?"

"To Eastward Fork, a village beyond the burn we visited yesterday."

We. Her use of the collective eased his guilt and gave him hope that they could come to accord. She would confess her sin and recount the details of her liaison with Edward. Another need niggled at Drummond, for the more time he spent with her, the greater his interest about her grew. "What will you do in Eastward Fork?"

A pensive smile lifted the corners of her mouth. Then she looked him square in the eye. "I'm going to do something I should have done years ago. I'll be home before Vespers."

Her cryptic reply and strength of purpose further roused his curiosity, but he decided not to pry. Instead he responded in kind, for he intended to change his tactics. "Then we'll both share surprises when you return."

Later that afternoon, Drummond stood in the

tiltyard and leaned against the quintain. A pleasant breeze cooled his skin, and the high, pillowy clouds blocked most of the August sun. A group of children ringed the yard, their parents looking on. The intermittent ringing of the blacksmith's hammer punctuated the laughter and conversation. From the open window of the barracks came the hearty snores of toilworn huntsmen.

Sween Handle, the master of the hunt, had spent the afternoon watching Drummond instruct Alasdair in the use of sword and shield. Even without hearing Sween's family name, Drummond would have recognized him as the butcher's younger brother, for they favored each other, down to the streak of pure white in their thick brown hair. Drummond liked the man's jovial and straightforward manner.

Earlier in the day, when Alasdair referred to another of Clare's expansive tales about Drummond, and he expressed concern about being perceived as a legend, Sween had been objective in his reply.

"Only the young ones believe Lady Clare's tales," the huntsman had said. " 'Tis the best way to get them to sleep — or so the married folks say."

At first, Drummond had been surprised to learn that Sween was a bachelor, a landless adventurer, as Alasdair called him. Then he'd been suspicious and wondered if Sween could have an affection for Clare. That had surprised Drummond more, for he'd never been jealous of another man or possessive of any of his women.

After a hour in Sween's company, Drummond learned that the huntsman's affections lay with another.

Alasdair was now sauntering around the yard. Wearing a too large helmet and carrying a sword and shield, he faced off against an imaginary foe.

"He struts like the cock o' the walk," Drummond said.

Sween folded his arms over his chest. "True, and he's stronger with his left hand, but quicker with his right."

Drummond felt a burst of pride. "He'll learn to wield a sword in either hand."

"Were you schooled in that fashion?"

Childhood memories came rushing back. Drummond thought of the happy times — before England had declared war on Scotland. "Some say it's a God given talent, but I doubt I was so blessed. With a bevy of sibling lads nipping at my heels, I had little choice but to fend them off from both sides," he said.

Tipping his head toward Drummond, Sween put his hand over his mouth. "I've heard the Highlanders fight naked. Is it true?"

After seven years among the English, Drummond was all too familiar with the misconceptions about his people. Unlike the taunting prison guards, Sween was asking out of curiosity, so Drummond took no offense. "Not in my experience — unless a man's caught in the wrong bed."

Sween threw back his head and laughed. "An ignoble way to die."

Drummond laughed, too. "Dying in itself is ignoble."

With a hand as big as the quintain counterweight, the huntsman slapped Drummond on the back. "Amen, and bless old Edward for sparing you his wrath. I've never seen him show mercy to an enemy."

Even though he'd heard that opinion before, Drummond sensed a familiarity in Sween's tone. "You sound as if you knew the late king."

Alasdair called out, "Watch me!" Jerking his elbow to and fro, he jabbed mercilessly at his phantom opponent and swore, "Take that, you scurvy toad."

After praising the lad's efforts, Drummond told him to keep his wrist steady and save his breath. Then he turned to his companion. "You were saying, Sween?"

Matter-of-factly, he said, "I fought with Edward the First in Wales, back in 'eighty-two."

"Against Llewellyn? That was twenty-six years ago. You must have been a lad at the time."

"I was ten and five. I left his service when he made war on the Scots. I've no taste for killing my mother's kinsmen."

"She's a Highlander?"

"Nay, from the Lowlands, but a Scot all the same. We make no distinctions here in the Debatable Lands. She was a Douglas, with a temper to match her red hair." Squinting, he stared into the sun. "She died the same year as Bertie lost his wife."

Drummond had forgotten the wrenlike woman who had accompanied his wife to the Highlands years ago. And why not? With Clare in a room, few of the other female occupants received more than a passing notice. His brothers had stood agog at the first sight of her. His mistress had become exceedingly pliable.

Standing beside Drummond on the steps to the kirk years ago, Clare had looked like a virginal goddess. He thought of the way she had looked this morning and the conviction she hadn't disguised. What was the purposeful errand she had been so driven to complete?

Images of last night intruded. He remembered the feel of her hands in his hair and her tongue sliding into his mouth. His loins grew heavy, and he again glanced toward the castle gates. Where was she?

As if reading his thoughts, Sween said, "She'll be back before nightfall."

"Does she never stay away?"

"Nay."

The helmet jostling on his head, Alasdair attacked the quintain. Drummond jumped out of the way just in time to avoid a blow from the short and deliberately dull blade. "Watch yourself, lad," Drummond warned. "Or I'll take that sword away."

Snickers sounded from the crowd. Alasdair flushed with embarrassment, then whirled and whacked away at the wind.

Drummond turned back to Sween. "Clare never calls on her overlord, Red Douglas?"

"She did once and came back with two of his wards. Fostered the lassies for three years." His eyes glowed with fondness and he shook his head. "She grieved for a fortnight when they returned home."

Then why didn't she want a daughter of her own? Most likely she didn't want another of Drummond's children. He'd disavow her of that notion. "How long ago was that?"

"A year or so. Alasdair pouted, too — missed having so many females fawning over him."

With his left arm, Alasdair held up the shield, and with his right, he brandished the sword. Lunging, he stirred up the dust and the crowd urged him on. A lassie of about six, her hair a mass of red ringlets, left the group and came to stand in front of Sween.

He smiled down at her. "Where did you get the tart, Curly?"

She wiped crumbs from her mouth. "From Mistress Glory," came the lispy reply.

Rumor had it that Glory was the village seamstress and midwife. She was also in love with Sween.

He winked at Drummond. "How fares the lady?"

The clouds moved away from the sun. Closing one eye, the girl peered up at Sween. "She's pot throwing mad, Uncle Sween."

"Did she mention me?"

The child's nod was almost imperceptible. "She says if you do not take her to collect simples, she'll rip off your ears and use 'em for fish bait."

Sween put his hands on either side of his head. "You tell her I'll do as I may. And she's welcome to try to steal my ears, but she'll have to catch me first."

Laughing, the lass dashed off.

"Warring is safer than women," Sween said.

Rumors of Sween and Glory abounded. Prideful, they called her. Stubborn as the church, they said of him. Drummond had yet to meet the infamous Glory, but suspected she was a match for Sween. "You could marry the lass," he said.

Sween kicked at a pebble. "That life's not for me."

Drummond caught a note of sadness in the reply, but before he could address it, the bannerman raced toward them.

Face flushed and gasping for breath, the fellow said, "My lady's coming, and she's got Elton Singer with her."

Sween's mouth fell open. "The devil you say."

"By my oath, I saw 'em, Sween. The watchman let me look through the spyglass."

Drummond had met dozens of new people today; Sween had told him stories about many of the other residents, but no one had mentioned the name of this newcomer. "Who is Elton Singer?"

The bannerman spat on the well-packed earth.

116

Sween said, "He's a boil on the butt of man and not worth the seed it took to sprout him."

"He's rotten to the core," the bannerman put in.

Drummond grew alarmed. "What's he doing with Clare?"

"More's the question," Sween murmured, "what's she doing with him?"

Johanna flipped the reins, and the horse trotted up the incline leading to the main gate. Although his clothes were freshly washed, her passenger smelled of last year's ale. "If you whine one more time, Elton Singer, I'll treble your punishment."

The worthless cur jerked his hands, which were bound at the wrists and tied to the cart seat. "But, my lady, I'll lose the use o' me hands."

"As well you should."

The gateman rushed forward and took control of the horse. Drummond helped her from the cart, his blue eyes anxious with concern. "What's happened?"

A surge of giddiness took her breath away, for she could grow accustomed to his attention. "Justice." She motioned for Sween to come forward. "Take Mr. Singer into the barracks."

The huntsman's face grew blank with disbelief. "Him? But why? He cannot even nock an arrow."

Johanna almost smiled, for Sween obviously thought she was enlisting Singer into service. In a way, she was. "I know," she said with fake pleasantness. "I had arranged for Mrs. Singer to help scour the barracks this week. Since she has been stricken ill, Mr. Singer has graciously offered to take her place. Haven't you, sir?"

Laughter rang through the throng of onlookers. Someone yelled, "Singer's doin' women's work."

Drummond looked confused.

Like a trapped animal, Singer scanned the men in the crowd. "Lady or not, she can't punish a man for doing what he's a right to. Ain't it so, brethren?"

Except for a few inquisitive rumblings, his speech fell on deaf ears.

Inspired and eager to carry her mission through, Johanna faced Singer. "First, the law that allows a man to beat his wife is unfair," she said through her teeth. "And second, your fist is not a rod the size of your thumb, as the law stipulates. Take him away, Sween, and if I learn that any other man visits cruelties on his wife, he will pay a stiffer price."

"My Lord Drummond," Singer wheedled, his bound hands held in supplication. "They said you had come home to us, and bless the saints for our fair fortune. We're sore needin' a man's justice. Tell my lady about a man's rights. She'll listen to you."

Drummond held his hands palms up, as if warding off a foe. "You'll get no allegiance from me. My lady cites the law true and to the letter." Then he gave her a winsome smile. "We'll abide by her decision."

Johanna felt like laughing and crying at once.

She hadn't expected the people of Fairhope to question her, but she could not have known what Drummond would do. She almost thanked him, before she regained caution.

She had come dangerously close to succumbing to him last night. She had lain awake for hours, reliving her mistake. If she yielded, he would know her for a virgin and an impostor. With time she could better play the role of wife and wield the female power she had glimpsed last night.

But now she had other work to do. "Sween, once Singer is settled in the barracks you're to take Glory to Eastward Fork. Maggie Singer needs tending."

"You had better have Bertie take her."

"Have you quarreled again?"

"She quarreled. I listened."

"I need Bertie here, so put your differences aside."

"Aye, my lady."

Singer looked crestfallen. "I'll look after my dear Maggie."

Johanna shot him a triumphant stare. "When fish walk on land!" Then she picked up her basket and walked to the steps to the keep.

"Mother!"

At the muffled sound, she stopped. Alasdair ran toward her, a war helmet bobbing on his head, the accoutrements of battle in his hands.

She lifted off his heavy headgear and put it in her basket.

His hair was plastered to his scalp and his face stained with dirt and sweat. "What did Elton Singer do?" he asked.

With her fingers, she combed his hair off his forehead. "He beat his wife. A man should never lift a hand to a woman or a child."

"That's why you never whip me . . . even when I'm bad."

"Yes. I'm stronger."

He stood taller. "And I'm a bright lad." Solemnly he added, "Violence begets violence."

It seemed an odd statement to Johanna, considering his warlike attire. She asked the obvious.

He banged the blade against the shield, which bore the symbolic wolf of the Macqueens. Chin up, he declared, "I've been learning soldiering. Father says I have quick feet and a right goodly balance."

In Latin, she said, "How were your studies today?"

He sighed dramatically and waved his arm before her. "Don't you see, Mother? I have a sword arm now. I must perfect it."

He seemed so determined, she knew she must nip his destructive obsession in the bud. "Who told you that?"

"I thought it up myself."

She hadn't heard Drummond's approach. He stood behind her. She was immediately reminded of last night, of his breath warm on her neck and his arm snug around her waist. The rapturous kiss. The hollow weakness that followed. The maidenly fear that even now tightened her chest and reminded her that she must fight her attraction to him. "Alasdair was supposed to study an extra hour with Brother Julian."

"Why did you not tell me you had lessons, Alasdair?" asked Drummond.

"Because you wouldn't have helped me get a sword arm."

Alasdair's skewed logic left Drummond speechless. Reveling in his predicament, Johanna sent him a what-will-you-do-now look.

He glanced from her to Alasdair. A long moment later, he bent close to his son and said, "A soldier never lies, nor shirks his duties. No custard for a week."

Alasdair threw down the shield. "That's unfair. Mother never takes away my custard for that long."

Drummond planted his feet and stared down at his son. "Well, unfortunately that's what's going to happen."

"Mother, do something," the lad pleaded. "I hate Latin. Brother Julian says I cannot carp it."

Pleased to her toes that Drummond had supported her, she gave her son a benevolent smile. "You'll like it better from now on, I'm sure."

His mouth, so like Drummond's, turned down in a pout. "No, I won't."

She calmly picked up the shield and sword and walked toward the steps. "Then you won't see these again soon."

"Give it back," he demanded. " 'Tis bad luck

for a woman to touch a man's sword."

Johanna froze. A woman. In one word Alasdair had made her a generality. She had always been "mother" and his authority figure. Someday he would outgrow his need for her, but until then, she would influence him in word and deed.

Turning, she stared him down. " 'Tis worse luck for a lad to sass his mother."

He clutched Drummond's arm. "Father, make her give it back to me."

"I suggest," Drummond began sternly, "that you get to the well and clean yourself up. Then you go to the chapel, apologize to Brother Julian, and ask him to give you your lesson."

Tears pooled in Alasdair's eyes, and he looked so forlorn, Johanna knew she would relent. As if sensing her capitulation, Drummond put his hand on her shoulder. Squeezing gently, he said, "Go along, Alasdair. Be a good lad. We'll see you at table."

A fat tear worked its way through the dust on Alasdair's cheek. "But I have to say the blessing. I'm the youngest."

His voice thick with emotion, Drummond said, "Then we'll wait for you and Brother Julian and discuss what you learned."

Alasdair sniffed and wiped his nose. "All right," he grumbled, then smiled. "But when do I get to give the orders?"

"To us? Never." Drummond patted Alasdair's bottom. "Off with you."

Choked with elation that Drummond had taken

an interest in both their son's education and Singer's punishment, Johanna turned away and started up the steps.

From behind her, she heard Drummond say, "I wonder why you chose today to confront that wife beater."

Not ready to broach the subject, she shrugged.

"I think I know where you got the idea." He moved beside her and lifted her arm. The sleeve of her bliaud fell back to reveal the small bruise he'd given her the night before.

She jerked her arm free. "I always believed Maggie when she claimed to be clumsy. Now I know that he's been beating her for years. I felt dreadful."

"So did I, and I apologized, Clare."

As always, bearing her sister's name had a sobering effect on Johanna. This time she gained strength from it, "You also promised to stay away from me."

His brow creased in confusion. "I agreed never to mark you again."

" 'Tis the same thing." Hearing that, his expression grew so calculating, she said, "You're up to something."

He gave her a bold, flirtatious smile and threw her own words in her face. "You're correct, of course."

Chapter
6

Unable to stop thinking about the day's events, Johanna paced the floor of Alasdair's small room. An image of Maggie Singer popped into her mind. Even with one eye swollen shut and her lip split and bruised, the woman would not accuse her husband of brutally beating her. Their only child, a sweet-faced girl of five, had clung to her mother's skirt and cast fearful glances at her father, who lay snoring on the cot.

Did he also abuse his daughter?

That possibility had kindled a fire of rage in Johanna. In a flash of insight she understood how a person could be driven to violence, for she had wanted to smash her fist into Elton Singer's nose.

He hadn't even stirred when she bound his hands and hobbled his feet. Only when she dragged him into the afternoon sunshine did he rouse himself. His indignation had sickened her. Gratification had come when Drummond and the others applauded her actions. Drummond's patronage hadn't stopped there.

From the moment she'd taken her place at the table he had been solicitous and charming in the extreme. He'd worn a pale blue jerkin that complemented his eyes and devilishly tight trunk hose that invariably drew hers. Never before had she been enticed to stare at a well-muscled thigh or to admire a sinewy calf. She had never dwelled on the strength and grace of a man's hands. She'd never appreciated the rumble of male laughter or contemplated a freshly shaven cheek.

Once, when he caught her staring at him, he'd given her a roguish wink and asked if she'd care to retire to a private place and have a closer look. The memory made her light-headed. Yet beneath the excitement, she felt a stab of longing and sadness, for he would never actually pay court to her, Johanna Benison. He didn't even know she existed.

Feeling melancholy to her soul, she hugged herself and walked to the window. Moonlight cast the yard in a silvery glow, and the long shadow of the keep fell like a great black spike over the inner wall and the bailey. A pair of guards stood near the main gate and spoke in low tones. Mingling with the male voices was the occasional barking of a dog and the ill-timed crowing of a cock.

The peaceful sounds lulled her into a yawn, and she considered returning to Alasdair's small cot and trying again to fall asleep.

The squeak of leather hinges stopped her. Someone had opened the door leading to the battlement on the roof of the tower. Who, and why was someone prowling the keep in the middle of the night? If it was Alasdair spying on the watchmen again, he'd forgo dessert until Nutcrack Night.

From the pegs on the wall near the door, she snatched up a shawl and went in search of her incorrigible son.

She found Drummond wrapped in a tartan plaid and stargazing. Outlined in a crenel in the shoulder-high battlement, he seemed a solitary figure, completely at peace.

"Hello, Clare."

Her fingers curled around the hard edge of the door, and she retreated into the shadows. "How did you know 'twas me?"

"I'd know you anywhere."

The irony in that made her chuckle.

With a motion of his hand, he coaxed her to him.

She stayed where she was.

"Very well." He pushed away from the wall. "I'll give you proof. You're taller and more shapely than Evelyn, and I assume no one else wears white sleeping gowns or has hair that shines like spun gold in the moonlight."

Charming was too quaint a word for his methods; beguiling better suited him. "Thank you. You are too kind."

It was his turn to chuckle, and he extended

126

his arm again. "I'm hardly that, as you well know. Join me. 'Tis a glorious night, and we have much to discuss."

Returning to her room seemed prudent, but he had a point, and he looked so disarming she couldn't bring herself to walk away. He posed no threat to her here, at the top of the keep. Although they stood in the open, no one could see them. Guards patrolled the wall below, and if she called out, they would come running.

She moved toward him, her soft leather slippers cushioning her steps, the wind stirring her unbound hair. Gathering the wayward strands, she tucked them under her shawl.

"Couldn't you sleep?" he asked.

Unwilling to reveal the cause of her restlessness, she braced herself on a merlon, leaned into a crenel, and looked down. A cat strolled across the yard, its tail held as stiff as a ship's mast.

"Clare?"

She started, which was odd, considering how long she'd answered to her sister's name. "I awoke when you opened the door. The hinges are dry and noisy."

"You never roused so easily, not before noontime."

Sister Margaret used to say that even an invading army wouldn't awaken Clare before midday. Johanna had always been the early riser. In explanation, she told a half-truth cloaked in a midwife's tale. "Alasdair's birth changed my sleeping habits."

He hummed in agreement. "Praise be to the mother who answers the cry of her child in the night."

"And fortune bless the father who keeps the demons from their sight."

"I remember no more of the rhyme," he confessed. "Do you?"

Johanna did, but she grew brave and decided to speculate about this man she hardly knew. She faced him. "You never were one for poetry."

His appreciative gaze settled on her hair. "A condition you oft lamented."

She snatched up a full truth. "I haven't the time for lamenting now."

"Do you still play the harp?"

Johanna could easier strum a tune on a pitchfork. Years ago, she'd been forced to sell Clare's harp. The forty pence she'd received had gone toward Sween's first year's wages. An excuse, in the form of a fond memory, came quickly to mind. "I had my hands full keeping Alasdair fed and clean and out of trouble. He was forever on a quest to explore forbidden territory — especially up here."

" 'Tis the Macqueen in him, I'm sure. My father boasted that my grandmother had to swaddle him in leather braces."

Their easy conversation didn't surprise Johanna; since her return from Eastward Fork, Drummond had been as agreeable as an almsman at harvest. Since Clare hadn't mentioned Drummond's father, Johanna feared tripping herself up if she dwelled on the subject. "What did your mother say about you?"

"She died giving birth to me."

The squalling of cats pierced the silence. A weight pressed in on Johanna. "I'm sorry, Drummond. I'd forgotten. You must think me crass."

"Most often," he murmured, "I'm in a quandary about you."

Feeling defeated and wary of the husky sensuality in his voice, Johanna glanced at the door and contemplated a hasty retreat.

"Stay," he said.

Resigned, she pledged to be more careful. "What did you want to talk to me about?"

He propped an elbow on one of the mertons. His wrap fell open to reveal the jerkin she'd admired earlier. "Longfellow needs more shelter than the outer wall affords," he said. "He's used to warmer climes and greater comfort."

If he were concerned about permanent quarters for the elephant, that meant Drummond intended to stay here. Her spirits sank even lower, for she'd been certain he'd go home to the Highlands. Looking up at him, she could tell he expected her to comment. Dashed hopes robbed her of anything to say.

"I thought to build a closure against the inner wall near the main gate," he went on.

Drummond being agreeable was one thing, hesitance from him was something else. "Are you asking my permission?"

His fine straight teeth shone white in the moonlight. "And your opinion, too."

Her first thought on the elephant was that it would be happier somewhere else, such as France. Knowing Drummond wouldn't appreciate her sentiment, she gave him what he'd asked for. "I do not know if Longfellow will tolerate all of the goings and comings at the gate."

"You needn't worry over that. He's accustomed to people. They thronged to see him in the Tower, and he's not at all dangerous."

She remembered what Alasdair had said about the animal. "I thought he tried to knock down a wall."

"He did. But I was leaving without him, and he rather likes me."

Who wouldn't? she thought. When he chose to be congenial, Drummond could charm a spinster out of her only fond memory. Johanna couldn't afford to fall prey to him. "If Longfellow needs a shelter, then by all means, we'll have the carpenter build it. Shall I speak to him?"

"I'll do it on the morrow." He stared into the distance. Set against the starlit sky, his features thrown into darkness, his noble profile limned in moonlight, he looked like a leader of men and a master of women. No wonder the Macqueens named him their chieftain. He must have been glorious in the role. A pity Clare hadn't elaborated.

Appreciation of his physical beauty turned to a yearning that melted her heart and clouded her reason. Maybe he wouldn't notice that she was a virgin. Perhaps he wouldn't recall the placement of the brand on her skin. Intimacy might bridge the gap between them, and as time went by he would learn to accept her as she was. If she were truly fortunate, he would give her a daughter. She'd insist that they name the girl Johanna, for she did so want to hear the sound of her own name again.

She searched for a place to begin.

Cry peace with me, Clare, and I will try to forgive you.

The memory of his words tortured her, for Johanna realized the dangerous direction of her thoughts. In a moment of weakness she had contemplated the unthinkable: becoming his wife in the true sense of the word. He would know she wasn't Clare. Common sense would tell him she was a relative of his wife. If the truth came out, Sister Margaret would surely be held accountable. Johanna's burden grew, and she vowed to bide her time, guard her heart, and get rid of him.

"Why do you stare at me so?" he asked.

Lies, lies, lies. And she could seek absolution for none of them. If sins were scars, she decided, her soul was an ugly thing, and just now she hadn't the strength to carry the guilt of another. "I watch you because, strange as it sounds, we hardly know each other."

Drummond understood completely, for sometimes he didn't know himself. "You are quite different to me as well, but we'll never reacquaint ourselves if you keep me at a distance."

131

She moved closer, but he knew it for the concession it was. "That's better. The Clare I remember would never have brought a wife beater or any other criminal to justice. She would also have flown into my arms."

She stared at his throat. "As you say, I am not that woman. I am someone else now."

He would also add that she was complex, deceptively honorable, and exceedingly interesting. "Given the right circumstance, boldness in a woman can be an appealing trait."

"I thought men were more concerned with the size of a woman's fortune or the fairness of her form."

"They are, and when she possesses an abundance of both, he looks for intelligence and other complimentary traits."

She tipped her head to the side. "Why ever would he trouble himself?"

Drummond had expected her to demur and flatter him in return. He grew uncomfortable with her frankness, and if he wasn't careful, he'd tell her how much she intrigued him. "Out of boredom, most likely."

"Idle hands and all that?"

He could think of several ways to occupy his hands, and each of them involved the sensory pleasure of exploring her womanly charms. Especially when he considered that she was naked beneath her gown. In spite of the breeze he grew warm beneath his wool tartan. "A man could also be curious about how she came to be so bold."

Their eyes met, hers dark and mysterious in the moonlight. "Had I not learned to stand up for myself I would be a pauper and Alasdair a waif."

His list of misconceptions about her grew, for he added industrious. "I wasn't faulting your motives, Clare. Especially since the benefits are mine as well. Thanks to you, our estates prosper."

"But Fairhope is a small demesne when compared to your Highland holdings. How could you give it more than a passing glance?"

Was she being coy? He didn't expect that of this new Clare, and the last thing he wanted to discuss was the Highlands. He had other questions to ask and personal matters to broach. He chose the topic that had troubled him most of the day: her refusal to give him more children. "Fairhope will serve as dowry for our eldest daughter."

Her eyes widened in alarm, and her fingers knotted. "What of Alasdair's future?"

He glimpsed her protective nature again, and envied his son the luxury of maternal love. "He will inherit my mother's dower lands."

"In the Highlands," she said, sounding as if Scotland were at the end of the earth.

"Aye."

"I see."

"So you mustn't diminish Fairhope's importance."

Even in the pale light, he could see her blanch. "I was not. I simply assumed that your other property suffers from lack of your attention. What

133

will be left for Alasdair then?"

"You sound eager to be rid of me. Are you?"

"Of course not."

The insincerity in her hasty reply begged for a challenge. "You are my property. Do you wither from neglect?"

She laughed nervously. "It's safe to say that I've lost the ability to wither. Surely you'll concede that."

For every retiring trait she'd lost, she'd gained a measure of character, an enchanting aspect to an already interesting woman. "I'll concede only that you are not the same Clare I married, and as your husband, I have the right to explore the differences in you."

"Ha!" She danced away. "What you're saying is, you'll get me with child again, then leave me to birth it and raise it on my own."

He followed her, regretting that the battlement was round, for he could better trap her in a corner. "Even if I hadn't been away warring against Edward the First, I would have been denied entrance to the birthing room. And mothers usually raise the lassies."

"In this family, the mother raises all of the children."

Taken aback, he could only gawk at her. When he regained his wits, he grew defensive. "Pardon me for putting the future of a kingdom over the welfare of one pregnant woman."

"You should have negotiated with the English, rather than jump into war and jeopardize the safety of *this* pregnant woman. You put your wife's safety in jeopardy."

He grew incredulous at her self-indulgence. "Jump into war? With an army marching toward us, we had little choice. And I thought you carried a royal bastard."

The fight went out of her. "You could have been killed on the spot and Macqueen Castle reduced to rubble."

The events of that black day long ago hung like a bad memory in his mind. He had been certain that death would find him before dawn. He hadn't considered Clare's plight.

"Who am I to upbraid you for defending yourself?"

He had no reply to that, so he addressed another worrisome topic. "You should have asked me to go with you to Eastward Fork today."

"It wasn't necessary."

" 'Twas *my* place."

"Actually, it's Sheriff Hay's responsibility."

Would she never recognize that she had a husband who had sworn to protect her? "Your safety is mine."

"I was in no danger. Singer was suffering the effects of too much ale. He had difficulty putting one foot before the other."

If every woman was as capable as she, men would become as useless as ballocks on a barbican. "Was that before or after you hobbled him?"

Her chin came up. "Both."

He wanted to rail at her, but she looked so

135

proud, he decided that logic was the better approach. "He's prone to violence, Clare. That was the reason you went after him."

"Do you know, I didn't really think of him or what he might do to me. I was concerned with Maggie's safety."

Unselfishness joined the list of her attributes. But he couldn't help wonder if she would ever be as concerned about him or their sham of a marriage. "A woman's safety often depends on the mood of her mate."

Her expression reeked of disbelief. "A woman's happiness depends on her husband's good humor? That's rubbish."

"Then how do you account for telling me that you'd never known happiness before marrying me. You said you'd devote your life to pleasing me."

She bowed her head and murmured, "I must have been besotted with you then."

He gave her high marks for courage. "But you're not now."

"I do not know what to think about you. I'm in a quandary, too."

Having his words tossed in his face made Drummond cross. She needed a strong, guiding hand, and he'd had seven years to contemplate what he wanted of her. He leaned closer to her and said, "You could end your uncertainty by being a good wife."

She rose on tiptoe, and when their noses were a breath apart, she declared, "I'm as good a wife as you are a husband."

She had him there. "Then perhaps we should both start over again."

"How?" she scoffed.

"By doing what other husbands and wives do."

"Which is?"

He almost laughed out loud at her naivety. "They become close."

"And if one of them refuses to get close?"

"The other would surely demand an explanation — that, or look elsewhere for his closeness."

Gone was the bold woman. In her place he saw a shy and tentative girl, her fingers toying with the edges of her wrap. "You mean he would take a mistress," she said. "You've done that before and without provocation."

And she had lain with the man who was now king of England. Lord, what a farce they'd made of marriage. Drummond couldn't forgive her, not until she begged for forgiveness. But as matters stood between them now, he'd have more success in demanding she turn pigs into geese than insist that she bare her soul. If he were going to dictate policy to her, he had to go slowly.

He extended his arm and kept his voice even. "Now I merely want someone to hold my hand."

She glanced toward the main gate, then threaded her fingers in his. Her skin felt cool, softer than he remembered, and her wrist fragile enough to break with a snap of his fingers. He thought of Elton Singer, the wife beater. Did Clare refuse to share Drummond's bed because she'd seen firsthand the brutality of which a husband was capable?

Driven to know, he said, "Why do you sleep in Alasdair's bed?"

"Because it's too small for you."

He tried to stifle his laughter, but heaven help him, he could not. When she tried to pull her hand away, he clasped it tightly. "I should have asked why you skirt your wifely obligations."

"Obligations?" She yanked her hand free. "Is that what making love is to you, an obligation?"

Her chilly disapproval quelled his mirth. "It wouldn't have to be, not if we reacquainted ourselves."

"Please define reacquaint."

With long walks in the woods and quiet, private evenings up here, he almost said. Then he caught himself. By the saints, he was contemplating the seduction of his own wife. Part of him objected, but the freedom of the vast night sky lulled him into complacency. Call him weak, but for too long loneliness had been his constant companion, and he wanted her company.

She snapped her fingers. "I have it. Let's forget what happened before you were taken. Everyday we could share a story, something that occurred during our separation."

What trick was she playing? Before he could ask, she said, "I could tell you which word Alasdair uttered first. I could describe his first steps. Or recount the time he put salt in the oat bin.

I laughed beyond measure at that. So many of his doings were entertaining . . ."

He ceased listening. He didn't want to hear. If he'd known about his son, the dark and lonely times in prison would have been unbearable. Instead he'd fantasized about Clare. He had pretended that she visited him often, bringing his favorite foods and warm new clothing that she herself had stitched. Although she looked like Clare, the woman he had conjured was not the faithless wife but the devoted helpmate. More's the pity, he thought.

"Drummond, are you listening?"

He banished the fantasy and addressed the reality. "And what can I tell you, Clare?" he said through gritted teeth. "Shall I describe the lavish furnishings in an English cell? Perhaps you'd care to hear about the delicacies they served me or the minstrels they provided."

"Oh, Drummond. I did not think of you as . . ." Her teeth closed over her bottom lip, and her eyes turned starry.

"As what?"

She embraced him and laid her head on his chest. "I did not think of you as simply a man deprived of his freedom."

She had always rushed to tend the sick in his village; yet he didn't want her sympathy; he wanted a confession, then a plea for forgiveness for the crime of adultery.

She felt warm and yielding, and his physical needs overrode his principles. He'd been without

139

a woman for too long, and if she continued to caress his back, he'd have her on hers.

"They had no right to imprison you and tell us you were dead. Why did your family not send word to me?"

"After the first year, they told the Macqueens I'd been hanged and —" His voice broke; he could not face the horror. No matter what had occurred between them, he could not tell her the gory particulars of Edward I's explanation of Drummond's demise. "Hanged."

"Those years must have been wretched for you."

Bitterness burned inside him. She'd valued this piece of land in the Borders more than her wedding vows. Her heart beat strong and steady against his chest and comfort streamed from her in gentle waves. Give me your burden, her body seemed to say. Worry not, for I'm here to share your pain.

His knees trembled, and he no longer felt like the wronged husband; he became the ordinary man of whom she'd spoken. His arms engulfed her, and he rubbed his cheek against her hair. She smelled of home, and her tender touch brought to life one of a thousand lustful dreams.

In this one, he stood atop a well-fortified castle, freedom as far as his eye could see, a golden haired goddess at his side. She caressed him from temple to waist and lower, her soft lips and dancing fingers playing an erotic melody upon his skin. Then she grew eager and, moaning wan-

140

tonly, guided his hands over her feminine form. When he expected the woman of his dreams to beg him to love her until dawn, the woman in his arms gave him a final pat and stepped back.

Desire blurred his vision and buzzed in his ears. When he could focus, he saw an expression of wonder on her face. Or was it confusion?

"I, ah . . ." She paused, staring at the exit door. "I must say good night, Lord Drummond."

Her formality checked his base urges, for he instinctively knew that she was gripped by emotions she neither welcomed nor understood. As bizarre as it seemed, he felt as if he were still seized by his own fantasy. For she was Clare and yet she was not. He couldn't let her go.

"And if I command you to stay?"

She pulled the shawl tighter around her shoulders. "I would ask that you do not."

A more honest appeal he'd never heard. "Do you take back your words of comfort?"

"No." Her voice was thick with grief. "I would wrap them in tinsel thread and lay them at your feet."

"Then you are tired."

She stared at his knees. "I have never been less tired in my life."

"You suffer from an illness?"

"I am exceedingly hale and hearty."

Her eyes met his, and he felt an odd stirring in his chest, for he saw agony and soul deep fear. "You are beset with bad humors."

"I could as like call up the merrymakers."

Desire poured over him like hot honeyed wine, and he lifted his brows in invitation.

Backing away, she said, "Tomorrow is Wares Day, and I must up with the dawn. Good night, Lord Drummond."

Moonglow pearled on the moisture in her eyes before she turned and disappeared through the dark doorway.

A moment later Alasdair stepped out, battle shield and sword in hand. "What's wrong with Mother?"

A reply lodged in Drummond's throat, and he stared at the gaping black portal, willing her to return to him, to finish what she had started, to tell him what was in her heart.

"She didn't even see me. You won't tell her I'm here, will you, Father? You said I must begin my soldiering, so I thought to patrol the battlement up here. To protect Mother and Bertie."

Shaking his head, Drummond tried to cast off the image of her, her turmoil and her quiet dignity. Would she have yielded? He didn't know for certain, but he'd wager all his sons to come that she'd wanted to, and it both thrilled and frightened her.

"Will you promise, Father?"

With a pledge to further test the boundaries of her self-control, Drummond devised a plan. His strategy set, he ruffled his son's sleep mussed hair. "I'll keep your secret, Alasdair, but you must do something for me."

Chapter
7

"Mother, may I have a quince?"

Smothering under a blanket of regrets, Johanna leaped at the diversion. If she couldn't stop thinking about how much Drummond had suffered, she might as well rush into his arms and tell him precisely why she hadn't inquired after him.

"Curly and her little sister have quinces." Walking backward and facing her, Alasdair pouted. "May I please have one?"

Thinking he was due a haircut soon, she reached out to scruff his head. "Will you promise to keep your appointment with Brother Julian?"

He dodged her admirably. "I gave you my word of honor. 'Tis a manly thing."

In another few years he'd grow away from her. In manhood, he would make her proud. Later he would bring his children to visit. Engulfed in motherly love, she wanted to hug him, but he'd balk at so public a display. "You're to be there before Vespers."

He nodded. "I'm hungry, Mother. I'm as starved as a mouse in Glory's pantry."

"Where did you hear that?"

"From Sween." Looking back over his shoulder he steered himself to the clean edge of the lane. "But he says she can keep her sweets to herself."

The latest episode in the ongoing war of the lovers promised to outdo the rift at Whitsunday last. *Whitsunday.* Drummond's birthday. How many of those days had he spent alone and hungry in the Tower of London? The grief returned to weight her shoulders and prick her conscience. She should have inquired, for she knew the old king practiced brutality against his enemies. It followed that he would hardly account for their needs or address the concerns of their families. That still didn't excuse her; she could have asked through a third party.

"Mother, what's wrong?"

Everything. Alasdair had stopped to stare at her. His fretful expression mirrored a worried frown from Drummond. "Nothing's amiss, dear, and yes, you may have a quince, but only one."

"And one for Longfellow." He spun around and darted down the cross path that would take him to the market.

Johanna dodged a herd of yearling sheep and continued on her way to the tanner to find a protective glove for the cook. Merchant stalls and larger businesses lined either side of the lane. As they displayed their wares, the craftsmen and the castle folk exchanged morning greetings. It was still too early in the day for visitors from the surrounding hamlets, but by noontime the bailey would be filled with carts and wagons and the thoroughfares clogged with customers.

The baker called out to her. "Have a scone, my lady. Lord Drummond said they was as good as his aunt Fiona's. Ate an even dozen of 'em and said I should deliver up a batch to the keep every morning."

The aroma of fresh baked bread teased her nose, but she doubted she could swallow even a crumb. She had succeeded in avoiding Drummond this morning, and knowing his whereabouts would allow her to keep it that way. Facing him would come later.

She smiled and hoped she didn't sound like a woman who'd lost her wits over a man. "When was Lord Drummond here?"

The baker raked his forearms, stirring up a cloud of flour. "Just 'afore he and Sween set off for the tanner. My lord said you'd want to look for him there."

So much for going to the tanner. She had expected Drummond to be at the carpenter's shed and had planned her errands to avoid that establishment. That he wanted her to look for him didn't bear addressing.

"Elton Singer left his harnesses to dry-rot," the baker was saying. "Sween brought 'em in with him this morning. Mistress Glory's still in Eastward Fork, y'know. Suppose he'll fetch her in a day or two. I look for a pleasant makin' up from 'em.''

Sween and Glory's troubles were their concern; Johanna had problems of her own. "Thank you." She put the scone in her basket, which already contained a broken trivet and several jars of honey; then she bade the baker good day and set out for the smithy.

On the way, the shoemaker waved her into his shop. His mouth puckered, he aimed a coarse thread through an outsized needle. Behind him, his fragile wife lounged on a bench.

"Lord Drummond's at the tanner," he said, concentrating on his task. "He said you'd be asking after him."

Johanna would as soon inquire after a doomed hog. "He did?"

When he'd succeeded at his task, the shoemaker smiled and, with a flair, rolled a knot into the thread. "Finer man you couldn't want. Commissioned Alasdair a pair of boots."

Wishing Drummond were sending messages from the Highlands and spending money there, she thanked the cobbler and moved on. Just ahead and coming toward her, Morgan Fawr led a basket laden donkey. She'd never met the man, but Alasdair had described the rail-thin fellow perfectly. His closely cropped brown hair and chest length fiery beard made him easily recognizable.

She stopped before him. "I haven't had the pleasure of welcoming you to Fairhope Tower,

Mr. Fawr. I'm Lady Clare."

"Stories tell you how a person come upon knowin' 'em."

Garble-mouthed Welshman, Bertie had said. Johanna understood why. "You're Longfellow's caretaker."

"Herdin' creature, he is for company. Oncet, he shined to a mouser and her kits a crawlin' all over him. Skin tougher than a ship's deck's next to him."

She had hoped to glean information about Drummond from this man. Although she already doubted her success, she plunged onward. "Have you known Lord Drummond long?"

"Coming on the time since the wall crumbled at the water gate."

"The water gate to what?"

The donkey nudged him. With sticklike fingers, he scratched the animal's snout. "At the piling o' the rocks the Conqueror threw up on the Thames."

Garble-mouthed was beginning to sound like a flattering description. Pile of rocks. William the Conqueror. Thames. "You mean the Tower of London."

"Onliest keep on the river with prisoners wearing out the stairs."

Now that she was getting somewhere, she jumped on the lucid thought. "You were a prisoner, too?"

His hand stilled. The donkey let out an ear-splitting bray. Over the noise, he said, "Wasn't there hirin' a room and a bucket o' eels."

Even if she did pry information from him about Drummond, Johanna knew she wouldn't understand much of it. "I hope you enjoy your stay with us."

"I'll run it to ground before it gets away. Plantagenets keep their booty close."

Ignoring the placement of the words and the verbs, she concentrated on the nouns. "The king keeps you close by. He won't allow you to return to Wales?"

Miraculously, he nodded. "He's a-certain I'm after shoveling a mountain of elephant dung."

Baffled, she said, "Are you?"

He blinked, one lid moving slower than the other. "The new king'll never wear the leek upon Saint David's Day."

She jumped at the chance for common ground, for she knew that David was the patron saint of Wales. "Then you're a religious man."

"What's the church got to do with the king?"

At a loss and wanting to yank out her hair in frustration, she handed him the scone. "Here, this is for you."

He reared back, bumping into the donkey. "Begged food falls into a meek belly."

She decided that his thinking was as skewed as his speech. "I always pass out scones to the newcomers."

He peered into the basket. "Full of glad-you-came's today, eh?"

"Yes," she ventured. When he smiled, she thrust the scone into his hand. "Eat hearty. Enjoy."

He turned it over in his hand and mumbled, "A crown upon your head."

Picking up her step, Johanna vowed that the next time she tried to converse with Morgan Fawr, she'd insist that Drummond interpret. A foolish thought, for she intended to stay as far away from him as possible.

Approaching the smithy, she drew off her mantle in deference to the heat. At his forge, the blacksmith clutched a clamp that held what looked suspiciously like a small helmet. "I hope that's not for Alasdair."

The clamp slipped from his hand, and the helmet plopped into the water that hissed and boiled. "Lord Drummond came himself to commission it. There's to be a mail shirt and a breastplate, too."

An acrid smell made her stomach roil; so she moved upwind. "Perhaps for another boy, but not for Alasdair."

"My lady," he pleaded, drawing the sweat-soaked rag from around his neck. "You're husband was particular in his instructions. He's at the tanner now, asking after gauntlets for the lad. Said to tell you he was there so you wouldn't lose track of him."

Lose track of him? His whereabouts could be the fourth biggest mystery, for all she cared. She handed the blacksmith the broken trivet. "I sug-

149

gest you put your efforts into repairing this, should you value my patronage. Eastward Fork has a new forge, or so they say."

Wearing a downtrodden frown, he nodded and fished the helmet from the water. He gave it a fond look, then tossed it aside.

Ready to do battle with the despotic Drummond Macqueen, she went to the tanner.

"Not to worry, my lady. He said you'd come looking for him. He's in the tiltyard with Sween. If you take the alley behind the cooper's, you'll get there quicker."

She almost snapped that she knew the way, but the tanner did not deserve her anger. She went in search of the man who did.

Drummond stood in the center of the yard. Shirtless, his hair tied back with a strip of leather and sweat glistening on his muscled back, he looked like the ancient gladiators Homer had immortalized. Garbed in indecently tight trunk hose and soft leather boots, he had drawn a crowd of adoring women. He seemed unaware of their attention, for he concentrated on the task of uprooting the rotted quintain post. Good, she thought; Fairhope needed no weapons of war. The thing was an eyesore, and the men never used it.

Flexing muscles and long sinewy legs drew her eye. Miffed that she could appreciate a man who would turn his perfectly sweet son into a bully, she marched up to him. "I came to speak with you about the items you commissioned the blacksmith to make for Alasdair."

Glancing at her over his shoulder, he gave her a devilishly inviting smile. "You found me."

"How could I not when you left a trail of verbal mouse droppings for me to follow?"

Amusement danced in his eyes, and his lips puckered with mirth. "You look lovely in that color. The shade brings out the yellow in your hair. You must have worn it for me."

That he had, purely by chance, guessed her exact thoughts while dressing this morning miffed her even more. Chance was all it was. She liked the dress, and that was precisely why she'd worn it. For her, certainly not for him. "Alasdair is not to have a suit of armor."

He straightened and draped an arm over the top of the post. His gloved hand looked large enough to cup her head, and his massive shoulders blocked out the sun. "Are you always so frisky in the morning?" he asked.

How could she both welcome and despise his cajoling tone? Having no answer, she said, "Will you please address the matter at hand."

He sighed and shifted his weight to one leg. "Were it up to you, our son would only excel at kissing altar cloths and speaking foreign languages."

Pride stiffened her backbone. "I speak Latin."

He laughed. "To whom? Evelyn? John Handle?"

Some of the starch went out of her, for he

had a point. But Latin was a language of scholars, the very thing she had in mind for Alasdair. "He must be taught."

Turning over a hand, he said, much too reasonably, "Then teach him something useful."

He smelled of leather and hardworking man. To her dismay, she found it particularly appealing. "Like killing?"

"He should learn to protect himself." He swept an arm in a circle. "And defend everyone here. There's also philosophy, Roman governing, and Scottish history." The last two words were said with marked emphasis.

She had intended to find a well-versed Scotsman to school Alasdair, but not yet. "I cannot afford another tutor, nor do I think it wise to disrupt his studies at this time."

He gave her a sugary grin. "Worry not, my dear. I'll teach him everything he needs to know. Leave it to me."

Already the craftsmen were deferring to him and the women gawking. Johanna hadn't the time to go along after him, cancelling commissions or wondering if he'd settled accounts. She couldn't bring up the subject of money now, not until she learned if he had means of his own. "I insist that you begin by telling the blacksmith that Alasdair has no need for chain mail. I've taken care of the helmet."

He leveled her a smoldering look that could have melted an ice maiden. "Easy now, Clare, or I'll have him make you a chastity belt."

152

Mortified, she gritted her teeth. "You'll do no such thing."

Staring at her hips and lower, he murmured, "On second thought, it might be a sin to lock you up. Tell you what —" He rubbed his back against the post. "I could be persuaded to alter Alasdair's training, if you could be persuaded to . . ."

Unsaid words hung between them. When the silence grew, she couldn't help anticipating the rest of his thought. He'd say that she could give him a house full of children, or that she could share his bed starting tonight. Feeling her cheeks flame, she stared at his broad chest. "I could what?"

"Scratch my back."

Her gaze flew to his. "Your what?"

He jiggled his brows, then turned, presenting her a broad expanse of muscle. Loud enough for even the gateman to hear, he repeated, "Scratch my back."

She'd rather tell him to wallow on it in the dirt, but with half the eligible women within hearing distance, she checked the thought. Since she had no choice, Johanna put down her basket and did as he asked. He gave a contented groan and shivered beneath her touch, reminding her of the power she could wield over him. But last night she had glimpsed the control he could as easily exercise over her, a talent she had yet to perfect. The trouble was, he'd had vastly more experience than she. As a consequence, she must approach every encounter with caution. She must also be certain they were never alone.

To better accommodate her, he bent his legs and braced his hands on his knees. "I'm glad you stopped biting your nails. Did Alasdair's birth change that, too?"

Sister Margaret used to say that bad habits aided Johanna and flocked to Clare. "You might say that."

Leaning to the right, he said, "Yes. Just there. Ah. You slept well?"

She'd hardly closed her eyes. In a cheery tone, she said, "Famously."

"You said you had never in your life been less tired."

Blast his memory. "It was a fleeting feeling."

"Hum. Then the next time we dally, I'll strive to make the experience a lasting one."

A memory stirred vividly to life; she felt sheltered again, safe in his arms. More disturbing, she had wanted a greater closeness with him and not only the physical kind. Sharing the events, both sad and joyous, of his life, held particular appeal.

"There is no Wares Day," he said. " 'Twas a feeble excuse to run away from me and your vows last night."

"Feeble?"

" 'Twas easily verified."

"I sought only to comfort you."

In a husky whisper, he said, "Oh, and you

did. I still recall the feel of your head resting on my chest."

She withdrew her hand. "I met Mr. Fawr."

Facing her again, he gave her a look that said he wasn't fooled by her conversational zigzag. "Fawr's not his family name. 'Tis rather a description."

"Meaning what?"

He rubbed his stomach. "The great."

"He thinks well of himself."

"As he should. He was the last one standing on the Welsh side of a battle."

"Edward the First took him prisoner."

"He told you that?"

"I managed to untangle a word or two."

A mischievous twinkle brightened his eyes. "Careful, or you'll be gathering up enough double *l*'s and stretched out *o*'s to get sight of a friend."

Laughter burst from her. "You've been around him too long. You sound as garbled as he."

His expression sobered and he wiped a glove across his brow. "Seven years."

Sympathy welled up inside her. "What can I say to you, Drummond? Had I been in a position to do so, I would have set you free."

He paused, his elbow in the air. "Your position with the new king has never been in question. You knew him well enough."

"That was precisely what I had in mind when I —" She clamped her lips shut. He had tried to trick her. She could not, would not, address Clare's sin, not to him, not to anyone.

155

The expression in his blue eyes turned chilly. "When you what?"

His deceptively calm tone didn't fool Johanna; he wanted a confession from her. He'd go to his grave wanting it. Clare had sinned to save him. Johanna would not belittle her sister's decision.

She moved away. "I thought you were building a shelter for Longfellow this morning."

He cupped his hand to his ear. "Hear the hammers?"

With her mind dwelling on regrets about last night, she hadn't noticed the pounding noises coming from the direction of the main gate. She turned toward the sounds and saw Sween in the lane, a freshly cut post over his shoulder, a skipping Alasdair beside him. They were headed for the tiltyard.

Anxious to conclude her discussion in private with Drummond, she said, "Why are you replacing the post?"

"Because as it stands you could knock it down."

"I forbid you to teach Alasdair to use it."

"I say he does."

"Then you face disappointment."

"You can forbid until your Roman centurions return. I'll do as I may."

"How will you pay for it?"

"With the profits from this demesne, which I intend to double by raising Spanish cattle."

"Fairhope belongs to me."

" 'Twas left to the widow of Drummond

156

Macqueen. You are not that woman."

Fear crawled up Johanna's throat. Had he guessed? Swallowing back the panic, she searched his stern expression but saw no sly motive lurking there. "What do you mean, I am not that woman?"

"She does not exist, for I am hale and hearty." He peered into her eyes. "And you are as white as snow on ice. What's amiss, Clare?"

Clare. Relief poured over Johanna and she thought her sister's name had never sounded sweeter. She grabbed a snippet of his conversation. "I am committed to supplying grain to the overlord. I have no spare pasture for cattle, Spanish or otherwise."

"That and other things are changing."

Only the Second Coming could have altered her life more than the arrival of Drummond Macqueen. "I would have things stay as they are."

His brows shot up and his mouth dropped. "For heaven's sake why?"

Determined to have the last word, she picked up her basket. "I rather like being a widow."

Certain that the plan he had devised last night would now work, Drummond bowed from the waist. "And I rather like friskiness."

To his delight, her pretty mouth pursed in frustration. If he could keep her off guard, he could get her into bed. Once there, she'd tell him what he wanted to know, for she'd never been able to keep her secrets from him in the dark.

"Who's frisky?" demanded Alasdair, staring at

157

the both of them.

A cunning smile blossomed on her face. "The horse your father is going to buy you."

She marched off, leaving Drummond to deal with an excited Alasdair and a brooding Sween.

Alasdair gulped down a mouthful of spoon cake. "Father said I could nail the horseshoe over Long-fellow's door. That'll keep the witches away from him."

Johanna opened her mouth to caution him about the dangers involved in scaling a ladder, but paused, for advice would sound like another lecture. Feeling left out of his life, she raked the garnishing hazelnuts to the edge of the bowl.

"I doubt a spirit would go seeking the beast," said Brother Julian. "God made few provisions in the scriptures for beasts of burden."

Drummond rested an elbow on the table. "Then what was Noah doing?"

Eager to defend his territory, the cleric pushed the trencher toward Alasdair. "He was obeying the will of God and preserving all of his creatures."

Huffing, Drummond said, "Sounds like a provision to me."

"I meant to say that animals do not merit further concern, my lord. They lack souls."

"What say you, Clare? Does Longfellow have a soul?"

How delightful that she'd been consulted on something other than the reasons for Glory's jealous nature or the cause of the cobbler's wife's fainting spells. Hearing the peevishness in her own thoughts, she glanced at the man beside her. "I believe that God put animals here to serve man."

Interest twinkled in his blue eyes. "Not for his own purposes? Surely God can appreciate a fine hound or a skilled falcon. They are also his creatures."

So, Drummond Macqueen fancied himself a philosopher. She, too, enjoyed a lively discussion on the higher purpose of man. "True, but they are trained by man to do our bidding."

Drummond waved his spoon. "Dogs are not trained to hunt. 'Tis natural for them in the wild. Domestication only trains them to obey the will of man. There's a difference."

"A subtle one," murmured Brother Julian.

Scanning the others at the table, Johanna saw proof of how easily Drummond commanded attention. Alasdair stared, enraptured; Brother Julian looked keenly attuned, and Bertie seemed unable to turn away. Once they had preyed on her every word. She knew that jealousy fueled her ill-humor, but Johanna couldn't help saying, "When it comes to domination, man is seldom subtle."

His faith engaged, Brother Julian said, "My lord, next you'll have me shriving animals and Lady Clare setting a place at table for them."

"Is Longfellow going to Mass with us?" said an incredulous Alasdair.

159

The cleric huffed, "Of course not."

" 'Twould be a waste." Drummond leaned close to Johanna. "Since he doesn't speak Latin."

"Do you?" she challenged.

"Nay, Latin is for the frisky at heart. I'm but a simple man."

She scoffed. "And I'm Robert the Bruce."

Joining in, Alasdair declared, "And I'm a landless adventurer."

"You're an exhausted, landless adventurer. Find your bed," Drummond said. "And rest well."

The boy's excitement vanished. Something passed between father and son. A moment later, Alasdair grew animated again. "Mother, will you tell me a story?"

Bertie rose, bless him. "Come along, lad. It's late, do you see, and we're all toilworn."

As if to verify his loss of interest in her, Alasdair murmured good night and left the table. When Brother Julian excused himself, Johanna rose.

"Stay." Drummond put a hand on her arm.

With gentle pressure he kept her there until Evelyn had cleared the table, banked the fire, and excused herself.

"I'm sending Sween to Spain to purchase a bull."

Her heart jumped. Had he discovered her carefully hoarded savings? "How will you pay for a bull?"

Looking very much like the chieftain, he said, "I have my own funds."

"Shouldn't you go yourself? Who will lead the hunt?"

He shot her a who-do-you-think look. "According to you, I can fell a hart with a blunted arrow from three hundred paces."

Had she erred? On reflection, yes, but her intentions had been pure. Same as Clare. Oh, dear sister, she thought, did your heart beat fast and your logic flee in the presence of this compelling man?

Feeling like a fool, Johanna caught him staring at her. "Can you fell a hart with a blunted arrow?"

He shrugged. "I haven't had the opportunity, but rest assured that in Sween's absence, I will contrive to keep meat on our table. We will not starve."

"I'll sleep ever so much better knowing that. Did you find Alasdair a horse?"

"Nay. The blacksmith says Red Douglas has the best stock. I'd like for you to write to him and say we are coming to visit — you, me, and Alasdair."

"As a family?"

"Aye. I have no other wives or sons hidden away."

He hadn't the one wife anymore, much the pity.

"I also intend to discuss your grain obligation to Douglas. 'Tis unfair."

"He lent me money when I had none."

"According to the ledgers, you've already given

him a fair return and more. He's taking advantage of you."

If he continued to usurp her authority she'd soon be relegated to supervising the porter, the cook and Evelyn. "I will abide by my agreement."

"I'll renegotiate it."

Just as she was about to object, Alasdair returned. Wearing his long nightgown and cap and a forlorn expression, he straddled the bench and laid his head on her shoulder. "I cannot sleep, Mother. Will you tell me a story?"

Her heart melted, and she embraced him. "I would, but we'd awaken Bertie."

Drummond got to his feet. "I'll say good night."

Deciding that Alasdair could sleep in his bed and she'd make a pallet on the floor, she led him away.

Giving them time to get settled in Alasdair's room, Drummond paced the rush-strewn floor of his chamber. The dried grasses had been liberally laced with basil and thyme, and the pleasing odors permeated the room.

Nowhere, he thought, were the changes in his wife more evident than in this cozy chamber. She'd lost her penchant for expensive looking glasses and fancy silken tassels. Instead of bouquets of rosebuds in delicate vases, she now favored clay pots from the wheel of a local potter, filled with bundles of heather.

The spacious bed sported linen sheets and woolen blankets, rather than lace and ruffles. To his great relief she no longer slept on a mountain of pillows, for he'd often awaken with a painful crick in his neck. But he'd been young and his wiry body quick to recover from minor discomforts. After seven years on a hard cot, he shuddered to think of how he would feel after a night on a cloud of goose down.

He'd brave it, though, for the chance to possess her again.

Wait, his conscience said. 'Tis too soon yet.

Resolved, he strolled to the waist-high table by the window. On a finely embroidered cloth lay an assortment of keepsakes from her son. Among them were an almost square box containing a lock of curly black hair, a leather pouch filled with dried rose petals, a faded red ribbon, and a sheet of vellum with the words *A Joyous Day* printed in a lad's scrawl above the date of her birth, *19 March 1286*. Drummond remembered the day for another reason, same as all Scots did; their beloved and capable Scottish king, Alexander III, had died that night. Some said he was rushing to see his new wife, Yolande; others told of a breakneck ride to witness the birth of his illegitimate twin daughters, delivered of a noblewoman named Margaret.

A search for Alexander's lover and his identical lassies yielded only the rumor that Edward I, in his quest to claim Scotland, had spirited them to England. Alexander's favorite and his offspring were never found, and the tale was relegated to fiction.

Drummond was reminded of the tales Clare had spun to amuse Alasdair. The lad had responded by laboring to make the items on the table. Loving gifts, gifts to warm a mother's heart. Upon Drummond's arrival, she had removed her book of days and her prayer book and left her treasures. She had wanted him to see them. Why? To soften the heart of a husband wronged?

Her ploy had worked, for Drummond did feel closer to her, and with each passing day he found that he liked her more. He smiled, thinking about their first meeting this morning. Lord, she'd come to the tiltyard ready to brave the lion himself to defend her kit. As if Alasdair needed her defense. Clever beyond his years, the lad had carried out his part of tonight's plan to perfection.

Anticipating the gratifying meeting ahead, Drummond extinguished the lamp and went in search of her.

He heard her voice before he reached the open door to Alasdair's room.

". . . women and children, and even the clansmen trembled in fear of the crazed boar, but not Lord Drummond."

"It was the biggest and most enormous boar of all times, wasn't it?" Alasdair put in.

Looking at his wife's back, Drummond leaned against the doorjamb and made not a sound. He couldn't see Alasdair; Clare sat on a stool near the head of the bed, blocking the lad from view.

"Yes," she said, drawing out the word for added drama. "It was the meanest boar that ever lived.

164

His tusks were razor sharp, and his nose and eyes were as keen as the best hound in the land. Alone, with only his dirk for a weapon, your father stalked the beast, night and day, for a week."

"But Father never tired, did he?"

"Of course not. He was the best hunter in Scotland, and he was on a great quest."

Alasdair peered around her until he spied Drummond. The lad's eyes widened, then he snuggled deeper into the mattress. His mother noticed and turned around. Surprise enhanced her youthful appearance, and Drummond wished, for the hundredth time, that she'd been constant in her wifely devotion. Even as he admired her beauty, her expression changed to acceptance, then suspicion. She glanced at Alasdair, then back to Drummond.

"Please continue," he said, stepping into the room.

Alasdair sat up straight. "Oh, hello, Father. Fancy seeing you here."

Drummond winced at the practiced cadence of his son's words.

Clare gave him a smile that smacked of punishment to come. "Do join us, my lord. I was just about to tell Alasdair a new tale about you."

He didn't like the sound of that, but followed his plan and sat on the edge of the bed.

"You have to finish the tale about the boar, doesn't she, Father?"

Stiff with anger, she arched her brows. "Perhaps

your father would care to do the honors himself."

"I wouldn't think of it," Drummond said.

"Well, good. Now." She fairly wiggled with satisfaction. "This is the tale of the flying, fire-breathing dragon that once preyed upon the Macqueens."

Alasdair gasped. "A flying dragon?"

She sidled a glance at Drummond. "That breathed fire and wreaked havoc upon the land."

Second thoughts turned to misgivings.

"Once upon a time, Lord Drummond was out collecting berries so his stepmother could make him a pie. He was a dutiful son and always obeyed his father's second wife. Didn't you, my lord?"

Her skin shouldn't glow so prettily in the lamp-light. Her mind shouldn't work so quickly, either. "Aye." It came out as a squeak.

Folding her hands primly in her lap, she continued. "His search led him to a forbidden cave. He knew he wasn't supposed to go in, for his stepmother had told him not to. But the berry vine had spread and grown into the opening, and the fattest fruit lay just out of his reach. So he ignored the advice of his stepmother and crawled inside to pick the vine clean."

"Did the dragon come after him?" Alasdair said.

"Most definitely, and Lord Drummond ran as fast as he could, but the enormous dragon flapped his wings and took to the air."

Enthralled, Alasdair clasped his hands and drew them to his chest. "Wha-whatever did Father do?"

She snapped her fingers. "Quick as could be, he ripped a limb off a tree and, with his trusty dirk, fashioned himself a bow and an arrow."

"And he killed the dragon dead!" cheered Alasdair.

"With only one shot, straight through the heart." Giving Drummond a cheeky grin, she added, "He was dubbed the finest archer in all of Scotland."

Lord, he'd underestimated her. But beneath the guilt, deeper emotions stirred inside Drummond. His convent-bred wife had grown into an exciting and challenging woman.

"Oh, Father. Can I have a bow and arrow? Will you teach me to shoot? I'll practice until my fingers fall off. I swear by my oath, I will. Please?"

Knowing whatever he said would worsen his lot, Drummond took the easiest way out. "I'll . . . uh . . . I'll think about it."

"I'm sure you'll make an admirable teacher, my lord," she said. "But let's not overlook the lesson in this tale. Do you know what it is?"

He was reminded of the time he'd been called to task for using his father's battle ax to chop firewood. Still, he wasn't about to grovel, no matter how clever she was. "The moral is, picking berries is woman's work."

Disappointment pinched the corners of her mouth, and Drummond knew he'd compounded his mistake.

Calmly, she said, "Picking berries is the work

of anyone who wants to eat the pie." To a confused Alasdair, she said, "What is the moral of the story?"

He screwed up his face and stared at the beamed ceiling. "A lad should always obey his parents?"

"Yes, but more specifically . . . ?"

The lad brightened. "His mother."

"You're the joy of my life, Alasdair Macqueen." She kissed his cheek. "I shall say good night to you both."

"Wait." Drummond rushed after her and grabbed her arm.

She turned slowly, and the lamplight glistened on her shiny hair. Their eyes met.

"Talk to me, Clare."

"I hope you are proud of yourself. You used an unsuspecting boy for your own selfish reasons. I never thought you'd stoop to manipulating a child."

"Stop being facetious. Tell me what's on your mind."

"Only one more thing. Let go of my arm."

He released her, and she walked slowly away.

Her silence lasted three days, and when she did speak, Drummond could not believe his ears.

Chapter
8

"The sheriff holds an affection for me."

Johanna held her breath and waited for Drummond's reaction. She had expected his features to harden with disgust. He didn't disappoint her, but beneath the glaring disapproval she noted regret. It made her want to cry, for life had been woefully unfair to Drummond Macqueen. Greatness had been his destiny, misfortune had become his lot.

"How thoughtful of you to prepare me."

Unwilling to cower or confirm his base speculation, she faced him squarely. "Sheriff Hay is an honorable man, and if you would but try to engage a friendship, I think you will admirably succeed. I have never encouraged his intentions, and I certainly have never —" The words stuck in her throat. When the intensity in his eyes fled, replaced with cool acceptance, she marshalled her courage and told him a truth. "I have never lain with Sheriff Hay, nor any other man."

"I see." Fake wonderment tinged his words, and he reached up and grabbed a beam that supported the nearly completed shelter. His upper arms bulged and his naked torso rippled beneath the strain. "We wore out our marriage bed, conceived a son, and after a seven-year absence, God has blessed me with a virginal wife. Hear you that, Longfellow?" he said over his shoulder. "I am truly a son of providence."

Transfixed, Johanna watched the elephant wrap its trunk around Drummond's waist in the strangest hug she'd ever seen. When the tip of the animal's snout mussed Drummond's hair, her jaw went slack. "He does like you."

Drummond responded with a halfhearted lopsided grin. "You were telling me about your association with the honorable sheriff who is, as we speak, plodding across our outer bailey."

Our bailey. Our marriage bed. Nothing in her life had prepared Johanna for this discussion; she was accustomed to people, strangers and friends alike, thinking the best of her. Drummond's scorn opened a wound, but she hid her pain. "Red Douglas is with him."

"How cozy." Drummond's arms went loose, giving the impression that he dangled from the beam. "Tell me, do they flip a coin or roll the dice to determine who lies first with you?"

Anger shimmered through her, and she balled her fists to control her rage. Ramsay and the overlord seldom came to Fairhope together. Ramsay had been visiting Douglas when Johanna's message reached him. "That's preposterous. Douglas is my overlord."

"Not a king? Tisk, tisk. 'Tis a pity you had to lower your standards."

The watchmen scrambled for position on the wall. Bertie hurried the dung cart out of the lane. Perched on stilts, Alasdair and another lad raced toward a group of cheering children near the well. Outwardly life went on as it should.

Inwardly, Johanna cringed. Especially when she looked up into Drummond's face. Even in pique he commanded admiration. His blue eyes glistened like gems in the sunlight. Black curly hair fanned across his chest and dwindled to a thin line that stopped at the waist of his gray trunk hose. He inhaled, and she could see that the line of hair continued downward, past his navel. Shocked that she had seen that part of him, she looked up. He was watching her like a hawk sighting prey.

His strength of will surpassed hers, and she yielded. "Ask me to swear on something, Drummond, for I would have us declare a truce during their stay."

The tip of Longfellow's trunk skimmed over Drummond's arms, neck, and legs. The odd caress seemed so erotic that Johanna wondered how many women had touched Drummond just so. The strain of their three-day separation still dragged at her. Pride and anger had prevented her from approaching him. Necessity and the imminent arrival of guests had forced her to relent.

He had used the unsuspecting Alasdair to get her alone.

"If you disgrace me again, Clare, I will take Alasdair away." With deadly calm, he added, "You will never see him again."

The heart went out of her. "Someday you will regret your treatment of me, for I harbored no ill will toward you before you made that threat."

" 'Tis no threat, but a promise."

"Oh, Drummond. Your perception of me is tarnished."

"You expect me to sing hosannahs to your name?"

"Of course not." His true wife had committed a crime; Johanna could only pay the price. But she would not grovel. She had loved Clare and often wondered if their special closeness hadn't begun before birth, for they had shared their mother's womb. Now they shared the same sin and the same man. "I'm merely saying that should you look long enough for flaws in me, you will surely find them."

Wearing a particularly menacing grin, he looked her up and down.

She swallowed her pride. "All right. I will occupy your chamber if it will ease your mind."

"How generous, but I must decline," he said, much too cordially. Then his tone changed to insistence. "You will stay in Alasdair's room. The lad will stay with me. Bertie can barrack with the huntsmen. Our guests will occupy his chamber."

"I have always given them my bed."

"Not," he said, "in my presence."

Sweet Saint Mary, her words had come out wrong. Just as she grew weary of convincing him, his expression softened. Taking advantage, she moved close enough to see her own image in his eyes. "When important guests visit, I always occupy Alasdair's room, and he stays with Bertie. Ask anyone, Drummond. You know the custom well, so don't pretend otherwise. You're just being wicked to me because you think I deserve it."

He said "cuddle up" to the elephant. Longfellow's trunk snaked about both their waists, bringing her flush against Drummond's half-clothed body. She gasped at the feel of the elephant's cushiony snout, for it held her immobile. As unyielding as a stone wall, Drummond's body dwarfed her. She trembled in fear. "Drummond, tell him to let me go."

"You must learn to trust your husband." His grip tightened on the crossbeam overhead. "You were saying?"

When she realized that Longfellow would not squeeze the life out of her, she calmed, but only a little. "I was saying that you have the wrong impression of me. Look around you, Drummond. I could not command the respect of these people did I behave with abandon. I am a respectable widow."

His brows rose in mock surprise. "Your husband is very much alive."

He'd labored most of the morning to complete

173

Longfellow's shelter, yet he still smelled of minty soap. "You mean you're — ah . . ."

He writhed against her. "I mean that a certain one of my ungovernable extremities is 'touched' by your nearness and quite sympathetic with the plight of a lonely widow."

She recalled the first kiss he'd given her, the strength of his passion stirring beneath her hand. Even through his clothing his desire had been evident and shocking that night. The tight trunk hose he now wore would leave nothing to the imagination. "You'll be embarrassed, too."

"Aye, but 'twill be tempered by the envy of every man who hears the tale. If not, I shall contrive to abide the shame."

The jangle of harnesses and the pounding of hooves told her their guests were nearing the main gate. They would enter the yard momentarily. "What must I do to make you release me?"

He took his time appraising her. At length he said, "Put your arms around my neck and kiss me."

Drat her for walking into his trap. From her vantage point her view consisted of him from his naked shoulders up, and Longfellow's huge head behind him. "They'll see."

Seemingly unconcerned, he scanned her face. "Now that I think on it, I would have you kiss me on the lips."

Leather creaked; their guests had dismounted. Against her breast, Drummond's chest rose and fell. "Please, Drummond. Stop being foolish."

He licked his lips. "Having time to think truly stirs the imagination," he went on conversationally. "I would have you kiss me with your tongue."

Behind her horses danced restlessly, and a man, probably her overlord, cleared his throat. Were they close enough to hear? Incensed that they might, she hissed, "You'll regret this."

"I could order you to rip off your coif and let down your hair."

Like dread, awareness of his ploy seeped into her shocked senses. "If I do not kiss you now, on the lips —"

"With your tongue," he reminded in a chiding tone. "And they cannot hear us."

She sighed. "If I do not kiss you on the mouth and with my tongue, you will think of other, more intimate ways of embarrassing me."

His response was a sly wink. "Bright lass."

Banishing her good sense, she twined her arms around his neck. He made a great show of rearing back, his face a mask of shock. But under his breath, he commanded the elephant to hold them tighter.

He was making her act the wanton! The beast.

"You begged for a truce, Clare. I offer you what you asked for — only don't look so long-suffering when you claim me for your own."

Through a haze of mortification, she recalled the adoration that Glory on occasion bestowed on Sween and copied the expression.

"Splendid," he murmured.

175

Feeling the rumble of his voice, she cupped his nape, pulled him down, and pressed her mouth to his. His lips parted, waiting; his heart hammered, or was it her own? Hollowness spread through her, and when shame threatened to fill the void, she forced it away, rallied her feminine power, and slipped her tongue into his mouth. His response was immediate and expected; he became the aggressor, twisting his mouth for a better fit and radiating a heat that seeped through her clothing to warm her skin.

Fearful that he was pushing her too far, she hummed a scold into his mouth, and he grew still again. With a final twining of her tongue against his, she brought the kiss to an end. Leaning back to see the results, she was disappointed to find him staring past her.

He murmured, "If the sheriff is not your lover, why then, does he look like a calf taken too soon from the teat?"

"Because he has an affection for me, not a passion."

When he huffed in disbelief, she said, "Savor that kiss, Drummond Macqueen, for it's the last you'll get willingly from me."

His gloating grin faded, and she hoped his ardor with it. "We'll see," he said. Then he spoke to Longfellow, who released them. Johanna stepped back, fighting the urge to fuss with her surcoat before she faced the sheriff and her overlord. Pretending normalcy, she turned.

If manly envy had put the grin on Red

Douglas's craggy features, it had made Ramsay Hay look like he'd swallowed a snake.

Drummond came up beside her and pulled off his gloves. Folding his arms over his chest, he held the work gauntlets in the hand nearest to her.

Ramsay Hay stood ramrod straight, his chain of office slightly off center, his dark green jerkin dusty from the road. His hazel eyes normally brimmed with humor, but today they were clouded with disappointment. A kind, intelligent man, he commanded the admiration of everyone she knew. He was horribly uncomfortable, and for that she was completely sorry.

Red Douglas, as stocky and solid as a stunted oak, removed his bonnet and gave her a perfunctory nod. Then he turned to Drummond. "Macqueen."

Drummond flicked his wrist, bringing the gloves to rest on her shoulder. The possessive gesture shocked her, but she did not move away.

"Welcome to our home, Dubhghlas," Drummond said.

The overlord brushed the air with his hand. "We seldom speak the Gaelic in the Borders."

They seemed to be squaring off like dogs ready to fight. Before being declared a traitor, Drummond, as chieftain of the mighty Macqueens, outranked Douglas, who commanded only his clan and the landowners in Drumfries. To quell the unexplained animosity between the two men, Johanna considered throwing them a conversational

177

bone, but thought better of it. Their behavior was not her concern.

Instead, she took pity on Ramsay Hay, who put on a grim smile to hide his disappointment. "How nice to see you, Sheriff Hay. May I present my husband, Drummond Macqueen."

Ramsay stepped forward. "When did His Majesty set you free, my lord?"

Tonelessly, Drummond replied, "Two months after his coronation."

That would have been in April, over three months ago. Where had he been since then? The gloves grazed her upper arm, as if to remind her of his presence and his authority over her. Bother him, she silently scoffed, and decided that she didn't care a rusty needle where he'd been.

Red Douglas pitched the reins of his mount to one of the dozen clansmen who had accompanied him. "The new king also gave you the elephant? I've heard of its existence."

Drummond shrugged. "Edward the Second had little choice, for Longfellow follows me everywhere. I doubt the king opines the loss, for I now shoulder the enormous cost of feeding the beast."

The overlord stared at Longfellow, who sent his trunk dancing in the air near the newcomers. Lifting his bushy eyebrows, Douglas said, "Just as well. The king can use the coin to pay off the debt his father left him."

Drummond made a chopping motion with his hand; Longfellow went back to coiling his trunk around snatches of hay and tucking the food into his mouth. " 'Tis for certain he'll not fill his coffers by raiding the Highlands."

"He knows that," said Douglas. "I expect that we in the Debatable Lands will suffer for it in higher taxes."

"For the war Edward the First waged on my people?" Drummond asked, incredulous. "Pardon me if I'm unsympathetic for your loss of gold."

Douglas's eyes narrowed. Drummond seemed unconcerned. Ramsay glanced cautiously from one man to the other, before sending Johanna a searching look.

Drummond didn't miss the silent exchange between his wife and the sheriff. To again illustrate his command of her, he handed her the gloves. "Will you fetch my shirt, Clare? 'Tis draped on the manger in Longfellow's castle."

She opened her mouth, but closed it before stating her mind. A curse for him, most likely.

"Of course, my gracious lord." She retrieved the garment and waited until he'd pulled it on. "Perhaps our visitors would like to come inside and refresh themselves."

"The alehouse'll do," said Douglas.

Drummond wanted to talk to both men — alone. "My lady, you go along and have that talk with Bertie. Tell the cook we have guests."

On the surface, she appeared the dutiful wife, but Drummond saw past her civility; underneath she was angry enough to slap his face. She wouldn't, though, for she was scared to her soul

179

that he'd take Alasdair away.

"Your wish is my command, my lord."

Guilt nudged Drummond, but he paid no mind. She had been unfaithful once, she could do so again. Should that occur, Drummond would make certain Alasdair did not witness her shame or pay the price.

He watched her speak again to their guests, then start up the steep steps leading to the keep, her back as stiff and straight as a new lance. Out of the corner of his eye, Drummond saw Alasdair skipping across the yard toward them, his face alive with youthful exuberance. The lad skidded to a halt a few feet from Douglas, then gave him a wide berth.

Drummond was reminded of himself and his siblings when in the presence of their father and the other Highland chieftains.

"Good day, sir. Father's going to buy me one of your fine horses."

Douglas completely ignored the lad.

Drummond, too, had expected Alasdair to speak only when addressed, for that was the way lads his age were treated. Seeing it happen to his own son, however, gave Drummond a prejudiced view of the practice. Douglas could have at least acknowledged the lad.

"Alasdair," said the sheriff. "I've brought you something." From a pouch on his saddle, Ramsay Hay produced a package wrapped in oilskin. He handed it to Alasdair, who fairly beamed. "Thank you, Sheriff. Did you know that I'm getting a

180

set of armor and a — ?" He glanced cautiously at Douglas. "A horse."

Unabashed affection shone on Hay's face. He laid his hand on Alasdair's shoulder and said, "You'll make a fine knight, lad. Your father's a bit of a legend in that regard." Looking up, he caught Drummond's eye.

Drummond saw acceptance and sadness in the sheriff's expression. He remembered what Clare had said: *Sheriff Hay is a delightful fellow, and if you would but try to engage a friendship, I think you will admirably succeed.* Knowing it now for a fact, Drummond smiled.

With a slight nod, the sheriff dropped his hand and stepped back. Alasdair ambled off, pretending great interest in the book. Drummond suspected that the lad was confused and his feelings hurt. Knowing this couldn't be the first time, Drummond lamented the years in prison; Alasdair had needed him.

Turning to Hay, he said, "Go with Douglas to the alehouse and tell the barkeep to tap a laird's keg. I'll meet you there."

Drummond moved in the opposite direction. He caught up with Alasdair near the well. Pulling him aside, he said, "That's a very fine book."

He rolled it over in his hands and continued to stare at his feet. "Aye."

The words "a good parent" flashed in Drummond's mind, and he understood what his wife had meant. Carrying out his responsibility to Alasdair posed a challenge, for he knew not

181

where to start. He squatted so they were eye to eye. "You like the sheriff."

"Aye, he taught me to piss off the curtain —" He stopped. "Oh, I told you that story already. Mother says I'm not to repeat myself, especially to you."

"You worry too much, Son. What else does your mother say?"

"That you've forgotten what it's like to be a lad, and when I'm as old as you, I'll wish I was still making mischief. Do you?"

"On occasion, especially when there's a custard about."

"You like custards, too?"

Drummond made a great show of licking his lips. "More than you know."

"Mother says I used to yap like a puppy for custards."

"Came from me, most probably."

His eyes glazed with pleasure. "You did that?"

To his own surprise, Drummond threw back his head and yipped.

Alasdair roared with laughter. "I look like you, too."

"You're a limb off the mighty Macqueen tree."

"Truly? Tell me about my grandfather. Do I have hundreds of uncles and cousins? Will I be as good a soldiering as they are?"

"We'll discuss it at length tonight, should you want to sleep in my bed."

"Hoorah!" As quickly, his expression fell.

"Mother will sleep in my bed again?"

"Aye."

"I saw her kissing you. Does that mean you're not a beef-witted troll anymore?"

"Did she call me that?"

"You made her very angry."

"Do you know why?"

He replied that he could say nothing more on the matter. "I gave her my oath, do you see."

Bertie, too, had influenced Alasdair, for the lad copied the man's speech. "Then you must keep your word; 'tis the honorable thing."

"Aye, sir. A Macqueen must always be constant and faithful."

It was the motto of Clan Macqueen. "Did your mother tell you that?"

"Nay. Sheriff Hay found out about it for me."

So, thought Drummond, Clare couldn't be bothered to educate Alasdair. Look for flaws and you will find them. He was guilty of both. "You must thank the sheriff warmly at table tonight."

Drummond's astounded son clutched the book to his chest. "I can sup at the table with Red Douglas there?"

Had Clare allowed the slight? Another flaw. Douglas would pay the lad no mind, but that wasn't Alasdair's fault. Old habits rule men like Red Douglas; they had once ruled Drummond, but he vowed never again to carelessly disregard Alasdair's feelings. "Aye, Son. You'll sit between your mother and me."

Alasdair scampered off. Drummond thought of

183

a way to celebrate Alasdair's first meal with the overlord. He went to the cutler's shop, then hurried to the alehouse. No sooner had he taken the first swallow from his tankard than Douglas said, "I expect your oath of fealty, Macqueen."

He had the right to expect allegiance; Drummond would have thought less of him had he not demanded his due. But before he went down on his knee to a marcher lord, Drummond would have to reconcile his Highland loyalties. If Douglas were smart, he'd pick a more insistent matter on which to take a stand.

To pacify the man, Drummond held up his tankard in salute. "We'll come in a fortnight for Alasdair's horse."

"In October, the king comes for the salmon. Make it then."

He was probably conniving to have Drummond swear fealty to Edward II, too, or at the least have a royal witness. Then later, if Drummond went against the king, Douglas would not be held responsible. Watching his back, as Drummond's father used to say. "I favor a go at the salmon myself."

Douglas nodded, half his attention on the maid tending tables. " 'Twill wait."

Drummond broached the subject of the field pledged to Douglas.

The overlord scratched his shoulder. " 'Tis a matter agreed and done."

"In lieu of the funds Clare borrowed to build the chapel, she agreed to give you one-third of the grain from a given field. The land has been overprosperous, and you have taken advantage of her."

"A bargain is a bargain."

"We'll not give you another grain on account of the loan. 'Tis paid and more."

"I also gift her with a beef every Michaelmas."

"You may keep it. Henceforth, we will raise our own."

"I have a fine bull, if you're interested." He spoke to Drummond but his attention kept straying to the serving girl.

"Thank you, nay. I'm importing fresh stock from Spain."

"Will your clansmen be bringing the beasts?"

Was he worried? Odds were he knew more about the comings and goings of Clan Macqueen than Drummond did. "My kinsmen do as they may."

"There's trouble with Clan Chapling. That young laird Revas Macduff thinks to claim the sword."

Clan Chapling was a mighty alliance of Highland clans. United, they presented a formidable defense. Edward I had dissolved the union. His son's indifference toward Scotland had obviously allowed the Highlands to consider uniting again. Drummond knew little about Macduff; the Macgillivray clan had always claimed leadership of Chapling. "Revas Macduff will have to claim his bride first." And Drummond knew precisely where to find the lass, Meridene. He'd wager his sword arm that Macduff did not know where Edward I had hidden her.

The serving maid sauntered over to refill their mugs. She'd unlaced her bliaud, and the garment fell open almost to her tightly belted waist. Stopping near Douglas, she put her hands on her hips and swayed from side to side. "Yer lookin' fit, milord."

"Fit enough to put a twinkle in your eye, Meg." In an odd sort of surrender, he slammed coin down on the table. "Have Jake tap a Douglas keg, and don't expect me for Vespers." Then he led the smiling girl through the side door.

Hay chuckled "He supports his by-blows."

"Would that all overlords did," Drummond said.

"My lord, I know of a ship's captain who harbors in Maryport and plies the Orkney trade. He could bring news of your clan and not pass it on to everyone he met."

If Hay was offering to get news from the Highlands, then he knew Drummond hadn't been hiding out there for seven years. "You knew I was alive."

The sheriff huffed. "I'd never set eyes on you, dead or alive."

"So you let Clare and Alasdair think me dead."

"She'd already grieved. The king should have hanged you. Why break her heart again?"

A steely calm stiffened Drummond's spine. "Tell me about her grief."

"She had no family left, except Alasdair, and he was still suckling a wet nurse."

Drummond had always thought her as close as sisters to the other two girls at the abbey. She had called Johanna and Meridene her family. Or had the then Prince Edward turned her out? Had she mourned the loss of her royal lover rather than her lawful husband?

But Edward could wait; Drummond had Ramsay Hay to deal with now. "You no doubt extended your sympathies?"

"She's a decent woman, Macqueen, and yes, I'd have her."

"If you *have* had her I could beat you to porridge and every man here would sing hosannahs to my name."

"She has not dishonored you."

Drummond laughed.

"Shall I employ the ship's captain on your behalf?"

"I could send a messenger and find out for myself."

"Certainly you could, and when and if the king moves against the Highlanders again, what will you do?"

Drummond hoped to be fighting shoulder to shoulder with his kinsmen should that happen, but Hay needn't know that. "I should rely on gossip?"

Hay emptied the tankard and tapped it on the wooden table. "You're outlawed and forbidden any contact with your clan."

Drummond grew uneasy; he had hoped to keep the stipulations of his release a secret. "How did you know that?"

" 'Tis my business to know, and only mine. I'm certain Lady Clare does not know."

"She's hardly a chatterbox where I'm concerned."

"She thought you dead. I heard the old king even sent your body home to your kinsmen in parts."

Drummond couldn't help thinking about his stepmother. She would accept his fate and go on with her life, but not out of any avarice toward him; it was Highland custom. He thought about Clare and how fiercely she protected Alasdair. A good parent.

"Have I broached an unhappy subject, my lord?"

"Nay. By order of Edward the Second, the Highlands are forbidden to me. Should I choose to travel elsewhere, Sheriff, I'll not leave my wife or any other of my possessions to your tender mercies." Drummond would return to the Highlands someday, but he would keep his plans to himself.

Hay reddened and ground his teeth. "Worry not about my tender mercies. Since you doubt me, ask Sween Handle."

"I'm sending Sween to Spain."

"For the cattle?"

"Aye."

"Glory'll wish him farewell, pout until he returns, then give him her back for leaving in the first place."

"What causes their quarrels?"

"Ask Lady Clare."

"Is she involved?"

"Hardly. It's a tale better told by a woman, and who spins better yarns than Lady Clare?"

Drummond doubted he'd ever hear the story, for his wife certainly wanted nothing to do with him. What a fool he'd been for refusing her offer to share his bed. Look for flaws and you'll find them. Her correct assessment of his methods made Drummond uncomfortable, so he changed the subject. "My lady took the law into her own hands in your absence."

"Was the miller slighting the weights again?"

"Nay." Drummond told him about Elton Singer.

"I thought we'd shielded Lady Clare from his ilk. How did she ever learn of it?"

Drummond gritted his teeth against the guilt, for had he not bruised her, she would not have recognized Singer for a wife beater. "I cannot say."

"Where was Sween?" Hay asked.

"He's innocent. She told no one what she was about. What will you do about Elton Singer?"

Hay stared at the ceiling. "Nothing. I have no grounds. And I will not invent one for any price. Even if I did, Maggie would lie for him."

So, Hay was as honest as Clare had said. "Then I'll insist that they move to the village."

189

Hay took off his chain of office and put it on the table. He would not compromise his office, so he'd momentarily abandoned it. "How will you manage that?"

"I'll make living here so appealing, Singer will come willingly."

"And if he does not?"

The exchange of information with another man on a leadership matter awakened a long-dormant need in Drummond. He'd grown up in the company of important men making vital decisions. He'd spent seven years where every decision vital to his life was made for him. "I'll make the offer irresistible. Have you a comment?"

Hay tipped his head toward the barkeep. "Have Jake water down Singer's ale and send him home, with an escort, before dark. That should help, my lord."

Drummond's respect for the sheriff trebled. "Macqueen will do."

Hay again donned his chain. "Then Macqueen it is. Have I other criminals awaiting justice?"

"Two. A thief and a poacher."

"Have you an opinion on either?"

"I'll abide by yours."

He nodded. "I'll address them tomorrow. Who is the fellow with the red beard?"

"Morgan Fawr? He helps me care for Longfellow. When did you see him?"

"He was standing on the other side of the elephant when . . . uh . . . we arrived."

"How long will you stay?"

"Three, four days. Red should have his fill of Meg by then. His men will hunt while they are here, so do not despair of feeding them after to-night."

Drummond thought of the evening to come. Discretion told him to approach his wife before the meal and in private. He finished off the ale and went in search of her.

Chapter 9

Johanna had just lathered her hair the second time when a knock sounded on the pantry door. "Who is it?"

"Your gracious lord."

Yanking up a towel, she drew her knees to her chest and covered herself as best she could. Should he barge in, the soapy water would afford her some modesty. She should have latched the door, but she was unaccustomed to having a resurrected-from-the-dead husband interrupt her toilet. He was supposed to be entertaining guests; she hadn't considered that he'd abandon them. "I'm unavailable."

"Because you're bathing?"

Drat that Evelyn for her loose mouth. "Yes, and I prefer privacy."

"I prefer to talk to you." The door swung open, and he stood on the threshold.

She looked past him into the kitchen, but

Evelyn and the cook were nowhere in sight. The traitors.

He stepped inside and latched the door.

"Where are the servants?" she asked.

"The market and the buttery."

The urge to cower was almost overpowering, but she fought it. With a casualness that she was far from feeling, she tied the towel around her neck to hide the brand that would betray her secret and cost her all that she held dear. Then she draped an arm on the rim of the wooden tub and strummed her fingers to hide the shaking. "Can you not wait half an hour?"

"Nay. I may have left the matter too long as it is."

The cryptic remark said, he rolled a barrel near the tub and sat down. Light poured from the high window and threw his shadow across the pantry floor. He'd raked his hands through his hair and laced up his jerkin. He looked all legs and arms and beguiling blue eyes. The beast.

She had often been at a disadvantage with him, but those former occasions paled. Sitting naked, him towering over her with something weighty on his mind, made her feel completely at his mercy.

"Alasdair will sit between you and me at table tonight," he said.

It was the last thing she expected. "I'm certain he's very excited. Thank you for telling me."

He half smiled and made a slow inspection of her hand, her wrist, and her arm.

A shiver worked its way up her spine, and her fingers stilled. "Was there something else?"

His eyes narrowed with mischief and his grin turned cocky. "I imagine so."

Borrowing one of Glory's particularly successful remarks, Johanna said, "Don't be tiresome."

"I thought I was a beef-witted troll."

She'd wring Alasdair's neck, and then she'd seek Glory's counsel on how to avoid a husband she did not want. "A beef-witted troll will do for now."

He scanned her face and the mane of wet hair trailing over her shoulder and pooling in the water. "You enjoyed kissing me."

"I'd as soon watch milk clabber."

Laughter fluttered his belly, and she remembered the dark mat of hair that tapered to a thinner line and led past his navel and pointed the way to his —

"And if I command you to kiss me again?"

Her heart thudded against her ribs. He'd said those same words on the night she'd comforted him on the battlement. At the time she had answered honestly, because she'd been genuinely moved to heal the wounds of the past. But he'd spoiled the occasion, and now she faced a mother's worse terror. "I would refuse to kiss you, unless you threatened to take my son away."

He winced, but she wasn't fooled by a prick to his conscience; Drummond Macqueen was heartless to his core. "If that will be all . . ."

To emphasize her dismissal, she lifted her brows in query.

Grabbing his ankle, he drew up his left foot and rested it on his right knee. "What of our hard-won truce? We've not discussed provisions."

Heaven help her. He was settling in for a chat. With the door latched. "Provisions?"

"Aye. We both make concessions to show that we are earnest about keeping the truce."

When her hands began to shake again, she curled her fingers around the edge of the tub. "I've done my conceding."

"You did it exceptionally well, if I may say so."

"You may say it to the Pope."

Bracing his arms on the barrel, he leaned back and stared at the bundles of drying heather that hung from the ceiling. "I'm certain you felt desire for me."

The jerkin fit too snugly across his chest and upper arms. The seams would rip if he didn't stop flexing his muscles or have the garment altered. She hoped his tailor lived in London. "I'm certain you will color up the event as you see fit."

In a lithe move, he stepped off the barrel and picked up the bucket of warm water. "I'll rinse your hair. You never liked doing it yourself."

She stared at the wall shelves and tried to ignore her nakedness and his insistence, but sacks of dried peas and crocks of honey did little to ease her trepidation. She was his wife. His faithful wife. "I've changed."

He sniffed her hair. "In your choice of soap as well. You know 'tis my favorite."

She knew no such thing. She also found the fragrance pleasing, but he seemed destined to claim responsibility for that, too. "Heather is abundant here, and I haven't the coin for expensive scents."

"You chose it for me. 'Tis another of the ways you've changed."

His eyes turned hungry as he gazed at her. Her skin turned to gooseflesh. "Think what you will, Drummond. Just think it elsewhere."

"Why order me out? You were never so modest before. Quite the contrary. You were proud of your body and the predictable effect it had on me. Why do you blush now?"

With tremendous glee, she said, "I am not the woman you married."

He was staring at her breasts. "I like you better now."

Kindness from him would never do, not if she hoped to keep him at a distance. "I like you less."

A self-effacing grin added charm to his already handsome features, "Even a beef-witted troll can see that you're angry with me."

"Stop being so accommodating; that only makes me question your motives."

"I could tell you my motives outright, for they concern you," he said in a silken whisper, his cheek very close to hers. "Then you wouldn't wonder."

As if the oaken bucket were a lightweight crock, he grasped it in one hand. "Lean over, unless you want water everywhere. And take off that towel."

Not for all the world's riches would she risk exposing the brand. "I can rinse my own hair."

"Indulge your husband."

Trapped and disgusted, she hugged her knees and kept a tight hold on the towel.

"Close your eyes."

She did. A moment later warm water trickled over her head, and his fingers kneaded her scalp. She'd been correct about the size of his hand, for the span of his fingers captured her skull, and like a man prone to thriftiness, he rationed the water, spreading it carefully over every strand of her waist-length hair.

Soap stung her eyes, and she pressed the soaked towel against them. Even though she tried to ignore him, she felt the heat of his body and the rush of his breath very close, too close. She tried to move out of reach.

"Be still. I have always wanted to taste heather on your skin."

Clare had favored lilacs or roses, and she had never mentioned Drummond's penchant for tasting skin. Then he pushed her hair aside and kissed her unmarked shoulder and her neck.

Johanna's toes curled. Thank God the servants would be back soon. With so many visitors, Evelyn and the cook wouldn't tarry at their errands. Johanna felt moderately safe, and if she kept talking to herself she could ignore the voice of weakness and its never-ending plea for her surrender to Drummond Macqueen.

"Do you remember my recurring dream?" he said. "The one you thought vulgar."

A brilliant excuse came to mind. "I forced myself to forget it."

He spoke against the cap of her shoulder, his teeth lightly grazing her skin. "I lay on the grassy bank of a fast running burn. 'Twas a glorious summer morn. Eagles soared overhead, and forest creatures scurried in play. The world and all in it seemed on display just for me. Then you rose, naked from the water."

"I walked on water?"

He nipped her skin in a playful bite. "Hush. Irreverence is not allowed." In a too husky voice, he continued. "You smiled and knelt beside me. You told me you had been sent especially for me. Then you granted me three wishes."

The sensual cadence of his voice lulled her, and the tale sounded harmless so far, except the naked part, but it was fitting. The troubling part was, he thought she was his wife. *No,* she realized, would not be a big enough word to extricate herself if he didn't stop nibbling her skin.

"What did you wish for?" she said.

"That depends on which time I had the dream."

Humor him, she thought, and perhaps he would leave. "The first time."

"I asked for a sword, a bed without two snoring

198

brothers, and a pony."

Laughter burst from her. He joined in, and the sounds of their mirth felt so natural she wondered if they might find lasting accord after all. He hadn't seen the brand today. He hadn't once called her a whore, either. He hadn't even mentioned Clare's sin. Pray God he would soon forget it.

"How could you have a dream about me when you were a lad? You didn't even know me then."

" 'Twas fate."

When it came to fate, Johanna Benison could go him one better. "What did you ask for the last time you had the dream?"

"Very adult things." He gathered up her hair. She snatched the ends of the towel in a death grip.

Making a rope of her hair, he wrung out the water, then picked up the brush and began to work out the tangles. "A room with many windows at the top of Fairhope Tower." His lips fluttered down her spine, leaving a trail of shivers on her skin.

"Drummond . . ."

"Shush." He breathed the word into her ear, and she had to strain to keep from crying out. Showers of pleasure cascaded over her, refreshing, taunting, bringing to life a picture of the idyllic scene he'd described, complete with her kneeling naked beside him and awaiting his bidding.

"Aren't you curious about my second wish?"

199

"Wish? What wish?"

His arrogant, manly chuckle sounded a warning. She grasped the gist of the conversation. "Your second wish."

Brush forgotten, he lifted her arm, ducked under it and kissed the tender side of her breast. His other arm went around her shoulder and tried to rake the towel aside.

"You must stop." The feeble request sounded unconvincing even to Johanna's ears.

His mouth hovered over the tip of her breast, his breath puckering the nipple. " 'Twas a wish to find you here bathing in the pantry and in need of someone to rinse your hair."

His sensual tone and romantic words lulled her, and she squeezed her eyes shut. "What was your third wish?"

He took her nipple into his mouth and dragged his lips back and forth, around and around, stealing her breath and clouding her thoughts.

"Do you know," he murmured. "I think I've forgotten."

"Try," she gasped, "to remember."

"You're too distracting."

"No. I'm conceding to you again."

"Admirably so."

He sounded so satisfied by her answer that Johanna almost rejoiced; they were conversing easily. Conversing? She could lay claim to the title of second biggest fool if she equated having her breasts suckled to carrying on a conversation. But if she didn't stop him, he would expect her to

200

take her wifely duties one step further. She was already in over her head.

Yet the need to yield blared like a seminal call, summoning deep emotions, compelling her to pair up with this man and build a nest and a future. He was luring her to forget the harm her discovery would cause others. What of the bride of Christ who'd devoted her life to raising the daughters other people hadn't wanted? What of Johanna herself? What would become of her? To the world, she lay buried beneath the consecrated soil of Scarborough Abbey.

Fear of dire consequences fled when his mouth moved to her other breast, and he busied his free hand with soothing the nipple that he'd just abandoned. Tension stirred deep in her belly and her neck went limp. Words and phrases spun in her head, but she could not string together enough of them to form a coherent thought, not when his mouth settled on hers in a kiss that sent rivers of pleasure flowing to her toes.

Seeming to know how she felt, he laid his hand on her stomach and gently kneaded the ache. Her thighs relaxed and her hips tightened, then lower she felt a dampness as different from bathwater as conversing from suckling. He continued in his role of wizard by tipping his head to the side and deepening the kiss just when she thought to make the move herself. He slid his hand lower and dipped into her dampness.

She gasped and pulled her mouth from his. The expression in his eyes bordered on dreamy, and she asked if he hadn't drunk too much of the ale she'd tasted on his mouth.

"Oh, nay. I intend to remember every moment of our lovemaking."

Lovemaking. What a beautiful word.

Then his arms were lifting her, hauling her up and against his chest. She clung to him as he sat on the barrel, put her on his lap, and drew up her legs to straddle his hips. Naked and exposed, she felt his straining need even through the fabric of his trunk hose. The tightness began again in her belly, and when she shifted her position, the tension magically eased. His hands caressed her back and exerted gentle pressure as he thrust upward, then down, settling into a rhythm that made porridge of her brain and nonsense of her will to resist him.

He rocked against her, sliding his hardness against the precise spot that craved his touch.

"Be adventurous with me, Clare."

Clare.

Like a scream snapping her from a nightmare, the sound of her sister's name awakened Johanna to where she was, what she was doing, and with whom. Desire urged her to forget the consequences and step completely and irreversibly into her sister's life.

She rebelled. With the keep full of extra mouths to feed, the cook and Evelyn should have already started the evening meal. They would return, and if she could but bide her time an escape would surely present itself.

She gave opportunity a nudge. "You haven't told me all of your wishes."

His mouth grazed over her cheek and ear, nibbling and nudging. "One is moot now, thank heavens, and I'll tell you the other afterward."

Afterward. Dread tightened her chest. He'd have something to say all right, but it would involve the wondrous fact that after bearing him a son and committing adultery, his wife was still a virgin. Unless? — she recalled what he'd said when she'd asked if he'd drunk too much ale.

I intend to remember every moment.

Did that mean ale could make him forget? Only once had she overindulged, and the details of the event *had* been blurry. If he were in his cups when he made love to her, he might not notice the difference in the brand. *The brand.* Oh, lord, she'd forgotten the brand.

The door rattled. "My lady, are you still in there?"

It was Evelyn. And the towel was still snug around Johanna's neck. Praise God twice. "Yes, I am."

He hissed an expletive.

"Sorry to disturb you, but the cook forgot to fetch the ham before you went in for your bath. He says if he don't start it a-boiling now, the Douglas men will go to bed hungry."

"Where's the damned ham?" Drummond whispered harshly.

Relief thrumming through her, Johanna pointed to the barrel beneath them.

When he opened his mouth to let out what she knew would be another angry curse, she slapped her hand over his face. "Will you be quiet? I'm embarrassed to my toes, and I refuse to be discovered dallying with you in broad daylight."

He nodded, and she took her hand away. "Tell her you're almost done." His hands tightened again on her hips, and he winced. "God knows I am."

"What's that supposed to mean?"

He gave her a strange, searching look, as if he'd expected her to understand. " 'Tis not important. I just hope that water's cold enough by now."

"Cold enough for what?"

He gave her that same, queer look, as if her question puzzled him. "Cold enough for my purposes," he grumbled and set her on her feet.

Her knees buckled and she clutched his arm to steady herself. Glaring he said, "That ache in your belly is your own fault. You'll get no sympathy from me."

She wanted to ask why he thought she wanted pity, but her last two questions hadn't been well-received. So she fought the dizzying weakness and pulled on her clothing. When she had located the brush, she unlatched the door and came face-to-face with a perky Evelyn, who wore a posy in her hair and a saucy smile. Probably the work of one of Douglas's men.

The maid's gaze moved to Drummond, who

was so angry he nearly tore off his jerkin. She looked him up and down, then moved back as if burned. "I'll just get Amauri to fetch that ham."

Johanna understood completely; she wanted nothing to do with Drummond, either. She escaped to find Glory. There were questions she needed to ask about how to handle a man.

Two hours later, Drummond threw open a window in the solar and searched the yard for his wife. He spied Alasdair demonstrating his sword technique for Sheriff Hay, Sween, and a group of huntsmen. In the lane, merchants folded up their stalls, and the departing crowds wended their way to the main gate. Spread-eagled on the sloping roof of Longfellow's shelter, Morgan Fawr secured the last bundles of thatching.

Drummond again scoured the throng until he spied a familiar yellow surcoat and a white coif. Her movements were unmistakable: the confidence of her carriage, the swing of her arms, and the pleasure she derived from sharing a greeting or waving to a child.

A respectable widow, she called herself. He was beginning to believe it. Not the woman he'd married, she was wont to say. That statement concerned him, for she was as different from the Clare he remembered as the Thames Pool was from Loch Maree. Had he changed as much to her? She hadn't said so, but she also hadn't cared enough about their life together to commit it to memory.

Asking after his mother was proof of her disinterest. Once at table, she had asked Drummond's father to describe Drummond's mother. Gavin Macqueen had been so angry that she would pose the artless question in the presence of his second wife that he'd banished Clare from table for a fortnight.

She'd cried for days, begged Drummond to intercede on her behalf and he had, to no avail. How could she have forgotten? Or was it that he'd had too many idle years to remember the past?

Looking for new memories, he followed her progress as she made her way to the steps at the base of the keep. She stopped to speak to a woman with two small daughters. After fussing over the girls, she touched the sleeve of the woman's frock, obviously admiring the garment. They conversed for a moment more, then Clare continued on her way. She looked at ease, her stride purposeful. The people here adored her. Everyone except Elton Singer, who she'd banned from the alehouse until after Vespers.

At the memory of her clever method of administering justice, Drummond smiled. Had she learned authority from Ramsay Hay? When he'd approached her in the pantry, Drummond had intended to confirm her high opinion of the sheriff and admit he'd been wrong to accuse her of again breaking her marriage vows. An apology hadn't been necessary, for she'd already forgiven him.

Why else would she have been so responsive to his ardor? She harbored no ill will, and didn't she have a delightful way of showing it.

In some respects he was courting her for the first time. Since she'd been delivered to him by the old king, Drummond had been spared playing the gallant to gain her favor. Her dowry had been a promise of peace from a warring English king. Her destiny had been a singular life on this patch of land.

Drummond rather enjoyed bandying words with her, for he did like her better now; she'd developed a stinging wit and a delightful sense of humor. She was also more passionate.

When she was halfway up the stairs, someone called out, "Lady Friend." She halted, her features sharp with alarm. Drummond saw Bertie Stapledon rush down the steps to meet her, no doubt to pass along the message that her husband awaited her here in the solar.

They conversed in tones too low for Drummond to hear, but he had the impression that Bertie was reassuring her, for she began to relax. He envied the special bond that existed between them, but she had been without father or husband for seven years.

She thanked him, then hurried up the steps. Moments later, Drummond heard her voice in the hall. She was telling the cook to send Amauri to the baker to fetch extra bread.

Anticipating another rewarding exchange, Drummond turned. When she entered the room he said in a pleasant voice, "Where have you been?"

Blinking in confusion, she put down her basket and removed her coif. "Visiting with Glory. Did you want me for something other than satisfying your lust?"

Her boldness baffled him; he'd asked an innocuous question. "What's gotten into you?"

Wisps of freshly washed hair framed her face in a spray of ringlets. The finely woven linen of her surcoat fitted snugly over her breasts and fell to the floor in gentle folds. According to the ledgers, she could afford a wardrobe of costly silks and velvets, but possessed only a few finer gowns. Or so Evelyn had told him just before he sent her to the market.

"Please be more specific," she said.

His good humor fled. "By all means. You appear angry now. Yet not long ago you were naked and bouncing up and down on my lap. 'Tis proof you were hot for me, so why speak only of *my* lust."

"I said be specific, not lurid. You're demented if you think you can embarrass me and seduce me, all in the span of a day."

Where was the melting, moaning, passionate Clare? "Then I take it that by being cold to me now, you are returning the favor."

"How could I when I do not in the least favor you?"

He felt as if he'd been slapped. "You do. Pray explain why you first ordered me out of the pantry and ten minutes later, begged me to suckle your breasts."

Color blossomed on her cheeks. "I never begged you."

He held up his thumb and index finger. "You were this close."

"Delude yourself as you see fit." She seated herself behind the desk and opened a ledger.

"What do you think you're doing?"

A determined glimmer shone in her eyes. "I *know* that I am recording the day's provisions." She flipped through the ledger until she found the page she sought. With a flourish, she inked the quill and began writing. "Let's see. That's hay for twenty-two extra horses. Oats, four bushels. Ale, already reckoned. Bread, two bushels."

The scratching of nib on vellum grated on his nerves. "Will you stop that?"

As calm as a cleric at Mass, she replaced the quill and folded her hands on the book. Then she gave him a bland smile. "Of course, my lord! Have you something meaningful to say?"

At a loss, he strolled behind her and stared over her shoulder. Satisfaction filled him, for she wasn't so composed as she wanted him to believe. "You've entered the figures on the wrong page. These are the reckonings for Longfellows' expense and mine."

She tapped the top of the page. "It's the accounting for visitors."

Frustration made him cross. "I am *not* a visitor!"

She eased off the stool and headed for the door. He called her back.

She stopped, sighed, then turned around. "Yes, my lord?"

Naked, she had trembled with desire; now she acted like an uninterested virgin. Only hours ago, her eyes had turned the warm color of cinnamon. Now they looked coolly brown. She was fickle, and one way or another he'd put an end to it. "I would have accord between us," he said.

"Why? You care little for me."

Was she being coy? "Not two hours ago, I cared very much for you."

"You as easily could have bestowed your 'caring' on a leman."

"You expect me to take a whore?"

"I expect you will take whatever you want. Now, if you will excuse me —"

"I do not excuse you."

"Have you a command for me?"

He wanted her willing and currying favor with him. She would; he'd make her. "Aye. Come here."

She searched his face, trying to discern his intentions. Drummond lifted an eyebrow, daring her to refuse him. The slender column of her neck worked as she swallowed, but praise her courage, she did not look away. She walked halfway across the room and stopped.

To encourage her closer, he said, "We'll be visiting Red Douglas in October. I thought to discuss the arrangements."

"The purpose of our visit is . . . ?"

"He has demanded that I swear fealty to him."

"Will you?"

"What do you think?"

She studied him carefully, her brown eyes bright with intelligence. "I think you have not decided yet."

Damn her intuition. "Would you swear fealty to me?"

"I must decline. Wedding vows take precedence over civil promises. Although some would have it that Highlanders are completely uncivilized."

Drummond laughed. " 'Tis one of the nicer descriptions of us."

She tried and failed to keep from laughing. "I once overheard the farrier in Carlisle say that Scotsmen hike their legs on their houses to keep their clansmen away."

"What do you say?"

"I think each of us has an opinion."

"I think you remember little of your life in Scotland. Why else would you evade the question?"

"It's a habit I learned from you. Every time I asked you if you loved me."

She hadn't forgotten that part. "You picked odd times to ask."

"I only thought of it when you came home reeking of your mistress's cloying odor."

"I've taken no woman here." Hell, he hadn't even enjoyed his wife, not completely.

"Then you must not be looking in the right place."

"You care not if I take another woman?"

Her haughty expression was unpracticed, her jaw too rigid. "It's your right."

"You were wild for me in the pantry."

Her gaze wavered, then fixed on the laces of his jerkin. "You never did tell me what you wished for the third time."

"I wish to know why you will not answer me."

She waved a hand in dismissal. "Because there are more aspects to marriage than the physical."

The truth of her statement gave him pause. He desired her physically, but he wanted more from her. He had asked for an accord; discussion seemed a perfect place to begin. "Just as there are more aspects to being a father than the obvious?"

"Yes, and how admirable of you to recognize it. Alasdair was very comforted by your attention earlier. He's quite excited about staying in your room."

The verbal praise felt like a caress. "I'm certain you are, too."

She demurred and quite prettily. "I would know you better."

"Then you'll be pleased to know that I'm taking him on the hunt tomorrow."

"Have you already told him so?"

"Why?"

"Because if you haven't, he won't be disappointed."

"I intend to bring him back, and I do not need your permission."

"Nor my opinion, it seems."

Be reasonable, he reminded himself. She was frightened of losing her son and would go to any ends to protect him, the second best thing about her that Drummond liked. "I was certain you would object."

"So you chose to disregard my feelings without even knowing what they are."

He had been guilty of that, but with good reason. "I know what you will say. You will argue that he is too young."

"Then you have erred. I believe he is old enough, he just doesn't know how to hunt. He will ask you a hundred questions, and you'll either be too busy or simply won't want to answer. You'll lose patience with him, and he'll get his feelings hurt. You'll both be miserable, and you will bring your ill humor home to me."

She'd made her case logically, dispassionately, and she might be correct. Drummond hadn't thought how troublesome Alasdair's demands and questions would be on a hunt.

"However," she added, sparing Drummond a feeble reply, "I believe I have a solution. You could teach him to hunt, but privately." A quirky little grin made her eyes twinkle. "He's more attentive without a crowd."

Her thoughtful compromise was an example of what she'd called good parenting. And they were sharing the responsibility. The exchange surprisingly pleased Drummond as few things in his life had. "You love him very much."

"More than my life," she said thickly.

"I'll watch him, Clare. You have my word."

"And fell game at the same time? You exaggerate your prowess more than I ever have."

After seven years in a cell, Drummond doubted he could throw a spear true, but he hadn't considered that he'd have to practice before attempting to live up to her tales. "You're probably correct."

She picked up the ledger. "I believe we've executed the first provision in our truce."

Her mood had warmed; he intended to take advantage of it. "I think I'm conceding."

She smiled as if she remembered making the same statement earlier. "How does it feel?"

"Encouraging, since we must seal our bargain with a kiss." He held out his arms.

She eyed him cautiously and glanced at the open door. "No." Then she whirled and left the room, stirring the air with the earthy smell of heather.

Chapter
10

"Mother?" Alasdair said for the twentieth time.

Johanna gave up listing the harvest tasks in her book of days. She capped the ink pot and stowed her writing things in her trunk, which the porter had moved into Alasdair's room.

Alasdair sat on his bed, his fingers clutching the edge of the mattress, his legs swinging. He wore new trunk hose in a shade lighter than his oak brown jerkin.

"Mother." He sprang from the bed and took up his sword, which he jabbed at an invisible opponent. "A sister would *also* be a good idea because she could marry an important lord and I" — he poked his chest with his thumb — "would have someone to spar with."

This talk of a little sister had to stop. She'd managed to evade Drummond, and given the time, she knew she could convince him that a marriage in name only would perfectly suit their purposes. But each time he made her laugh or put a smile on Alasdair's face, she found herself wanting him for a true husband. When he pulled her into his arms and kissed her, she couldn't help wishing that they'd just met and he was beginning to love her.

She could eradicate the brand. She could make certain, on a given night, that Drummond drank too much ale. She could approach him, smiling, and reach for his hand. He'd wrap her in his arms, and she'd ask him why his kisses made her feel hollow inside. The thought made her shiver with excitement.

But sooner or later, he'd call her Clare and his mouth would pinch with distrust. Love would shrivel in her heart — until the next time, when he managed to forget what Clare had done.

"Did you hear me, Mother? A sister will make me a better leader of men."

The price of loving Drummond Macqueen was too high for Johanna Benison to pay. The devil with husbands. "Who told you that?"

"Father did, and Sheriff Hay said 'twas so."

She snatched up the chance to change the subject. "You must thank him for your new book."

From his pouch he pulled out a narrow strip of leather decorated with feathers and wooden beads. "I made him this. It's for tying game to his saddle."

"That's very thoughtful of you."

"I thought it up myself. Except the feathers. Glory said they would sweeten a huntsman's game. Is that true? Sween said Glory wouldn't know sweet if it crawled in her bed."

"I expect Sween's opinion of Glory is tainted."

"Aye," he said solemnly. "Because she wet another man's wick."

"What did you say?"

He drew in a breath, but held it, his gaze blank with confusion. Then he focused on her. "No one will tell me the gist of it, but I shan't need a lucky charm to make me a good hunter. Father will teach me."

She let the crude remark pass, for if she belabored it, he'd wear out the phrase until she explained its meaning. Drummond could better define male vulgarities. He'd probably excel at that.

"When will you give the sheriff his gift?" she asked.

He puffed out his chest and slid a glance at the door. "At table."

He was excited about being included tonight, and she wanted to be sure the evening went smoothly for him. "You could give it to him there. I'm certain the other men will admire the gift."

He watched her closely, his intelligent mind sensing that she'd given him something to ponder. After a lengthy consideration, he hesitantly said, "Will they laugh at it?"

"Certainly not. I should think they'll praise it. What will you say if they do?"

He examined the contraption, his shoulders slumped, his face a picture of regret. "I'll want

217

to give them one, but I cannot make more to-night."

He'd always been a bright child. "And you will feel uncomfortable."

"Yes. What would I do?"

"The sheriff will be here for a few days. You could give it to him tomorrow or the next day."

"Whew!" He plopped down on the bed.

The bell rang; Evelyn would begin serving dinner in half an hour. Thinking she should check the preparations, Johanna rose.

"Wait!" Alasdair took his time returning the game cord to its pouch. "Does Red Douglas eat carrots?"

The innocuous question, coupled with his slow movements, piqued her curiosity. "You're dawdling, Alasdair. Why?"

"Me?" He stared at the ceiling, the floor, and the hem of his jerkin.

His expression was so sheepishly innocent she almost laughed. "Yes, you, Alasdair Alexander Macqueen."

Bottom lip protruding, he shrugged and tucked his chin to his shoulder. "I had many things to discuss with you. Now seems a good time." He glanced at the door. He was certainly in no hurry to eat.

To test him, she said, "I hope Brother Julian doesn't come to table early and start sampling the baked quinces."

Alasdair ran to the door, leaned into the hallway and looked left and right. Johanna followed him.

Spying her, he jumped back inside and blocked her way. Fumbling behind him, he closed the door. "You had better brush my hair again."

"You little trickster. I just brushed your hair."

He took her arm and dragged her back into the room. "Please?"

"What are you up to?"

"Nothing." Guilt made his voice break. "I'm just . . . just preventing an embarrassing moment." Grabbing the brush, he shoved it in her hand. "Red Douglas might think me a ruffian."

She raked her thumb across the bristles. "I doubt he would think you anything but a trustworthy, honest lad, who never lies to his mother."

Wincing, he stepped closer and bent his head. "Please?"

It seemed important to him that she relent. He'd tell her what was on his mind, but in his own good time, and she had patience aplenty.

She drew the brush through his hair; it crackled with life. She thought of his father's overlong mane and reminded herself to take the shears to him.

He'd been motherless since birth. Drummond hadn't known the special love a mother and son could share. His mother had missed hearing his childish garbling. She had been denied the wonder of his first steps. Who had brushed Drummond's hair or nursed his ills and tended his soul?

"Why do grown people hate children?"

Alasdair's question interrupted her thoughts.

Why was it that even in a crowd the sound of her son's voice could distract her? She didn't know but accepted it for the special gift it was.

"Mother?"

He often seemed too wise for one so young; tonight he seemed particularly vulnerable. "All grown people do not hate children."

"Oh, yes, they do. The tailor chases me and the other lads out of his shop."

"That's because young lads have sticky, dirty fingers that ruin his cloth."

Alasdair stood and stuck out his arms. "My hands are clean." An idea gripped him, and he raced to the basin. "But I should wash them again."

In the order of dislikes, washing his hands ranked just below studying Latin and having his cheeks pinched by the cobbler's wife. Now Johanna knew he was up to something. She folded her arms. "Say what's on your mind, Alasdair Macqueen, or you'll be facing a truly embarrassing moment — when I make your excuses to your father and Red Douglas."

"You cannot!" He screwed up his face in concentration. "Red Douglas is sure to like me now that I have a father."

He was troubled and captive to a young man's hesitance. Feeling guilty, Johanna moved to reassure him. "It's not that Douglas doesn't like you. He simply has a different way of speaking with children."

"I know." Drying his hands on a towel, he

declared in a booming voice, "Keep the lads in the nursery till they learn where the privy is. And once they can sit a horse, foster the cubs out." He shivered with too much revulsion.

Was Alasdair suddenly worried that she might send him away? "You will not go to foster. I've told you that."

Again, he glanced at the door. "What does Father say?"

An ugly suspicion banished her motherly concern. She'd bet her chance for redemption that Alasdair was waiting for Drummond. The father was again manipulating the son for his own purposes. If so, she'd make Drummond wish he'd gone home to the Highlands. "Why don't you ask your father?"

Exasperated, he flapped his arms. "I would, but he's not here yet." At her sharp glance, he winced.

A knock sounded at the door. Alasdair scrambled to answer. "Father!" He tipped his head back and propped his hands on his hips. "You're late."

"You're impudent." Drummond stepped inside. His hair was still wet and slicked straight back, and his face was freshly washed. He wore a new leather jerkin, dyed black, and gray trunk hose. Under his arm he carried a small casket, and in his hand he held a bouquet of white heather and night-blooming sallies. "My apologies," he said, then handed Alasdair the casket and Johanna the flowers.

Alasdair squatted on the floor to examine his gift. Johanna smelled the posies, but her grip was so shaky she had to clutch the stems with both hands. How dare he stroll into the room looking as handsome as sin and bearing gifts? He wasn't supposed to want her, and she couldn't risk falling in love with him.

"The white heather's for good luck," he said.

She suspected the gift was a ploy, but she'd never expected to have a husband bring her flowers. She felt a powerful urge to simper, but vanquished the weakness. He wasn't the first man to bring her flowers. She wouldn't lose her head over a simple gift or an endearing grin.

The present for Alasdair confused her. Why had Drummond given it to him here and now when guests awaited?

She sneaked a peek at him and found him staring at her clothes.

"The green favors you well," he said, his brow smooth with contentment and his lips curved in a smile.

It was her best dress, a feather light wool with wide bands of black satin ribbon at the hem and the sleeves. She *had* considered his opinion because she'd wanted him to admire her tonight. She'd also chastised herself for doing so silly a thing.

Flustered, she murmured a thank you.

"Look, Mother!" Alasdair stood and held out one of a set of table knives. The blade had been finely honed and the wooden handle looked as if it fitted smoothly in the hand. Johanna was grateful that Drummond thought of Alasdair, but she was also curious. "Beautiful, Drummond, and an interesting gift for a lad, are they not?"

He glanced up quickly. "You've forgotten that, too?"

Here was another occasion of which she had no knowledge, but Clare would have. Would she never learn to keep her mouth shut? "Please jostle my memory."

"We must commemorate Alasdair's sharing his first meal with a clan chief. 'Tis a Highland custom. Do you not recall the night the Mackenzie chieftain dined with us and my younger brother Randolph received his knives? You fussed beyond measure over them and the practice."

Although she'd been caught in another error, Johanna took heart. He had recalled a pleasantry about a kind and loving soul who'd reaped a bitter harvest of life. Poor Clare.

"What's wrong?" Drummond said. "You look sad."

Would that she could tell him and cleanse her soul. Instead, she committed another sin. "I'm not." Then she took refuge in her son. "What do you think, Alasdair?"

His blue eyes rounded with awe, and he rubbed the knife handle with the pad of his thumb. "It has a wolf carved on it. See?" He handed it to Johanna. "It's the symbol of the Macqueens. Did you know that I'm a branch off the mighty Macqueen tree?"

Tears thickened her throat. A father in Alasdair's life was the answer to an oft-made prayer. But she'd never imagined that his true father would fill the role, for his presence spelled doom for her. However, her own troubles could wait. Drummond had kept his promise to teach his son about Scotland. Alasdair was happy. She intended to rejoice with both of them.

She tested the blade. "It's very sharp, and the workmanship is as fine as any I've seen. Your guests will be most impressed, Alasdair."

His sweet face broke into a grin that would one day win him the heart and the troth of a woman. Pray God they found harmony.

"Oh, thank you, Father." He lunged at Drummond, who swept him up and perched him on his hip. "Tell me everything about my knives."

"If the overlord takes one with him," Drummond said, "it means he accepts you as his kinsman and feels welcome at any table in your kingdom."

"His kinsman." Alasdair mulled it over. "Do I have to stop being a Macqueen?"

"Never. You're a Macqueen, Son, until the day after forever. God has deemed it so."

"God sent you back to me."

"Aye, he did." Drummond winked and tossed a screaming Alasdair into the air.

Seeing them together, so alike in physical appearance and so happy with each other, filled Johanna with pride. Alasdair had always been a confident lad, and with Drummond's influence, he'd have an understanding of the Macqueens who'd come before him. Regardless of what happened between her and Drummond, Alasdair would have the father and the future he needed. Any sacrifice on her part seemed worthy by comparison.

"Mother?" Regret shone in Alasdair's eyes. "I told Father he could help me escort you to table, but I couldn't let him face an embarrassing moment by being late to table. That's why I was dawdling, and why I didn't tell you the whole truth. Do you forgive me?"

Love twisted inside her. "Yes, I do. It was a very small omission, and your motives were honorable." She glanced at Drummond and added, "And your own."

A self-effacing grin enhanced his masculine appeal. "Even a beef-witted troll has his admirable traits."

None more than you, her heart cried.

Alasdair hooted. "Mother called you a troll. A troll. Father's a troll."

"Enough, Son," Drummond said. "And remember, you mustn't repeat everything she says. Unless I command you."

Silly and cocksure and enormously happy, Alasdair poked his father in the chest. "I command you to tell us why you were late."

Drummond put him down. "Since you insist, Lord Alasdair, the woodcarver worked as quickly as he could, but he only just finished."

Alasdair nodded and glanced from his father

to Johanna. Then he stared at her flowers, his face a picture of concentration. What deep thoughts had him in their grip, she wondered. She glanced inquiringly at Drummond, who shrugged, amused.

"You know, Mother," Alasdair finally said. "Heckley says that if you give me a sister, I'll trip her in the lane and throw mud in her face. But you mustn't believe him."

If Drummond was enjoying her discomfort he didn't show it, for his expression was serene. Since he didn't seem interested in the subject, she would ignore it as well.

"I give you my word of honor, Mother."

She'd had years of experience as a parent, and steering a young mind was her forte. "When did you see the fletcher?"

With the tip of his new knife, Alasdair gently ruffled the tiny white blossoms of the heather in her bouquet. "Today. Father's going on the hunt tomorrow and he needed Heckley to make his arrows."

Drummond said, "I told Alasdair he could go a-hunting when he's older."

"I have to practice with my bow —" Alasdair slapped his hand over his mouth and sent his father a pained expression.

If Drummond had ignored her wishes and told Alasdair he could join the hunt, she'd put bitters in his beer and thistles in his bed.

He sensed her disapproval and had the gall to look surprised, "Alasdair," he said, putting the lad down. "Tell your mother what else I said about the hunt."

Alasdair began pacing the floor, his arms behind his back, the knife clutched in his hands. "Hunting is dangerous, Mother. I may be old enough, but my pony's too slow, and she might get hurt. A good hunter always looks after his mount. Valkyrie is my trusted friend. I also have to practice."

As cheerful as a rooster at dawn, Drummond said, "And tell your mother when you will practice."

"After my Latin lessons."

Drummond fairly beamed at her, and Johanna felt her stomach float. Fatherly pride was a new experience for him, and she was reminded of all the times Alasdair had enriched her life. She felt a kindred spirit in Drummond. Could their shared concern for Alasdair become the cornerstone on which to build a future as man and wife? She didn't know.

"We're a family now, aren't we?" Alasdair said.

Johanna could feel Drummond watching her, willing her to look at him. She did and was immediately sorry, for she saw regret, as only a wronged man could express it. She'd seen the look often enough on Sween.

"Aren't we a family?" Alasdair repeated.

"And hungry at that," she said and started for the door.

Satisfied, Alasdair replaced the knife and hefted the wooden box.

"One thing more," said Drummond. "If Douglas brings up a subject of which you have knowledge, you may join in the discussion. You do not have to wait for him to specifically address you."

Alasdair hitched up his hose and swaggered out the door. In the droll speech of a Yorkshireman, he said, "I shall endeavah to be entataining."

Red Douglas adhered to the custom that dictated silence during meals. Little was said until Johanna signaled for Evelyn to clean the table and serve dessert.

"My lord," she said to Douglas. "How do Mary and Bridgit fare?" Johanna had fostered the girls for three years.

With little feeling, he said, "They would as soon return to you."

Alasdair said, "I taught Bridgit how to catch a lizard."

The overlord leaned back and stretched. "Catching a husband is better sport for an unpromised girl."

"Have you found them husbands?" Johanna asked.

"Both, and to titled Englishmen. They'll wed at Michaelmas."

To good men, she hoped. "Give them my best."

Douglas belched and rubbed his belly. "Nothing like talk of a wedding to inspire a man to wet his wick."

Alasdair piped up. "Sween says Mistress Glory's

228

good at wetting a man's wick."

Johanna's mouth dropped open. Douglas burst out laughing. Drummond was choking with laughter. Brother Julian blustered. Sheriff Hay chuckled. Thank God Bertie wasn't here; he'd've howled just to spite her.

Brother Julian cleared his throat. "Douglas, the bishop at Sweetheart Abbey says the king is sure to name you a baron."

A suddenly serious Douglas glared at Drummond. "I'd keep a peace with the Plantagenets. If Edward the Second goes against the Highlanders, where will you stand, Macqueen?"

Shoulder to shoulder with my kinsmen, Drummond wanted to say, but his wife spoke first.

"Lord Drummond says our new king has not the taste for Scotland that his father did. Edward the Second also doesn't have the funds to finance a war against the clans."

Douglas sucked his teeth. "An English prison changed your mind, eh, Macqueen? We thought the old king had quartered you and nailed a piece of you on every city gate in England."

A feminine gasp sliced the air. Her complexion turned as white as snow on ice, and her jaw went stiff with shock. She was staring at Alasdair, who'd lost interest in his custard.

Drummond glared at his guest. "A sorry subject to address at table, Douglas."

"Indeed," she said, her color returning with a vengeance. "Lord Drummond has returned to us, and we praise God and his angels for the kindness."

"He was caught —"

"What he did," she interrupted, all righteous champion, "is his affair, Douglas. We shall leave it at that."

He shrugged. "Ramsay thinks the king'll hand carry your pardon, signed and sealed by Parliament. You'll be a free man and respected."

Stunned by her defense of him, Drummond wanted to hug her.

"A pardon?" said Alasdair. "Who was in prison?"

Douglas got to his feet. "Your father was, lad, and he looks none the worse for seven years in a London hellhole."

Alasdair balled his fists, and his face turned red with rage.

"My father was not in prison. He was in heaven with the angels. Weren't you, Father?"

Douglas guffawed.

Regret flooded Drummond. He should have told Alasdair, but he hadn't known how. He glanced at his wife. Her expression said, Oh, God, why didn't we tell him?

Because we were too consumed with our own troubles, he silently replied.

To Alasdair, Drummond said, "These are not proper subjects. We'll discuss them later."

Douglas excused himself, but Alasdair didn't notice that his overlord had hefted the knife, nodded his approval, and taken it with him. The lad had even abandoned his half-eaten custard. "May I retire?" He stared at the table.

Everyone else stared at him.

A fist squeezed Drummond's chest. He hadn't considered what effect his beliefs and actions would have on his son. He hadn't considered that Alasdair didn't know about greedy English kings who covet other men's land. He hadn't taught his son to love Scotland. But Clare had taught the lad to love Fairhope, where peace reigned. The lad must be told about victors and the vanquished, and Drummond prayed he could find the right words.

He caught his wife's gaze. "Enjoy your dessert."

At the word *enjoy,* she rolled her eyes, and he knew she'd enjoy nothing save an end to Alasdair's misery. Drummond would do his best to oblige. He rose and rested his hand on his son's shoulder. "Come with me, Alasdair."

The lad jerked away, but scrambled off the bench and stomped from the room with his father.

Johanna watched them go, her heart breaking. Brother Julian mumbled his excuses and followed them out.

"The lad'll get over it," said Ramsay.

The heartless statement ignited a fire in Johanna. "You knew Drummond was alive. Why else would you expect the king to deliver his pardon?"

He sat up straight, assuming his official posture. Candlelight winked on his golden chain of office, and his angular features appeared harsh. "He was under death sentence. The king could have hanged him at any time."

Oh, sweet Jesus, she thought, Drummond had carried that burden alone, for seven years. Had he awakened every day wondering if he'd live to see the sunset?

"No one thought Edward the First would spare the chieftain."

Least of all Drummond, she thought. Enraged, she pushed the custard dish aside and leaned forward. "Ramsay, you've sat at this table a dozen times and heard Alasdair ask me if his father loved him. You could have saved me the grief his questions wrought."

"I thought you'd done your grieving."

"You hoped I had, but I never led you to believe that because my husband was dead I'd want you."

The insult stung, for he made a fist and pounded the table. "You never so much as mentioned him except in fable."

"What I carry in my heart is my affair."

"No longer, Clare," he spat. " 'Tis plain you love your husband."

Had she fallen in love with Drummond Macqueen? She felt many things where he was concerned, but she wasn't sure if she loved him. She'd sooner ponder that question without an audience. "You had no right, Ramsay, to keep the truth from me."

His commanding air turned chilly. "I thought it best. What would you have done?"

"I would have done as *I* saw fit."

"You're unsuited to be a wife," he grumbled. "You're too independent."

She had not encouraged his affection. Rather she had considered him a trusted friend, and he had betrayed her. The painful shattering of an ideal was new to Johanna. Glory always said men and women couldn't be true friends to each other. Sadly, she'd been correct.

Resigned, Johanna said, "You've corrupted our friendship, Ramsay, and for that I am truly sorry."

"He will not find contentment here."

For the first time, Johanna felt the brunt of Ramsay's oppressive will. No wonder little crime occurred in his domain. "Whether Lord Drummond prospers among us or returns to Scotland is not your concern."

"Ah." He relaxed and toyed with the handle of his mug. "So your devoted husband told you nothing about the terms of his pardon. You're strapped with him, Clare, for he'll be put to the horn should he step foot in his beloved Highlands."

"Vengeance is unworthy of you."

"Clare?" he pleaded.

Johanna's mind whirled with denial. "Never address me by that name again. You tried to court me knowing my husband was alive. You would have made me an adulteress."

He cursed and stormed from the room, his golden chain clinking.

She could erect a wall of politeness between

her and the sheriff. Now she must insulate herself from a husband, for a husband she would have.

Her search for him ended in the stables.

"He and Alasdair took off on the stallion," said Sween, who was sharing a pint with the farrier.

"That explains why Longfellow is so restless. Did Drummond say where they were going?"

"Nay, but he took a blanket and his flint and steel. I wouldn't fret, my lady. The lad wanted to go. Macqueen'll put things to rights with him. Alasdair never could hold his temper for long. It was rough news for him."

"You heard?" She desperately hoped Drummond could build a bridge across Alasdair's shattered illusions.

He moved his head from side to side. "Bloody Plantagenet devils."

"And the sheriff, too, Sween. He knew." She blinked back tears. "All these years, he knew."

Sween took her hand. "You and Alasdair thought well of him. For that I am sorry."

With men like Sween in his life, Alasdair would soon forget the sheriff. She gave Sween a half grin. "Glory was correct, you know."

He huffed. "She's as wrong as beaks on badgers."

Arguing the point offered a respite from the cruelties of the day. Johanna grasped it. "And you're as stubborn as faith on sin. You do not deserve her."

"So she tells me. I'll do as I may with the wench."

Johanna knew that for a truth. "I wish you peace, Sween Handle."

"To you, my lady. Your men'll not return this night. Shall I walk you back to the keep?"

"Thank you, no."

She had business better done alone. Her sister had sinned by lying with a man who was not her husband. Johanna would do the same. Pity she couldn't tell Drummond the truth. Perhaps she could some day. But now was her chance to take an irrevocable step toward becoming his wife and consigning herself to a life of new sins.

Chapter

11

They'd fashioned a shelter and built a fire in the heart of a stand of beeches. Woodsmoke scented the air. Stars filled the sky. Biting insects were content to buzz, and the fire was inclined to blaze. Droning and crackling, the night came alive with sound. Most compelling was the hushed breathing of a father who didn't know where to begin and a son who didn't know what to say.

Drummond stared at the fire, and on the edge of his vision he saw Alasdair's boots. Seated beside him on a log, Alasdair tapped his feet together, scuffing his heels in the dirt and displaying his indecision. Dust from the road coated the lad's hose, as did an assortment of dried leaves and twigs.

On the short journey, a silent Alasdair had ridden before Drummond on the stallion. Gamely, the lad had gripped the horse's mane and used his legs to keep his balance. Once at the clearing, Drummond had ambled off to collect firewood.

Alasdair had foraged in the opposite direction.

Where to start? Instinctively Drummond shied from the cause of the trouble; best to begin with a cheery topic. What would lighten Alasdair's heart and encourage him to talk? In his silence, he was like his mother. But Alasdair wasn't exactly ignoring Drummond, for if wounded feelings were sounds, the lad verily shouted in pain. Where did an inexperienced father begin?

With the toe of his boot, Drummond nudged a smoldering log. Plumes of sparks whooshed into the air, and an owl screeched in protest. Nothing in Drummond's past had prepared him for the discussion to come. In the Macqueen family, lads weren't allowed to suffer bruised spirits or confused emotions. Ill humors and melancholy were female conditions. Drummond saw the error in that conviction; if a lad or lass hurt, a parent should ease the pain. More than anything, he wanted to ease Alasdair's.

"Did you know that Douglas took your knife when he left the table?"

In a small, sad voice, Alasdair said, "He laughed at me."

"He thought the knife fine."

Alasdair drew up his legs and rested his chin on his knees. "Before that he laughed. When I talked about Glory wetting a man's wick."

So the lad wasn't ready to brave the lion's den of their problem either. Drummond took heart; given enough time, he'd find a way to set things right with Alasdair. "You should worry more over your mother's reaction to what you said than Douglas's. He was entertained. She was taken aback."

Alasdair glanced up, his gaze clear and direct, like that of his mother. "She wouldn't talk to me. That's how you know when she's truly angry with you. You can jump up and down and howl like a wolf, and she pretends you aren't even there."

"She's a master of it." Drummond felt the weight of his burden ease. "She ignored me for the last three days."

Alasdair contemplated the fire. "The longest she ever ignored me was one day. I broke wind in church on purpose. What did you do?"

He had not uttered the word *father*, and Drummond missed it dreadfully. "I did a dreadful thing. 'Twas the night we tricked her into telling you a story. She had a right to take offense."

Picking up a twig, Alasdair began snapping it into pieces. "But she always tells me stories."

Unsure of how to proceed, Drummond chose honesty.

" 'Twasn't about the story. 'Twas because we connived behind her back. She doesn't like being tricked."

Alasdair swung his head toward Drummond. Hurt dulled the luster in the lad's eyes. "Why did we do it then?"

Dozens of answers came to mind, but they involved husbandly pride, intimate promises, and other adult complexities that Alasdair wouldn't understand. " 'Twas not *we*, but *me* who shoulders the blame."

"Why?"

"Reasonable circumstances forced her to decline to read you a story. I gave her no choice in the matter."

"Bertie was already asleep?"

"Aye. I was wrong to prey on her love for you."

"Did you tell her so?"

"Nay, but I will."

"Good. She likes to talk about love."

"Does she? What does she say?"

"She loves to see Sween smile at Glory, but he doesn't often." He pursed his lips. "She loves to hold little babies, and doesn't even care if their nappies are soiled —"

Something rustled the bushes. Alasdair started. "Do you think it's her?"

Drummond listened for a whinny of alarm from his horse, but heard none. He hadn't expected her to follow, for she'd voiced no complaint when he and Alasdair left the table. Just in case of trouble, Drummond had told Sween where they were going.

Hearing no alarming sounds, Drummond searched the shadows and saw that the stallion was content to nibble at the forest floor. "Would you like it if she came?"

Alasdair shrugged and tossed the broken twigs into the fire. Then he eased closer to Drummond. "She knows I'm safe with you."

"Did she tell you that?"

"Yes. She said you loved me well."

Would that all mothers were so thoughtful. "I do."

"Father, will you tell me what it means for a man to wet his wick?"

Contentment vibrated through Drummond. "Aye, but I'm not sure I can make you understand. 'Tis a manly remark, one of the things men say among themselves, but never in the presence of a lady."

"Like bragging that you need two hands to hold your balls when you jump from the loft into the hay?"

What a joy this lad was to a man who had given up hope of ever having a healthy son. Praise Clare for her guidance and care of him. Out of habit, Drummond remembered her great sin as he did every time he felt pleasure in something she had done. But this time his stomach didn't tighten and he didn't grind his teeth. Perhaps he could forget and forgive her. He wanted her with the intensity of a lad who'd found his first sweetheart. That too surprised him, for he hadn't expected to desire Clare Macqueen. He'd still hear her confession, though.

"Did you hear me, Father?"

Drummond harkened back to the subject. " 'Tis exactly like that. Only ladies are generally uninterested in speeches about a man's private parts, one of which is often called his wick."

Alasdair gasped. "Mine's bigger than a wick!"

With the exception of his lips, which he'd inherited from his mother, Alasdair looked just like Drummond's younger brothers. He fought to control his mirth. And lost. " 'Tis not a statement of size."

Now adamant, Alasdair propped his hands on his thighs. "Willie Handle says his uncle Sween's wick is so long he can piss over his shoulder with it."

Summoning brevity, Drummond said, "You mustn't say that in front of your mother or any other female."

"Very well. Wetting my wick is the same as going swimming, isn't it?"

"Nay. 'Tis a crude reference to what men and women do in the privacy of their bedchamber. You'll do these things with women when you are older." Reflecting, he added, "Much older."

"What do older people do?"

"They practice their marriage vows and celebrate their feelings for each other in a physical way."

Confusion wreathed Alasdair's face.

"If they are fortunate," Drummond went on, "they make little sisters and brothers."

His interest piqued, Alasdair straddled the log and faced Drummond. "How?"

Clare's words came back to Drummond. *He'll ask you dozens of questions. You'll lose patience with him.* But patience wasn't the problem, inexperience was, for Drummond felt like squirming. "A man uses his wick to give a woman his seed."

241

"But how does it get wet exactly?"

Avoid nuances, Drummond told himself, and get to the bloody point so they could move on to more comfortable subjects. "God created women to complement men. Physically women are different, so they can accommodate a man's 'wick.' "

Alasdair blinked, waiting.

Oh, Lord. Drummond felt lost at sea without rudder or sail. "Parts of a woman are very soft and wet."

Chewing his lip, the lad stared into space. "Curly Handle gave me a wet kiss once. I almost retched on her."

Drummond chuckled. "You will not vomit when you're older and a woman kisses you. I vow this is true."

"Do you like kissing Mother?"

He thought of her naked and dripping with heather scented water. God, he'd been hot for her, and she had wanted him, too. But other images of her rose in his mind: Clare the diplomat who tried to turn the subject from Drummond's imprisonment; Clare the storyteller who'd inspired pride in a fatherless lad; Clare the mother who'd taught this lad to defend the father he hardly knew.

"You're thinking about kissing her, aren't you?"

Chagrined, Drummond cleared his throat. "Aye, and other things about her."

"Sheriff Hay drank too much ale and tried to

kiss her. She slapped him and said if he ever did it again, she'd toss him out and bar the gates."

"What did he do?"

"He groveled like a starved pup, because he has an affection for her." Then sagely, he said, "The widow Macqueen is no easy mark."

She was also no longer a widow. "The sheriff can take his affection back to Dumfries."

"What about the cloth merchant from Glasgow?"

Stunned, Drummond searched his son's expression to see if he lied. "He also harbors an affection for her?"

"Yes. She's so pretty and —" He paused, scratching his head. "And she begs for a man to tame her wild spirit."

Drummond vowed to be the only man to accommodate her. He'd do more than bar the gate to any man who dared approach his wife in an unseemly way. After all, she was Lady Clare Macqueen.

His irritation rose; by right and title, she was his. "Where did you hear that?"

"Well, when we have visitors of lesser rank, like the cloth merchant, Sween and the watchmen always sleep in the hall. I sleep there, too." He shook his finger in mock reproof. "To keep those rascally knaves away from her. She's a prize, you know."

Drummond wondered if Clare had fostered that plan or if the men had taken it upon themselves to protect her. "Aye, she is bonny, and I shall talk to her very soon about that sister."

Alasdair's nod was quick and emphatic. "Brother Julian says she toils overmuch and that she needs a husband. Now she has you back."

She didn't want a husband, of that Drummond was certain. The only time she approached him was out of necessity or when he'd displeased her. Which was often, especially where Alasdair was concerned. "She has you, too."

Alasdair sat straighter and smiled mischievously. "Did you know she was a prankster as a girl? Bertie told me about her dressing up like a boy and sneaking out of the abbey to watch the villagers dance 'round the harvest fire."

"You have it wrong, Alasdair. She tells that tale about her friend Johanna. Your mother was afraid of everything." Clare had been the timid one, too shy to wander about at night. But not too shy to wallow in a royal bed.

His face pinched with incredulity. "Mother, afraid? No. She's as brave as anyone."

Drummond saw his mistake; any lad should think the best of his parents. Perhaps Clare had outgrown her fears. "She is brave, Alasdair, just don't put a lizard down her dress or expect her to pet a dog."

"She always liked lizards, even as a girl. Sister Margaret sent the baskets she used to catch them."

Again, the lad had gotten confused. "Nay, 'twas Johanna who caught lizards to eat the insects in the abbey's kitchen garden."

Slowly, succinctly, Alasdair said, "Mother

tended the garden, same as she does now. She also fawns over the puppies and brings bones to the dogs."

The lad seemed so vehement that Drummond did not protest.

"Father?"

At Alasdair's serious tone, Drummond grew alert.

"Did Douglas tell the truth about you?"

Drummond took a deep breath and hoped for the best. Scooting back, he straddled the log so that he faced Alasdair. Futile hope shone in the lad's eyes. "Aye, Son. He did."

Alasdair's mouth tightened, an expression very much like his mother's. "I thought you were with the angels in heaven. Were you truly in a hellhole?"

Ugly images rose in Drummond's mind, and although the fire radiated warmth, he felt chilled. "I was in a prison."

"Elton Singer says he's in prison, but it's just the barracks. Were you in a barracks?"

"Nay. I was in a keep called the Tower of London."

"What was it like there? Were you ever lonely?"

His first thought was to fall back on the teaching of his own father and keep his feelings to himself. Instinct told him to speak from the heart. "Aye, Son. I ofttimes was lonely."

Eyes brimming with concern, Alasdair rested a comforting hand on Drummond's knee. "I would have scaled that tower and rescued you, had Mother told me where you were."

Drummond didn't question where Alasdair had learned compassion. It was one of many fine qualities Clare had instilled in the lad. Drummond intended to praise her for it. "Your mother did not know I was there. She thought I'd been —" He searched for benign words for the cruelty he, and now Clare, had expected.

"Cut up in pieces?"

Drummond's guards had often threatened him with the "fate of the Welsh princes," as they termed dismemberment. Even now he shivered with revulsion. "Your mother thought I'd been hanged."

"Why?"

"Because I fought against the old king."

"But I cried when he died and said prayers for his soul."

Drummond had cursed the monarch every day and wished him to hell more often. "Old Edward hated the Macqueens."

"Mother says hating is no reason for a man to die, especially if he has a family who will miss him. We missed you."

They'd also kept Drummond's memory alive. Considering the events of the past, the noble tribute was an unwarranted gift. "I missed you, too."

Leaning back, Alasdair braced his hands on the log. "Did the king capture you?"

"Aye, 'twas a black day for the Macqueens. My clan had been skirmishing his army for weeks, but fortune left us, and we were separated."

"What happened?"

Regrets and better tactics whirled in Drummond's mind. "I was outnumbered."

A skeptical frown made Alasdair look endearingly young. "By how many men?"

To this day, Drummond was haunted by his poor judgment. "Twenty to one."

"But you battled fifty heathen Vikings to save the church's holy relic. Why could you not slay a mere score of Englishmen?"

Compared to fable, the true story became what it was: a desperate young man's tactical error. "My sword was broken and my horse lame."

"You could have used your dirk. You killed the terrible boar with it."

Knowing the discussion could go on for hours, Drummond told another truth. "Your mother may have embellished the tale of the boar hunt."

"That's what Sheriff Hay said."

Drummond's anger rose. Ramsay would pay for his sin of omission, not to mention the crime of coveting another man's wife. "In future, you will listen to me, Alasdair, not Sheriff Hay."

He nodded. "You might not know it yet, so it's best I tell you. I'm an easy lad to teach and clever."

"Who told you that?"

"I heard Mother say it to Brother Julian."

"Were you hiding behind a door?"

He stiffened with righteous indignation. "I was in the solar tallying my accounts. The door was open."

"Your accounts?"

"Yes. Grain for my six chickens and oats for my pony. I must be prepared for manhood."

"What kind of man do you think you will become?"

In imitation of his elders, he rubbed his chin. "A respecter of persons, I should think."

" 'Tis a commendable ideal."

All seriousness, Alasdair folded his arms over his chest. "A man must protect the poor, the sick, and the contrite."

He sounded so worldly, Drummond couldn't help but say, "Know you much of contrite?"

Alasdair sighed and stared at the sky. "Only that I'm a poor master of it."

To hide a smile, Drummond scratched his cheek. "Well said."

"Father? When we return, will you talk to Mother about that sister for me. She isn't at all interested in getting me one."

"I shall endeavor to change her mind."

"Will you also take me to the Highlands?"

Drummond hesitated. Dreams of returning to his home and family had sustained him through the bleak nights in that wretched tower. Now Scotland was forbidden to him unless he defied the new king. If he did, Alasdair would become a traitor's son and Clare the wife of a fugitive. Unless Edward II intervened. Would he agree to ignore Drummond's flight if she again yielded her favors? Would she agree?

Why had she said yes so many years ago? Or

was the long-ago affair, as Drummond had so often rationalized, a single act performed for the purpose of embarrassing a young and popular Scottish chieftain?

Drummond despaired, for what had once been a foregone conclusion had now become a complicated dilemma.

"Will you take me, Father?"

Drummond dodged the issue. " 'Tis too cold there for you to swim."

"Whatever do the lads do for pleasure in summer?"

Pleasure. With Edward I bringing army after army into Scotland, life had offered scant recreation for the children of the Highlands. " 'Tis much better here, Alasdair." Drummond knew it was true; yet he felt disloyal to the depths of his soul.

"I'm glad you're here, Father. Will you tell me a story?"

No fairy tale would do; Drummond wanted to teach Alasdair about the Highland spirit. He searched for an event that would hold the lad's interest, but most of the stories ended unhappily. Except one. "I'll tell you a tale about the Tablet of Scone."

"What is it, and what does it do?"

" 'Tis a block of stone that once resided in Scone Abbey. By tradition, the kings of Scotland stand on the tablet to receive the crown. But the old king Edward took the stone and put it in Westminster Abbey. At least that's what everyone believes happened to the stone."

"What *did* happen?"

"Therein lies the tale, my eager friend, but before I tell you, you must promise never to speak the lad's name or reveal his secret."

"Oh, Father, I swear on my oath," Alasdair gushed and jumped up and down. Then he grew pensive. "I wish Mother was here. She loves stories and she's ever so good at keeping secrets."

"If, after hearing it, you decide to tell her the story, you may."

He looked toward Fairhope, longing in his eyes. "Mother will miss us."

According to his mother, Alasdair had never spent the night away from home without her. Drummond felt compelled to say, "Do you want to go back?"

"I'm not sure, and you haven't told me the story."

"You can decide later."

Absently, Alasdair nodded. "I wonder where she is now?"

Johanna entered the darkened hall and peered into the shadows to be sure she was alone. Her fingers gripped the heavy iron. The metal felt cool and smooth against her skin. And harmless. The tables had been dismantled and put away and the fire banked. Certain all had retired, she walked to the hearth.

Before she could again change her mind, she knelt and plunged the rod into the coals. Sparks flew. She jumped back to protect her best dress.

The coward in her urged reconsideration. She couldn't be certain Drummond would notice a difference in the brand: Clare had said he paid the mark little mind. Neither had he been repulsed. But what if he noticed that the imprint of the tiny blunted sword was upside down on Johanna's shoulder? When he'd stormed into the pantry and watched her bathe, she had managed to cover the mark with a towel, but she could not always hide the brand. Even if he did not grasp the difference the first time he saw the mark, he could the next, or the next.

She must get rid of it and only a hot iron would do.

What of putrefaction? If the burn fevered, she could die.

Not from so small an injury. As an infant she'd survived the burning from the branding. She would dress the new wound quickly and well and sleep warm and cozy in Alasdair's bed. Her discomfort would be small. She wasn't in the forest bereft of aid and mortally wounded. Heavens no.

In the time it would take to ink a quill, she would lay the thumb-size rod on her skin. She would obscure the one physical trait that marked her as Johanna Benison. Her stomach roiled.

She wasn't afraid of illness. She feared losing her own identity.

As her hesitance grew, she stared at the hearth.

251

The handle of the rod protruded from the coals. Farewell Johanna.

No. She couldn't. So she ran from the hall. At the stairway, she pulled a lighted torch from its sconce and raced to the top of the keep.

The cooling wind sharpened her senses. The sky twinkled with stars, and moonlight blanketed the land. She could hear the village sleeping, the creatures settling, the wind soughing through the trees.

This place had been wild before she came and the people poor beyond measure. Now the demesne bristled with life and prosperity.

The watchman at the main gate swung his lantern in a wide arc. In answer, Johanna waved the torch, then thrust it into a brace on a merlon. The familiar ritual fueled her sense of accomplishment, for she often came to this spot. She grew melancholy, thinking of the progress her leadership had wrought.

From behind her, she heard footfalls. Turning, she saw Bertie framed in the threshold. "Would you like company?"

Gratitude flooded her. "Please."

Wearing a dark cape and holding another, he came to stand beside her. "Here."

She took the wrap and draped it over her shoulders. Together they surveyed the village below.

After a companionable silence, she said, "I was just thinking about how much this land has changed since we came here."

" 'Twas forest and moor and little else, save

the naysayers who had of it that you would fail."

A sense of accomplishment comforted her. Bertie's support had always been a given, a constant. He had been with her during every dark moment. It seemed fitting for him to be with her now. "I could not have succeeded without you."

"Bother it," he scoffed, his kind features pulled into a self-effacing grin.

"More than anything, I wanted a home of my own. Remember how jealous I was when word came that Clare would marry before me? I hated the king for that."

" 'Twas God's will, not His Majesty's. I'm thinking that's also why Drummond was freed."

At the mention of his name, her heart ached. She had doubted her feelings for him, but after tonight Johanna faced the sad truth that she had fallen in love with Drummond Macqueen. Rather than bolster her confidence, the knowledge added weight to her burden.

"He deserves better, Bertie."

"Better than what?" he challenged, waving an arm over the battlement. "A prosperous estate? A strapping son? A capable and beautiful wife?"

Battered by doubts, Johanna felt the old misery return. "I wasn't pursuing compliments, Bertie. I was thinking about what he feels in his heart. You should have seen him at table. A lesser man would have crumbled beneath Douglas's harsh words, but Drummond thought first of Alasdair."

"He has a father's fondness for the lad, and

he's too clever to lose Alasdair's admiration. He'll make a fight of it, do you see?"

"I do not envy his task."

"And what of yours, Lady Friend?"

"He deserves a truthful wife." Then she told him what she planned to do.

"Sweet Jesus!" he cursed. "You cannot put a hot iron to yourself. What if you take a fever?"

Defending herself had never come easy to Johanna, but Bertie was her friend. "I will not. What are they saying in the village about Drummond?"

"They're saying that Edward the Second should be canonized for freeing your husband from prison. *I'm* saying 'tis foolishness you contemplate."

Under different circumstances she would have cherished Bertie's advice. "I was little more than a girl when we came here. When have I never listened to you, Bertie?"

"Now."

"I cannot."

"You've a good soul, Johanna Benison, and given the time, Drummond Macqueen will see it. Then you can tell him the truth."

"But what of the danger to Sister Margaret? The old king was emphatic about keeping secret the fact that Clare had a sister, especially a twin. Sister Margaret gave him her word."

"Why would he ask for such a pledge unless your existence threatened his rule? He's dead, and who's to give a gelded goose now?"

"You're missing the point, Bertie. Sister Margaret stood over that grave and wept for me." She tapped her breastbone. "With the entire village looking on, she prayed aloud to God to take Johanna Benison into heaven. She accepted condolences from the people. There are witnesses aplenty to swear that Johanna Benison died and was buried. If word gets out, do you think the church will sit by and do nothing? I'll wager they'll strip Sister Margaret of rank and privileges." Sorrow choked her. "I cannot allow that to happen."

He opened his mouth, but closed it and bowed his head. "Nay, Lady Friend, you cannot. 'Tis a nettle."

She knew the way out. She had but to find the courage.

An hour later, she knelt before the hearth, her bliaud bunched at her waist. She slid shaking fingers into the cook's thick leather glove. Then she picked up the iron. The tip glowed red, and a thin line of smoke floated upward.

Bile rose in her throat, and a dozen new objections came to mind. Thoughts of Sister Margaret held sway.

Resigned and braced for the pain to come, she moved the iron close and whispered, "Farewell, Johanna."

Chapter
12

Drummond leaned against a plum tree on the periphery of the kitchen garden and watched his wife. At one time she hadn't known celery from heather and now she looked perfectly at home, sitting on a pallet among the maze of flourishing plants. She wore a smock of coarsely woven linen over a faded blue underdress. Sans coif, her hair had been loosely restrained with a green ribbon. In a gilded waterfall, it trailed down her back and past her waist to pool on the mat.

On her left hand she wore a stained glove and, with little vigor, wielded a small spade. Her right arm was cradled against her breast, as he expected. But she didn't look sorely ill, as Sween had insisted. She looked endearingly young and far too tempting.

Nearby Evelyn used a clawed hoe and fierce determination to hack at the soil around a waxy leafed bush.

Clare lifted her head and sighed. Then she

caught sight of him. Holding the pouch containing Glory's medicine, he walked into the sunny garden. Her smile seemed forced, and on closer inspection, her eyes were rimmed with fatigue.

"Fare you well, my lady?" he asked.

"Very well, and you, my lord?"

Why would she forswear her injury and not ask about Alasdair? When last she had seen the lad, he'd been distraught. Why was she unconcerned? Or was she angry at Drummond for staying away all night with their son?

Determined to find out, he moved closer, snapping off a leaf as he went. "The sorrel thrives." He sniffed the lemony smelling plant but didn't take his eyes from her.

"The plant's well rooted. I brought it from the abbey garden."

Still no mention of her son. "You've become a fine gardener."

Her gaze wavered and she went back to working the soil. "None of us here favors bland food. Did you know that the sheriff and Douglas are anxious to speak with you?"

Where was her vibrancy, her constant motion? Where was the kind concern he'd seen at table last night when Douglas spewed his venom?

"My lady," squealed Evelyn. "You've pulled up a basil."

"Oh, so I have. Here, you put it back."

He glanced at Evelyn. Her mouth was pinched with disdain. Their gazes met. Her expression grew intense, as if to say, *Do something!*

"Bother it, Evelyn," Clare said into the silent exchange. "It will not be the last time I mistake basil for thistle."

"You?" said Evelyn. "You know more about growing things than Glory, for all her misfitting ways."

Clare said, "For that flattery, you shall have an afternoon to yourself on Sunday next."

Her too cheery tone didn't fool Drummond. Why would she make light of her gardening skills? She seemed uncomfortable with the changes in herself. Why? The answers could wait; he was more concerned with verifying Sween's conviction that she was too ill to stand.

"My lady, I'm thirsty and rather toilworn," he said. "Will you fetch me a tankard of ale?"

"Evelyn, fetch Lord Drum—"

"Nay," he interrupted. If she were truly ill and too proud to show it, he'd make certain she did as the midwife had instructed her. "Unless you are unable. Did Glory not tell you to stay abed?"

The morning sun had cast a pink glow over her nose and cheeks, but she seemed indifferent to her appearance or the elements. She certainly had no inkling of how appealing and feminine she looked to him, or how confounding.

"Glory has her opinions," she said, flicking weeds out of the way. "I have mine. I suffered only a slight burn."

Evelyn huffed, then mockingly said, "My lady says she's fine as crimson silk, my lord. That's what she'd have of it."

He lifted his brows expectantly. "The ale, Clare?"

She glowered at him, her brown eyes darkening with anger. "For Evelyn's sake, I must decline."

The wind tossed her hair into her face. She lifted her right arm, but winced. Dropping the spade from her gloved left hand, she tucked the wayward strands behind her ear and left a smudge of dirt on her cheek.

Defiance lifted her chin. "Fetching and carrying is maid's work."

Determination rippled through him. "What happened to your hair?"

Again, Evelyn huffed. "As I'm an honest girl, my lord, I refused to braid it for her or tie her coif. Mistress Glory was insistent that my lady stay abed today."

"Bite your tongue, Evelyn," Clare snapped.

Drummond opened Glory's package and took out the vial.

Through tightly clenched teeth, Clare said, "I will not drink that drug."

He stepped closer. "Aye, you will, and you'll rest till Glory says otherwise."

She had to crane her neck to look up at him. "Be off, Drummond. Glory makes much of nothing. I fare well enough."

"You'll fare better off your feet and inside."

As if he were a nuisance, she sighed and held out her gloved hand. "If it will make you happy. Give it to me."

He did, and she dropped it into her basket.

He chuckled. " 'Twill make me happy if you drink it now."

Her hair again blew across her face. She turned into the wind, but the movement was slow and cautious. "I'll have it later with a slice of bread and cheese. Did I mention that cook is roasting a fat moorhen with chestnut pudding today?"

No query about Alasdair. Patience gone, Drummond planted his feet. "Clare, you will drink it or have it forced down your throat."

Eyes cool with retribution, she retrieved the vial. With a flick of her thumb, she sent the wax sealing cap flying into a bed of leeks. Then she held out her arm, twisted her wrist, and poured the brownish liquid over a patch of celery. Tossing the empty vial onto a pile of dried dung, she said, "You'll pour nothing down my throat, Drummond Macqueen, least of all that mind dulling swill."

Dumbfounded, he watched her pick up the spade and go back to the weeds again.

Evelyn mumbled something about the dire consequences of stubbornness.

"Find a chore elsewhere, Evelyn," he said.

That got Clare's attention. "You'll hoe that row of spotted beans, girl, or go back to your family. Drummond," she appealed, her mouth full and pouting and much too missish. "I'm perfectly capable of directing the staff. I have only a laggard's work to do here, and you surely have more im-

260

portant tasks, such as granting Red Douglas an audience."

Under different circumstances he might have welcomed her subtle display of sensuality. Tucking the memory away, he looked at Evelyn and tipped his head toward the keep.

The maid propped the hoe on her shoulder. "My lord, shall I warm the broth she refused?"

"I'll sup when everyone else does," came his wife's angry reply.

Drummond nodded. The maid marched out of the garden.

He held out his hand. "Come, Clare."

Perspiration dotted her brow, and her eyes looked dreamfilled. "I pray you, trouble yourself no more on my account, my lord. I do not wither as your bride did — as I did when I was your bride — as a bride would. Oh, bother it!"

Her befuddled speech convinced him. Vowing to make her come inside, he bent from the waist and touched her elbow. "Get up."

She cried out and jerked away. When she teetered, he scooped her into his arms, being careful not to touch the injured side of her body.

Her complexion looked ashen, and her eyes were dark with pain. "Clare?"

She buried her head against his shoulder, but said nothing. Through the fabric of his tunic, he could feel her hot, pained breathing. Her right hand was fisted so tightly between them that her knuckles gleamed white.

Her hair trailing over his arm and raking the

plants, he navigated the winding path out of the garden and carried her up the steps to the keep. He kicked open the door to his chamber and put her on the bed.

Blanketed and blinded by her hair, she tried to sit up.

He put his hand on her hip. "Be still."

"You're making too much of this," she said in a weary voice.

"Humor me." He began gathering her hair, which smelled of basil and savory and felt like silk in his hands. Strips of soft white cloth circled her neck, and on the right side, the skin looked puffy and red. A bandage there? But Glory said she'd injured her shoulder.

"It's really nothing."

"Then why does everyone from the farrier's apprentice to the goosegirl fear for your recovery?"

She peered up at him through the curtain of her hair. "Because the goosegirl is Glory's sister, and the apprentice worries overmuch."

When he'd managed to tame the mass of her hair, Drummond coiled it around his fingers. "What happened to you?"

She stared at his neck. "I thought to have some warm milk last night. The mulling iron slipped from my hand. The mug shattered. I made a mess of the hearth."

As if he cared about the condition of the hearth. "Look at me and tell me what you've done to yourself."

Her gaze moved to his chin. "A minor burn."

He didn't for a moment believe her. "Show me."

She shrank back and bit her lip to stifle the pain the movement caused. After a few deep breaths, she said, "Glory tended it, and she doesn't take well to having her handiwork disturbed."

Undeterred, he tugged on her hair until she again lay back on the mattress. "I want to see what you've done."

She stared at the tapestry on the wall. "Then I'll be certain to summon you when she changes the dressing. Truly, Drummond, I'll mend." She shook her left hand until the glove slipped off. Covering her mouth, she faked a yawn. "Perhaps I *will* rest awhile."

He didn't believe that, either, but he had her on her back and out of the sun. "You didn't ask about Alasdair."

In the blink of an eye she went from laconic to alert. "Oh, Drummond. Did he misunderstand the explanation of your imprisonment? You failed to reassure him?"

Drummond couldn't help smiling. "*I* assured him. Longfellow ate him for breakfast."

A chagrined smile curved her lips, but her eyelids dropped. "And I'm a Venetian moneylender."

He'd made that facetious declaration on the day of his arrival at Fairhope. He had seen her cry at the mention of her friend Johanna. She'd denied shedding a tear because she missed the woman.

He lifted a brow in recognition of her cleverness. "Rest."

She closed her eyes. "Where is Alasdair now?"

"Strutting in the lane and bragging about his adventure."

"Bring him to me."

She sounded so queenly, he was compelled to say, "As your lord and master, shall I *command* thee to rest?"

"No. As your wife and the mother of your heir, I shall be bound to refuse."

He sensed a new confidence in the way she said the words "your wife." "Why?"

Turning her head away from him, she murmured sleepily, "He needs a bath and his hair scrubbed." She cuddled her cheek against the bed linen. "And lessons."

Drummond smiled at her kittenlike movement. "I'll see to it."

She drifted off, her lips slightly parted, her arm still resting between her breasts. She hadn't needed the sleeping potion.

Moving a bench from beneath the windows, Drummond sat and watched her slumber. In repose, she looked like an angel, her hair a halo and her mouth curled in a saintly smile. But he knew the earthy passion her mouth could inspire.

He remembered the first time he'd seen Clare, the blessed, as they called her. In physical appearance, she'd been perfectly chosen for a Scottish chieftain, for her fair hair and elegant features were easily mistaken for Highland nobility. Some of his clansmen doubted the old king's sly assertion that she came from good Lancaster stock. Among themselves, his kinsmen compared her stately good looks to the Scotswomen of the royal House of Dunkeld. But that was only clan talk; all of the Dunkeld offspring were accounted for, save the mythical twin daughters of Alexander III, and even the expert spies of Edward I could not have located a progeny that existed only in fable.

Drummond thought of the tales she'd invented about him, flattering tales, exciting tales, tales designed to foster legend. Then he thought of her great sin.

Anguish seeped into his soul. Better that he'd lost his sword arm than suffer a faithless wife, especially one who'd lain with the son of the "Hammer of the Scots."

Some Highlanders compared Drummond's marital misfortune to that of Llewlyn Fawr. But the great prince of Wales had wed Siubhan, a king's daughter. Those same gossipers said the princess's faithlessness stemmed from her father's carousing and her own illegitimate birth.

Nothing was known of Clare's lineage, except the obvious: Her parents had been bonny well favored. Unknown misfortune had left her in the care of the Crown. Her family's poverty had become the Macqueen's providence, for she'd come bearing a dowry of peace between England and Scotland.

Even after placing her hand in Drummond's, old King Edward had said no more about her.

And like a buck primed for the rut, the newly wedded Drummond had been more interested in mounting his doe than quizzing the king on her bloodlines. The humor was, Drummond had planted his seed and, through her, secured his own bloodline. Alasdair stood as indisputable proof of that.

Look for trouble, and you'll find it. Against his will he was beginning to admire her. To counter the weakness, he sought out her faults.

As he watched her now, sleeping as peacefully as the angels she resembled, he wondered if she had confessed her sin and received absolution. Had Brother Julian been the one to carry her transgression to God?

Drummond cringed inside at the thought of anyone in Fairhope knowing that she'd made him a cuckold. But surely they did not know, for these people loved and cherished her. From the moment Drummond and Alasdair had entered the gates this morning, they had been inundated with the news of her injury. Worry wreathed the faces of the villagers and huntsmen, and en masse they'd begged him to command her to have a care for herself and follow Glory's advice. Only the approach of an eager and trumpeting Longfellow had swayed them from going directly to her.

Bertie Stapledon's reaction had been most puzzling, for he had stared accusingly at Drummond, as if to say her injury was his fault. Before Drummond could question the man's motives, Alasdair had dashed off toward the kitchen garden in search of her. Sween ran the lad to ground and deposited him with Bertie.

"It's a man's task you've ahead of you, my lord," Sween had said, his soldierlike demeanor comical with exasperation.

And so it had been, Drummond reflected, still watching her. But why? No one in Fairhope would think her slothful for time spent recuperating from what they called a perilous injury. According to Sween, since after matins she had listened to a steady stream of lectures and queries before escaping to the kitchen garden and declaring it off limits to all save Evelyn.

Perhaps Clare's stubbornness stemmed from concern for Alasdair. She probably expected the lad to fret insufferably over her when he heard about her injury. What would the lad do when he saw her?

Drummond found out half an hour later, when Alasdair entered the room, a garland of flowers dangling from his wrist and a pewter mug in his hand.

"Evelyn said you should make Mother drink this broth."

"Shush!" Drummond held up his hand.

Looking as forlorn as the first spring lamb, the lad peered at his mother. Drummond's heart went out to his son, and he patted his own thigh. Alasdair sat down.

Taking the mug, Drummond set it beside him

on the bench, then leaned close to his son. "She's resting well, but you must be very quiet."

Alasdair nodded so vigorously, he teetered on Drummond's knee. Steadying him, Drummond pictured the three of them through a stranger's eyes. He saw a father and son sitting vigil at the bedside of the woman they both needed and loved. He saw a family enduring one of life's misfortunes. Sadly, he wondered if he, an exiled Scot, were destined to always want a family of his own.

"Father, I'm afraid."

Drummond hugged his son. The lad smelled of the forest, and he trembled with fear. "She's on the mend," Drummond whispered.

"God won't take her to the angels?"

"Nay. She said so herself."

Leaning back, he dashed away tears. "You swear?"

"As I'm a Macqueen."

Alasdair sagged, so great was his relief. "I wanted to give her this."

They had gathered the wildflowers during their return to Fairhope this morning. Drummond had helped him fashion the chaplet. "You may, when she awakens. But we must not disturb her now."

"What if she doesn't wake up until tomorrow?" he asked, eyes wide with confusion.

She was sleeping soundly, and Drummond intended to see that she continued to do so. "Then she will have enjoyed a good night's rest."

The lad stared at her and sighed. "She's very beautiful, isn't she?"

"Aye."

"Will my sister look like her?"

Clare's words echoed in Drummond's ears. *He'll ask you dozens of questions. You'll lose your patience and hurt his feelings.*

A good parent. Softly, Drummond said, "Of course she will. Bide quietly with me now, and later you can go with Morgan when he takes Longfellow to the burn."

The request proved an impossibility, and when Alasdair began to squirm, Drummond excused him.

Alasdair cupped his hands around his mouth and moved close to Drummond's ear. In a wet and loud whisper, he said, "I'll come back after sword practice."

Wincing, Drummond waved the lad out the door. Then he touched her cheek to see if she'd fevered. Her skin was cool to the touch.

Relieved and unable to resist the lure of her hair, he stroked the thick mane, delighting in the silky texture and smelling the odd aroma of kitchen herbs.

The wall of disdain he'd erected between them began to crumble, as it had every time he kissed her or they shared a companionable moment. He imagined himself cradling her head and spooning a nourishing broth past her lips. He saw himself as the lovestruck husband blustering orders to the servants and demanding that Glory heal his wife or suffer the consequences. He pictured her on the mend and imagined himself lying beside her, holding her and murmuring words of comfort. In return for his devotion, she declared her love and said she would have no other but him.

No other. Except a prince cum king.

Drummond couldn't want her now, not for more than obvious and base reasons. He understood his physical craving for her; Clare possessed beauty enough to ignite his desire. Baffling were the unexpected ways that she pleased him. He could not deny that he enjoyed her sharp wit and her ready sense of humor; neither could he spurn her forthright manner and her integrity.

Bother her admirable traits, he grumbled to himself, and vowed he would not share her bed until he'd observed her with her old lover.

In October, he would take her to Douglas's in Dumfries and present her to the visiting Edward Plantagenet. If the new king had been telling the truth about his continued liaisons with Clare, Drummond would surely know. If she acted with decorum and proved to him that Edward II had lied, Drummond would consider forgiving her. If his suspicions proved valid, and she showed too much favor to her old lover, Drummond would suffer the moment. Then, when everyone else slept, he'd take Alasdair and make for the Highlands. Morgan and Longfellow would travel north at their own pace.

If Edward the King followed, he risked striking the battle anew with Scotland. Drummond gambled that the newly crowned king would avoid the conflict, for he had neither the treasury to finance another siege of Scotland nor his father's loyalty from the troops. The Highlanders, however, after learning of Drummond's treatment at the hands of the English, would crave revenge.

Anticipating the bloody battles that would result, Drummond shifted on the bench. The wooden legs squeaked loudly.

Her eyes drifted open. She'd ever been slow to awaken.

Her gaze focused on him. "It's bad luck to watch a woman whilst she sleeps."

"Your friend Meridene used to say that."

"She's a superstitious Scot."

Delivered without rancor, the remark inspired a friendly reply. Striking up conversations, he was beginning to realize, came as easily to her as nurturing a garden. "We're not all beholden to our fears."

She looked fatigued but not muddled. "What are you beholden to, Drummond?"

Considering he'd been contemplating the possibility of another war between England and Scotland, Drummond steered his thoughts to her. "I'm beholden to getting you well, so your son will stop mewling like a lost kitten, as Sween would have of it."

She smiled, but her eyes radiated little humor. "Now that he's a nuisance, he's *my* son. When he behaves, he's a branch off the mighty tree of the Macqueens."

Ready humor. Quick wit. Faithless wife. Damn her for remembering his every word and making him glad he'd said each one. Damn him for bringing her into this room; she looked too appealing in his bed. "Aye, and I wonder how you tolerate him once each month, when your menses send you to bed."

Her mouth rounded in surprise; but then she relaxed. "I told you, I no longer suffer as I did."

He had not listened, and now, shocked, he scanned her slender and very womanly form. "You've lost the ability to bear more children?"

She turned away, murmuring, "No. It's just another blessing from Alasdair's birth. I'm well-suited to motherhood."

Again sleep claimed her.

When next Johanna awakened, the sun was low in the sky and Drummond sat on a bench beside her bed. He picked leaves from her hair. She squeezed her eyes shut so he would think she still slept.

Her shoulder throbbed mercilessly, as if the blacksmith were flaring it with a hot mace. She had expected to feel pain, but not this bone deep ache. On reflection her plan had been faulty from the start. The hall had been too dark. The iron had been too hot. The pain — just thinking about it brought a return of the agony, and she could not stifle a moan.

Something touched her lips.

"Drink," came Drummond's soft, commanding voice.

The moment a drop of Glory's musky tasting brew touched Johanna's tongue, she drew back. A tearing sensation ripped through her shoulder, and pain shot up the side of her neck. Blackness narrowed her vision and her head went light.

"Clare?"

Through a tunnel of pain, Johanna heard her sister's name. She was alive, for no one in the hereafter would call her Clare. "No potions. Water."

"You're in pain."

She forced her eyes open and saw beguiling blue eyes. The insistent set of his mouth promised a battle.

Again the vial touched her lips. "Drink it."

She had seen what the drug could do, even to a grown man; last year it had turned John Handle into a babbling penitent. He'd confessed to every misdeed from stealing quinces as a lad to taking pleasure in seeing his wife naked. Johanna Benison had far more sinful secrets, and she intended to keep them.

She pressed her lips together and willed the pain away. When it receded enough, she said, "Water, please, Drummond. I'm fair parched."

He hesitated, his gaze raking her face, looking for the truth. If she so much as flinched, he'd scour deeper, and heaven help her, she hadn't the strength to hold on to her secrets for long. Reaching within herself, she found the will to

273

return his probing gaze.

She saw a man who'd dropped his barriers, and beneath the bold and handsome exterior she spied a worried and wounded soul. She saw a man who'd lived for seven years in a cell with no one to call his name in friendship or seek his counsel in need. She saw a man beset by miseries too great for a single heart to bear. Could she convince him she would share the burden? If love were the means, she surely would succeed.

Her vision grew blurry with tears and she reached for him.

Her shoulder screamed in pain. He flinched, but whether from surprise at her outcry or in defense of her intrusion, she did not know. Like a cloud moving over the moon, the moment of discovery passed and Johanna was left with a feeling of emptiness and a throbbing pain.

Aching, she watched him cap the vial and produce a pewter mug. Using her left arm, she levered herself up enough to drink. He held the mug to her lips but stared at the garden glove she'd discarded earlier. The metal felt as cool as his mood had become.

But he had the right to conceal his emotions from her, just as she had the option of pursuing him again, and she would. She intended to make a life with this man, and now she could begin the campaign for his affection. The telltale brand was gone. She was his wife and bound to appease his physical needs.

She had almost emptied the mug of broth before

rational thought returned and she realized the consequences of taking so much liquid. In the next instant, she felt the need to relieve herself.

Lifting her chin, she let him know that she'd had enough. He reached across her and slipped a hand around her back, then eased her onto the mattress.

His face was inches away from hers. He smelled of woodsmoke and a night in the forest. "You've a gentleness about you, Drummond Macqueen."

He pulled his arm free and took his time putting the tankard on the floor. "You're injured."

She took a risk, hoping he would warm to her again. "Some hurts are not so obvious, are they?"

Like slamming shutters before a storm, he covered his vulnerability. "Or so easily healed."

Striving for congeniality, she said, "What is that I smell?"

"Basil and . . ." He brought a handful of her hair to his nose and sniffed. "Chervil. There's a nest of it in your hair."

She'd pretended ignorance in the garden when he noted her skill with plants. She had even uprooted a basil to prove it, but thanks to Evelyn's tart mouth, Johanna's attempt to emulate her sister had gone awry.

"How long did you think you could keep the truth from me?"

Johanna's heart sank. He knew. Just when she'd found the courage to obliterate the last evidence of her true self. But she would gladly suffer the same pain again, if it meant she could tell him the truth and hear her own name spoken softly by this man who tried to conceal kindness and vulnerability behind a warrior's veneer.

"Clare?"

Her fear eased at the sound of her sister's name. Even as she relaxed, Johanna knew that one day she must tell him the truth. But not yet. She couldn't take that chance until she'd captured his heart.

"How long did you intend to keep the truth from me?" he repeated.

Grappling for an answer that would appease him, she chose an equally general reply. "As long as I could."

"Why?"

"It was a foolish accident."

His guarded expression softened. "And you dislike acting foolish?"

"Immensely so."

His gaze flicked to her shoulder. "What happened?"

"I was clumsy and careless with the new mulling iron."

"You?" He mimicked Evelyn's border drawl.

"I may be different, Drummond, but I haven't lost my pride."

A rueful grin gave him a rakish air. "Nay, you've trebled it and your stubbornness, too. Why else would you disregard the danger of putrefaction?"

Fatigue dragged at her, but they were conversing easily on a moderately safe topic. "You haven't actually spoken with Glory, else you'd know she's confident my wound will not fester."

One side of his mouth tipped up. "I haven't actually ever set eyes on the elusive Glory. As Sween would have of it," he mocked the huntsman's local speech. "The lass flits about like a new midge on a fresh pile of dung."

"Then call up the trumpeters," said a familiar and compelling voice from the door. "It seems His Majesty Sween Handle has admitted to thinking like the royal insect he is."

Drummond turned toward the door. As Johanna expected, his eyes grew wide in surprise at his first glimpse of the unusual Glory Roade.

Chapter
13

As always, Johanna enjoyed seeing a stranger's first look at Glory. In defiance of custom, the healer kept her wavy chestnut hair sheared shorter than that of most men. Unlike *any* man she was as lithe as a doe in an open meadow. It was often said that if Brother Julian tended the souls of Fairhope, the twenty-six-year-old Glory tended their bodies and tried their Christian patience.

Openly beholden to no one, the outspoken woman had smokey gray eyes and pale skin. Her upturned nose and high cheekbones were dusted with freckles. Today she wore forest green trunk hose and an ankle-length overdress slit up the sides and embroidered with overlapping rainbows. The nail on her right index finger was inordinately long. For poking it where she ought not, Sween liked to say. Draped over her arm was one of Johanna's favorite bliauds, and slung over her shoulder was a leather pouch bulging with the tools of her trade.

Glory was independent, forthright, and deeply in love with Sween Handle.

She glanced at Johanna's reclining form, nodded approvingly, then in graceful strides, marched up to Drummond. He sprang to his feet and studied her from head to slippers.

"Disapproving of me, are you?" Glory shrugged. "Take yourself off then, so the sight of a woman in trews doesn't bruise your manly pride."

Drummond folded his arms over his chest and shifted his weight to one leg. " 'Twasn't my pride, lass, but surprise that you would so casually order your betters about."

Johanna winced, for the unsuspecting Drummond had fallen into Glory's favorite verbal trap.

"Think you, you are better than me?" She bowed from the waist. "Please allow me to introduce myself. I'm Glory Roade, a woman of wealth and taste."

Some men were angered, others appalled at her boldness. To his credit, Drummond appeared intrigued. "I wish neither to eat you, nor to take your purse, Mistress Glory."

Taken aback, the normally redoubtable Glory examined her one long fingernail. A moment later, she glanced up. "What *do* you want?"

Drummond burst out laughing. "Sween was right about you."

Her lips thinned. "Sween has never once" — she held up the elongated fingernail — "in his meaningless life been correct."

Wiping a tear of mirth from his eye, Drummond said, "I beg to differ. He said you were the only woman in Christendom for him, and 'twas his penance that God put you here."

Like a spider on a newly trapped beetle, she pounced. "Pray tell me where on your chart lies Christendom? Is it located in the bloated bellies of hungry babes? In the blackened eyes of Maggie Singer?"

Turning, Drummond faced Johanna, a curious expression lifting his brows. She felt bound to say, "Continue at your own peril, my lord. She will defend all women against the evils of men, and she seldom loses."

His features grew serene with confidence, and he addressed Glory again. "The hungry are soon fed and the guilty punished."

She lifted her arms. "And praise be to your God for that?"

"God answers the prayers of man."

"Man." Glory nodded, but Johanna knew that her compliance portended greater insult. "What makes men better than women that God should speak directly to them? Speak you a different tongue, you and God?"

" 'Twas meant in the broadest sense," he grumbled. "You must concede that God favors man. He created him first."

"And made a poor job of it, so he corrected his error." She planted her hands on her hips. "You see before you his perfection: woman."

"He gave man greater strength."

280

"Indeed." She grew contemplative, a posture that usually sent men running for the safety of a malleable female or a fair measure of spirits. "So you can wield your sword and slap each other's backs in celebration of your blessed camaraderie?"

"God made man for a higher purpose."

"Higher purpose, you say. Let us review your lofty callings." Using her long nail, she tapped the index finger on her opposite hand. "You cannot give birth." She tapped her middle finger. "You cannot survive the evening without four pints of ale." In a wilting pose, she brought the back of her hand to her forehead. "You cannot abide a soiled nappy or the travail of the birthing chair."

Angry, but disguising it well, Drummond said, "What can *you* abide, Mistress Glory?"

Her mission accomplished, Glory now soothed her wounded prey. "How gracious of you to inquire," she purred. "I can abide a day without looking into the dung-ugly face of Sween Handle."

Somewhat mollified, Drummond resumed his casual pose. "Do you speak this way to him?"

"I do not speak to Sween at all, if I can prevent it. His thinking is as skewed as the speech of your Welshman is garbled. A fall at birth, I should think. Will you oblige me by banishing him to Norway?"

"I will oblige you as you oblige me, Mistress Glory. My name is Drummond Macqueen, lord of this domain and protector of this injured woman, whom we seem to have carelessly forgotten."

At his sensible and polite answer, her face went blank. The calmness only accentuated her earthy beauty. "A win to you, my lord," she conceded amiably. "If you will excuse us, I'll tend my lady."

"After you challenged my manhood?" He laughed, but more at himself than her. "Nay, Glory. I'll stay and offer what assistance a feeble man may."

Glory's mouth twitched with humor, revealing what Sween called the devil's own dimples. "You succeeded in getting her to bed, my lord. Hardly feeble work in any man's guild. With luck you may rejoin her in it in a fortnight."

Outraged, Johanna yelled, "Glory!"

"Perhaps a sennight," she revised, and sat on the edge of the bed. "At least her sensibilities are rallying."

Either Drummond hadn't heard or did not care, probably the latter, thought Johanna, for he stared at the small pouch he'd had in the garden.

"How fare you, my lady?" Glory asked. "You did not take the sleeping potion."

Johanna swallowed. "Nor will I."

"Mind-dulling swill, she called it," Drummond said to Glory, and pitched the pouch onto the bed.

Glory shrugged and helped Johanna to sit up. Lying down had offered a respite from the pain, but now it returned with a vengeance. Drummond stepped forward to offer his assistance, but too late.

"I altered your dress." Glory held up the garment. The right sleeve and the neckline of the bodice had been removed, the side now closed with laces. The dress design would easily facilitate tending the wound.

"How clever," Johanna said, wishing she were wearing it now so she wouldn't have to bare herself to the waist before Drummond. As her husband he'd have to abide a scarred wife. Better he see only the result.

"I'll help." He reached for the fastenings on Johanna's surcoat.

"Really, my lord. Glory and I can manage."

For reply, he gave her a bland stare.

Forced to move or challenge him, Glory scooted to the foot of the bed and began taking medicinals from her pouch and arranging the salves and bandages on the bed. Drummond took her place near Johanna.

Grinning, he said, "Tending the sick might be my higher calling. Think you I should trade my sword for a healer's pouch?"

With his winsome ways, he had even disarmed the formidable Glory, who huffed halfheartedly in response. In spite of herself and the situation, Johanna smiled.

"You *are* on the mend," he said.

Disarmed better suited her feelings at the moment, for when he chose, Drummond Macqueen could charm the whitewash from the walls. How

283

much stronger could her love for him grow? Considering Clare's romantic descriptions of the private moment they had shared as man and wife, Johanna both feared and longed for the intimacies to come.

"I'll be very careful, Clare." His hands were deft in their movements, probably from so much practice undressing his former mistresses, Johanna thought peevishly.

"You're frowning," he said, all attentiveness. "Is the pain suddenly worse?"

Which pain and from what source? She had a variety to choose from: jealousy over his penchant for mistresses, regret from the past, and doubt about the future. Better she address the simplest ache. "My shoulder is better now."

Seemingly satisfied, he unfastened her surcoat, taking great care to avoid her injury. His fingers felt feather-light on the closure of her bliaud, and she couldn't help wishing that his insistence and tenderness stemmed from affection for her rather than duty. *Lord of this domain and protector of this injured woman.*

Only on her fanciful days had Johanna wished for a man to help ease her burden of responsibility, fill her lonely moments, and give her a keep full of children. If she were lucky, Drummond would grant her one of the three, for she could not picture him as helpmate and comforter. Even at the risk of suffering greater heartache, she must try to build a life with him. But not until she'd recovered.

"Now, let us see what havoc you've wreaked."

Alarmed again, Johanna grew desperate. Over his bowed head, she glared at Glory, who frowned in confusion. Johanna shot a pointed glance at him, then willed Glory to help her get him to leave the room.

Glory blinked in understanding. "My lord," she said, still fishing through the contents of her pouch. "Before you remove that dressing, will you ask Evelyn to fetch hot water and cold?"

He had loosened Johanna's underdress and reached for the placket to ease the garment off her shoulders. He paused and shot them a look that indicated he knew they were conspiring to get rid of him, but he went.

The moment he disappeared into the hallway, Johanna said, "Help me into that dress, Glory, and quickly."

The midwife paused, a roll of clean cloth in her hand. "Why do you shy from him? He doesn't seem the sort to go green at the sight of injury."

"I have my reasons."

"I believe he's truly concerned. More than Sween would be should I lie injured."

Drummond was concerned, but only out of curiosity. Sween Handle was Glory's business.

"My lady?"

Johanna didn't reply, but peeled off her clothing herself; she'd learned years ago that the best way to deal with Glory was not to try. Just as she stepped into the newly altered dress, she heard Drummond in the stairway passing on the request for water to Evelyn.

Biting her lip to stave off the pain, Johanna held the garment in place with her injured right arm and threaded her left through the sleeve. She had to work the dress up over her hips. The gown had been altered in other ways.

"What have you done to my dress?"

Glory's eyes glittered with mischief. "A tuck here, a smaller one there. You have Lord Drummond's pleasure to consider. It's obvious he finds you beautiful, why not give him more to admire?"

Now that Drummond had returned to Fairhope, Glory probably expected Johanna to commiserate on the intimate side of marriage; the women often talked among themselves on personal matters. Johanna had always avoided the discussions. She could not speak knowledgeably when she knew only the rudiments of the subject. "Why indeed? At the moment I hardly feel like enticing him." That much was certainly true.

"You admit that you should have stayed abed?"

She did feel better since coming inside, so Johanna gave Glory the answer she wanted. "Yes, and you were correct. I cannot use my arm. It's too sore. Will you please help me!"

Her objective met, Glory laced up the dress, but not too snugly. "Do you promise to rest?"

Listening for Drummond's return, Johanna said, "I promise." But her agreement came too late, for he stood in the doorway, his gaze moving from her waist to her naked right arm and settling on the trail of bandages that began at her shoulder, wound beneath her right arm, partially covered her right breast, and circled her neck.

Glory produced shears from her pouch, and with her mouth set in concentration, she cut away the old dress. The shears felt cold against Johanna's skin, and she shivered, both at the hard touch of the metal and the cold dread about what Drummond would say.

"My lord," Johanna interjected, using her good arm to hold the now loosened bandage in place. "Glory is capable — more cable than the king's own physician."

Disregarding her, he crossed the room and reached for her wrist. "I want to see what you've done to yourself."

"Oh, very well, but it looks worse than it is." She waited until he released her wrist; then she peeled back the dressing.

He winced and his gaze fled to hers. "By the saints, Clare. I've seen men suffer lesser wounds and claim debility for weeks and more. You've hurt yourself badly."

If she hadn't lost her grip on the iron the moment it touched her skin, the wound would have been the size of her palm, as she had planned. But the wayward iron had fallen back to her shoulder and rolled toward her neck, searing a patch of skin larger than her hand.

Glory peered over Drummond's shoulder. "The salve has brought down the swelling."

"Brought it down?" he asked, engrossed in the wound. " 'Twas worse?"

"Yes. My lady swooned," Glory said. "Bertie found her in a heap near the hearth. Her shoulder is tender from the fall, which is why she favors her right arm."

His gaze captured Johanna's. "What were you doing swinging a hot mulling iron over your shoulder?"

Did he doubt her story? She hadn't considered that he would ask for a detailed explanation. Finding the courage to carry out the deed itself had taxed her no end. He couldn't know how long she had grappled with the decision. The harm was done. She must go forward from here. "I was not swinging it over my shoulder. 'Twas an accident." From which he would also benefit, for she could now truly become his wife and hopefully fulfill his wish for more sons.

His mouth pulled into a tight line, his eyes brimming with regret, he shook his head. "We'll discuss your accident at another time."

"Why?"

"You've obliterated the old brand on your shoulder. One might wonder if you did it on purpose — to obscure the mark."

Over the pounding of her heart, Johanna heard Glory gasp.

"Mark?" said the midwife. "What mark?"

Battling back fear and pain, Johanna struggled to keep her voice even. "The mark is my affair, Drummond. I had forgotten it."

His gaze turned steely, and she had the distinct impression that he did not believe her.

"You've left me no choice in the matter, have you?" he said. When she made no reply, he continued. "You're to stay in this bed until Glory gives you leave to move about the keep."

She'd willingly chain herself to the floor if only he would take himself elsewhere. Discretion gave way to exhaustion. Later she would contrive a plausible explanation for the mishap. "I promise."

"I'll bring Alasdair to see you tomorrow." Then he did the unexpected, he kissed her forehead and gave her hand a gentle squeeze. To Glory he said, "Have you everything you need, Mistress?"

"More, if you count the unwelcome presence of Sween Handle in my life."

Looking distracted, he rose. "Heal my lady, and I shall oblige you by sending him away."

"What?" Glory's mouth fell open and she almost lurched at Drummond. "When? To where will he go?"

"You do not wish him to leave?"

Glory started, then tossed her head. "Of course I wish him gone. He's another canker on the pocked face of man."

Drummond turned to Johanna. "After I meet with Red Douglas, I'm off to Eastward Fork. The tanner's son wants to try his hand at farming, so we'll be moving him to the Singer place and the Singers into his house here."

Guilt compounded Johanna's misery. Moments before she had judged him a poor helpmate, and now he was taking up her causes and assuming her responsibilities. "Thank you," was all she could manage.

He looked at her strangely, his bearing suddenly rigid. "I need no thanks for carrying out my duties, especially when I doubt you will approve of all the changes I intend to make."

On that cryptic statement, he exited the room, leaving Johanna to wonder what he meant.

A week later, alone atop the keep's battlement, Drummond still wondered if she had spoken the truth about the accident. Time and again he had pictured the motions involved in plunging a hot mulling rod into a tankard to warm the contents. How could the iron have touched her shoulder when the motions were downward in direction? Logic told him she had lied. But why and how had the mishap occurred? Or had it been a mishap?

The "why" especially troubled him. If she were now ashamed of the mark, that would account for the discrepancy in her explanation; yet his wife hadn't possessed the courage to maim herself. Few people would go to such extremes, and she had been proud of her beauty. But as she had so often reminded him of late, she was not the same Clare he'd married.

Thinking perhaps the brand had turned ugly with age, as some scars did, he had casually questioned Evelyn. To his surprise, she had never helped Clare dress or assisted with her bath. Queries to Alasdair about their summer swims had yielded no information on the brand. Odd as it seemed, the two people closest to her had no knowledge of the unusual mark on his wife's shoulder. The day he'd seen her naked in the pantry and almost made love to her on a barrel, he had not seen the mark. She'd covered it with a towel, and when he had tried to move the cloth aside, she'd held it tightly. Why? She always wore concealing clothing. She bathed alone. She dressed herself.

Dressed. *The dressmaker.*

Drummond applauded himself, for he'd discovered the one person who would have knowledge of his wife's body.

Except Edward Plantagenet, his pride protested. Drummond rejected the thought, for he had no proof of her continued infidelity save the king's word. But in less than a month, when they traveled to Dumfries, Drummond would know.

Pray she told the truth, his heart cried, for with each passing day, he found something new to admire about her.

Still, the mystery of the accident niggled at him. But now he had a plan, and although he'd never pictured himself visiting a dressmaker, he relished the prospect.

For seven years he'd been deprived of honest companionship and intelligent conversation, and he felt starved for the camaraderie Glory had damned. Yet he found the healer interesting and wondered what had brought her and Sween to such a romantic blockade.

In some ways Drummond felt blessed to abide among people with more on their minds than torturing and hanging. None of these people called him an animal and cursed his ancestors for cave dwelling creatures.

Suddenly hungry for a slice of the rare beef the cook had served earlier in honor of the overlord's and the the sheriff's departure, Drummond made his way down the stairs and walked softly past Sween, who slept soundly on a pallet near the hearth.

In the pantry Drummond found the plate of meat wrapped in a cloth. He poured himself a mug of cider and took a long pull of the sweet juice. Just as he rewrapped the roast and returned it to the platter, he heard a soft gasp behind him.

His wife stood in the doorway. Beneath a modest shawl, she wore a flowing white gown, and the rope of her braided hair lay over her shoulder and dangled at her waist. The faint light from the hearth behind her was too dim to shine through the fabric, but from past experiences, he knew well her feminine form. In this very room he had pulled her from a bath and held her on his lap. His fingers itched to trace the tapered curve of her waist, and he remembered vividly the contours of her breasts, the texture of her pert nipples, and the taste of her skin. He thought of the brand, gone now.

"I thought you were abed," she said.

Since her injury, Drummond had moved his pallet into the hall. As tonight, Sween often joined him. But Drummond seldom slept there for more than an hour at a time. He liked the freedom of the battlement and the solitude and safety of the keep at night.

He held up the slice of beef. "Would you care to join me?"

"Hum, yes." She crossed the small room, leaving the door open. "The beef was the best we've had all year, thanks to Red Douglas. Do you like him?"

"Well enough, and we'll soon have our own cattle."

"Have you decided when to send Sween to Spain?"

"Aye, he'll leave on Sunday."

"Does Glory know?"

"He told her after Vespers."

The light was faint, but he could discern Clare's smile. "I wish I'd been a flea in the rushes during that discussion," she said, spreading a cloth over a waist-high barrel.

When she reached for the platter, Drummond stopped her. "Let me, Clare." He put it on the barrel.

"You needn't coddle me, Drummond. I'm truly mended, and there's little meat left on the bone."

That was true, for everyone, even Alasdair, had asked for a second portion, and the once sizable haunch of meat would now provide them with only a light repast. She could easily have lifted the platter, but Drummond rather enjoyed seeing her assert herself, even though he always prevailed. She had been agreeable and pleasant. Too much so to Drummond's way of thinking. What was she about?

They had just begun to eat when a feminine yet compelling voice whispered, "Sween! Wake up."

He recognized Glory's husky tones.

"Shush." Drummond stepped lightly to the door and went down on one knee. Through the arch of the open hearth, he could see into the hall. Glory knelt beside Sween's pallet and jostled his arm.

The huntsman stirred and sat up. "What do you here, woman?"

She spoke so softly, Drummond couldn't make out the words, but he couldn't mistake the question in her voice.

Sween looked around. "He must be sleeping on the battlement."

"Or with his woman," Glory said. "Which is where you should be."

Rubbing the sleep from his face, the huntsman stood. Drummond took his wife's hand and pulled her with him behind the door that opened into the pantry. He flattened himself against the wall with her beside him, just as Sween moved into the kitchen. Pewter clanged, liquid sloshed.

"Will you share your ale with me?" Glory said.

"Nay," Sween growled.

"Why not?"

"When last I saw you, you called me a dung-ugly monster and cursed me to Spanish hell."

"I meant it not, Sween. I was angry, as you often are with me."

Drummond leaned close and whispered in Clare's ear. "Know you how to play at being a flea in the rushes?"

She buried her face in his chest to smother a giggle. He wrapped an arm around her, but loosely, still concerned about her injured shoulder. Holding her and snickering like wayward children felt natural, and the joy he found in the moment overrode any guilt he felt at eavesdropping.

"I have just cause to be angry, Glory. Stop that!"

Glory fairly purred. "You lay with Mary Heckley and gave her a stillborn babe."

"There's none to say the babe was mine. Everyone took their pleasure of Mary."

"Everyone laughed at me." Her voice was thick with tears. "I was ten and five, Sween, and I thought you loved me. But you went to her."

"So you went to another man."

"I felt unwanted. But not now."

"What are you doing?"

Clare had grown still against Drummond, and he knew that she was comparing her circumstances to Glory's. He wanted to soothe her but couldn't bring himself to offer comfort. She had willingly lain with another man. Even when confronted, she had not denied her sin. Look for trouble and you'll find it. He'd look for trouble in Dumfries; then he would know what to do about his wife and his future.

"Kiss me, Sween."

In the ensuing silence, Drummond tried and failed to marshall his randy body. Tucked against his side, his wife was also affected, for her breathing grew labored and she pressed closer.

"Stop just there, girl," Sween said, but the command held little authority. "Someone could come upon us."

"They're all abed. You like my breasts. I know you do."

"What have you done to your nipples?"

"I stained them with berry juice. Will you have a taste?"

"Glory, if you take off those trews I'll do more than fondle you, and you'll be sorry tomorrow."

The rustling of clothing told an erotic tale. "I'm sorry now, Sween, and I want you. Touch me here. And here."

A manly groan vibrated on the still air and settled in Drummond's groin.

Glory sighed. "Oh, yes, Sween."

Christ.

"You've the body of an angel."

"Then be my devil, Sween. You cannot deny that you want me. The proof swells in my hand."

"You'll have my seed in your palm, too, do you keep that up."

"Hum. I want to kiss you there and take you into my mouth."

Clare gasped, but the sound was muffled against

Drummond's chest.

"By the saints, no!"

"Shush! Can you not be a man about this?"

"Not with so much woman in my arms."

"Your woman?"

In a groan rife with surrender, Sween said, "My woman."

They were kissing again or moving on to more intimate pleasures, and imagining the reasons for their sighs and moans proved a powerful aphrodisiac to Drummond. Seeking a diversion from the lustful torment, he wondered what his wife was thinking.

Since her accident, she'd been agreeable, even cheerful, as if she'd made a decision and was greatly pleased with herself. Upon questioning she had said, "I've decided to follow your advice and Glory's. If you are calling me to task for it, I shall resume my duties."

She had been complimentary of his plan to grow oats and millet in the field she'd sacrificed to Red Douglas. She had applauded Drummond's idea of harvesting the nuts and selling them to the swineherds to fatten up their stock rather than letting the beasts forage at will in the forest.

"The children can participate in the harvest and earn a penny of their own."

She had dubbed the next Friday Foraging Day and set Evelyn and Bertie to passing the word through the village: All were invited, especially the children.

Sween grunted and Glory moaned, and they

panted as if they were running uphill. Were they actually coupling on the kitchen floor? Driven to know, Drummond peered through the crack between the door's leather hinges. And held his breath, for Sween leaned against the wall, a naked Glory standing before him, her hand wrist deep in his trunk hose.

His face a grimace of either pain or pleasure, Sween grasped her upper arms and set her away from him. "Get your clothes, Glory."

"Where are we going?"

"To the buttery."

"Will you take me with you to Spain?" Looking like a wood nymph, Glory crouched before him. "Please."

"Will you accept me as your lord and master?"

"My husband."

"Lord and master," he insisted.

"You're cruel, Sween Handle."

"Nay, Glory. I'm desperate for peace between us."

"Lord and master," she conceded. "But only in the privacy of our home."

"It's a start."

She squealed in delight and threw her arms around his neck. He enveloped her and turned in a circle.

"What are they doing?" Clare asked.

Hoarsely, Drummond said, "Coming to accord, I believe."

Glory scooped up her clothing and they hurried from the room.

Drummond cleared his throat. "They're gone."

She cupped his neck and pulled him down for a kiss. Her lips felt soft, and she tasted pleasantly of sweet cider. Vowing to stop the seduction before it went too far, he bridled his own need and tested hers. When her breath rushed against his cheek, he slid his tongue across the slick seam of her lips. She opened herself to him, but rather than plunge into her sweetness, he held back, curious to see how far she would go. Her tongue peeked into his mouth, and her fingers curled around his wrist for balance, for she was beginning to sway.

Her breasts heaved against his chest, and when passion spiraled to his loins, Drummond seriously considered hiking her gown and having her here, against the pantry wall. What if she took his capitulation for forgiveness? What if she resumed her position as mistress to a king?

Doubts dashed Drummond's desire, and summoning strength, he set her away from him. "Shall we eat?"

Her eyes were glazed with passion, but she rallied. "Yes. I'm suddenly famished."

Chapter 14

The next afternoon, Johanna stared at the ledgers, but her thoughts kept straying to the night before. She relived the giddy moments when she and Drummond had dashed to shelter behind the pantry door. She'd felt carefree and young and at ease in his company, and she instinctively knew he had felt the same. The titillating exchange between Glory and Sween had inspired Johanna. Glory's erotic words had chipped away at Sween's stalwart resistance. If Johanna and Drummond could reach accord, they too could enjoy the freedom of expressing their affection.

In the next breath, Johanna's naivety fled, replaced by a woman's desire for love, countered by a male's concern for her health. Or was it resistance?

The wound had almost healed, leaving a patch of smooth pink skin. The mark had been a part of Johanna, and puzzling as it was, she almost missed the tiny symbol. Her tribulations over losing her sense of herself had proved groundless. In every movement and method, every deed and action, she was still Johanna Benison. She would continue to thrive as she had since coming to the Borders, and she would stop craving to hear the sound of her own name on Drummond's lips. He was coming to care for the person she was; why else would he show so much concern for her welfare?

Yearning filled her, and she clung to the feeling, for she knew the end was near. Tonight she would ply him with wine, then entice him to take her to bed. A delicious shiver coursed through her, and she anticipated the event, pictured waking in his arms and being sheltered by his embrace. By God's grace, she would one day labor in their bed to bear his children.

Too distracted to concentrate on the figures before her, she checked the store of wine and changed the bed linens herself. She scattered sweet marjoram in the rushes and put a heather scented candle on the bedside table. Then she languished in her bath.

When she returned to her room she found Drummond sitting on the bed. In his hands he held her green surcoat.

He looked up. His face was set in stern lines and his gaze seemed intent, yet detached.

"Come in." He motioned her forward. "I've been waiting for you."

She felt like a servant caught stealing the salt and called to task before the master.

"I've been asking myself how you came to burn your shoulder the way you said you did. How could you hold a mug just so." He draped the garment over his forearm and held his left hand in the air. "And an iron like this." He raised his right arm. "And manage to burn yourself up here." He touched his shoulder.

Johanna went hollow inside. His theory didn't trouble her, for she had anticipated this interrogation. What hurt was the surety that he had already made up his mind. She could counter his objections, but what if the doubt remained and surfaced again when next she erred?

As part of her defense she affected nonchalance. "It's simple, Drummond. Rather than return the iron to its hook, I put it on the mantel. Being round, it rolled off and struck my shoulder."

Unmoved by her display of indifference, he nodded and stared at the garment in his hands. "Miraculously you did not ruin your dress. 'Tis free of even the smallest ash. I find this odd, Clare."

He'd pilfered the key to her trunk. Like a thief in the night, he had plundered her keepsakes. Had he noticed the significance of the twin locks of golden hair, or understood why she kept a pair of matching rosaries? Must she now destroy the only remaining mementos of her childhood? She'd lost her sister. Was she to have nothing of her past?

She didn't know whether to laugh or cry, and

his lack of emotion only complicated her indecision.

"How did you accomplish so baffling a feat?" he said.

She had removed the green surcoat and pulled the bliaud off her shoulder. When the deed was done, Bertie had helped her upstairs, then fetched Glory. The version told to Drummond would stand. "The dress is unharmed because I wore another that night."

His blue eyes glittered with accusation. "Bertie claims 'twas this one. He found you."

"Yes, but Bertie is disremembered of it." She went to the larger trunk and took out an old sack where she kept the rags she used during her woman's time. Pulling out a handful of the clean cloths, she said, "I was wearing an old dress, which was burned beyond repair. From the remnants I made these items for my personal use."

As she had hoped, he reddened. Exhaling, he raked a hand through his hair. Doubt still lived in his eyes. "You burned yourself apurpose, Clare. Why?"

Without doubt, she knew this was not the last direct lie she must tell him. Pity. "I did not, Drummond, and I am wounded that you would doubt me."

"I'll find out," he said reasonably. "Perhaps not today or tomorrow, but I will. Do you not care?"

"Care that you doubt me?" Hope for the future dwindled, and the years stretched before her, end less and infinitely lonely. He would never return her love, and she must keep her affection to herself. "I would name this the sorriest moment since your return."

"As would I."

She must change his mind, but how? Only the truth would suffice, and she couldn't endanger Sister Margaret for the sake of her own romantic yearnings. To aid Johanna in her quest for independence, the abbess had willingly stained her kind soul with a lie. One was plenty for the abbess.

"Have you nothing more to say?" he asked.

Volumes of unspeakable truths weighted her conscience. "May I have the key to my trunk?"

"Certainly." He stood and handed her the dress. " 'Tis still in the lock."

His quiet words and slow movements as he left the room gave proof that he, too, was troubled. Bother it, she told her breaking heart. She had fallen in love with him, and she could bloody well fall out of love with him, but she would not betray the first person to show her kindness.

There would be no tiny infant girl to suckle at her breasts and fill her life with joy. There'd be no sons to tag along after Alasdair and inherit his trinkets and wear the shoes she'd carefully packed away.

Without the brand, Johanna was Drummond's wife and no one could gainsay her. But she wasn't truly his wife, nor did she care to be. Until the very next day when Alasdair resumed his campaign for a little sister.

He'd come into the solar still wearing his chain mail shirt, his gauntlets, and his sword strapped around his waist. Since acquiring his accoutrements of war and practicing every afternoon, Alasdair had grown more confident. He'd even come to morning table dressed for battle. He'd quickly learned the maneuver of retreat.

" 'Tis a poor excuse, Mother, for denying me a sister. She can have *my* room."

Lord, he was even beginning to speak like his father. "And where will you sleep?"

He puffed out his chest. "I'm old enough to stay in the barracks with the men."

And she was a Venetian moneylender. Drat her for also affecting Drummond's ways. Now she must outwit both of them, day in, day out. "That's a fine way to show your affection for the beloved sister you cannot live without. I thought you wanted her."

Arms flapping at his sides, Alasdair stared at the ceiling. His sword rattled, and the belt slipped low on his skinny hips. "I do want her, but I'll be becoming a man soon. You cannot deny that."

"If you're a man, then that makes me a grandmother, and much too old to bear another child."

"You must!" He stamped his foot, and the sword belt fell to the floor. Squatting, he yanked the belt back up to his waist. "A knight's belt must not bind," he murmured.

If she challenged his tantrum, he'd grow more peevish. Changing the subject seemed best. "Where is your father?"

Suddenly alert, he toyed with his gloves. "If I fetch him will you wet his wick and get me that sister?"

Mortified by his crude speech, she shot to her feet. "The last time you said that to me, you did not understand what it meant. Now you do."

"Aye." He folded his arms over his chest. "Father told me all about what older people do. Will you do it now?"

She'd have Drummond's head on a pike. "Where is your father?"

"I want a sister."

She clasped her hands when she wanted to wring them in despair. "Answer my question."

Lips pursed, he squirmed. "He's grooming Longfellow's feet. If he knows you're angry with me, he'll never let me sleep in the barracks."

She wanted to laugh at that, for Drummond couldn't give a rotten nut for her feelings. He'd named her a liar. Pray God he did not learn she was also an imposter. But how could he? The brand was gone. She was Clare, wife to the mighty chieftain of the Macqueens and mother to this rascally lad. "No, your father will not punish you." When Alasdair relaxed she added, "I will."

"But I've only had custard once since the last time you punished me."

She had intended to unpack Drummond's sword and have him present it to Alasdair. Now he'd have no sword at all. "This time you will yield your sword."

His mouth flew open, and he spat, "Nay."

"And if you protest further, I shall carry it 'round from sunup to sundown and ask every woman in the village to touch it."

Once he would have been crestfallen; now Alasdair screwed up his face in anger and fisted his hands in defiance. "I'll find another."

"Then I shall begin a collection."

Unsheathing the sword, he threw it down and ran from the room yelling, "I hate you."

His words cut deeply, but she knew he did not intend to be cruel. His life had changed drastically since Drummond's return, and he was too young to accommodate the changes with grace. But he was a resilient and kind child at heart. Guidance was what he needed.

Johanna left the weapon where it lay and went in search of Drummond. From across the yard, she saw Alasdair gesturing wildly and pleading with his father, who stood near the elephant, a file as long as her arm in his hand.

Would Drummond stand by her? He had before, and even if he didn't believe her about the burn, he wouldn't be petty enough to spoil Alasdair just to spite her. Would he? No. In his heart, Drummond Macqueen was a good man. Fate and politics had conspired to alter his destiny. He loved Alasdair, and although he still struggled with the role of father, his intentions were good.

At her approach Drummond nodded. "My lady."

If he wanted formality, she could oblige. But

why did her heart have to ache and her stomach float at the sight of him? Because she loved him. "My lord. I wish —"

Longfellow trumpeted and sent his trunk dancing on the air before her. She waited for the elephant to complete his inspection before he went back to devouring a hayrick.

"What brings you here?" Drummond asked.

"Absolute justification." She stared at Alasdair. "I wish to talk to you about this bully's foul mouth and ill manners."

He patted his son on the head and cheerfully said, "This Alasdair? A bully? Surely not."

Chin up and reveling in self-worth, her son seemed a veritable stranger. The changes in him both troubled and challenged her. She had expected him to outgrow his need for motherly approval; all lads did. She had not counted on it happening this year or next or with such lack of grace.

"*That* Alasdair indeed." She told Drummond what the boy had said. "I took away his sword."

His jaw worked in agitation as he stared down at his son. "Did I not tell you 'twas rude, and warn you never to repeat the remark in the presence of a lady, especially your mother?"

Alasdair's nod was almost imperceptible.

"Did you say it to her, Alasdair?"

"Nay."

Drummond looked at Johanna, and he seemed so detached that she wondered if he thought she had lied. "Alasdair, tell your father the truth," she said.

With the toe of his boot, Alasdair nudged a pebble. "Aye, I said it."

"Why?" demanded Drummond.

Alasdair's sweet face turned pitiful with misery. "I want a sister and there's no one else to get me one."

Drummond studied the file. "Alasdair, do you understand what a lie is?"

Alasdair's shoulders slumped and he rolled his eyes. "A lie is when you say something apurpose that is not true. You lied to me, so why cannot I?"

Drummond reared back. " 'Tis a serious accusation, Alasdair. When did I lie to you?"

"When we stayed the night in the forest. You said Mother hates lizards."

Johanna's head began to pound.

His face drawn in a worried frown, Drummond spoke softly. "Your mother does hate lizards."

Swinging his head, Alasdair dragged out the word. "Nay. You said when I was so little I wasn't born yet, you put a lizard in her dress and she squealed. You said she hates lizards, but that's a lie. She even makes baskets for catching bugs, and she never squeals." Looking up, Alasdair pleaded with his eyes. "Is that not a lie?"

From beneath his lowered brow, Drummond glanced at Johanna. She cringed at the confusion he did not try to hide. "Clare, I defer to you."

She grew uneasy under their dual scrutiny, but too much was at stake. Fairness dictated that she corroborate Drummond's statement, but Alasdair knew better. She must find a way to appease both of them. "Alasdair, lizards are harmless to me and beneficial to the kitchen garden."

Drummond's gaze didn't waver. "That's no answer for the lad. Explain to him."

They looked so much alike, father and son, and so united in their cause that Johanna felt the outsider. Caught in yet another trap of her own setting, she seized her only escape. "I misspoke the tale, Alasdair. Your father did not lie. Sister Margaret taught both Johanna and me how to weave the baskets and trap lizards. Johanna was always braver than me, but I was too proud to admit it. When I came here I conquered my fear of insects."

"You told a lie," Alasdair insisted, as disillusioned as the night he'd learned his father had been declared a traitor.

A stab of guilt pierced her. She looked at Drummond. "How do I explain a nuance?"

"You do not. I have tried." To Alasdair, he said, "Two wrongs do not make a right, Son. You spoke a vulgarity to your mother after I expressly forbade you to do it. That is the crux of this discussion."

"But I lied for a sister. 'Tis a cause good and true."

"But 'tis no excuse for rudeness toward your mother."

Through clenched teeth, Alasdair hissed, "I want a sister."

Drummond sighed. Johanna's heart went out to him. He could not retreat. Alasdair must learn to respect and obey his father. "Give me your gauntlets."

Bottom lip protruding, Alasdair refused. " 'Tisn't fair."

Drummond glanced at Johanna. He seemed at a loss, and she willed him to hold his ground.

He did, saying, "Life is not always fair, Alasdair. But you must behave with honor and chivalry. I'll have your chain mail, too."

"Father!"

"Do it now, Alasdair." Tucking the file under his arm, Drummond held out his hand. "Or you will stay here on Foraging Day and clean the barrack's privy."

Alasdair looked like he'd bitten into a sour plum. " 'Tis servant's work! And the other children will get a penny for gathering nuts."

"The other children have not offended their mothers, and they are not your concern."

"But I must govern them. I'm their betters."

"A better man would honor his mother. On Foraging Day, Elton Singer will show you where he keeps the shovel."

Alasdair ripped off the gauntlets and raised his arm as if to slap them against his father's palm.

"Should you do it, Alasdair," Drummond warned, "you'll feel the kiss of those gloves on your naked backside."

"Mother." Alasdair turned pleading eyes to her. "You cannot let him beat me."

Johanna abhorred the practice of whipping, but Drummond had done his best to avoid it. Their gazes met, and she felt a jolt of satisfaction in their communal triumph, even if it was over a misbehaving, seven-year-old boy. "I love you well, Alasdair, but drastic times warrant drastic actions."

Alasdair held out his prized possessions, offeringlike, to his father. "Here."

Drummond took the gauntlets and mail shirt and waited, praying the lad would apologize to his mother without being prompted. She disguised her feelings on other matters, but not where Alasdair was concerned. She was hurt to the core. Drummond remembered the words of his maternal uncle. *A mother's heart is a thing of glass. Have a care that you do not break it.*

When Alasdair made a dash for the keep, Drummond called him back. At least the lad had stopped strutting like a cock o' the walk. "You're to apologize to your mother and then spend the afternoon doing something nice for her."

Out of the side of his mouth, he said, "Doing what thing?"

Drummond wanted to shake his son, but violence would rob him of his pride. From experience, Drummond knew that a shamed man could not order his thoughts, let alone express affection, and Clare needed reassurance before she could forgive Alasdair. " 'Tis up to you to choose," Drummond said. "You know the things she favors."

"Perhaps," she said, her voice stiff with dignity, "Alasdair should spend some time phrasing his apology."

The lad looked up at her, but glanced quickly away. "I'm the only one who knows where the white heather grows — except father. May I be excused?"

"Aye, and put on a jerkin before you go a-fielding." Drummond watched him go.

"What are you thinking?" she asked.

"How simple was my father's method of child rearing."

"The flat of his hand just so?" She laid the back of her hand against her cheek.

The comparison seemed odd, for her cheek was smooth and her hand soft and supple. His father's hand had been clublike in both size and texture, and his aim had been forever true. "Just so."

She stared after Alasdair as he made his way up the steps to the keep. Drummond felt bound to say, " 'Tis natural for him to go his own way and to misbehave."

Sadness ringed her mouth, and he'd wager his last plaid that her heart was breaking. "I was thinking that very thing."

"He's making a poor job of growing up."

She nodded, but her breathing had turned choppy and her nostrils flared. Drummond grew desperate to cheer her. "We could pledge him to the church."

She swallowed. "They'd pay us not to."

"Aye. The Pope'd yield up his last fine raiment for the cause."

Even as he watched, she rallied. Interest sparkled in her eyes and her hands grew still. "For how long shall we punish him?"

"You mean depriving him of his war weapons?"

"Yes."

She shouldn't look so beautiful, not when he burned to possess her. Not when she'd lain with a king. Not when she kept important secrets. "Lying is a serious matter, Clare. And a poor quality in a son or a wife."

She did not mistake his meaning, but whatever her reasons she guarded them well. "Especially *your* wife?"

Pray God she would offer an explanation. "Especially so, since I only have the one."

On a half laugh, she said, "Then let me assure you, your wife did not burn herself apurpose."

She spoke as if his wife were someone else. She had changed, and the greatest difference seemed her ability to separate herself from the past. Neither in carriage, nor attitude did she seem like an adulteress. Rather, she appeared innocent in the ways of intimacy. Where had she acquired the skill, and where could he find the means to ferret out the truth?

A direct approach seemed best. "Aye, you did set out to burn yourself. Why?"

"Fatherhood suits you well."

Her attempt at flattery was so artless, Drummond laughed. "At best, I muddle through."

She tilted her head to the side and smiled. "Modesty becomes you. I, on the other hand, was a wretched mother from the start."

The diversion didn't fool Drummond; it made him curious. "You?"

"More than wretched." A self-effacing grin lit up her face. "The first time I gave him a taste of plum sauce, he cooed and giggled for more. He was just learning to crawl. I gave him as much of it as he would eat. I never stopped to think it would make him sick. Glory and I walked the floor with him for two days. I thought I'd killed the poor mite."

In a heartbeat, Drummond's animosity fled. She suffered a poor memory, but, by the grail, she'd mastered diplomacy and the art of disarming conversation.

"Another time," she went on, looking completely at ease, "I took him with me to Carlisle to find buyers for our first harvest. It was a glorious summer day, and we rode in the hay wagon. The sun blistered Alasdair's plump cheeks and nose, and I was too selfish and inexperienced to notice."

Blistered. Burned. How, Drummond wondered, could he have been distracted by her winsome ways? Because she possessed the rare ability to charm and deceive in the same breath. "You've become an expert on burns, have you not?"

315

She blinked, but could not disguise her disappointment. An instant later, she cheerfully said, "How came you to befriend Longfellow?"

The change of topics was so obvious, Drummond almost challenged her. Better to wait, he thought, and observe her, for he knew with certainty that she'd give herself away. Deceivers always did. "His keeper died, and his quarters were next to mine."

Shock sharpened her features. "You were kept with the . . ."

A chill went through him. "Animals."

"Oh, Drummond. I'm so sorry."

In her clear gaze and her heartfelt tone, she radiated truth. He committed the impression to memory. He had patience aplenty and time to sleuth out her lie. Then he would reap the bountiful harvest of her feminine charms. "As you say, I have a friend in Longfellow to show for it."

"You also have your freedom and a prosperous keep," she said reasonably.

And a faithless, lying wife. Like a raw wind, the reminder cut him to the bone and dashed his lovestruck ideals.

She must have read his thoughts, for she said, "Better to count your blessings, Drummond, than to dwell on your misfortunes. You have Alasdair, who is a mix of both, and he needs you."

He fought back a smile. He would not allow her to diffuse his anger; if he let down his guard, she would slip into his heart again. "A veritable bounty."

"Just so. Shall we celebrate your bounty?"

Was the question a sly attempt at seeking his forgiveness? She'd not so easily gain a pardon from Drummond Macqueen. But he was intrigued; how far would she go? "You mean to toast our success as parents?"

Suddenly eager, she said, "Why, that's a splendid idea, Drummond. We'll do it tonight."

So, immediacy *did* hold appeal for her. In that case, he would stall, for he rather liked being the object of her attention. He would, of course, keep his ambitions on a short rein. "Aye, 'tis," he said. "You may have the alewife start a batch of sennight mead."

"Sennight?" She stepped so close he could smell the heather on her skin. "But would not wine do as well?"

His mouth watered, and he clutched the gauntlets in his hands to keep from touching her. The bodice of her bliaud hugged her breasts, and the dusty rose color of the garment matched the enticing shade of her lips. Lips that could intoxicate. "Think you to get me drunk, Clare?"

She huffed with indignation, an expression that accentuated her regal bearing and reminded him of Alasdair. The sunlight played on her skin and gave her brown eyes a cinnamon hue. He longed to see them darken with passion again. But he would see honesty first.

"Why would I give you too much drink, Drummond?"

A number of answers came to mind, but they all seemed groundless. She had never practiced seduction; this new Clare was too forthright. Did she think to pry forgiveness from him? An interesting prospect, but far too naive, even for the old Clare Macqueen. Thinking to turn her plans around, he said, "What if *you* get drunk and reveal to me why you burned off that brand?"

"I have nothing to reveal, but we have much to celebrate. You were wonderful with Alasdair."

There it was again, a statement of praise that felt like a loving caress. Her confidence spurred him on. "In this I shall be relentless."

And relentless he was.

He knelt beside her at Vespers and whispered, "Did you grow ashamed of the mark?"

Head bowed, she touched her shoulder to his. "No, but I'm ashamed of you."

As innocent as the Virgin Mary, he said, "But I've only begun."

He stood over her as she fabricated bedtime stories for Alasdair. Leaning down, he said, "Did you think *I* would grow ashamed of the mark?"

Looking up, she said, "Rather, I prayed that you would come home and care for me yourself."

As if struck, he jumped back.

If kindness would counter his insistence, he was in for a flood of generosity.

He accompanied her to greet important guests.

Behind his hand, he said, "Did you think to gain my sympathy?"

"The devil with your sympathy, Drummond. It's your heart I'm after."

His surprised gaze had settled on her mouth. Borrowing one of Glory's bold moves, Johanna licked her lips. On a manly groan of frustration, he excused himself.

She wanted to race after him, but he was forever in the company of Alasdair or Bertie or Amauri. Never alone with her. If anything, Drummond seemed determined to avoid chance meetings like the one in the pantry. He slept on the battlement and barred the door. To outward appearances they were lord and lady, parents, a family.

But they were not man and wife.

Since the departure of Sween and Glory, Drummond had often been occupied with training and leading the huntsmen. He even lingered at the bog an extra night to find a fat frog because he knew she favored the meat.

But he was not her devoted husband.

She tallied the nut harvest. She inventoried the stores. She pruned the kitchen garden until no decent weed would dare take root. Just yesterday, she accompanied Drummond to the tailor and watched as he was fitted for new clothing. He had even suggested they visit the dressmaker so she could have a new gown for their journey to Dumfries.

"Something with a cowl at the neck to hide your self-inflicted burn," he'd whispered.

Patience gone, she murmured back, "Perhaps I'll choose black to remind me of my happy days as a widow."

With his thumb and forefinger, he had grasped her chin. "Another win to you, Clare."

"Then I demand a boon."

"In exchange for the truth?"

She'd lost the bigger battle, for no matter how often or shamelessly she tempted him, he avoided her seduction.

But she was a woman with a mission, and at week's end, when the sennight mead had fermented, Johanna seized her opportunity.

Chapter 15

Excitement lightened her step and buoyed her confidence. Wearing a berry colored bliaud and a new surcoat of pink velvet, Johanna made her way to the hall. Outside the entryway, she stopped before the polished shield to check her appearance. She had braided her hair and coiled it at the crown of her head. Over a whisper thin veil that framed her face and flowed down her back, she wore a garland of fresh white heather.

Alasdair had thrown mud in Curly Handle's face yesterday. As punishment, he'd been denied dessert and ordered to pick flowers for Curly. He'd also brought some to Johanna.

"For the next time I'm bad," he had said sagely. "That way your heart won't break."

"How came you to know about breaking my heart?"

"Father told me."

Drummond's influence on Alasdair showed in many ways; more often than not, the lad made decisions for himself. Although some were mistakes, Alasdair was learning to accept his setbacks with good grace. Had she planned a friendship between father and son, she could not have imagined better for them, and if Drummond excelled at the begetting of children as he did at fatherhood, he'd give her a score of lads and lassies.

"Shall I tell you what Father said?" Alasdair had asked.

"Of course."

"He said, 'Your mother's heart is made of glass, Son. Have a care that you do not break it.' " Proud of himself, Alasdair had squirmed as he twisted the white heather into a garland. "Morgan Fawr says Father's doing a lurk and waiting for the right turn of a head."

Johanna laughed. "Do you know what he means?"

"Nay." He had shrugged. "But no one else does, either. Heckley says Morgan himself doesn't even know his own mind."

Now Johanna smiled at the memory. Gazing at her reflection in the shield, she adjusted the garland, then stepped into the hall.

Evelyn knelt before the hearth and banked the fire. Drummond was nowhere about.

Over her shoulder, the maid said, "Good evening, my lady. His lordship'll make a fancyman's bow when he sees you."

Johanna had taken extra care in her toilet. Tonight was the most important of her life. "Thank you, Evelyn. Where is Lord Drummond?"

The maid stood and deposited the banking rake in an iron bucket. "He's waiting for you at the alehouse."

The alehouse? Johanna's temper flared. After a week of toe-stepping out of her reach, the blackguard had tonight resorted to hiding in a crowd! Was there ever, she pondered, a man more resistant to seduction than Drummond Macqueen? Yes, a cloistered monk.

But he wanted her, of that she was certain. He talked of Spanish beef and next year's crops, but the expression in his eyes spoke of husbandly need and banked passion. He was trying to wait her out, but his patience was no match for her conscience. She would win, and tonight he would make her his wife.

That happy thought in mind, she sailed down the steps and let the noise lead her to the alehouse. Tucked into a long, narrow space between the brewhouse and the cooper's shed, the tavern entrance was marked with twin barrels and jackjaw lanterns. Inside, the hard-packed earthen floor and thick wooden tables with long benches gave the room a cozy feel.

Drummond sat at the table against the far wall with Morgan Fawr, the butcher, a dozen huntsmen, and Bertie. The latter whistled at her arrival. Like peas rolling off a knife, they slid from the bench so she could sit beside Drummond. Cornered and against the wall. Could she manage a graceful exit for them? Yes, she could.

Sidestepping, she moved between the bench

and the table. Drummond followed her progress, his brows lifted in appreciation. Waving her forward, he rested his arm on the window casement. To everyone at the table it would appear that he'd wrapped his arm around her. A loving couple. Man and wife.

Tonight, her dwindling patience screamed. Tonight.

As innocent as a newly christened babe, he grinned. "Did I disremember a special occasion?"

So close she could count his feathery black eyelashes, she said, "You know perfectly well you did. We were to tap the sennight mead and celebrate our success as parents." And get too tippered to notice that his wife was a virgin, she thought.

" 'Tis hardly fitting today. Your son lopped off the donkey's tail."

From her perch on her father's lap, Curly Handle yelled, "Alasdair's a wretched lad!"

Johanna would not be deterred. "Rest assured, Curly, he's paying the price. He's cleaning Longfellow's harness."

"Dawn'll fly in his face does he grab a wink," said Morgan Fawr. He sat across from her, his long red beard tucked into the placket of his jerkin, his hands cupping a battered pewter tankard.

Accustomed to his undecipherable speech, everyone went about their conversations. Meg set a brimming mug before Johanna and handed another to Morgan Fawr.

"To my lady." Drummond held up his tankard. "A goddess of grace and beauty."

"And a heart good and true," said Bertie.

Drummond wiggled his brows. "Just so."

They all toasted her. She demurred, her mind fixed on the man beside her, the gleam in his eye, and the event to come. As always, her mouth went dry at the thought. She sipped the mead, and almost choked.

"Have a care, Clare," Drummond said.

"You made a rhyme," chirped Curly. "Flutter, flutter, the sparrow's in the butter."

" 'Tis a hearty brew," he said.

Hearty? Even the breath she inhaled turned to potent fumes. But the mead would serve her purpose, and the taste was sweet with honey. The second swallow went down easier. "I like it, my lord? Do you?"

" 'Tis as hale as the king's own ale," he said, which set Curly to giggling again. Then he grinned, looking like a man with the answer to the first great mystery. Her mystery.

He leaned close. "You wouldn't want to get tippered and spill your secrets, lass."

Lass. He hadn't called her that before. She rather liked the endearment, but then, even if her name was goose grease, she'd love the sound of it on his lips.

Catching his gaze, she murmured, "Just watch that you don't get tippered, my lord, lest *you* reveal *your* secrets."

To the table in general, he said, "I'm a blank

and waiting slate where my lady's affection is concerned."

The men guffawed. Curly's hands flew to her cheeks, and her childish laughter rang through the room.

For a week, Drummond had often spoken flattering words to Johanna in public. Tonight she would repay the favor. "Shall I write you a story, my lord?"

He lowered his arm and dropped his wrist over her shoulder. "Only if I'm the knight in shining armor and you're the damsel in distress."

Happiness rippled through her, for tonight he'd carry through with that sentiment. He'd rescue her from the chains of innocence. Please, God, let her conceive. "You play the gallant well, my lord. Just remember that you ceased rescuing other women when we wed. My distress is your only concern."

Bertie hooted. "My lord's got a sally for that, do you see."

In salute, Drummond tipped his mug toward Bertie. "My lady's good humors are a pursuit I verily relish."

Murmurs of approval rumbled around the table.

Basking in his attention, she touched her mug to his. "To my stalwart angel and silver-tongued devil."

The others chortled.

Mirth softened his profile, and tiny lines of laughter fanned the corners of his eyes. Handsome didn't begin to describe him. Lovesick couldn't touch her feelings.

He gulped. She sipped. And wondered if the physical aspects of marriage inspired affection. Eager to find out, she leaned into him.

The ever efficient Meg took his tankard to the server and returned it, then flitted off to a group of huntsmen at a table near the door.

"You've something on your mind, Clare," he said softly.

Staring into her mug, Johanna smiled.

"Hum. Methinks 'tis a woman's secret."

The din at the table grew; the others talked among themselves. The familylike atmosphere said much about the people of Fairhope. They deserved a man of Drummond's stature and competence. Let the same be true for her. "Perhaps I plot a man's downfall."

"Shall I offer a sporting challenge or simply collapse at your feet now?" Lowering his voice, he added, "You look bonny."

She wanted to squirm and fall swooning into his arms. "Thank you."

"Like a princess."

It was too much. "Then collapse later, my prince. When we are alone."

He set the mug down and laid his palm over the rim. "You play with fire, Clare, but then you have a great mastery of it, do you not?"

Her confidence faltered, but his taunts would not dissuade her. Not tonight. "Passing so, but whatever expertise I lack or have forgotten, I

327

trust you will provide."

"You've forgotten much of our time in the Highlands."

In a voice as sultry as Glory's, Johanna said, "I yield, then, to your tutelage." She looked up at him. "And your —" Promise smoldered in his eyes. The sentence melted on her tongue.

"Have you a thirst, Clare?"

"Of a sort." She put the mug to her lips.

Meg held up a pitcher. Only the Welshman accepted.

"Me! Me!" Curly squealed.

"None for this mite," said her father.

Meg pinched Curly's cheek. "I'd sooner serve Elton Singer a pint after dark as give your poppet a taste of brew." From her apron, she produced a honey treat and presented it to a beaming Curly.

"Does the mead revive you, Clare?"

Johanna gathered her composure. "Aye, and the company. What did you do today?"

"We cleared the deadwood from the forest near Anderson Hollow. Tomorrow we'll build a charcoal oven. And you?"

"I sliced apples and plums until my fingers ached. John butchered a fat hog."

"Have we mincemeat from last year?" he said, looking as eager as Alasdair when a custard was set out to cool.

"Yes. Shall I have cook make you a pie?"

"Two. I'm fair starved for the taste."

And she was famished for him, but beneath the yearning lay understanding. He had been de-

328

nied simple favors such as a pie made from the remains of a barrel of pork preserved with fruit. She could spend a lifetime providing him with the comforts he'd missed.

For the next hour, between conversations with the occupants of the alehouse, they traded meaningful phrases and poignant looks. When John Handle swung a sleeping Curly into his arms and made for the door, Bertie and the others followed him. Like a corpse awaiting burial, Morgan Fawr lay in a stupor on a nearby bench. He'd had four tankards of mead. Drummond had had three.

Anticipation set Johanna's pulse to hammering, and her hands twitched with idleness. A graceful exit awaited. "Shall we?" she asked.

His expression turned thoughtful. "Nervous?"

"No. Why?"

"You're strumming your fingers."

Oh, dragons! She stilled her telltale hand and assembled her wits.

"Have you something to tell me?" he said.

He expected her to tell him why she had burned herself. He'd fare better waiting for the Second Coming. "Yes, Drummond, I do."

His gaze sharpened; yet he stared straight ahead.

She put down the mug and took a deep breath. "I love you."

Shock widened his eyes, and he grew still. " 'Tis an odd time for you to tell me. Did you just think of it?"

Anger ripped through her. "Look at me, you wretched snake."

Turning, he propped his elbow on the table and rested his chin on his open palm. His raven black hair fell over his forehead, and his blue eyes glittered with challenge. "Did you?"

An invisible shield stood between them. "No, I did not just think of it."

"When, then?"

"The exact moment?"

"Aye, and do not spare the details."

She must break through to the gentle, compassionate man beneath. He wanted her. She loved him. They could make a good life together. He would give her children. One day she would tell him the truth. He would come to love her; she would make it so.

"If I tell you will you leave off with the other?"

"The 'other' being my conviction that you put a hot iron to your skin rather than have me see the mark?"

One lie. "Yes. That erroneous belief."

"Tell me when you began loving me."

The words rolled off his tongue as if he were asking when she inventoried the linens. "The day you upheld my judgment of Elton Singer."

"Why did that make you love me?"

Was he taunting her with the word? The troll. "You've never taken my side before. In the Highlands, we were both too young."

"You speak of the time when I did not stand by you after my father banished you from table.

330

I should have chosen my wife over my sire."

According to Clare, he had agreed to the marriage in hopes of gaining a peace with England, the noblest of reasons. Even a monarch could not command a man's heart. "You never *chose* me, Drummond. The king forced you to marry me."

"And I did — willingly."

He spoke truths so easily. She longed to repay his honesty in kind. Since she could not, she sought to lighten the mood. "You married me so you could have a chamber with a woman in it, rather than two smelly brothers."

He tried not to smile, but failed. "You never said as much at the time."

"As you say, we spent our private moments in endeavors other than talking."

He squinted, as if looking into the memory and finding humor there. "Rabbits, we were."

An interesting picture, she thought. Drawing on it, she said, "We verily wore off our fur."

He burst out laughing. "Heavens, Clare, you do brighten the soul."

It wasn't his soul she was after; she wanted his heart, and that was serious business. "Actually, I was too inexperienced to think of what your life was like before I arrived in Scotland, and I was too selfish to earn a place for myself among your clan."

He gave her a meaningful look.

Had she erred? Please, God, no. "What are you thinking?"

"Where other people's feelings are concerned, you are worldly now and considerate," he said.

"Thank you."

"And proud of it."

The burr in his voice put a shiver in her breast. "Well, yes. I have responsibilities beyond stewardship of the land." She also had a mission. "At all events, the word *worldly* holds particular appeal for me tonight."

He rubbed her veil between his thumb and forefinger, and his interest lingered there. "In many ways, we are strangers, Clare."

Suddenly she felt drawn to him. He'd lowered the barrier. She rushed onward. "This stranger loves you, Drummond Macqueen." Like sunshine, the truth made her glow inside. She put her hand on his thigh. "Shall I say it a dozen times? I love you. I love you. I love —"

"Enough," he growled.

The muscles beneath her hand rippled, and she moved higher. "Take me to bed, Drummond, and I'll show you."

A grin spread across his face. He tipped his head toward the door. "After you."

Why was he so deliberate? He should be slurring his words.

"Having second thoughts?"

"Of course not." She scooted to the end of the bench and stood. Her vision wavered, and her head spun. A moment later, the effects of the mead diminished.

"Feeling light-headed?" he asked, working his way toward her.

"A bit." She took heart, for Drummond had drunk fully three tankards to her one. "Are you?"

"I feel . . . pleasant," he said.

Feeling magnanimous, she extended her hand to him. He took it and stood. Towering over her, he offered his arm. She laid her hand on his forearm and noted the warm and steely strength of him. Later she would notice all of him.

They bid farewell to Meg and the alewife and a dead-to-the-world Morgan Fawr; then they stepped into the cool night air. Johanna's senses sharpened. The quarter moon glowed brighter than she remembered; the frogs croaked in a resonant harmony; and from the depths of the forest, came the distant howl of a wolf. Deep in her breast, Johanna felt the vibrations of the creature's lonely lament, but solitude was not to be her fate this night.

Another sound, low and unfamiliar drifted to her ears. "What is that noise?" she asked.

They started up the steps to the keep. " 'Tis Longfellow. He snores when he's content."

With absolute confidence, she said, "So do you."

He scoffed. "Your memory has deserted you."

She waited until they'd entered the keep. Turning, she stepped into his arms. "Then refresh my memory."

His hands lingered at her waist, as if uncertainty

ruled him again. Waning yellow lamplight glittered in his blue eyes, turning his irises a darker, richer hue. The shadow of his lashes fanned his cheekbones, softening the manly planes of his face.

She couldn't resist cupping his jaw. A slight stubble tickled her palm, and the idea of lying naked with him tickled her in places that made her blush.

"What are you thinking?" he said.

"I was thinking that thanks to you, Alasdair will make a handsome man."

Beneath her hand, the muscles in his cheek relaxed, then worked. "He's a wizard at finding white heather."

He reached for the garland and drew it off her head. The veil drifted to the floor.

"Are you a wizard, Drummond?"

He rolled his eyes. "If you've forgotten that part, I'll divorce you where we stand."

She'd won! Pound the drum and call out the merrymakers. He'd soon love her and make them one. "I seem to remember you liked looking at my hair."

"Let it down."

At the low, insistent command, she pulled the precious silver pins from the coil of her braids and let it tumble down her back.

He breathed deeply. "Heather everywhere."

In places he'd never suspect, she thought wickedly and smiled. Then she took the garland from his hands and placed it on his head.

"Think you to ply me with trinkets, lass?"

She worked her hair free of the plait, then shook her head. Standing on tiptoes, she wound her arms about his neck. "Not trinkets," she said, and pulled him down for a kiss. "Something much more earthy."

Indecision lingered in his gaze, which was oddly sharp, as if the mead had had no effect on him. But that was impossible, for no one could drink three mugs and keep his wits. Then his lips brushed hers and she forgot doubts and strong drink and languished in the lazy sensuality that seemed so much a part of him. His mouth toyed with hers, nibbling, skimming gently until finding a fit that suited him.

Inhibitions freed, she kissed him with all the finesse he'd taught her. She felt his hands roam her back, and when her balance wavered, he pulled her into the wall of his chest. His mouth slashed across hers, and his tongue prodded in a slow rhythmic movement that begged for accompaniment. She willingly joined in, tasting the sweet flavor of honey and reveling in the joy of his embrace. Against her breast, his heart beat strong and steady and his arms engulfed her in a cocoon of steely warmth. He was man enough to give her children and a future; was she woman enough to please him and make him forget the past? Pray God and his angels yes, for she wanted a lifetime with this man, here in the nest she'd spent years building.

He pulled back and studied her. "Shall we retire?"

"I'll help you up the stairs."

Indignation gave him a kingly air. "Think you I will stumble?"

"I *know* you drank three tankards of mead. You must be tippered."

"I'm sober enough to put a smile on your face come the morrow."

But would he remember any of it? Not the miraculous purity of her body. She was certain of that. "But I'm already smiling now."

"Aye, you are, and 'tis a bonny sight."

"Shall I frown to spur you on, or will we remain here for everyone to see?" She waved her arm toward the stairs.

"Privacy is your desire?"

"And immediacy my method."

Laughing, he swung her into his arms and carried her up the stairs to their chamber, his steps sure and his task seemingly effortless.

Light from a brace of scented candles cast wavering shadows on the walls, and the pleasing aroma of heather filled the room. The flame of a single taper illuminated the tapestries that curtained the bed. The bedchamber was modestly furnished, but fine enough to serve a chieftain and his lady.

She looked up at him and saw a man happy with himself and at peace with the world. She understood the feelings completely.

He drew his arm from beneath her knees and let her feet touch the floor, but his other arm held her snugly. She turned and laid her head on his shoulder, her fingers winnowing through his hair. His chest heaved and his arms engulfed her; then his mouth closed over her ear and his tongue did a devil's dance with her lobe.

Her knees buckled, and desire raced through her veins, spreading excitement and awareness from the tip of her nose to the soles of her feet. When his hands cupped her breasts, she closed her eyes and set her fingers to exploring new parts of him. Just as his thumbs teased her nipples, she discovered the ropy muscles of his neck and the shieldlike shape of his chest. About the time he caressed her bottom and drew her to him, she clutched his lean waist. When he undulated against her, showing her vividly the extent of his arousal, she tunneled beneath his jerkin and spread her palms over the sensually swaying contours of his buttocks.

He groaned and reached for the clasp on her surcoat, his fingers clumsy at the task.

The effects of the mead.

Inspired, Johanna trailed her fingers up to his waist again, then around to the tie of his hose. She encountered him, thick and straining against the fabric.

His mouth moved back to hers. "Hold me."

Her hand curled around him, and he winced before his features settled into a dreamy smile. Confidence soaring, she caressed him, acquainting herself with the bold length and rigid strength of him.

His breathing grew ragged and he jerked back. "A respite, love."

Love. She sighed and waited as he unfastened her clothing and peeled it off her shoulders. He paid the scar little mind, seemingly more interested in sight of her naked breasts, her navel, and her femininity below. When her garments pooled at her ankles, he carried her to the bed. The quilted thickness of his velvet jerkin felt soft against her skin, and when he lowered her to the mattress the linens felt crisp and clean at her back.

Looming above her, he gave her lips a quick smack, lowered his head, and took a nipple into his mouth.

Her back bowed and her hands flew to his head, holding him there, feeling his eagerness as he made a feast of her breasts. Her thoughts grew hazy and her vision blurred, turning the tapestry at the foot of the bed to blotches of green and brown and yellow. Warm, agile fingers trailed over her hip and slid with gentle purpose between her legs, spreading her, then fluttering like butterfly wings over places so sensitive she cried out for more.

"Shush. I forgot to throw the latch."

Desire hummed in her ears. "I'll do it."

"You'll as soon swim to France as leave this bed now."

His will spoken, he moved to her other breast where he laved and suckled while his fingers prodded and fondled until her breathing grew labored

338

and her hips rose and fell with the timing of his tender ministrations.

She couldn't help thinking about the myriad nights she'd lain alone in this bed and dreamed of having a mate to lie here with her. A mate to ease life's burdens and end her loneliness. A mate to give her children.

A familiar hollow feeling spread through her belly and she yearned to feel him naked against her. "Take off your clothes."

"Not yet." He twisted his wrist, wedging her open and sliding a long finger inside her. "Or you'll have a rabbit buck at you."

She moaned and curled her fingers in his hair.

"For certain I'll be a buck at rut the first time," he lamented.

First time. Her heart soared, for he already knew he would want her again. Then his thumb joined the fray and he caressed her as he had that day in the pantry. With the expertise she remembered, he tended her gently, allowing her passion to soar ever upward, ever increasing her need, until heaven burst inside her, only to give way to an even greater paradise. The sweet release swept her up and sustained her at the crest of mind-numbing pleasure.

Rising from a fog of ecstasy, she opened her eyes and saw him staring down at her, his eyes glowing with banked passion.

" 'Tis time to bar the door, Drummond."

With pointed insistence, he warned, "I'll tie you to the bed, should you move."

She stretched her arms over her head and squirmed against the clean linens. "Not even for the promise of eternal life."

He grinned and levered himself off the bed. As he crossed the room he tore off his jerkin, and when he threw the latch, he pulled off his boots. Turning, he strolled toward her, garbed only in tight hose that drew her eye to his manliness and her thoughts to how he would please her. At the bedside, he stopped and peeled off the hose, revealing a boldness that made her heart flutter and her belly cramp.

"I ache for you," she said.

"Aye, lass." He touched himself. "I know the feeling well. Have you room there for me?"

At once he looked masterful and endearingly young. She moved over and held up her arms. He lowered his weight, matching breast to chest, thigh to thigh; then he slid his legs between hers and nudged ever so gently at her innocence.

All eagerness and accommodation, she eased his way and bid him welcome. All insistence and determination, he moved forward, sinking deeper and pulling her hips up to meet him.

Fullness turned to pressure, and she fought to disguise her discomfort.

"God, but you're slick and ready and as tight as our first time. Relax, lass, and I'll try to go easy."

"I cannot, Drummond."

"Then I'll not argue. Draw up your knees and lift your hips."

She did and in the next breath, her world went white with pain. On a groan she clamped her lips shut and waited for the moment to pass. When it did, she was left with the fullness and stillness of him. His chest heaved like a bellows, and against her ear she heard the rasping of his breath.

"Drummond?"

"If you move one muscle, lass, you'll unman me."

"Then what shall I do?"

Through clenched teeth, he said, "What you always told me to do when we arrived at this pass — although I swear age has changed the feel of you."

He rested within her, still vigorously full yet content to linger. And he had yet to notice that she'd been a virgin.

At a complete loss for words and actions, she held him and marveled at the beauty of two bodies twined in mutual passion and contentment. His love would follow, of that she was certain; he wanted her, and she was obviously pleasing him. Given time, he would forgive her and forget the past. Henceforth, they would share this bed and join forces to build a future. They'd share a hundred nights in the company of their friends, and later she would languish in his arms. They would reign over a kingdom of prosperity and love.

"You seem distracted," he said.

She couldn't hold back a chuckle. "I thought I was plying you with trinkets."

"Move that wee trinket of yours now," he murmured, "and I'll take us both adventuring."

With deep rhythmic strokes he took her through a whirlwind of sensual bliss that washed away her inhibitions and flooded her with erotic visions. When the storm built to a tempest, he drew her legs up and over his naked buttocks and sank so deeply into her that she felt him touch her soul. "Yield now, lass," he rasped, "seek your paradise."

Her mind a mass of swirling ecstasy, Johanna clutched his shoulders and gave herself up to the pounding exhilarating release.

Chapter
16

A virgin.

Drummond stared at the woman sleeping beside him and tried to deny the truth. He could not. He knew a maidenhead when he breached it, and until several hours ago, this angelically beautiful woman, who passed herself off as Clare Macqueen, had been innocent.

Innocent? A double-edged term. Did she think he would not notice? Yes, and she had plied him with sennight mead to assure her success. For a week, she had been relentless in her seduction: smiling suggestively when she'd come upon him while he labored to repair the postern gate; moving past him closely enough so that her breasts brushed his arm; or requesting his aid to inventory the stores, a task she performed with ease.

Tonight he had suspected another trick and had outsmarted her by asking Meg to weaken his drink with water. Now he knew why she had wanted him besotted with drink. She had thought he wouldn't notice. A wildly naive and erroneous assumption. The gift of a woman's innocence was a memorable event even to a rogue.

Who was she? A sister or a cousin to Clare? The resemblance was uncanny; even a husband estranged for seven years would easily mistake her for Clare. But his wife had sworn she had no family; on occasion she had even garnered sympathy for being orphaned at Scarborough Abbey.

Was Clare dead? The possibility saddened him, for the lass had been a pawn in a game of kings. Or had Edward the Second spoken true when he claimed an ongoing affair with her? Was Clare tucked away in some hunting lodge awaiting his divine pleasure? Had she abandoned Alasdair to this capable woman and taken up the life of royal mistress?

Did she cuckold Drummond still?

He should bellow and curse and upturn the furniture. He should toss this woman from his bed. That he did not was as surprising as finding a virgin beneath him had been.

He'd called her whore and worse. The woman beside him had not taken his condemnation to heart, because his words had not wounded her; this woman had not lain with young Edward Plantagenet, not eight years ago, not ever, and not with anyone else. Except Drummond Macqueen.

Had she and Clare cooked up this scheme? Had Edward played a part? Did they think Drummond fool enough to believe their ruse?

Answers to other questions blazed in his mind like signal fires on a dark night. He'd been wandering, lost in a forest of confusion, but enlightenment had found him.

He wanted to examine her at his leisure, learn the reason for every doubt, see the truth behind each of his suspicions. He must look for proof.

The brand.

She had burned herself, not to hide a mark, but to disguise the fact that she had never born the brand. Like vanquishing an irksome enemy, he put that question to rest.

Shifting, he angled his head so he could see her neck. She purred sweetly and nuzzled against him. A loving woman, living a lie.

Like a cool wind on fevered skin, understanding swept over him.

I am not your wife.

No. Before tonight she'd belonged to no man.

This stranger loves you, Drummond Macqueen.

His pride reeled, and he willed his anger to flow. She had conspired with Clare to trick him. When had the unholy pact begun? Surely years ago, for Alasdair called her mother; Bertie addressed her as Lady Friend.

Drummond named her beguiling imposter.

She did not remember the events of her marriage in the Highlands because she hadn't been there.

Who was she?

I am not the woman you married.

Too agitated to stay abed, Drummond eased off the mattress and pulled on his hose, but his interest stayed fixed on her. His heartbeat quickened, for she looked like a woman well loved and content. Her glorious hair was prettily mussed, and her lips curved upward in a secret smile.

Secret.

He ground his teeth, and from the clothes chest, snatched up his tartan plaid. Drawing it around his shoulders, he slipped from the room and escaped to the battlement. But even in this favored spot, peace eluded him.

She had admitted the truth. On a dozen occasions she had told him she was not Clare.

I am not that woman. I am someone else now.

Who *had* she been? What life had she abandoned to become Clare Macqueen? And why? Upon his arrival, she had called him an imposter. She must have chuckled inside at her own cleverness. Even that revelation failed to stir his anger, for she loved to laugh.

She. What name did she speak in her heart? He must find out, but how? He couldn't publicly denounce her for an imposter; the brand on her shoulder had been his only proof. No one here would take his word. They'd sooner name him idiot and chain him away in a dungeon.

He looked out over the village and the farms beyond. She had built this prosperous estate out of moorland and forest. She. A woman who ciphered as well as a cleric. The woman whose penmanship was neat and efficient and unfamiliar. A woman who defended the weak. When her funds had been spent, she had borrowed money from Red Douglas. Not Clare, but the virgin Drummond had deflowered earlier tonight.

Never again would he call her Clare.

Who was she?

The question stabbed deeply.

Bertie knew of her deception. Did anyone else? No, not Alasdair and not even Brother Julian, Drummond wagered. She could not confess the sin of adultery; she had not committed it.

The door to the battlement swung open. "I grew lonely without you."

In a flowing night rail, she seemed to float toward him. In the faint light she was the image of Clare Macqueen. Yet she was as different from the woman he'd married as rock was to soil. This woman possessed depth of character and a deep sense of loyalty to these people and this land. She was also a liar.

In spite of that, his heart soared, and a confrontation died on his lips. Eventually she would reveal herself. If he gave himself away now, he'd never learn her secrets.

He pulled her into his arms, but not out of affection, he told himself. She could catch a chill. "We are truly one."

So great was her relief that she sagged against him. "Aye, and a glorious feeling it is."

Truly? She had lied from the beginning. He saw only folly in believing her now, and advantage was what he sought.

To verify what he already knew, he dreamed up an event to see if she would play along. "Do you remember the afternoon we made love in the loft of my uncle's stables?"

"If you tell anyone else about that tryst I'll . . ."

A skillful evasion, but she'd had much practice at avoiding direct questions. She also wielded cunning as well as a master archer aimed his bow. But Drummond was the master now, and he intended to enjoy the role. "You'll do what?"

"I'll tell Alasdair you intend to take him to Londontown."

Reality intruded. At the heart of the complicated issue of why this woman pretended to be Clare Macqueen was Alasdair. The lad was innocent, and no matter what occurred between Drummond and this woman, Alasdair would always be his son. Their lives would go on.

If the lad thought he was going to Londontown, he'd hound Drummond mercilessly. "You wouldn't dare tell him that."

Her arms slid around his waist, and she tucked her head beneath his chin. Tendrils of silky, golden hair caught the wind and furled around him. Heather. It filled his senses with the sweet smell of home and hearth. But Scotland was denied to him, and the woman he'd come to love was a stranger, a clever imposter who'd made him forget the past.

"You could put me to the test," she said against his neck.

Unwittingly he already had, and he could not remember winning a sweeter prize than her innocence. But to her mind, they were bantering words, not promises, for in spite of her other lies, she was too honorable to use Alasdair as a pawn.

"Very well," Drummond conceded. "I'll keep that lover's mischief a secret."

She grew still. "Was it as you remember?"

Of their own volition, his arms tightened around her. "Making love to you?"

In the slope of her shoulders and the shallowness of her breathing, she radiated vulnerability. "Yes."

Women always asked that question, usually in pursuit of a compliment. Not this imposter; she wanted confirmation that her ruse had succeeded.

Suddenly he felt like the chieftain of a well-armed clan facing an enemy without weapons. The day was his. Having the advantage allowed him the luxury of telling the truth. " 'Twas better than before."

"Truly?" She came to life in his arms. "You were pleased?"

She had a way about her, an ability to draw him into conversations that both enlightened and entertained and begged to be recalled and repeated. She had a bonny sense of humor, too. Thinking of that, he said, "Crying out to God is fair testimony, lass. I enjoyed you well."

"St. Ninian."

"Pardon?"

She tipped her head back and looked up at him. Moonlight bathed her features, and her eyes twinkled with mischief. "You did not cry out to God, Drummond. I did. You invoked St. Ninian."

Laughter churned inside him, but he would not allow himself to be cheered by her wit. He failed, and she laughed with him, swaying from side to side, playing the loving wife. Loving liar.

The sensual embrace was pure torture, for his randy body enjoyed a different humor, and even as his desire swelled anew, he fought the urge to take her again, here and now.

She was a deceiving conniver, and he'd given her his heart. Now he must guard her well. " 'Tis natural for a Scot to cry out to St. Ninian. Surely you understand, for you are forthright yourself."

"A timid woman alone often becomes a man's prey. Now that you've come home, I feel safe, and definitely not alone."

I'm different now.

Indeed; she was now a deflowered imposter.

How much had Clare told her about him? Some things, for she had abided by his wishes and named their home Fairhope. *We verily wore off our fur.* Clare would not have uttered that earthy remark. Neither would she make up tales of his heroism or take his side against the likes of Red Douglas.

"What makes you smile, Drummond?"

"How do you know if I am smiling?"

"Are you?"

She shouldn't know him so well, not when he knew so little about her. He remembered wondering, after their first meeting, if someone else had inhabited Clare's body. Now the observation seemed providential in the extreme. Now was also the time to learn how much she knew. "I was thinking about those gardens you wanted. Remember?"

"No," she said thickly. "I do not recall the gardens."

Of course she wouldn't. Clare had wanted manicured lawns; this woman wanted prosperity and a future for Alasdair. Clare had feared water; this woman had taught the lad to swim. She had also taught Drummond to be a good parent.

If she were Clare's relative, surely she held some affection for her. Where was Clare?

The unknown intricacies robbed him of ire. "My pardon, then."

"I will not tease Alasdair in your name."

"I know."

She had duped the lad as well, but she had also raised him with kindness and taught him respect for others. She loved Alasdair as her own, and he knew no other mother. Drummond remembered the first time he'd taken Alasdair up on Longfellow. Without saddle or second thought, she had ridden after them. She'd been terrified that Drummond would take Alasdair from her.

Weeks later, when he had threatened to do that very thing if she did not kiss him in front of Sheriff Hay and Red Douglas, she had played the smitten wife. Out of fear, not affection or desire.

Now she wanted him.

Forget her generosity and her mothering skills, his pride demanded. She was a deceiver. To his dismay, his body ignored character judgments and craved a different kind of gratitude. As if sensing his need, she cuddled closer.

The tether of abstention had been loosed. Why not enjoy her as often as he pleased? She took pleasure in the tender sport, and if hand movements were signals, she wanted him to love her again. If she conceived, he'd provide for the child. What to do with her would be decided later.

What to do with her now held particular appeal.

"Perhaps we made Alasdair happy tonight," he ventured.

"By making him clean Longfellow's harness?"

"Nay." He smiled at her innocence. "He wants a wee sister."

Her fingers clutched his back. "Do you think I could have conceived? We've only —"

Lain together once, he silently finished her thought. She'd almost given herself away. She would again. He could feel her fear, and he wondered how often she worried that he would see through her charade? Her effort seemed oddly gallant. The trick was to discern when she lied and when she told the truth. Direct questions seemed a good place to start. "Want you more children?"

"Oh, yes, a keepful."

The truth spilled from her lips and his loins heard. By the saints, he'd been deprived for seven years, and she was as willing as a true wife. Only a fool would deny her.

Only a scoundrel would take her again tonight. Then she moved her hands to the tie of his hose and nestled her cheek against his chest. His loins turned to iron.

"Would you have me love you here?" he croaked, wishing he could trust her reasons, wishing he didn't enjoy her company so much, wishing he could take back his heart.

"Hum." After a moment's contemplation, she said, "No, I'd not have you telling the tale that our firstborn was conceived on a battlement."

"Firstborn?"

She rushed to say, "I meant our firstborn daughter. Of course."

A slip of her tongue, but not the last. He would keep at her, and putting a distance between them now seemed a good place to begin. But he couldn't think logically with her breasts pressed against him and her fingers toying with the tie to his hose. "You must be sore."

"Why? I've told you before, I'm hale and hearty." Her hands moved lower to caress him intimately. "Motherhood suits me well, and you appear rather attentive to the idea. Yes?"

Desire blurred his vision, and he banished his

conscience and lifted her for his kiss. "Aye, I want you, lass."

She came willingly and melted against him in a surrender too sweet to deny. Even as her tongue swirled against his, he wondered which of them was truly yielding.

"Shall I carry you?" she teased.

"I am not besotted with drink."

"Not anymore."

Confidence made her coy. Drummond could disavow her of the belief that he'd been too tippered to notice the obvious. But she was smiling sweetly and his body craved *this* woman, whatever her name.

He swung her into his arms and returned to their bed, where he taught her new ways of making love. She proved to be an exceptionally bright student.

Sometime later, she lay on his chest, her knees hugging his waist and another part of her hugging him elsewhere.

"I could fall asleep like this," she purred against his neck.

Replete to his bones, Drummond said, "When 'like this' loses appeal, lass, I'll be too old to care."

"I cannot imagine being too old to love you."

Love? Not from her, a liar. The truth tainted his contentment but could not spoil the memory of the pleasure they had shared.

Still astride him, she sat up straight and

winnowed her fingers through her hair, flipping it back over her shoulders. Her naked breasts looked deliciously pert, and her eyes glittered with satisfaction. "Shall I fetch you a sleeping gown?" she asked.

Holding her waist, he thrust upward. "I have one."

Her hearty laughter left him completely naked.

"Oh," she pouted, so openly disappointed at his withdrawal that he smiled.

A liar. Who made his heart sing and his soul soar. An imposter. Who'd built a life and a future here in the Borders and expected him to share it with her.

"I command you to rest." He rolled to his side, pulled her against him, and drew up the blankets.

Confusion robbed him of sleep. He should have guessed the truth, but he'd been too interested in condemning her for a whore and lusting after her.

Questions stood out in his mind. From this moment forth, he would be relentless in his pursuit of answers.

I am not the woman you married.

She had taunted him with the truth. Now he would repay the favor. She would reveal her secrets, and he would relish watching her squirm to keep them.

Thinking the sky couldn't be prettier even if God had painted the clouds gold, Johanna climbed the steps to the keep. Her leap of faith last night had proved successful and worthwhile. Her cheeks ached from smiling, and her body sang with contentment. She wanted to plow a field or milk a cow, but most of all she wanted to rush into Drummond's arms and tell him who she really was and explain why she'd deceived him. But she could not, not when she couldn't trust him and not when Sister Margaret's fate hung in the balance.

Methods and consequences aside, she loved him and through deed and action she would demonstrate her devotion. One day he would forgive her, and now she would build a foundation of friendship on which to lay his pardon.

Decorum behind her, Johanna almost skipped down the hall and into the solar. She found him seated at her desk, a stack of ledgers at his elbow. At the sight of her, his interest sharpened. She knew the feeling well.

"Good day, my lord."

Putting down the quill, he rose. "How fare you, my lady?"

Waving her arms in the air and dancing a jig seemed a natural response. But she composed herself. "I fare well, and you?"

He tapped the ledgers. "Wealth always sweetens a man's humor."

What had happened to the adoring and tireless lover of last night? He had no words of affection. "Wealth?"

From the stack of books, he withdrew the

king's writ. "Shall we burn this now or have a ceremony?"

How could he not feel cheerful and at peace with the world? Because he still knew her for an adulteress. "What do you mean by that? Why burn it?" she asked.

" 'Tis simple. You are not the widow Macqueen."

Sweet Jesus, he knew. Her hands trembled and her euphoria fled. Or did he know? "Of course I am."

"Only if I'm dead, lass, and you keep me very much alive."

The compliment soothed her fear and brought a return to her high spirits. "The writ proves ownership of the land."

"True." He rubbed his chin, and his eyes glowed with cunning. "With this decree, we could sell the land and have a healthy purse for it."

She had dedicated herself to making this land prosper. He could not sell it. Fear made her bold. "Where would we go? Sheriff Hay said the king has forbidden you Scotland."

Hurt flickered in his eyes, but then he laughed. "There's France and England and a wee bit left of Wales."

"I would rather stay here."

"You?" Grinning, he waved her forward. "You'll have to convince me you've changed your mind about exploring every corner of England."

Oh, Clare, Johanna lamented, you should have come to this man for guidance instead of taking the word of a demented Plantagenet prince. But poor Clare was dead, and Johanna had no right to scour for faults. She must abide with this man. "I've lost the wanderlust, my lord. In that, too, I have changed."

With male pride to spare, he folded his arms over his chest. He looked at home among her possessions, perfectly suited to the role of lord and master. Pray God she could keep him that way.

"For the better, I must say. You were as spoiled as any queen," he said.

Loyalty to Clare made Johanna defensive. "I was not so bad as all that."

"Nay?" He chuckled, but without humor. "You struck your maid and refused to rise before noon."

An excuse popped into her mind. "Because I dallied with you until almost sunrise."

He regarded her closely. "Our most recent dalliance has made you brave."

According to Glory, a woman could enthrall a man with her body, and at the moment Drummond was not attentive enough for her purpose. She resorted to flattery and feminine wiles.

Crossing the room, she stood before him and placed her hands on his chest. "I am your servant, my lord."

"Perhaps now, but what of your pouting and complaining?"

Why was he speaking so cruelly about Clare? It was almost as if he wanted her to defend her sister or herself or both their actions. Oh drat.

Johanna wasn't sure what he wanted, so she told the truth. "I am subject to neither of those weaknesses."

"Good. Alasdair pouts and complains enough for the three of us. I just hope his siblings do not learn from him."

Drummond did want more children, and the knowledge filled Johanna with hope that she would soon conceive. "As do I."

With a work-worn finger, he traced the edge of her ear. "It must have been lonely for you at the abbey, growing without siblings. I recall you did not speak often of your life there."

Johanna fought the sensual pleasure his touch inspired. She was treading dangerous ground. Clare could not have spoken in detail about her childhood. The old King Edward had forbidden her to reveal that she had a twin sister. "On occasion it was lonely, but I did have friends in Meridene and Johanna."

"They were as sisters to you, did you not say?"

She could put the matter to rest and end her fear of discovery by telling him now that Johanna was dead. God help her, but the words would not come. "Yes, we were close."

"Were there other orphans there?"

Guilt dragged at her conscience and made her cross. "I have no family, Drummond, save you and my son. Can we not embrace a cheerier subject than relatives I'll unfortunately never know?"

"You never cared about my relatives, either," he challenged.

How could he have been so loving last night and so callous today? She did not know, but she had no intention of yielding her pride. "I tell you, I was too young to know better."

"You refused to attend the funeral of the child my mistress had borne the winter before. The wee lad offered no threat to you."

Had Clare been so selfish? Had she not even offered him comfort? The possibility brought tears to Johanna's eyes. She could not justify her sister's action, but neither could she listen to more charges. Unsure of what to say or do, she murmured, "I'm sorry," and returned the ledgers to the wall shelf.

"Lass?" he said, his voice thick with regret. " 'Twas cruel of me to recall that day. You couldn't have known my feelings. 'Twas natural for a prideful young man to keep them to himself."

Misery choked her. "But I should have. I'm very sorry, Drummond. The poor lad was a gift from God. I will pray for him today at Vespers."

He embraced her, sheltering her in his arms and showering her with comfort. "Worry not now, lass. He was well-shriven and his passing honestly mourned."

Compelled to right the wrong, Johanna lowered her guard. "What was his name?"

" 'Twas Evander."

"Then give me another son, Drummond, and we shall name him for the lad you lost."

He kissed her then with an intensity of passion

that was new and yet as old as time. No barrier existed between them save the trappings of propriety, and when his breathing grew ragged and his need too great to ignore, Johanna pulled away and bolted the door.

All roused and ready male, he leaned against the desk. "What mischief are you about, lass?"

As wanton as Eve, she began peeling off her clothes. "Only my mischievous wifely duties. Have you an objection?"

He lifted his jerkin and looked down at the bulge in his hose. "See you an objection here?"

"No. I see a man wearing far too many clothes."

He loved her there, on the desk, with rare September sunshine pouring through the windows and the promise of forever hanging in the air.

An hour later, their clothing righted and their eyes aglow with the remnants of passion, they went into the yard to oversee the building of the charcoal oven.

Their task was interrupted by the arrival of a messenger from Sister Margaret.

Chapter 17

*Praise God that Lord Drummond has been spared.
We at Scarborough Abbey are visited of the Archbishop of Lancaster until Michaelmas, else I would
tender personally my greetings to your husband.*

*Stay true to the one who resides in your heart,
my child. Confess often and only to God, and should
the opportunity arise for travel, know that our doors
are always open to you and yours.*

Johanna crushed the vellum. Although cloaked
in good advice, the abbess's meaning was clear;
Johanna was not to reveal her identity, and if
she wished to flee, she would find sanctuary at
Scarborough Abbey.

Her heart rebelled. She had intended to tell
Drummond the truth, for he deserved honesty
from her. Could she share his bed and bear his
children and deceive him all the while? The lie
would grow with the passage of years, and the
weight of her burden would eventually crush her
spirit.

Raindrops splashed on the window casement, and the dreary turn of the day matched perfectly her mood. Suddenly chilled, she moved to the stool near the hearth and stared at the rushes on the solar floor.

For seven years, she had lived a borrowed life. Now she was being called to task for it. But, oh, the physical aspects of marriage gave her an inner glow. In this very room only hours ago, she had found comfort and bliss in Drummond's arms.

Even so, she knew he would continue to recall the mistakes of his young wife, and Johanna would have to shoulder the guilt and accept the blame. Today it had been Clare's lack of sympathy over the death years ago of Drummond's son Evander. Tomorrow Drummond would condemn her for another of Clare's transgressions.

Unless Johanna fought back. But with what weapons? Patience was easily exhausted, for she sensed in her heart that she and Drummond could build a prosperous life together would he but look to the future. Defense offered a partial strategy, but she had only limited knowledge of Clare's life in the Highlands, and those precious bits of information had come during the last hours of Clare's life. Each time Johanna must defend her sister, she recalled her own loss. But therein, too, lay a defense, for she could not let him defame her sister's memory.

Clare had been young and carefree. On the day word had come to Scarborough Abbey of her betrothal to the legendary chieftain of the Macqueens, she had danced on air.

At the memory, heartache burned in Johanna's chest. She had been wildly jealous. As was often the case, Sister Margaret had known and taken her aside. After showering Johanna with affection, the abbess had made her understand that happiness would come to her in time.

"Fret not, my child," Sister Margaret had said, her brown eyes filled with love. "You could as well wed a prince. And pity his majestic soul when he learns that his bride is worthy and as strong willed as any king."

Life's irony made Johanna smile. She was possessed of an inner strength, and where her heart led, determination would follow.

According to Clare, Drummond had made mistakes. Perhaps if Johanna reminded him of his shortcomings and those of his family, he would cease recalling Clare's. Then, and only then, would they abide in happiness and joy. Johanna would fight, for she knew no other method. She had fought her distractors to build this keep. She would fight for the man she loved.

Sooner than she expected, a new battle was struck.

The rain continued through most of the afternoon, turning the lane into a quagmire and making the walk to the chapel an ordeal. At the close of Vespers, Drummond began his verbal nit-picking.

" 'Tis odd, lass, that you did not fashion the

chapel within the confines of the keep."

The rain had dwindled to a heavy mist. Johanna and Drummond walked the clean edge of the lane. Alasdair ran ahead of them, hopscotching from puddle to puddle and splattering his boots and hose with mud. "The church is for all the people of Fairhope, and a walk never did any harm that I know of."

Drummond ducked beneath the cobbler's sign, "You no longer grouse over muddying your slippers?"

Passersby nodded, and Johanna smiled in return. Inside she wanted to scream, but a tantrum would yield her nothing. "I was only ten and three when you met me, Drummond. If you'll recall, I came to you with a pair of slippers and my serviceable boots."

"Are you charging that I could not support my wife? I gifted you with the best velvets in the Highlands."

She must show him the error of his thinking and steer the conversation to familiar ground. "I would have preferred your patronage to your purse, and you made a practice of imparting both elsewhere and often. But those times have passed, my lord, for I have all of the velvets I require."

He clutched her elbow and steered her around a pile of refuse. "What of my patronage?"

She gave him a saucy smile and leaned close. "In case you have forgotten, you properly patronized me earlier today."

"Then you have no complaint?"

"As I said before, my lord. I began loving you when you took my side against Elton Singer."

The stiffness went out of him. "Your love is a formidable weapon, lass."

"As is your long and *un*forgiving memory, my lord."

"I anticipate falling prey to your affection again — tonight."

"I pray for . . . for . . ." She paused, unwilling to beg a pardon for a crime she had not committed.

His fingers tightened on her arm. "You pray for what?"

Build a new memory, her logic insisted. Think not like Clare, but Johanna. "I pray for a dozen sons to keep you occupied."

" 'Twill be costly," he teased. "If I must outfit them all with weapons of war."

He was taunting her, for he knew well her feelings on the subject of war. "You will not make mercenaries of my children."

"As their father, I will do as I may with the lads."

"Unless they are as stubborn as you." She laughed, picturing him surrounded by his own obstinate offspring.

"What cheers you?"

"Oh, nothing, save the future."

"I'll wager 'tis at my expense," he grumbled.

"Just so. I was imagining you trying to lead a dozen battle-hungry lads who bristled at being governed. Better you should *not* teach them all the tricks of war you know."

"Better you should mind our daughters."

Her ploy worked, for he was responding to her rather than a memory. "I've not done badly with Alasdair, but I'm sure you will have of it a different opinion."

"Did you see him in the tiltyard before the rains came?"

She'd been reading Sister Margaret's letter and lamenting over the past. "Nay."

"Then boast not yet, dear wife. Since we forbade him a sword, your son announced that without weapons, he had no need of his eyes. So he pretended to be blind. He used a stick to find his way and a porridge bowl to beg for alms. For the better part of an hour, he recanted his every ill word and deed, all the while bemoaning the fact that his parents would not forgive him. I swear on the soil of Scotland, he wailed like a lass who'd been jilted by her beau."

She could see Alasdair doing those very things. "What did you say to him?"

"I bade him pretend to be a mute on the morrow."

Johanna burst out laughing. "A perfect response, my lord."

He fairly preened, shoulders squared, arms suddenly swinging at his side. Gazing after Alasdair, he murmured, "His vision returned with miraculous haste."

Drummond wore fatherly pride like a magnificent mantle. "His time of punishment has been worthwhile. What say you to giving him your old sword? You have another finer blade now."

His expression grew blank with surprise. "Where did *you* acquire it?"

Taken aback by the accusation, Johanna could not think of a reply. It was almost as if Drummond knew her secret. Impossible. Both the brand and her maidenhead were history. The prince had given the weapon to Clare, along with a promise to intervene with his father on Drummond's behalf. In that, Prince Edward had been true to his word, for Drummond had survived. Young Edward's largesse had not stopped there, for upon his father's death last year and his ascension to the throne, he had pardoned Drummond.

Emboldened, Johanna said, "Where do you think I acquired it?"

"I meant to say that I'm surprised you kept it."

"Well, I did. I hoped one day to give it to Alasdair. I'm sorry to say it's probably rusted, for I packed it away."

"And forgot about it."

"As I forgot about you." She finished his thought, and her words hung like specters between them in the misty air.

To her surprise, he let go of her elbow and wrapped an arm around her shoulders. Close to her ear, he said, "Did you, at Vespers, thank God for my return, and ask Him to keep me well?"

When Drummond turned on the charm, he

could win over a nun. Basking in his affection, Johanna looked up at him. "I prayed that He would gift you with humility."

Mirth glimmered in his eyes. "Then your prayers have been answered, for I'll gladly submit to your tender mercies."

"I believe, my lord, that you have confused the carnal and the spiritual."

As sly as a hungry fox, he said, "At a given moment, they have been known to converge."

He was speaking of their lovemaking and his habit of calling upon a saint at the moment of his greatest pleasure.

" 'Tis impolite to whisper," Alasdair grumbled, now standing before them at the base of the steps to the keep.

" 'Tis rude to correct your parents," Drummond said.

"I'm only curious. You would not tolerate an ignorant dolt for a son."

Drummond choked in surprise. "Where did you hear that sally?"

Grinning, and looking very much like his sire, Alasdair glanced at Johanna.

"Aha!" Drummond said. " 'Tis your mother's influence. That being the case, lass, I insist that you tell Alasdair what we were whispering about."

If he thought to embarrass her in front of Alasdair, he could think again; she'd had more practice than he. "Of course, I'll tell him." Looking Drummond square in the eye, she said to Alasdair, "Your father was just lamenting that he has only invoked St. Ninian once today."

His mouth fell open, but he recovered quickly. With a look that promised retribution, he said, "You clever —"

She slapped a hand over his mouth to cut off the diatribe. "Careful what you say," she warned. "Unlike his Scottish ancestors, your son has a long and *forgiving* memory."

Shaking his head, he ushered her up the stairs and into the hall. Excusing herself, she went to the solar and fetched his sword from the chest where she'd stored it years ago.

Wrapped in an old woolen blanket, the heavy weapon had been spared the ravages of rust. The scars of battle, however, were plain to see, for the scabbard bore myriad pocks and scrapes. What she could see of the sword itself was unadorned, save the pommel, which featured an engraving of the rampant wolf of the Macqueens. The leather grippings on the handle had dried and stiffened with age, revealing the fine wood beneath.

Years before, out of curiosity, she had tried to pull the blade from its sheath, but the weapon would not budge. Now she hefted the heavy weapon and tried again. Pieces of the leather wrapping crumbled against her palm. She gritted her teeth and jerked with all her might, but the sword would not come free of the scabbard.

What if Drummond could not draw the sword? Would he be embarrassed in front of Alasdair? No, she did not think so, for Drummond seemed secure in his own masculinity. He would take the weapon to the blacksmith and seek the craftsman's expertise.

Her course decided, Johanna lifted the blade to her shoulder and returned to the hall. She stopped on the threshold. Alasdair sat cross-legged atop the table and Drummond lounged on the bench. A fire blazed in the hearth. The shutters had been drawn and the lanterns lighted.

"You've never even drunk goose milk?" Alasdair was saying.

It was one of his favorite jokes, for it always garnered smiles and chuckles from his audience.

Eager to hear Drummond's response, Johanna leaned the sword against the wall and approached the table. Drummond looked up, and the tender plea in his eyes was unmistakable. He took his customary seat at the head of the table and patted his knee.

"Sit here, lass," he said. "Alasdair professes to know the secret of acquiring goose milk."

Squirming with self-importance, the lad said, "Care you to listen again, Mother?"

She cared a little more for the chance to sit on Drummond's knee. He drew her down. The muscles of his thigh rippled beneath her buttocks and his hand felt secure at her waist. To maintain her balance, she wrapped an arm around his shoulders.

"Now?" said Alasdair.

"Now," answered Drummond.

All animation, the lad leaned forward. "To acquire the rare and precious milk of the goose, you must first acquire a pail and then chase a goose to ground."

Drummond said, "How does one tell a goose from a gander?"

Alasdair's face went blank. Then he rallied, pointing a finger in the air. "Only a skilled goose hunter can know for certain."

Drummond nodded sagely. "One such as yourself."

"As myself," Alasdair chirped. "Well, once you've caught the goose, you hold her over the pail and say, 'Give up your milk, goose. I do command thee.' You must say it three times with no mistakes."

"And then what happens?" Drummond asked.

Scooting close, Alasdair tweaked Drummond's nose. "The goose pinches you, because everyone knows there's no such thing as goose milk!" Holding his sides, he fell back onto the table and chortled with glee.

Drummond rolled his eyes and laughed so hard his shoulders shook.

"You'll toss me to the floor," Johanna complained.

Eyes twinkling, Drummond murmured, "Only when I've a mind to invoke St. Ninian."

Johanna blushed to her toes. "A win to you, my lord."

His pleasure filled gaze scoured her face. "Then for my boon, I'd have our rowdy lad sleep in the barracks tonight."

As quick as a cat, Alasdair rolled onto all fours. "May I, Mother? May I please?" The drawn out plea, accompanied by soulful eyes and a pouting lower lip, robbed her of denial.

"Very well, but I forbid you to bring home bad habits from the huntsman."

"Hooray!" As quickly as it had come, Alasdair's exuberance fled. "Mother, can a man learn to snore?"

"I wouldn't know." Anticipating her next words, Drummond's hand tightened on her waist. "But your father has perfected the skill. They say he's the most resonant snorer in Christendom."

Awe rounded out Alasdair's features. "Are you, Father?"

Under his breath, Drummond said, "I'll get you for that." To Alasdair, he said, "Trouble yourself not over it now, Son. You've years to perfect the craft, and your mother has something to give you."

"The item we discussed earlier?" she said.

"Aye, I saw you bring it in."

She went to the door, fetched the weapon, and put it on the table. Alasdair's earlier excitement paled.

Fidgeting, the lad drew close. "What is it?"

" 'Tis my sword."

Sucking in his breath and looking as if he were about to touch a holy relic, Alasdair reached out for the weapon.

"I haven't the strength to free it from the scabbard," Johanna said.

Drummond seemed distracted, probably reliving the many battles he'd fought. Smiling in support, she placed her hand on his shoulder.

He glanced up. "Then you've never seen the blade?"

"No, but I'm sure it's very fine. I mean I remember it being fine."

"I want to see it," Alasdair said, transfixed.

Drummond emitted a half laugh and picked up the weapon. With one hand on the scabbard and the other on the frayed leather grip, his well-muscled arms bulged as he pulled. The tendons in his neck grew ropy from the strain. To Johanna's surprise, metal scraped against metal as the double-edged sword emerged from the sheath. But the blade itself was a ragged stump no longer than her forearm.

"What happened to it?" she said.

"It met the knee of Edward the First."

Containing her shock, Johanna spoke softly for Alasdair's benefit. "You wounded him in battle?"

"Nay." He handed the sword to Alasdair, who cradled it as if it were a swaddled babe. "He broke it over his knee. 'Tis a custom of English kings, to blunt the swords of vanquished enemies."

Drummond had been forced to surrender his sword. Johanna's heart ached for him and the great blow his pride had suffered. "Well, I hope he had a healthy bruise to show for it."

With his eyes, Drummond smiled at her. "We'll

see if the blacksmith can fashion a new blade," he said.

Encouraged by his good spirits, Johanna said, "Had I known it would render Alasdair speechless, I would have given it to him years ago."

"Now that I've yielded my sword for a second time, lass, have you trinket to replace it?"

As Drummond expected, she gasped in mortification and stepped back.

As prissy as a spinster, she lifted her chin. "I'll just see how the meal's coming along."

He watched her go, wondering how he could find out her true identity. He had intentionally spouted insults about Clare, hoping this woman would grow angry enough to trip herself up. Instead, he'd hurt her feelings. Clare had been deeply sympathetic at the death of Drummond's son. She had not cared that the lad was the child of his mistress. He must find a way to put that hurt to rights, but he could not, not until the lass opened her heart to him.

"Father, may I take this with me to the barracks tonight?"

"Nay, Alasdair." When the lad's face fell, Drummond added, "But you may take the scabbard."

Satisfied, he went back to examining the sword.

Watching him, Drummond wondered if his son could provide information about her. But Drummond felt guilty at the thought of prying information from one so young. Still, he must have answers.

"Alasdair, where is your mother's harp?"

"Harp?" He screwed up his face in confusion. "Heckley's otter dog has more musical talent than Mother. That's what she has of it."

Drummond wasn't surprised; the woman masquerading as Clare shared her appearance, but little else. "Did you know that your mother received a message from Sister Margaret today?"

The lad shrugged, engrossed in picking the crumbling leather wrappings from the handle of the weapon. "She sends me candles for my birthday."

Drummond peered through the hearth into the kitchen. He could see the blue fabric of her skirt next to Evelyn's plain gray smock. They conversed in normal tones, but he could not make out their words. Knowing the reverse was also true, he casually said, "Does anyone else write to your mother?"

Head down, Alasdair said, "Aunt Meridene. She sends me clothing that is embroidered with a very fine hand. She's an expert with a needle, you know."

"What of your aunt Johanna?"

Alasdair looked up and blinked in confusion. "She's dead, and it makes Mother very sad to talk about her. She loved her well."

Drummond struggled to hide his shock. No mention had been made of the woman's death. Clare had not — He stopped the thought. The lass was not Clare. But one of her actions would lead him to the truth, of that he was certain. "So no one else writes to your mother."

"The cloth merchant does." Using both hands, Alasdair brandished the sword. "I told you he has an affection for her."

A short-lived affection, Drummond thought. But as he stared at the broken blade of his sword, he forgot her correspondence. An ugly suspicion had entered his mind.

Clare could be an illegitimate daughter of Edward I. But Drummond would bet every drop of his Scottish blood that she did not know of the relation. His stomach soured at the alternative, for it meant that she had willingly lain with her half brother. No. Clare had not known. But if the old Edward was her father and the new king Edward her half brother, it all made sense.

Out of loyalty to his bastard daughter, Edward I had spared Drummond's life and given this plot of land to Clare. Through her, it would pass to Alasdair.

Where was Clare, and who was the lass who'd captured Drummond's heart? Surely another Plantagenet bastard, a cousin or a younger sister. A king's daughter. But why would a father brand his own flesh and blood? And why would a prince admit to an affair with his own half sister? Because he hadn't been told.

Although his mind swam with theories and possibilities, Drummond knew he was close to learning the truth.

When the table had been cleared and Alasdair delivered to the barracks, Drummond dismissed the maid. Then he took his woman's hand and led her to the hearth, where he'd spread a blanket. "Bide here with me, lass."

She came willingly, but this woman had boldness to spare. She also had a secret. "The floor, my lord?"

"I heard no complaints this afternoon. When I loved you on a desk."

In a move of pure grace, she lowered herself to the pallet and kicked off her slippers. "Nor will you hear a protest now."

He dropped down beside her, plucked an iron from the bucket of utensils and stoked the fire. The golden light accentuated her fair features and turned her hair to shimmering silk.

"Will you play your harp for me?"

Her gaze darted from the flames, to the mantel, to her hands. "I haven't played in so many years, Drummond, I doubt I could strum the simplest lay."

He had given the harp to Clare upon her arrival in the Highlands, and she played with the skill of the finest minstrels. "Have you the instrument still?"

"No. I'm sorry, for it meant much to me."

Had Clare taken the harp with her? Where was Clare? The longer the answer eluded him, the more anxious he became. "What happened to the harp?"

She glanced up at him, her expression rife with regret. "I sold it to Glory."

He noted that her eyes tilted up in the corners a tiny bit. Unlike Clare's. On closer inspection, her nose was straighter and the bridge higher than Clare's. She suffered his scrutiny with good grace, although she was clearly uncomfortable.

"I needed the money to hire Sween and to pay the glazier."

He basked in the honest statement, for a lie would have been easily discovered upon Glory's return. "I should like to hire the glazier back."

"Will you commission a window for the chapel?"

"I should, I suppose, but I rather enjoy the battlement. I thought to glass in the crenels and add a roof."

She removed her linen coif and let down her hair. "Do, and Alasdair will claim it for his own. He loves to patrol it at night."

Her hair was of a wavier texture than Clare's, and it varied with a dozen hues from sunny yellow to honey gold. He couldn't resist training his rough palm over the thick braid. "I had more intimate pastimes in mind for the battlement, and Alasdair will do as he's told."

"You show great confidence, my lord. A mistake, I fear, where our son is concerned."

Our son. She had no intention of baring her soul to him, not voluntarily, and the knowledge hurt. She must have good reason to keep her secrets. In her little finger, this woman possessed more character and strength of will than any noble he'd ever known. And why not? She was a king's daughter. Her courage troubled Drummond, though, for he had hoped to hear the truth from her lips.

"What weighty thoughts occupy you? Surely you do not worry over Alasdair?"

"Nay. I asked Bertie to stay with him." He gave her a lecherous smile. "We are alone."

Her brows lifted. "What have you done with Evelyn?"

"Evelyn has done something with herself, and I'm certain you will disapprove."

"Then it must involve John Handle's eldest son."

Drummond had to smile. "Does anything in Fairhope escape your notice?"

"Your long hair has not. Shall I shear it before we go to Dumfries?"

"You can trim it now."

"Oh, no. Alasdair fights like a badger every time I take the shears to him. I expect you to be a good example for him."

"We leave on Saturday."

"Why? The journey requires only three days' travel."

The fire popped and crackled; Drummond added another log. "Not on a plodding elephant."

"Can you not leave him here with Morgan Fawr?"

Drummond chuckled remembering the last time he'd left Longfellow behind. "When I left the Tower of London without him, I had walked only as far as Billingsgate when he trumpeted loud enough to wake the French. As soon as he started battering the walls, they let him go."

She laughed, too. "That must have been a sight, Longfellow barreling after you in Londontown. Some of the streets are narrower than he."

He'd caught her in a blatant lie, for Clare had never been to London. This woman could easily have traveled to London — to visit her father.

If she knew her birthright. But the more Drummond studied her, the less convinced he was that she knew. He craved knowledge of this woman, her past, and the needs in her heart. "When were you there?"

"Never. But I know many who have. Red Douglas, Sheriff Hay, even Sween. They all tell a different tale."

Relief flooded him, for he believed her. "Do you care to go?"

"No, Drummond. I am truly content here. But tell me, how do you manage to go a-hunting and leave Longfellow here?"

"He has a truly marvelous nose. His old handler swore that the beast could smell as far as an eagle could see. I believe 'tis true, but I hesitate to put it to the test."

"We can forgo a luggage cart?"

"True, unless you'd like to ride atop him with me? A tent would shelter us from the elements and prying eyes."

"Think you to . . . to . . ." Her face a picture

of maidenly modesty, she turned up her hands. "To do *that* on an elephant?"

"Have you no taste for adventure, lass?"

"I doubt I could feel at ease, Drummond."

"You mean, should I fondle your breasts." He reached for her, his actions matching his words. In caressing her, he decided that she was better endowed than Clare. The last time he'd seen his wife, she'd been big with child and her breasts swollen accordingly.

So many differences existed, and he'd been too obsessed with naming her an adulteress to notice. He noticed now, and the bounty he explored and the beauty he treasured had a predictable reaction. But this woman had also captured his heart.

Leaning into his hand, she closed her eyes, and her mouth curled up in a smile of pure pleasure.

"Do I please you?"

She opened one eye. "Silly questions are disallowed."

"If we are composing rules to this tryst, I would disallow clothing."

Her eyes drifted shut. "I shall not peek, my lord."

The door was bolted. He could enjoy her at his leisure. So he set about doing just that. In slow movements, he peeled off her clothing, and then his own. Anticipation thrummed through him, settling heavily in his loins, but he battled his own desire and focused on hers. Kneeling before the hearth and facing her, he took her in his arms and gave her a slow, wet kiss. She grew eager and clutched his shoulders, tilting her head to the side to deepen the kiss. When her tongue sallied forth, he suckled it gently, and she moaned and swayed against him.

Pulling back, he waited until her eyes fluttered open. Her dreamy expression fattened his pride and lengthened another part of him. "Slowly, love. I had in mind to savor you for a while."

"Savor me," she murmured. "I like the sound of that."

Only a hussy or a newly breached maiden would speak so artlessly. "You'll like the rest more," he teased, and laid into the kiss again.

When he thought he had her breathless and too weak to protest he drew back again. To his surprise, she took him in her hand and said, "How else do I savor you?"

Not Clare. Not by a bishop's mile. "I'll teach you, later." He moved her hand aside.

She pouted prettily and tossed back her hair. Her breasts beckoned, and he gripped her waist and lifted her so he could suckle properly and at length. The heather-sweet taste of her nipples whetted his appetite for a more precious delicacy, but he shelved the need for now and moved to feast on her other breast.

She shivered and moaned and wove her supple fingers into his hair, holding him there, an un-necessary but highly evocative gesture, for not even a clan war could distract him from loving this woman tonight. Her breasts felt pillow soft, a delightful contrast to the pebble-hard tips, and when he drew back enough to blow gently on her dampened skin, she gasped in both joy and shock.

Eager for greater delights, he eased her onto the blanket and worked his way down her body until his cheek rested on her thigh.

The hearth fire hissed as flames licked at the dry logs.

"What are you about, Drummond?" she asked in a breathy, quiet voice.

"I'm about my husbandly pleasure." He spread her legs wide and with his fingers, parted the petal-like folds of her treasure. "You've lost the freckle you had here on your —"

"Drummond Macqueen! You'll rob me of my dignity."

"I seek only my favorite trinket."

He tasted her, and at the touch of his lips, she moaned, "Oh, Lord."

Against her honeyed skin, he murmured, "Try invoking St. Ninian. He's always served me well."

He loved her thusly, until she squirmed and cried out to a dozen saints. Primed and ready, he moved up and over her. Her arms lay limp at her sides, but her fingers still clutched the blanket in a death grip. Her hair fanned out in a golden puddle and the firelight turned her complexion the color of old ivory. He noticed the patch of lighter skin on her shoulder.

His willpower was sorely taxed, and his manhood unerringly found the place it sought. As he drove into her exquisite softness, he glimpsed an old scar beneath the newly healed skin.

A tiny blunted sword.

Chapter 18

Sitting in the shade of Longfellow's shelter, Drummond assembled the harness that would secure the elephant's traveling saddle. Across the yard, his wife conversed with Elton Singer. Like an unsolved riddle, the puzzle of who she was tormented Drummond. In his surety that she was an imposter, he had only looked at the dilemma from one perspective: His own.

Hundreds of times since seeing the old brand beneath the new scar he had considered asking her outright. The query always died on his lips, for he feared that she would continue with the ruse. Why not? He had called her a whore. He had searched out her faults. He had threatened to take Alasdair away. How could she trust a man who had visited so many wrongs upon her? The answer saddened him, for he knew in his heart he had treated her cruelly.

As he often did, Drummond thought about the Clare he remembered. He'd last seen her at

Hogmanay, three months before her fifteenth birthday and four months before Alasdair's birth. For a New Year's gift, he had presented her with a bolt of fine white velvet. She had squealed with glee and spent the evening choosing and discarding dress styles for the fabric. It had been a girlish exercise and typical for one her age. She had no responsibilities at Castle Macqueen, no duties designed to aid in the seasoning of a convent bred Englishwoman. Growth and experience had come later for her, after Drummond's capture, after her flight from the Highlands.

Any woman would mature in seven years' time, especially so, given the circumstances. Look at her now, Drummond thought with pride, watching her give counsel and encouragement to a former drunkard and reformed wifebeater. Through patience and understanding, she had bettered Singer's life.

Could Drummond have been mistaken about her innocence? He didn't think so, but he hadn't loved a woman in seven years. No, that was incorrect. He hadn't *lain* with a woman in seven years. More to the point, he had never before loved a woman, not the way that he loved her. In their too brief time together, she had taught him to appreciate his freedom and rejoice in even the smallest of life's gifts. She encouraged him to lead the people of Fairhope and look to the future. In her presence, he felt like a king with the world at his feet and tomorrow at his command.

He would not risk losing her; yet he must know the truth, and only she could reveal it. He must bide his time, and with each word and every deed, let her know that he merited her trust. Instinctively he knew that much was at stake for her, this woman he could not, would not, live without.

He smiled as he finished the preparations for their journey to Dumfries, for he knew just the way to gain her confidence.

On the way to Douglas Castle, Evelyn refused to ride a horse or to climb aboard Longfellow, so a carter had been hired. Between broken wheels and the necessity to choose the best and longest roads, the trip had been lengthened by two days. Tempers grew short, but Drummond diplomatically soothed the men each night while Bertie cared for the horses. With a fire on one side and a wall of elephant on the other, everyone had slept warm beneath the stars.

At Douglas Castle, Johanna settled Alasdair in a room with Bertie, then returned to Drummond. She found him staring out the window of their chamber. His freshly cut hair drew attention to the breadth of his shoulders, but corded neck muscles testified to the tenseness he felt. He wore a leather jerkin and brown trunk hose beneath his tartan cape. Moving to the bed, he picked up a red velvet jerkin emblazoned with the Macqueen family symbol. Johanna knew he planned to wear the garment for his audience with the king, and she was surprised when he tossed it into a corner.

"You'll look unkempt tonight," she said.

He leaned against the casement. "Who'll notice a few wrinkles when a Highland chieftain falls to his knee?"

She couldn't answer. To avoid fidgeting, she strolled the room, pretending interest in the crucifix on the wall and the tassels on the bed hangings. The silence grew heavy.

In desperation, she finally said, "Then you've decided to swear fealty to Red Douglas and the king?"

Drummond pushed away from the wall and walked to the foot of the bed. "If I do not, will you come with me to Scotland?"

She drew in a sharp breath and stared at the pads of her fingers. The question risked his life. She could easily tell Red Douglas that Drummond planned to escape. His chance, and possibly his life, would be forfeit, for Douglas would detain Drummond until the scheduled audience. Edward II could return the man she loved to prison, or he could carry out the dire punishment that Red Douglas had described.

When she dared raise her gaze, she found Drummond watching her, his beguiling eyes luminous with vulnerability. The chieftain of the Macqueens had handed her his life. The latter chased a chill up her spine, but she held out her hand to him.

He took it and raised it to his lips. "Will you

go where I go, lass?"

Love filled her, and she threaded her fingers through his. "What of the people of Fairhope?"

He gave her a crooked smile. "You haven't a care for yourself or the hardships that await us in the Highlands. Your first thought is always for others."

"I will survive the Highlands."

"Because you are my hale and hearty wife."

Like a captive struggling for freedom, the truth she must tell strained within her. She opened her mouth, but long practice gave her pause.

He raised his brows, as if willing her to speak her mind. Squeezing her hand, he softly said, "I love you."

Her heart filled with short-lived joy. He loved her, he wanted to take her with him wherever he went. Their lives together were secure. She could no longer conceal her true identity. If Drummond could trust her with his life, she must trust him with her own. "I am not your wife."

"I know." Giving her a crooked smile, he added, "Thank you for the gift of your innocence."

Taken aback, she didn't know whether to rail at him for not telling her sooner that he knew, or fly into his arms and worry over it later. His quizzical expression ended her indecision. "I'm Clare's sister."

He seemed to nudge her with an expectant look. "Your name is . . ."

"Oh." She almost wilted at her own lack of

insight. "I'm Johanna. Johanna Benison."

That confused him, for he tilted his head to the side. "Alasdair believes you dead."

"As does everyone else in the world, save Bertie and Sister Margaret, and Meridene, of course."

He took a deep breath. "Where is Clare?"

Johanna crumbled. He caught her and pulled her against his chest. She hadn't shared her grief in so very long, and living with Drummond had brought back all of the memories.

"In a grave that bears my name."

He rocked her from side to side. "How did it happen?"

Between sobs she told him about their sisterly relationship, Clare's death, and Johanna's promise to care for Alasdair.

"Poor lass."

His chest quivered, and she suspected he held back his own grief. When the storm of sadness passed, Johanna looked up at him. "I had the chance to build a life for myself and Alasdair. Can you forgive me for deceiving you?"

He reached into his pouch and handed her a scarf. "Dry your tears — Johanna."

The soft caress of his words made her sob again.

"What is it?" he entreated, blotting her eyes and bestowing a kiss to take the place of each tear.

She struggled for composure. "I dreamed of hearing you call me by my name. I thought never to hear it on your lips."

"Shall I say it a dozen times? Johanna, Johanna,

Johanna." His crooning, lilting voice made a poem of her name.

Smiling through her sadness, she said, "That will do, my lord."

He led her to the bed and sat down beside her. "Why did you burn yourself? You bear the same brand as Clare."

"Not the same. Although we were twins, my brand is upside down. I thought you would notice."

His face went still and white. "Twins?"

"Yes. Does that make a difference?"

He stared at the far wall, squinting, as if trying to remember something important. At length, he said, "You were born on the nineteenth of March in twelve eighty-six."

"Yes."

He touched her scarred shoulder, then his hand cupped her cheek. "Do you know who branded you and why?"

As always, she grew defensive. "No, nor do I care to know who my parents were. They gave Clare and me away. I have nothing to give to them. If the mark or my lack of lineage troubles you, then I am truly sorry, but I will never seek out my family."

He fell back on the mattress and closed his eyes. "Fret not about your heritage, Johanna, for I have enough relatives and family tradition for the both of us."

"Will you swear fealty?"

"Aye, I will and gladly now. I have two bonny

reasons to make my home at Fairhope."

"Oh, Drummond." She lunged at him, and he hugged her tightly.

She felt like heaven in his arms, and Drummond couldn't help whispering her name over and over. Johanna — one of a pair of twin daughters born on the night that Alexander, the last king of Scotland, met his death.

The enormity of her identity robbed Drummond of breath and filled him with awe. Edward I of England had found the lassies, scarred them with his infamous blunted sword, and spirited them to Scarborough Abbey. Years later, in an act of supreme cruelty, he'd paired a daughter of the royal house of Dunkeld to the chieftain of the mighty Clan Macqueen. He'd put one of the Scottish princesses right under their noses, and he probably intended to hold Johanna for blackmail. Only Clare's death and Johanna's determination had foiled the second part of his plan.

Drummond rejoiced for his people, then quickly grew sober with the weight of a new responsibility. If news of Johanna's existence reached the Highlands, there'd be bloody hell to pay. The clans would rally round her and rattle their swords of war. Alasdair could look forward to a future of political intrigue. Their daughters would become alliance makers, pawns on the great chessboard of European nobility.

But not if Drummond kept their birthright a

secret, a privilege and a burden he must bear alone.

"Drummond Macqueen!"

From her angry tone, he knew he was in for trouble.

She squirmed free of his embrace and scrambled off the bed. Anger narrowed her eyes, and she propped her clenched fists on her hips. "You taunted me with Clare's faults."

Lashed by regrets, Drummond pleaded with his eyes. "She truly grieved for wee Evander. I'm deeply sorry, and said as much in my prayers."

"And the other accusations?"

He sighed. "I confess I colored them up to suit my purposes. I wanted to find out who you were." Lowering his voice, he said, "She *was* unfaithful to me."

As he watched, her anger melted. "I know. She told me so. But she had good reason, Drummond. The prince, Edward, promised her that he would intervene on your behalf. Now he's king of England The beef-witted troll."

Drummond chuckled, but without humor. "Better him than me."

"I swear I'll make you a good wife."

She still seemed so troubled, and Drummond hoped to end her melancholy. He knew just the way. "Impossible."

That caught her attention. "What do you mean?"

" 'Tis simple. We have not said words before

394

a priest, so you cannot be my wife."

Fire glittered in her eyes. "I'll not be your mistress."

"Nay. You'll be my lifelong mate — as soon as we find a priest."

Her gaze searched his, and he thought she had never been more lovely, more companionable. "I do not understand," she whispered.

Tamping back excitement, he took her hand. "You, Clare *Johanna* Macqueen, will say your vows."

Enlightenment sent her flying into his arms. "Oh, Drummond. You're too clever for words and for bad kings."

He drew her against him. "And you're too alluring to resist."

She swallowed and glanced toward the door. "You'd love me now?"

"I will love you always." Cupping his hand around her nape, he held her still and lowered his mouth to hers. It was a kiss of fulfillment, of belonging, and a passion neither place nor time could alter. Knowing he'd succumb to the lustful demands of his body, Drummond pulled back. "We'll invite Sister Margaret to serve as witness when we *reaffirm* our wedding vows."

"That's what everyone will think. That we are *re*affirming our troths."

He also planned to confer with Sister Margaret and confirm Johanna's heritage. "You're brighter than an Oxford scholar, my delicious love, but you must continue to style yourself 'Clare,' for we know not who else knows that she had a sister."

" 'Tis no real burden, for I loved her well."

"Then it's settled."

She folded her arms at her waist, hugging herself, holding a secret within. "How ever will I face Edward again?"

Drummond had thought the last surprise behind him. "Again?"

A troubled frown marred her perfect brow. "He came with his father to fetch Clare to the Highlands and to you. The old king commanded me to stay out of sight during their visit. Why, I do not know. Late one night, I went to the pantry to check the next day's provisions — I managed the commerce of the abbey."

Fond memories filled Drummond with hope. "Capable, dependable Johanna. 'Tis what Clare said of you. What else of Edward?"

"I saw him in the kitchen. It was odd beyond belief."

"What was odd?"

"He was with another youth, a swarthy fellow, not much taller than me, and only a few years older than me. They were speaking French, but too quickly, and the dialect was unusual. I know the language is romantic in sound, but it seemed to me they were conversing much too fondly." She shrugged, obviously at a loss for an explanation.

Even in the Tower of London, Drummond had heard rumors of the new king's unnatural affection for the Gascony knight Piers Gaveston. Had Johanna actually witnessed what so many others speculated about?

That prospect made Drummond warm with fear. "Did they see you?"

"Yes, but I told them I was Clare."

Like a spike of lightning, the truth behind Clare's unfaithfulness flashed in Drummond's mind. Young Prince Edward believed she had witnessed his unholy affection for Piers Gaveston. For no other reason than to discredit her, the prince had coerced her into an affair. If she had exposed him, no one would take the word of a known adulteress. How clever and typically Plantagenet. And how sad for Clare, who had been totally innocent of the knowledge young Edward had feared.

"What's wrong, Drummond?" She knelt at his feet, her best green gown pooling on the floor, her eyes wide with concern.

" 'Tis nothing. Do not fret." But his heart felt broken for the young woman, his wife, who had sold her fidelity to a perverted prince for the promise of her husband's release. Drummond had been blessed among men, for he knew both of the Scottish princesses as wife, and they had both loved him well. He silently swore to protect the remaining princess with his life and his false fealty to an unworthy king.

"Drummond, I will not shame you. I'm not at all like Clare."

Saddened that she had misinterpreted his silence, he cupped her face. "Aye, Johanna, you are, for she was a bonny lass."

"But I meant —"

"I know." Sliding his hands under her arms, he pulled her onto his lap. " 'Twas not her fault."

"Then you forgive her?"

Indeed he had. He owed Clare much, yet his soul felt lighter. "Aye. I shall say a prayer for her at Vespers."

Johanna's heart flowered with joy, and she cuddled into him. "Just do not say it to St. Ninian."

He chuckled. "Invoking my favorite saint 'tis easy. Anticipating what Edward the Second will do causes me great distress."

Later that evening with Johanna at his side, Drummond stepped into the great hall at Douglas Castle. At the high table, seated between burly Red Douglas and the swarthy Piers Gaveston, was Edward Plantagenet, king of all England and defender of the faith.

The observation made Drummond smile; he knew more of the man than most.

Over the din of the Douglas clansmen, Drummond heard Johanna say, "What humors you, my lord?"

Johanna. His love. He gazed down at her and found her warm brown eyes brimming with joy. She wore a new surcoat of rust-colored velvet trimmed in fox. Her glorious hair was coiled atop her head and covered with the white veil. Securing it was a garland of dried heather that looked like the crown she deserved to wear.

Only when they were old and their daughters safely married could he tell her the truth. Filled with weighty pride, Drummond diverted his wife. "What think you of the king, my love?"

Blushing, she scanned the dais. Behind her hand, she whispered, "His cheeks have grown fat and his mouth slack."

"What, no praise for his Plantagenet good looks?"

She made a slow inspection of Drummond's face and her interest settled on his new jerkin. "You are a thousand times more pleasing to my eyes and to my heart."

"You flatter me well, my lady."

"For many years to come, I pray."

He placed her hand on his arm. "As do I. Shall we?"

Her fingers tightened. "I love you more than my life."

Inspired and eager to make quick work of the upcoming farce, Drummond began the long walk across the cavernous hall. His scabbard slapped against his thigh, and he wondered what Edward would say when he saw the blade within.

He also took a moment to wonder what his kinsmen would say, and he knew they would condemn him for what he was about to do. But any dent to his Highland pride was more than offset. He would never again lay claim to the title of chieftain. In return, neither Johanna nor Alasdair would have to wear a bloody crown of Scotland.

Her regal head held high and her fearless gaze fixed on the king, Johanna moved gracefully beside Drummond. Noise abated in their wake, and the men of the crowd cast appreciative glances at her. She deserved them all.

Perpendicular to the other tables, the dais was draped in purple velvet and festooned with cords of gold. Jeweled goblets and plates of cheeses and brown bread marked the beginning of the feast.

As Drummond and Johanna approached, Red Douglas started to rise, but remembered his manners. When Edward stood, everyone in the hall came to their feet.

Drummond bowed from the waist. Johanna's curtsy was queenlike, and his throat grew thick with pride at the vision she made.

Rising, she murmured so that only he could hear, "Just remember, my lord. The king is but a man with grease on his fingers and crumbs in his beard."

Laughter almost choked Drummond; only his Johanna could find humor in so solemn an occasion.

Unaware of her artless comment, Edward put down his goblet and walked around the table to stand before Drummond. Red Douglas barreled after him.

When both men stood before Drummond and Johanna, she threaded her fingers through his.

In formal presentation, Drummond held her at arm's length.

The king eyed her cautiously, and Drummond read the fear behind his gaze. "Lady Clare."

"Your Majesty," she intoned. "May you long become your throne."

Edward the Second blinked, then nodded in respect.

Her part done, Johanna stepped to the side, but Drummond could feel her reaching out to him to stand strong and tall. He could not do otherwise, for pride throbbed strong in his chest.

Tipping his head back, Edward looked down his slender nose at Drummond. In a voice loud enough for all to hear, the king said, "What say you, chieftain of the Macqueens?"

Drummond thought of the happy, prosperous years ahead, years filled with peace and enhanced by the company of the woman he loved. She would bear him children; he would teach them well. Buoyed with a happiness he never before thought to enjoy, he bowed his head and went down on one knee.

"I style myself your servant and do submit me to your service, Your Grace."

"Rise, then, and rejoice," the king replied. "But give me your sword."

Drummond swallowed back apprehension and stood. With a firm hand, he pulled his broken sword from the scabbard and offered it up.

Red Douglas gasped in surprise. Murmurs rumbled through the crowd.

Edward took the weapon. "Do you present me with my father's symbol, the blunted sword of Curtana?"

"Nay. If it please Your Majesty, I give you the broken sword of Drummond Macqueen."

Edward's keen blue eyes scanned the blade before handing it back. " 'Twas my father's practice to break the swords of his enemies. I command you to carry a proper sword, Lord Drummond, and wield it in the name of peace. This, then, would content me and satisfy Lord Douglas."

Drummond sheathed his weapon. "Agreed."

Douglas clapped his hands. "Let us eat and be merry."

Heaving a sigh of relief, Drummond took Johanna's hand and led her to the high table.

Hours later, when the king finally said his farewells, Johanna turned to Drummond, "Will you walk with me, my lord?"

"What have you in mind, lass?"

He looked so endearingly handsome that her heart tripped fast. "Must I have a reason to stroll in the moonlight with my husband?"

"Your motives are suspect." He smiled and as he took her arm, his fingertips caressed the side of her breast. "And you know it well."

Undeterred, she walked regally across the hall. In silence they exited the castle and strolled the moonlit yard. Longfellow trumpeted their arrival. She patted the elephant's trunk, and when Drummond stepped closer, she said, "Longfellow, cuddle up."

His trunk snaked around both her waist and Drummond's, gathering them chest to breast.

"Clever minx," Drummond murmured into her ear.

"This clever minx loves you to distraction."

His lips met hers in a kiss of promise and soul deep love. When he'd taken his fill, he murmured, "Now that I'm distracted, too, what else have you on your mind?"

Her heart overflowing with love, Johanna cradled his cheek in her hand. "Only thoughts of you, my mighty chieftain."

"Will I be a chieftain when I grow up?" piped Alasdair from his perch atop Longfellow.

"Alasdair!" bellowed Drummond. "Get down here this minute."

Johanna craned her neck to see Alasdair but it was too dark.

"I could be persuaded to come down," the boy drawled, "if you could be persuaded to teach me how to be a chieftain."

Drummond rubbed his cheek against Johanna's. "What ever will we do with him?" he lamented, loud enough for the boy to hear.

More trials would come with Alasdair, for he was an inquisitive lad, eager to please. He also needed discipline.

"I have an idea," she said with much enthusiasm. "A chieftain must have kinsmen to lead. I say we give our son a dozen brothers."

"Nay," Alasdair protested, clamoring down the rope ladder and coming to stand before them.

"It's sisters I want — a whole passel of them. Please?"

"Hum." Johanna pretended to ponder the request. "If you will promise not to snoop on your father and me, I'll do my best to give you a sister."

"When can I have her?" Alasdair demanded.

"Oh, by Whitsunday next, I should think."

Drummond grew still. "Did you just say what I think I heard you just say?"

Alasdair laughed and danced in a circle. "Father's gone tongue tied, and I'm getting a sister."

Johanna smiled. " 'Tis early, but, yes. I carry our child."

Drummond squeezed her tight. "Thank you, my own dear love. If you have no objections, I should like to give her my favorite name: Johanna."

Tears clogged her throat, and Johanna Benison knew that she had at last fulfilled the prophecy of her name. She had truly been blessed.